BLOOD
BEFORE
SUNRISE

A SHAEDE ASSASSIN NOVEL

AMANDA BONILLA

A SIGNET ECLIPSE BOOK

SIGNET ECLIPSE
Published by New American Library, a division of
Penguin Group (USA) Inc., 375 Hudson Street,
New York, New York 10014, USA
Penguin Group (Canada), 90 Eglinton Avenue East, Suite 700, Toronto,
Ontario M4P 2Y3, Canada (a division of Pearson Penguin Canada Inc.)
Penguin Books Ltd., 80 Strand, London WC2R 0RL, England
Penguin Ireland, 25 St. Stephen's Green, Dublin 2,
Ireland (a division of Penguin Books Ltd.)
Penguin Group (Australia), 250 Camberwell Road, Camberwell, Victoria 3124,
Australia (a division of Pearson Australia Group Pty. Ltd.)
Penguin Books India Pvt. Ltd., 11 Community Centre, Panchsheel Park,
New Delhi - 110 017, India
Penguin Group (NZ), 67 Apollo Drive, Rosedale, Auckland 0632,
New Zealand (a division of Pearson New Zealand Ltd.)
Penguin Books (South Africa) (Pty.) Ltd., 24 Sturdee Avenue,
Rosebank, Johannesburg 2196, South Africa

Penguin Books Ltd., Registered Offices:
80 Strand, London WC2R 0RL, England

First published by Signet Eclipse, an imprint of New American Library,
a division of Penguin Group (USA) Inc.

First Printing, July 2012
10 9 8 7 6 5 4 3 2 1

PUBLISHER'S NOTE
This is a work of fiction. Names, characters, places, and incidents either are the
product of the author's imagination or are used fictitiously, and any resemblance
to actual persons, living or dead, business establishments, events, or locales is
entirely coincidental.

The publisher does not have any control over and does not assume any responsibility for author or third-party Web sites or their content.

ALWAYS LEARNING   PEARSON

For Drew because you are daily proof that a person can do anything they set their mind to and it inspires me to keep going. And for Jacquelyn, thank you for being my sounding board. You've always got my back no matter what. And you know I've got yours.

ACKNOWLEDGMENTS

Again, I find myself overwhelmed by what exactly it means to be a part of this amazing community of writers, readers, and book professionals. I have been reminded so many times over the past year of how fortunate I am, and I am truly thankful.

Juan, as always, you've been a trouper. I know it's been tough at times, and despite the fact that my laptop is sometimes considered "the other man," you've been supportive through it all. The fact that you tried to pimp my book to every person who passed it in Barnes & Noble with such pride in your voice is the only affirmation I need that no matter what, you're behind me.

Mom and Dad, thanks for bragging me up and being proud of me no matter what I do. Niki, Cassidy, Nancy, and Jess, what would I do without you guys? I spend most of my time with fictional people. The fact that you understand it and encourage it means so much to me.

Sarah Bromley, you are the brainstorming master of the universe! I know that when I'm stuck, all I need is to call you up and in an hour or so, you've helped me talk my way through an entire story. You're an idea machine!

Windy Aphayrath, I know I can count on you to call me out. Your eye for detail has saved my butt more than once. You get my angst and support me even when you don't agree with me. Plus, you survived the killer rooster. You get extra points for that!

Suzanne Hayes, I wish I had your talent for poetry. All I had to do was send you my thoughts and you helped to weave the words into music. I can't rhyme my way out of a paper bag. I owe you.

To my partners in mayhem, Shawntelle Madison, Sandy Williams, and Nadia Lee, I'm so glad we're on this journey together! Thanks for having my back. And Cole Gibsen, you rock out loud! Thank you for offering a shoulder to lean on when I needed it!

To my too-fab-for-words agent, Natanya Wheeler, and everyone at NAL, thank you so much for everything you've done for me. It's the most wonderful feeling to know I have your support and encouragement!

Jhanteigh Kupihea, my editor, you are amazing! You know exactly what to do to bring out the best in me. My craft improves every day because of you. Thank you. Thanks also go to my production editor, Zachary Greenwald; my copy editor, Jane Steele; and my cover designer, Katie Anderson.

And last but certainly not least, to the reviewing and book blogging community. Your passion for a good story is exactly why I write. Your enthusiasm is contagious. Many of you spend hours working for free, networking, maintaining blogs and Web sites, and hosting contests, charity events, and blog tours. Thank you for your hard work. You are so, so appreciated.

As always, if I've missed anyone, and chances are pretty good that I have, you know who you are and how I feel. I take full responsibility for my scattered state of mind. In fact, I may or may not be thinking about nachos right now.

Chapter 1

"*What are you looking at?*"

I tore my gaze from the delicate curve of the dagger's blade, my eyes drawn to Azriel's dark, handsome face like a magnet to metal. "Nothing," I said, though that wasn't entirely true.

"*Ever lacking patience*," he said with humor. "*You'll never make it as an assassin if you can't wait more than a few minutes to get a job done.*"

True enough, I supposed. I liked to wait about as much as I liked to be doused with gasoline and set on fire. "*Lorik's late*," I said. "*It's not like him.*"

Azriel stroked his finger along my jaw, and his eyes burned with an intensity that had nothing to do with business. "*It matters little to me if he shows or not. Either way, my night won't be wasted.*"

I flushed at the innuendo, knowing all too well where a jobless night would lead us. Not that I'd complain. . . .

An engine growled in the distance, followed by the squealing of tires. The Cadillac LaSalle Roadster came to a halt inches from where I stood, and the driver's expression was full of adrenaline-infused excitement. Lorik loved flashy cars, and despite his need to lie low, he could never resist showing off. What was the point in not putting that engine and sleek body to use? He'd consider it a waste. Besides, I had a suspicion that the fancy car coupled with his pin-striped suit and fedora pulled low over his brow, made Lorik feel as if he'd just pulled a bank caper. Driving into the sunset and immortal glory would be the icing on the cake. And I'd be willing to bet a Chicago Type-

writer rode shotgun to round it all out. I mean, what self-respecting gangster didn't have a machine gun in the front seat?

"Looks like your clothes will be on for a while longer, my love." Azriel leaned down and pressed his mouth to the pulse-point just below my ear.

I shivered at the contact, suddenly not caring whether Lorik's life was in danger or not. Though the guy's father did pay our bills, I supposed I could put my erotic thoughts on hold. But if he didn't get down to business—and soon—he could rot in hell for all I cared.

"What are you looking at?" Tyler asked again, his tone bemused when I didn't answer him right away.

"Nothing," I finally said as I stared at the spot near the alley where that LaSalle had come to a skidding stop all those years ago. "Not a damned thing."

God, I hadn't thought of that crazy Armenian in decades. He had to have been dead for a while now, if someone hadn't managed to do the deed in his youth. Lorik had been the closest thing Azriel had to a friend. I always wondered about it, the comfortable way Azriel had with him. Usually we lay lower than low, but with Lorik, Azriel had allowed us to let our guard down a bit. Maybe I'd do some digging just for shits and giggles and find out what really happened to him after he went off the grid. Because I had *so* much free time on my hands these days.

My annoyance wasn't so much about memories of Lorik—and Azriel—intruding on my thoughts, or even my lack of actual downtime. Rather, it was more about the fact that I stood at yet another dead end. It's damn hard to catch someone who's always one step ahead of you.

And chasing an Oracle is like chasing the wind.

I drove my katana into the scabbard at my back. Yet another close call, and the bitch had slipped right through my fingers. You wouldn't think someone as blind as a bat could escape so easily.

But she had.

For months.

Time and again.

A discarded can nudged at my toe and I kicked it, sending it sailing down the sidewalk toward the street where it narrowly missed a parking sign. Beyond frustrated, I felt my agitation settle as a knot between my shoulder blades, and I stretched my neck from side to side in a futile effort to ease my mounting tension. Raif, my mentor and the best friend I've ever had, laid a comforting hand on my shoulder. "Don't worry," he said. "We'll get her."

Tyler took a step closer, his body touching mine in more places than appropriate for work hours. He snaked an arm around my waist as he brought me against his body, his eyes narrowing in Raif's direction. Jeez, touchy much?

Raif shook his head. He looked to me, his expression saying, *Is he for real?* I raised my brows, the action as good as a shrug. I had no idea what had gotten into Tyler, but I could almost hear the predatory growl, the low rumble of a wary bear. "Relax, Jinn," Raif said, tucking a dagger into a sheath at his side. "You look a little wound."

"Not hardly," Tyler said, his tone just on the edge of becoming hard. "In fact" — he lowered his face to the top of my head and nuzzled my hair — "I'm pretty damned relaxed right now."

Again, Raif gave me a look. And again, I gave him the equivalent of a facial shrug. Hell if I knew why Tyler was acting like a high school jock facing off with the opposing quarterback. Maybe we all needed to take it down a notch and hang it up for the night.

As if he'd read my mind, Raif gave me a playful knock against the shoulder, eliciting another grumble and glare from Tyler. "I'm calling it a night. See you tomorrow?"

"You know it." There was no way I was letting up anytime soon. I'd search day and night until I found that mousy, pain-in-the-ass Oracle. "Meet me at my place."

Raif's brilliant blue eyes glowed against the backdrop of night as he gave Tyler a last questioning glance. He flashed one of his deadly smiles. "Tyler," he said with a nod, his tone dry. He scattered into a dusting of shadow and left us alone in the alley.

I turned a caustic eye to Tyler. I hated it when he got all territorial on me. It made me feel like a bone—and tonight, Ty was definitely the dog. He put his lips to my forehead, ignoring my accusing glare. Apparently he didn't think his behavior as juvenile as I did. That was saying a lot, considering Tyler had centuries on me in the age department.

Hunting a mark had never been enjoyable—exciting, sure, but also a necessity. Going out with Tyler put a whole new spin on "job perks." As my Jinn, personal genie, and sworn protector, he made it his business to have my back. But since he was my boyfriend, it was a pleasure to have him along. Although the word "boyfriend" didn't do justice to Tyler's role in my life, I thought he'd appreciate the more modern reference. He might have had centuries on me, but he was a modern guy, through and through. I doubted a word existed to describe what Tyler was to me. More than simply my lover, and definitely more than a friend, he had captured more than just my heart over the five years I'd known him. Tyler had claimed my soul.

He'd been out combing the city with me every night this week staying out even after Raif abandoned the hunt. I guess Ty was the only person with the stamina to keep up with me. And believe me, his stamina wasn't something I was about to grumble over anytime soon.

"We might as well call it a night too," he said, giving me a squeeze. "I think we should try Idaho again. Maybe next week. I know a lesser Seer in Coeur d'Alene who might be tempted to shelter Delilah—for the right price."

Idaho again. We'd already searched most of the panhandle, and I doubted another go-around would produce better results. "No," I said, leaning into him so I could feel his muscled chest against my shoulder. "I don't think she's that far away. Don't ask me why, but I can't shake the feeling that she's staying close to home. Delilah has unfinished business, and she never struck me as a quitter."

"Darian," he said, his fingers stroking up my arm, "let's go home."

I melted against him, loving the way my name rolled off his tongue like a sacred word—or a prayer. It never took much for Ty to break down my defenses, and the thought of spending the rest of the night naked and twined around his magnificent body beat the hell out of standing on the cold, rain-drenched street for another second. He placed his lips against my neck, his tongue darting out to trace my flesh. Chills rippled across my skin from the contact. Oh yeah. It was time to go home.

Side by side, we walked through the Queen Anne District just like any human couple would. Though nothing would have stopped me from becoming one with the shadows and traveling under the cover of darkness, I liked walking with Ty. As we headed down the street, the black tails of my duster floating out behind me, I was just a woman, one of thousands inhabiting the city of Seattle. It made me feel just a little less like a freak of nature, and more like the person I used to be. Night, day, dawn, or twilight—I could now pass through the world without the hindrance of being corporeal no matter the hour. I had to admit it was a nice perk, one that no other Shaede could claim, though the means to that end had been anything but pleasant. I never used to believe in ancient prophecy or rituals until I'd been the focal point of both. One attempted sacrifice and an eclipse later, and I had a whole new perspective on life.

Though months had passed since my transformation to something more than Shaede, it seemed only a matter of days. My former lover, Azriel—the one who had supposedly made me what I was in the first place—had made an alliance with the Oracle Delilah and a small army of nasty Lyhtans—violent, praying mantis–looking bastards who hold a serious grudge against any Shaede—to bring down Xander Peck, the King of the Shaede Nation. The fact that Azriel had been Xander's son made the situation that much worse. Hungry for power, he'd had designs on Xander's crown for centuries. And he'd been willing to do *anything* to get it. I'd been the pawn in their little power struggle. But I wasn't randomly selected for the honor. As it turned out, I was a creature created of my own will, and my superspecial blood had been used to awaken the Enphigmalé, hideous gargoyles with a serious binge-eating problem.

When I'd first been introduced to the gargoyles by the raven-haired children who'd made me their prisoner and served as the Enphigmalé caretakers, they'd been solid stone. But one eclipse and a sip of my blood later, they'd sprung to life, hell-bent on devouring anything that crossed their path. Of the gargoyles that had made the transformation from stone to flesh, I'd killed all but a single beast. And just like the Oracle who'd orchestrated its resurrection, the Enphigmalé escaped. Azriel had been Delilah's right-hand man, and he'd looked on as a spectator while I was almost killed. But since I was alive and well, and Azriel had gone into the shadow forever— meaning I had run my dagger across his lying, traitorous throat—it wasn't hard to tell who'd come out on top of his little attempted coup.

Delilah had been the one loose end I'd failed to tie up—so far. According to Azriel, she'd had more reason to hate Shaedes than anyone, though for the life of me, I couldn't guess why. She'd proved to be more slippery than I'd given her credit for, however, and that was a sharp thorn in my side.

Night wrapped me in its warm embrace, tickling my senses. I grabbed onto Tyler's hand as we continued at a steady pace, not as my shadow-self, but in my corporeal form. I liked the feeling of being *real*, substantial, and not just a whisper of something too foreign for even preternatural creatures to comprehend. The lonely anonymity of my life prior to my transformation was gone. Up until several months ago, I'd thought I was the only

Shaede in existence—part of Azriel's lie to keep the secret of my self-made transformation good and hidden. It's hard to hide under the cover of darkness when shadows are watching, though. Alexander Peck—Shaede High King, or to me, just plain Xander—had been watching me for a while. Once he plucked me from obscurity, there was no going back.

Splinters of muted silver moonlight shone between the taller buildings, casting shadows on the rugged, handsome lines of Tyler's model-worthy face. My pace slowed, and I released his hand as a strange urging pulled at my center. *Turn here,* intuition called, and as if I had no control over my limbs, I obeyed.

"Darian?" Tyler said. "What's up?"

I ignored his question, my mind too focused to answer. My legs followed a path down an abandoned side street, the stench of ripe garbage wafting from a nearby Dumpster. Clearing my mind of conscious thought, I moved on instinct alone, allowing the strange feeling to guide me past a fire escape and toward a gaping door where the street dead-ended.

"Darian!" Tyler's tone sharpened as something close to a growl rumbled in the lone word. A warning. He was bound to me as my Jinn, a mystical protector, and his Spidey sense must have been tingling. I held up a hand to quiet him as much as to reassure him. I wasn't in any danger—at least, not yet.

I walked through the opening, surprised to find a storage space large enough to park a car in. From the look of it—not to mention the stale smell—no one had used the space for a while. Through the dark, I perceived the presence of another, and the feeling in my stomach tugged lower, like a rope drawing me to the floor. Squatting down, I roved the space with my eyes, marking a path of dirty blankets and discarded food containers, grateful for the ability to see through the dark. And at the end of it all, a body sat huddled in the corner, knees tucked up and head hidden beneath thin, bony arms.

"Hello, Delilah," I said. "I've been looking for you."

* * *

"I'd never considered it." Raif's thoughtful voice echoed as we walked down the staircase into Xander's council room. The High King's brother rested his hand on his sword, his hand gripping and releasing the pommel as if it were a stress relief ball. "Perhaps it *was* the lack of decision making that allowed you to find her. If you hadn't settled on a course of action, there would be no future act for the Oracle to see."

Sure, it made sense. Why not? But something aside from knee-jerk reaction had led me to Delilah. I was certain of it. We'd been searching for months, and she'd stayed just out of our reach each and every time. But tonight, she'd been handed to me on a silver platter. The only thing missing had been a large, shiny apple shoved into her mouth. A strange, otherworldly force had guided me. I couldn't discount my feelings, though what they meant, I had no idea.

We came to a bookcase at the far end of the council room. Raif pushed on one of the books, *A Midsummer Night's Dream*, and I snorted before reining in my gasp of surprise. The bookcase gave way to admit us into what I can only describe as a prison cell. It wasn't your run-of-the-mill sparse concrete square like you see in the movies. Like everything of Xander's, this room bespoke a certain regality that almost made me laugh. A full-sized bed, decked out with pillows, a petite sofa, even a toilet complete with a privacy screen, furnished the cell — and a small flat-screen TV, for shit's sake. No windows — after all, the room was meant for containment — but the walls were adorned with lavish oil paintings of landscapes. The cell was nicer than most hotel rooms. And I'm not talking about a Motel 6. Muttering under her breath, Delilah sat on the bed, dirty, with downcast, unseeing eyes.

"Why didn't you keep Azriel here after we'd captured him?" I asked, regretting the words before I could take them back. Since his death, speaking of him was forbidden in Xander's house.

"Azriel was a crown prince." Raif's tone became stiff,

his usual formal self. "I would not have dishonored him so."

I opened my mouth to speak but reconsidered. Best to let sleeping dogs lie. "What are we going to do with her?" I asked.

"For the time being, she's Xander's . . . *guest*. We can't have her out roaming the streets and causing trouble. The PNT Council will hear her case, and I suppose they can decide her fate."

The Pacific Northwest Territories, as the area was called, encompassed the nonhuman population of Oregon, Washington, and Idaho. They met once per quarter to address business pertinent to the supernatural community. Who better to decide what should happen to Delilah than a jury of her peers?

"Do you think that keeping me locked up is going to do you any good?" Delilah's words came through clenched teeth, anger infusing every syllable. She rocked back and forth, her hands twitching in her lap. She brought a finger to her mouth and bit it, *hard*. Blood welled from her fingertip, and she passed it along the lines of her palm, studying the bright red pattern with frightening intensity for someone who supposedly couldn't see. "Of her blood, they'll drink like wine. Stronger, faster, changing still, she'll be forced to do his will! From herself she has been born. All will die and none will mourn!"

Oh, just great. "Listen, Delilah. I've had enough of rhyming words and prophecy to last me the next thousand years or so. What's done is done. You failed. It's over. Time to let go."

"He'll finish my business," she said, laughing like a lunatic.

"Azriel?" I asked, walking toward her. "Is that who you're talking about? He's dead, Delilah. He won't be doing anything ever again."

She burst into another fit of laughter that raised my hackles. "No," she said. "Not Azriel. The Man from The Ring is strong. Stronger than me. He gave me a gift of glamour! The Man will come, and he'll succeed where I failed. Then you'll know what true suffering is!"

"We should kill her and do the council a favor," Raif said, totally uninterested. "She's useless and half mad."

"Do it!" Delilah screamed, excited. "Do it now, and I can join my sister, who *you* killed!" She shrieked the last word, extending a bloodied finger in Raif's direction. "Your wife went willingly! She paid the price, and you killed my sister for it!"

I turned and looked at Raif in silent question. His story had been a tragic one: His daughter was missing, and with nowhere left to turn, he'd sought an Oracle for answers. Her price for information about his daughter had been the life of his wife. When he refused, his wife had sacrificed herself. Raif hadn't taken it very well. He'd killed the Oracle, Delilah's sister.

Brow quirked, I waited silently for his answer. Raif shrugged as if to say he'd killed a hundred Oracles in his life and couldn't tell one from another. A look of deep hurt, of past wounds reopened, marred his warrior's face as he turned on a booted heel and headed for the door.

"I know where your daughter is," Delilah said in a low, monotone voice.

Raif froze halfway out of the room, his hand jutting out to the wall as he steadied himself. I took several steps back, putting myself safely in the middle of the cell, shocked. "Raif." I didn't know what else to say.

He paused at the doorway and looked over his shoulder at the thin, dirty girl sitting on the pristine baby blue comforter. "Lies." Grief and doubt tore at his voice. "She lies. Her time has run out, and she says it to torture me. My daughter is dead."

"How can you be sure?" I said, wanting to comfort my mentor, my friend, and not knowing how. "What if—"

"No." In two quick strides, he was back across the room, his hands gripping me just below the shoulders. He pulled me close, his mouth next to my ear. "It is a lie. Her mind is gone. She knows nothing, and every word from her mouth is insanity." Without a parting word, he released his grip on me and strode from the room.

Delilah sat on the bed, her legs crossed in front of her as she rocked back and forth, back and forth. She'd resumed muttering to herself, laughing and pulling out strands of her matted hair, examining each like ticker-tape before letting it drift to the floor. I approached the bed and the mindless Oracle nested there. I bent low to her face, my voice a snarl as it tore from my throat. "Tell me the girl's name."

Delilah laughed, a smirk pulling at her thin, dry lips. "Brakae."

Chapter 2

"**B**eware the Man from The Ring."

Her lyrical voice echoed in my ears, so sure for a child so small. She couldn't have been more than four or five.

"Who is he?" I asked.

The little girl skipped around me in a circle, arms outstretched as if she played a game of ring-around-the-rosy with invisible playmates. "He is the wolf of the battlefield. Once the right hand of the goddess Badb, and the first true protector. Wronged, betrayed, exiled, by those whom he trusted most. He will hunt you down and use you for his own devices."

I just couldn't understand what it was about the supernatural lexicon that required everything to be spoken in rhyme or riddle. Besides being annoying, it flat-out pissed me off.

"Honey, how about giving me a straight answer?" I said, spinning around, trailing her movement. As she skipped, her waist-length curly black hair bounced like hundreds of springs, framing her lovely pale face and sapphire blue eyes. A bright but serious smile curved her lips.

"He is coming," she said, circling me one last time before running off toward a distant knoll where the swaying grass swallowed her up. "Beware."

I sat straight up in bed and gripped my head between my hands to stop the room from spinning. I still felt dizzy from turning in circles, and dreams weren't supposed to carry over into wakefulness. *Wonderful.*

The sun sat at the cusp of the horizon. I sensed its rising as a tingling of my skin, and its scent came to me as warm and smelling of earth after a long rain. As I lay in bed, the gray hour of dawn faded into bright morning, and no matter how I tried, I couldn't banish the disturbing dream from my mind. Her energy had felt so real, rippling across my skin like satiny shadows, and the faint luminescence of her eyes confirmed that she was a Shaede. I'd never seen a Shaede child, let alone dreamt of one for that matter. But a Shaede she was, and her warning stirred a moment of disquiet in me I'd been trying very hard to ignore. It seemed I just couldn't leave danger in my wake.

Slipping out from between the sheets, I padded toward the kitchen. I looked around the small space, took in the clean, polished concrete countertops, the soft white leather of the sofa. I breathed in the aroma of hardwood and carpeting. Cold air seemed to circulate through my studio apartment, twining around my ankles upward— or, at least, I thought it felt that way. Since my transformation, I had to recognize my senses in an entirely different way. And every day since then, I'd been relearning how to feel comfortable in my own skin—not an easy task.

Time ticked away inside my chest like a separate heartbeat; another souvenir I'd taken away from my Enphigmalé Island excursion. I'd changed during my time there, an evolution of my being that had come to completion under the black skies of a solar eclipse—a single moment in time when night became day and day became night. I tried for a moment to expel the sensation of time slipping through my body as I focused on the remembrance of quiet. How I longed for silence. But, like a cruel joke, the sound of seconds passing echoed in my soul, reminding me that I'd never have that kind of peace again. Yep, I was a lucky girl.

My phone rang, a pleasant distraction from time's steady cadence. I checked the caller ID. *Unknown.* I lifted the receiver. "Who is this?" I answered in a cordial-for-me voice.

"Xander wants to see you," a bitchy female voice on the other end said. "Now."

I didn't need to check the phone to know she'd already disconnected the call. Anya liked me about as much as oil liked water. I didn't exactly harbor any warm fuzzies for her either. It could have been natural female adversity that pitted us against each other, but I suspected that deep down, Anya hated me because I didn't regard her with the same level of fear and respect the rest of Xander's subjects exhibited. Or maybe she just didn't like my taste in clothes. I certainly didn't care for hers.

The early-morning sun peeked out from the remnants of last night's storm clouds and glittered through the skylights above me. I ran my hand through the yellow rays, my skin quivering like a mirage against desert sand. I watched in wonder as my arm began to fade into the light; then I sharply pulled away, rubbing my skin as if I'd been burned. It didn't hurt, not really. I just wasn't used to the sensation yet. My shoulders slumped, and with a sigh, I faded, becoming nothing more than a whisper on the air.

I traveled like a breath of wind through Xander's too-large mansion and found the High King seated at a table in the solarium, watching the eastern horizon and sipping from a porcelain cup.

As I stepped from nothingness into my solid form beside the chair, Xander's eyes drifted shut and the corners of his mouth lifted, hinting at a smile.

"Good morning," he said.

"You wanted to see me?" I allowed the aggravation to seep through my voice.

"Mmm," he answered with a sigh. "Yes, I did."

His voice reached out to touch me in a velvet caress. Xander had the most alluring voice I'd ever heard, smooth and seductive, and he tried to use it to his advantage.

"Well," I said, tapping my foot, "what the hell do you want?"

"Sit."

"Excuse me? Last time I checked, I wasn't yours to command."

"Sit."

He motioned to the chair opposite him just before a Shaede with bright platinum hair walked in, carrying a tray laden with a breakfast spread that would have put any of Seattle's best eateries to shame. Fruit, fresh-baked croissants, eggs Benedict, and a couple of other baked goods that looked like fancy breakfast Hot Pockets. She plunked down two plates, and I stifled a groan. The High King must have been pretty confident that I'd show up at just the right time. Xander was such a count-his-chickens sort of guy.

"I like your outfit, by the way," he said as he watched the platinum-haired Shaede leave. "I don't often see you in white."

I shrugged as I lowered myself into the chair, conveying my displeasure through the slits of my eyes. I hated his small talk. He didn't give two shits what color I wore. In fact, I was willing to bet he'd prefer to see me wear nothing at all. I didn't wear white—much—but since my transformation, I'd been wearing the color more often. He'd known I'd come straight over after Anya's call. And the fact that he'd maneuvered me with aplomb raised my hackles.

I ignored his smile and sparkling gaze and poured myself a cup of ultradark coffee. I added a splash of cream, paying more attention to my actions than they warranted. From the corner of my eye, I noticed Xander sitting very still, disregarding his meal the way I disregarded him. He watched me with hungry eyes.

"What does it feel like?" he almost whispered.

"What does *what* feel like?" I asked, stabbing at my food.

"The light."

I shrugged and popped a melon ball in my mouth. His curiosity about my *enhanced* state didn't surprise me. And he wasn't alone in his interest. I'd become a one-woman freak show—a new and unique creature, truly the only one of my kind.

"Neither Shaede nor Lyhtan be . . ." The words chanted by the suicidal teens who'd held me prisoner for the Enphigmalé echoed in my mind. "I don't know," I said, forcing the unpleasant memories away. "I guess it sort of . . . tingles."

Xander looked to his plate as if embarrassed by his question. I'd never known him to be anything but unapologetic, though, and I reveled in his awkward moment before changing the subject. "Are you going to tell me why I'm here?"

"Do I need a reason to see you?" he asked, the epitome of innocence. "Can't I just bask in the glow of your company?"

I rolled my eyes so hard, I thought they might fall right out of my head. I'd never been charming company by any standards. Plus, Xander didn't do anything without an ulterior motive, and I knew he hadn't asked me over just so he could "bask in the glow of my company."

A flash of canary yellow crossed the open doorway, followed by the creak of leather, and I rolled my eyes again, adding a disgusted snort. Anya, one of Xander's favorite attendants, had a leather fetish. I couldn't imagine what about it made her want to wear it every. Single. Day. But since I'd met her, I'd never seen her in anything else. I also knew that neither one of us was going to head up the other's fan club anytime soon.

"Xander, does Anya have to hover like that?" I asked, just a little on the loud side. "I'm developing an allergy to leather."

Xander gave another wan smile. I wondered if he was trying to play hard to get. "She's doing her job," he said.

"What job is that?"

"Protecting me."

I raised a dubious brow. "I thought that was my job."

Xander's smirk widened into an all-out seductive smile. Shit. He'd been fishing and pulled out the heavy gear. "I'm glad to hear you say that," he murmured in a voice that put my temper over the top. "Very glad."

Oh man, was I an idiot. He'd kept Anya close just to get a reaction. He knew how to play me, and I let him—every time. "But it looks like I've been replaced," I said, parrying his words like a sword thrust. "I guess I'm officially unemployed."

"Not quite," Xander said, and my stomach constricted into a tight, anxious ball. "I have other tasks set out for you."

"Other tasks," I repeated in a monotone. "I don't think so, Xander. You can't just order me around like one of your subjects."

He raised a challenging brow. "Can't I?"

I stuck my chin out defiantly. "No, you cannot."

With a robust, albeit exaggerated, pat to his well-muscled stomach, the King of Shaedes rose from his chair and headed for the door, effectively dismissing my previous statement. "I've enjoyed our time together this morning. But I have matters of state to attend to. We'll talk again soon."

I shifted in my seat, fingering the dagger strapped to my thigh. The thought of catapulting it toward his head made me feel all warm and fuzzy. "Aren't you forgetting something? You asked for me this morning. What did you want?"

His smile became that of arrogant satisfaction. "I got what I wanted. Good morning, Darian."

Not one single creature in all of my existence was capable of pushing my buttons the way Xander could. He hadn't needed me for a goddamned thing. Requesting my presence was nothing more than a test to see if I'd jump to attention when he snapped his fingers. And while in his eyes I'd passed with flying colors, in my own opinion, I'd failed miserably. I passed Raif on my way back up the stairs. A frown marred his chiseled features, and he stared at his feet as he descended the stairs, lost in thought. I doubt he would have paid attention to me at all if I hadn't brushed my elbow against his arm.

"What would prompt you to seek out my brother this morning?" Raif asked, running his hand through his usually well-kept, tawny hair. "Bored with the Jinn and looking for trouble?"

His words were spoken in humor, but there was no laughter in his tone. I ignored the slight against Tyler and gave him a quick once-over. His face looked drawn and unusually pale, the menacing spark gone from his eyes.

I cracked a grin, playing along so I'd resist the urge to question Raif about his haggard appearance. "You know me . . . always looking for a little trouble. What about you? Does His Royal Obnoxiousness have something planned for you today?"

A corner of Raif's mouth hinted at amusement, but the expression did not spread to the rest of his face. Azriel's little family feud had taken a greater toll on him than he'd let on. I assumed Delilah's statements the previous day hadn't helped the situation either. Her words had struck a chord.

"I'm going to work out, actually. I haven't beaten you in a while," he added, sounding a bit more like himself. "Want to join me?"

My grin grew into a full-on smile. "Love to."

I followed Raif back down the stairs and through another hallway into the west wing of Xander's sprawling estate, an area I'd never explored. Not that I was interested in every nook and cranny, but it did pique my curiosity. A gymnasium-sized room took up the entire wing, and, aside from weights and bags and a mirror-lined wall, the room boasted an open floor covered with the soft foam mats used in martial arts tournaments. I wondered for a brief and bitter moment why Raif hadn't conducted my earlier training in this room rather than in Xander's empty warehouse. But as I reflected on my teacher's nature, I realized he'd kept me at a distance from the king, his protection being Raif's highest priority.

As I looked around the gym, Raif pulled two bokken from a wall mounted with various weaponry, including a couple of war axes and a mace or two. The wooden version of the samurai sword, the bokken was useful when all you were looking for was a good workout. It was also the preferred training tool when the teacher feared he'd slice a less experienced student to shreds. I didn't think Raif was concerned about hurting me, so I had to assume the bokken was for his protection.

I was right.

Raif was at such a serious disadvantage that I would have squealed for joy if I'd been a girlier girl. Instead, I settled for smug satisfaction. We hadn't sparred since my transformation—and he wasn't even close to prepared.

Confined to his solid form, he had only his speed and strength to rely on, while I had all of that and more. His labored breathing and sweat-drenched face were sufficient indicators that I had the upper hand. I have to admit, I went easy on him. I tried to remain corporeal as much as possible, but I found at times the change was triggered subconsciously. The glorious crack of the hard wood resounded in the empty gym, and my abilities as a fighter had even me surprised.

Raif came at me running, the bokken twirling from side to side. I managed a back flip and landed, crouched low to the ground. It took only one swipe of my own weapon and my teacher landed like a stone. He lay flat on his back, a position I'd imagined putting him in more than once, staring up at the ceiling. The smile faded from my face as his sullen attitude stole the glory from my victory. Damn him.

"What's the matter with you?" I demanded, lowering the bokken.

I paced a full circle around him, slicing the air with my wooden sword before he decided to answer.

"What's the matter . . . ," he repeated, pushing up to sit cross-legged on the mat, "is that the air I breathe is being poisoned by that Oracle. This matter with her is not resolved, and I want nothing more than to turn her over to the council and have her gone from my sight."

He rocked backward, rolling onto his back and with a

fluid kick of his legs, propelled himself to a standing position. He spun, the bokken whirring as it sliced through the air before dropping to his side. "She'll cause nothing but trouble here. Her mind is gone, and all she does is sit in that room and ramble incoherent strings of words." Raif shook his head, wiping at his brow. "Damned Oracles," he said, disgusted.

"Raif," I began, willing to chance his temper, "I don't think we should disregard what she's telling us."

He turned, giving me his full attention, one eyebrow cocked curiously.

"I think Delilah knows your daughter's name."

"Her name is no secret. That the Oracle knows it is indicative of nothing. I can tell where your thoughts are leading, Darian. Leave it be."

No, he didn't. He didn't have a clue what I was thinking. And I knew Raif didn't really want me to let it be. He just didn't realize it yet.

"I mean it," he said as if he could read my thoughts. "Do not pursue this."

"But—"

"I said no."

"Raif—"

"Leave these notions like a stone on the road. Do not think on them again."

He seized the bokken from my hand and went to hang the training swords back on the wall.

"Brakae. Your daughter's name is Brakae—am I right?"

Raif's head hung between his shoulders. Delilah wasn't bullshitting us. Not in the slightest. It didn't matter if Raif's daughter's name was common knowledge. Delilah threw it out there to make a point. She needed a bargaining chip and this was it—Raif's daughter's life for hers. And he knew damned well I was right. Just as he'd assured me the night I'd killed Azriel, this was far from over. His daughter was alive; I knew it. And I was going to find her.

Chapter 3

If I hadn't run into Raif, I would've written the morning off as a total waste of my time. I had no interest whatsoever in playing Xander's games. The workout had been a welcome distraction; I hadn't stretched my muscles in a while. But Raif's obviously haggard state had left me feeling less than satisfied.

It had been months since we'd—well, *I'd*—killed Azriel. And though Raif's conscience felt the weight of his part in it, I wasn't the least bit sorry. Azriel had deserved the punishment I'd been paid by his father to dole out. But his death had raised more questions than solutions. And that had me worried.

I'd been arrogant before. Thinking you sit at the top of the food chain has a tendency to do that. Finding Xander and opening up an entire world of supernatural creatures had brought me down a peg or two. Despite my recent changes, I remained a small fish in a very big pond, and if my dream had any truth to it at all, it confirmed both Azriel's and Delilah's words: Someone was hunting me.

I wondered, as I recalled the dream, if there was a nursery somewhere full of little Shaede babies. Probably. Just because I'd never seen one didn't mean there weren't any. Kind of like Big Foot or the Loch Ness Monster. Could one of them dance right into someone's dream, though? Anything was possible at this point. Not that it mattered—Azriel had warned me long before my dream. Delilah backed him up with her own assertions as well. The coincidence of it all was just too perfect. I needed to watch my back. Hadn't the Shaede child tried to warn me too? *"He's coming for you,"* she'd said.

I felt dizzy just thinking about the skipping girl. *Shit.*

Stepping from pure sunlight, I became my solid self just inside the entrance to my apartment. Tyler sat at my table, working on a mammoth sandwich. He had a tendency to eat when he was worried, and he was chewing as if the damned thing were stuffed with nails rather than ham. I moved soundlessly across the hardwood floor, and he didn't even flinch.

"Where've you been?" The casual tone he'd been going for failed miserably. In fact, his voice sported something altogether darker. Worry, party of one. "You didn't call—"

"Because there was no reason for me to call." I walked around the table, my hand trailing across the sculpted muscles of Tyler's shoulders. He raised his hand to mine, his fingers pausing on the silver ring I wore on my thumb. He'd given it to me when I first met him. It was engraved with a bear, the protector—and his symbol. "I went to Xander's. Trained with Raif. Nothing unusual. Relax."

My short answers didn't do much to assuage his overprotective attitude. He'd been on me like white on rice for weeks. I could handle the protectiveness. In fact, it came standard issue with Tyler's Jinn nature. But for the past couple of weeks, that nature had grown from sweet to downright severe.

"I don't like the way you smell when you've been there," he said, setting down the sandwich as if it had a cockroach on it. "You smell like *him.*"

"Him" being the High King.

"You know there's nothing between Xander and me." Tyler's ego didn't usually need this kind of stroking. What the hell was up with him lately?

"I'm not talking about Xander," Tyler said.

Oookaaay. "Well, then, who the hell are you talking about?"

"Raif."

My jaw dropped on rusty hinges, and it wasn't closing

anytime soon. Come again? Raif? I couldn't even put my voice to the words of astonishment juggling around in my head. I mean—Raif? As in, like-a-brother-to-me Raif?

"You spend every day with him. Nights too."

Come on, mouth—work, damn it. I cleared my throat only to get a brooding hazel-eyed stare in response. One more try gave my vocal cords the get-up-and-go they needed. "Ty, what the hell's wrong with you? You *know* there's nothing between Raif and me. We're friends. I mean—I am allowed to have friends, right? Why the jealous-lover routine lately? And have you forgotten, I spend all of my nights with you too? During *and* after work hours."

Tyler's eyes lost a little of that hard edge, and he ran his fingers through his hair, making him look a good five years older. He sighed, flexing his arms as if his skin suddenly felt too tight. "I know," he said, his gaze cast toward the floor. "Sometimes the bond can make me a little twitchy. Darian, this is new for me. Usually the bond doesn't go hand in hand with romantic attachment. It's stronger *because* I love you. I guess I'm more worked up than I should be. Maybe I need to get a better handle on my feelings." He gave me a sheepish grin. "You gonna call me an ass now?"

Usually, Tyler was the most levelheaded person I knew. We'd been bound for years. In fact, Tyler had made the bond between us without my even knowing because he thought I'd shun his protection. Can you say overprotective? Aside from that, I didn't know much about the effects of the bond. As my genie, Tyler had more or less made a commitment to grant my wishes (but only when it was something I truly needed) and protect me to the point that he'd sacrifice his own life to keep me safe. But beyond that, I hadn't a clue how the bond affected him. He definitely wasn't acting like himself. He'd been just as keyed up as I'd been lately. Maybe we both needed a few weeks of vacation.

"I don't mind a little jealousy now and then," I said,

bringing his hand to my mouth so I could kiss each of his knuckles. "It's a turn-on." The spark returned to Tyler's eyes, no longer flashing with anger but with passion. "But not when it comes to Raif."

He brushed his thumb across my bottom lip, his eyes glued to my mouth. "Like I said, I'm a little twitchy. The bond just needs to settle a bit."

We'd been bound for five years. Jesus, how long did it take to settle? I laid my cheek against his cool palm. "I like that you want me all to yourself."

I left my chair and rounded the table to stand behind him, my hands kneading the tense muscles above his shoulder blades. "Ty, if I wanted to find someone, could I just wish for it?"

Tyler craned his neck around so he could look me in the eye, and he sat up a little straighter. "That depends on who you're looking for and why."

"Well," I said, peering at him through lowered lashes, "let's just say I want to find someone who isn't human. Could you deliver her to me if I wished for it?"

I pulled a chair right next to his and sat, rubbing the tip of my nose along his cheek, rough with stubble. I inhaled and held the scent of him in my lungs. His warm, spicy aroma had a homey quality and reminded me of comfort and trust.

"First of all," he said, his voice thick and husky, "if you don't stop that, I'm going to have you—right here on the kitchen table. Secondly, what are you up to?"

I smiled and took his earlobe between my teeth before gently pulling away. He groaned, and the sound sent a pulse of excitement zinging through my veins.

I knew the rules for making wishes, more or less. Tyler had spelled them out for me when I'd first become aware that he'd bound himself to me. Wishes, just like everything in the natural world, were regulated and restricted—balanced. So wishing for a million dollars or world peace was out of the question. I could wish only for something I needed. Just wanting something wasn't good enough to justify wish granting. I couldn't wish the dead back to life, or the living to be dead. I couldn't wish to change the natural order of things, so that secret desire of being able to shoot laser beams from my eyes was a definite no-go. And I could never wish to break the bonds of others, no matter what they might be. As far as our own bond was concerned, though Tyler had made the bond, only I could break it. He could choose to bind himself to another only three times in his life, and I had no idea if I was number one or three.

What I was about to wish for definitely fell under the "want" category. But someone I cared about needed it. So I thought maybe by virtue of the loophole, I'd get my wish. "It's just a simple question of finding someone," I said, building the framework for my request. "Can you do it if I ask?"

A curling strand of my strawberry blond hair drifted into my line of sight, and I huffed it away before fixing my gaze on Tyler's face. I tried not to stare directly into his eyes. They're gorgeous, and I sometimes lose myself entirely in the hazel orbs. What can I say; I'm a sucker for pretty eyes.

"Could you find a Shaede if I wished for it?"

"Maybe," he answered slowly. "There might be extenuating circumstances that would prevent me from granting that wish."

I leaned back in my chair and deposited my legs onto his lap. "Such as?"

He smiled, a good sign, and began to massage one of my calves. "Well, this particular Shaede might not want to be found. Or there could be magic stronger than mine protecting him or her. Also, is this something you need? Or just a passing whim?"

I raised a dubious brow.

"Who are you looking for, Darian?"

I sighed as I felt a tightening in my center that branched outward toward my limbs—the barest perception of the heavens shifting. The noon sun had reached its zenith, dipping lower into the sky. I pushed the sensation to the back of my mind and tried to focus on the matter at hand. How I hated unceasing time.

"I want to find Raif's daughter."

Tyler paused in midmassage, the dark shadow returning to his eyes for a fleeting moment before he shook it off. "Raif has already tried to find her, Darian. Unsuccessfully, I might add. Besides, didn't he tell you she died?"

"Yes," I murmured as he moved to my other calf, artfully rolling it in his palm. "But I think she's still alive. Delilah said something. Well, she said a lot of somethings actually, mostly incoherent ramblings, but I know she had her shit together when she told me Raif's daughter is alive."

"Did she tell you how she knew?"

I bit my bottom lip. "No. Raif thinks she's lost her mind."

"He tried to find her," Tyler insisted. "He couldn't."

"But he didn't have a genie."

"Do it," he said abruptly. His tone became serious, almost a dare. "Make the wish."

I stared into his eyes, momentarily absorbed by the brownish star that surrounded Ty's pupil. Something shimmered there, looking like an oil slick on water. My breath hitched. A wish was what I wanted, after all. He'd offered. Thrown it right in my face, actually. I tried to avoid making wishes; it felt too much like exercising control. But it wouldn't be an order, just a simple desire spoken aloud.

Swallowing down the bitterness that coated my mouth, I found it hard to speak the words. The last time I made a wish, I'd been a sacrificial lamb, my blood dripping into nine bowls to awaken nine dormant gargoyles. I'd needed Ty's help, and so I'd wished again and again for it. I needed his help now. "Tyler, I wish Raif's daughter were standing here right now."

Ty closed his eyes, thank God, and I could finally look away. A shudder passed along his body, and he inhaled sharply, every muscle in his body going rigid. I held my breath in anticipation as much as worry. I'd never seen the physical effect of the wish. Did it hurt him somehow?

Still silence consumed the apartment, but within me, time marched its steady cadence. Though the suspense was killing me, I waited while Tyler did his thing—whatever that was. His eyes flew wide open, and I felt the stirring of air as an invisible force ghosted past me. Startled, I pushed the foot resting in his lap against him, and my chair teetered on its back legs before coming down again on all fours. He exhaled an unsteady breath, his eyes watering.

"Nothing," he said. "If she's alive, she's protected far beyond my scope of power. I'm sorry."

He looked a bit shaky, and I cursed my selfishness. Had this happened every time I'd made a wish? Even the times before I'd known he was forced to obey my simple commands? "I'm sorry," I said, the shame welling up like bile. "I won't do that again."

Ty reached over and squeezed my hand. The reassuring gesture did little for my blossoming guilt complex. "It's part of the bond, love. No apologies. It's about damned time you started making wishes anyway."

Wrestling my hand free, I stood, the chair screeching against the floor as I pushed it back. Things had been a lot goddamned simpler when I was alone. For starters, I didn't have to worry about hurting the man I loved. "Delilah's got something up her sleeve," I said, crossing to the kitchen. "I don't know what, but I'm sure I'll find out soon enough. In the meantime, I want you to be more careful. Maybe you should keep a low profile until I'm sure it's safe."

A low snort of disgust answered me. Typical. Ever the knight in shining armor, Ty would never go down without a fight. "Keep a low profile," he replied in a caustic tone. "Yeah, right."

It was worth a try anyway. But I had ways of slipping through his fingers, and I refused to put him in danger again. I'd almost lost him forever when the Enphigmalé attacked him. And his only sin had been protecting me.

"Whatever." The smart-ass remark I'd prepared evaporated into the one word. I didn't want to fight with him.

Not right now. I had other things on my mind. "I smell like a locker room. I'm taking a shower." I walked toward the bathroom with a slow, languid gait, my hips screaming an invitation. A satisfied smile curved my lips as I heard Tyler's chair slide back.

I peeled the tight white T-shirt up the length of my body and over my head, tossing it behind me. I didn't hear it hit the floor, but I heard Tyler's breath catch. I paused, kicking off my boots, toeing both of my socks down and over my feet. Cool fingers traced a path up my spine, causing delicious shivers to race along my flesh. He worked the clasp on my bra with ease, pulling the straps down over my shoulders. His breath tickled against my ear.

"I'll help you wash," he whispered.

As I led the way to the shower, I heard items of his clothing drop to the floor.

I'd keep him out of trouble, all right. And if that meant using my body and all of my feminine wiles to do it—then so be it.

Chapter 4

Ty lay softly snoring in my bed. He was one tuckered-out genie. I admit, keeping him sedate with sex wasn't the best plan in the world, but I didn't have much else in my arsenal at the moment. I couldn't stop thinking about this mysterious Man. Azriel and Delilah could have been in on the secret, sure. But that didn't explain my dream. Had my subconscious conjured the Shaede girl and her warning? Who was this Man? Why did he want me? And what the hell did he plan on doing with me once he found me? I wasn't willing to draw Tyler into any of it. Wishing him out of danger was out of the question, even if it was for his own good. I didn't own him, regardless of what the bond said to the contrary.

I wriggled my feet into my familiar black boots, feeling a little more like myself. The sun had been past the horizon for an hour, and no matter the advantages my evolution brought, I still felt more comfortable at night.

Shrugging into my black duster, I tossed a note on the empty pillow, where I should've been sleeping. Ty would follow me when he woke up, but at least I'd have a head start.

Gone to talk to Levi.

If The Pit had been open twenty-four hours a day, I'd have moved in. I felt absolutely inconspicuous there—a feeling I cherished. Though the bar's clientele wasn't exactly limited to those of the human persuasion, it was just normal enough for me to blend in. Most nights I sat in the darkest corner of the place and people-watched to my heart's content.

Levi bartended two or three nights a week—mostly weekends. His college-boy looks made him stick out like a sore thumb in the decidedly rougher atmosphere of the bar, but it did wonders for his tip jar. Clean-cut and all-American, Levi had vapid frat-boy written all over him. Looks can be deceiving. Levi was a walking supernatural encyclopedia. If it wasn't human and walked the earth, he knew something about it. But his services weren't cheap; even information came with a price tag. Probably how Levi funded his Abercrombie wardrobe and teeth-whitening sessions.

"Don't worry about bringing a shit storm down on this place," Levi said, sliding a Midori sour across the bar. "This is neutral ground. You're safe here. What's after you this time?"

I sipped the froufrou drink, wrinkling my nose at the syrupy-sweet tang. He served me something new every time I came. First one of the night was always on him. "I wish I knew," I said, leaning into the bar. "Looking for someone to help me shed a little light on that. Want to throw your hat in the ring?"

Levi poured three shots of vodka and passed them over to the cocktail waitress. "I'll give it a go."

I leaned in even closer so I wouldn't have to shout over the music pumping overhead. The DJ was in rare form, House music being the flavor of the night. I less than loved his selection. "What do you know about a Man from The Ring?"

Levi pulled away and studied me for a second as if trying to decide whether I was joking or not. He didn't bolster my spirits much. "Could you get any vaguer, Darian? Please tell me that's not the only bit of information you're working on."

Fantastic. Hunter: one. Hunt*ed*: zip. I was getting nowhere, fast. "It's all the information I have. You don't have a clue?"

He thought it over while he mixed a few drinks. You

have to be a multitasker-and-a-half in his line of work. He could probably write a dissertation and juggle at the same time. "Ring," he finally said, shouting over the heart-stopping bass of the music. "It could mean anything. That's the problem. It could literally be a ring, like a spirit trapped in a ring. Maybe even a crown. Or it could be something else entirely. A place, or the notion of a place. I'll need more to go on before I can be any help."

Disappointed didn't even begin to describe how I felt about Levi's lack of knowledge. I'd formed the opinion there wasn't anything he *didn't* know. I guess it wasn't like I could just pop a quarter up his nose and have an answer spit out of his mouth. It would've been nice if it worked that way, though. "Sorry, but I'm pretty sure that's all I'm going to get." *Considering I killed the asshole who might know more than that little snippet. And my other lead is mad as a hatter.* "What am I looking at here? Can you ask around, see if any of your contacts know anything? Or am I basically fucked?" I slid a hundred-dollar bill across the bar, and he stealthily scooped it up and stuffed it into his pocket.

Levi laughed, showing perfectly straight white teeth. He reminded me of a toothpaste commercial. "You're not fucked, yet. Give me a few days. I'll rattle some chains and see what I can come up with. In the meantime, you'd better find a table. Drama's coming your way." He jerked his chin toward the entrance.

I recognized Tyler's shock of coppery curls as he fought through the crowd at the entrance. Even from across the bar, I could tell he was pissed. My jaw set, ready for a fight, I gave Levi a little toast and hauled my ass to my favorite dark corner. I sat with my back against the wall, the open area of the club visible from all sides. No one was going to sneak up on me here.

I sipped the girly green drink, which was starting to grow on me, and innocently trained my eyes on the dance floor. With Ty following my every move, I wasn't going to get anything accomplished. If I hadn't cared about him so much, I would have wished his ass permanently in my apartment. But, just like the drink in my hand, Ty had grown on me as well.

"Sneaky, aren't you?" he said, throwing himself into the chair across from me. He slapped his palm down on the Formica tabletop, the sound cracking, even above the blaring music. "Think you can just screw me into a coma and run?"

I pretended not to hear him, though my preternatural ears picked up every syllable. Well, I *had* thought screwing him into a coma would keep him safely out of trouble. Bringing the glass to my lips, I drained it in a couple of gulps, then ran my tongue over my now-sugarcoated mouth. Something stronger was in order, and I raised my empty glass to a cocktail waitress who changed course for our table. "Bourbon, neat." I turned to Tyler. "You want anything?"

The waitress looked to Tyler, recognition dawning on her face. A sultry smile replaced her regular customer-service grin. Her lids drooped almost imperceptibly, and she bent over, showing a sad attempt at cleavage, betrayed by one of Victoria's secrets. "Hi, Tyler!" she shouted. "The usual?"

Jealousy had never been natural for me, but I felt a stabbing twinge of it right in the center of my chest. Tyler glanced at me from the corner of his eye, a lazy smile creeping onto his handsome face. "Sure. Thanks." He plunked a bill down on her round, cork-covered tray. "Keep the change."

She turned to leave, and I stuck my leg out straight, pointing a booted toe to the sky. It wasn't entirely my fault that she tripped; she should have watched where she was going. Besides, she recovered well enough. The girl at the next table caught her before she hit the floor.

Our waitress had her wheels spinning for Ty; she made it back with our drinks in less than two minutes—impressive. She placed the Seven and Seven in front of Tyler, reaching from behind him to allow her breast to graze his shoulder. The bourbon, she set in the middle of the table. Someone wasn't going to get a tip from me, unless you counted a bloody nose and a couple of broken ribs.

I sat up from my slumped position and retrieved the glass, draining it in a single swallow. It burned all the way down, and I welcomed the heat. The warmth spread, real, comfortable, true. Despite what had happened to me, the liquor's effect hadn't changed. At least some things stayed the same.

The faint thrumming of an urgent pulse piqued my curiosity. Levi headed toward our table, sweat glistening on his brow. He ushered our waitress quickly out of the way and bent his head between Tyler and me. "Outside. You have company, Darian, and he's not the sort of patron we let in, if you get my drift."

Sounded like trouble, and I needed something to take my frustration out on. "Where?"

Levi cast a nervous glance in Tyler's direction. "In the back alley. Said he just wants to talk . . . but I've never known them to be peaceable."

"Don't worry," I said, giving a playful smile. "I'll go see what he wants."

"*We'll* go see," Tyler interjected.

Fine. "We'll go see," I said, standing.

"The back exit's open," Levi said. "No alarms. It'll take you right out to the alley."

Ty followed hot on my heels—literally. He bumped into me more than once. Had it been anyone else, I would have been tempted to give him an ungracious shove. What the hell did he think was going to happen anyway? No one had managed to kill me . . . yet. "This is exactly why you can't continue ditching me, Darian. You need protection. You need me."

"I can handle myself, Ty." Had something happened during my transformation to make me suddenly too weak to take care of myself?

"That's not the problem, Darian. I know you can handle yourself. But even *you* need backup every once in a while. That's where I come in."

I didn't answer, not wanting to fight with my boyfriend in front of my "visitor." As we walked out into the back alley, I heard the Lyhtan's grating breath before I actually saw it. *Him.* That was what Levi had called him anyway. With their androgynous, insectlike bodies, I still don't know how anyone could tell their gender. I approached cautiously. I'm not stupid. Regardless of having the upper hand, I didn't feel like I did. Lyhtans are deadly. They fight amongst themselves as much as they harry their enemies. Violence is their cup of tea, and it doesn't matter who serves it up.

When the Lyhtan laid eyes on Tyler, he took a defensive stance. Green-tinged drool leaked from his mouth, and he bared his teeth. A low hiss issued from between the sharp points. "I asked for the marked one. Not you, Jinn," he said in his many voices, which melded into a single ominous chorus. "You have no business here."

Marked one. Didn't realize I had an actual title. "His business is my business. Don't worry your pretty little head about Ty." *Pretty. Ha.* "What's your name, Lyhtan?" I had little hope he'd supply it. They rarely do. But then again, even sometimes *I* am surprised.

"I am called Chianshank."

Sounded a lot like a sneeze the way he pronounced it. *Chi-an* with a quick *shahnk.* I wanted to follow up with a *Bless you.* No wonder they didn't often supply their names. How in the hell was I going to remember that one?

"Well, *Chian*," I said, going for something a little less formal, "what do you want?"

"I bring a warning." His breath came foul and loud, echoing in the alley. "And you'd best heed it."

His voice, like so many tones layered together, reminded me of less than happy times. The threat of becoming a sacrifice choking every ounce of air from my lungs as I lay helpless on a slab of moss-covered stone, impending death on the wind. I thought of my soul, screaming for release from torturous love and betrayal.

I envisioned blood—so much blood streaming from twin slashes on my wrists.

Thank whatever gods are out there, I'm no delicate flower. I pushed the unpleasant memories away and widened my stance, caressing the dagger hilt at my thigh. It wouldn't kill the bastard, but it would wound him enough to get him out of my hair if his intentions were less than honorable. "Why warn me? The last time I met up with your kind, saving my skin was low on the Lyhtan to-do list."

"Neither Shaede nor Lyhtan be," he crooned. Sheets of gooseflesh rose over my skin. "You are Other. Dangerous to some, a savior to others. And I've been instructed to warn you."

From around the corner, a door slammed. Chianshank flinched, crouching low. A warning grumble bubbled from his thin lips. His taloned fingers flexed, and he cast a furtive glance to either side. "Come close, creature. I will deliver my message to your ears alone."

Creature, huh? If that wasn't the pot calling the kettle black. "I'll come a little closer on your word that you won't attack."

"On my word," the Lyhtan seethed.

Tyler snorted in protest behind me, and I held up a hand to silence whatever argument was about to spill from his lips. Taking a step toward the Lyhtan messenger and then another, I wondered at my own state of mind. The smell of Lyhtan that I'd thought of as especially foul didn't offend my nostrils the way it once had. To my new senses, the Lyhtan smelled of strong musk, pine, and wilting lavender. Heady, though not exactly pleasant.

As I moved within killing distance of the segmented body of my would-be enemy, he straightened from his battle stance just a little—enough to meet me eye to eye. I stared into the amber orbs, beady black pupils fixed on my face. Suppressing a shudder, I inclined my head toward the Lyhtan's slobbering, sharp-toothed mouth. I sensed Tyler stiffen behind me, his anxiety pulsing in soft invisible waves at my back. "Speak your piece, Lyhtan," I murmured. "And then get the hell out of my space."

Chian's face passed close to my cheek—so close I felt a whisper of slimy contact from his glistening mouth. He took a breath of me deep into his lungs before looking me in the eye, and his tongue flicked out, licking his lips as if in anticipation of a lover's kiss. I held perfectly still and forbade my body to react. I forced my lungs to expand and contract at a normal rhythm. Tyler's pulse quickened behind me, thrumming double time to the seconds that ticked in my soul.

I waited.

"You will be the instrument of destruction. Creature of nothing and everything—he is coming for you. You must seek out—"

A swooshing sound interrupted his ominous speech. The Lyhtan jerked, then stood erect. His amber eyes rolled back in his head, which lolled on his sharp, hunching shoulders. A shimmering wave, like sunlight on water, shivered across his skin. He jerked again, and turned to the side. The long shaft of an arrow poked out from the back of his head, which seemed to glow hot and somehow cold all at once.

I stumbled and fell back into Ty's waiting arms, which pulled me farther away toward cover. Chianshank pitched forward, and the arrow's shaft glowed blindingly bright, encompassing his body in a brilliant luster that forced me to avert my gaze. His long, lanky body crumpled to the pavement, sizzling and curling in on itself until there was nothing left but a greenish pool of steaming goo.

Before I could reach for my dagger, Tyler spun me around and slammed me against a brick wall. He pressed me hard against the unyielding surface, my face smashed against his chest. His arms spread wide as his palms pressed against the wall behind me. Another arrow cleaved the air, singing in the night, and stuck in the brick inches from my head. The tip burned crimson, eating away at the hard brick and turning it to sand. Its grip lost, the arrow dropped to the pavement with a hollow echo beside my boot and disintegrated into nothing but ash.

I did *not* have time for this shit.

Chapter 5

I don't know how he did it, but Tyler kept me pinned to that damned wall. The cool chill of his personal brand of magic snaked over my skin, holding me in a grip that refused to let me leave my corporeal form. "Ty, let me go!" My muffled command lost some of its impact in his shirt. "Goddamn it! Let. Me. Go!"

A third arrow zinged toward my head, and Tyler moved, damned fast I might add, flinging me to the ground. Like the second arrow, this one stuck in the brick, burning the masonry to grains of spilling sand. Tyler spread his arms wide, his palms tracing the air above me, and a dome of tangible energy pinned me to the pavement. I guess I should've been glad I wasn't lying facedown in a puddle, but close enough.

"Stay." The one word came harshly through Tyler's lips, making me wonder just where the hell he thought I'd be going, trapped as I was.

The air became saturated with magic, tugging at my senses and settling against my skin like the caress of a thousand downy feathers. Without a backward glance, Ty evaporated from where he stood. Just—poof!—and he was gone. His magic seemed to dissipate as well, crackling in the air like tiny sparks in his wake. Too bad his leaving hadn't released me from my invisible prison. I tried to push myself to at least a sitting position, but that attempt proved futile. The tight dome of energy held me down nice and cozy against the cold, wet, trash-strewn pavement. *How completely charming.*

The cold soaked through my black nylon pants, right

into my bones. I hate the cold—*hate* hate it. But could you imagine me walking the beaches of Florida, head to toe in black—combat boots, long-sleeved Under Armour and all? Me neither. Tyler hadn't even left me enough room in my little prison to maneuver the long tails of my duster beneath me. Sharp pieces of asphalt-covered rock jabbed into the palms of my hands and knees. I looked like a replica of a tarantula—the kind with a bubble of clear resin poured over it. If Tyler showed back up in one piece, I was going to take great pleasure in showing him how much I appreciated his gentle care of the woman he loved.

I'd been lying on the ground for twenty minutes before he returned. Again, I felt a strange weight in the bottom of my gut, and the atmosphere sparked as if in warning. In the blink of an eye, Ty stood beside me, his expression that of barely controlled rage. My own mood had become less than hospitable, and during Ty's absence, I'd graduated from wanting to give him a few scrapes to wanting to give him a black eye. With another sweeping motion of his hands, he traced the air above me, and the invisible dome lifted like the weight of too many blankets. I filled my lungs with air, preparing to give it to him with both barrels.

"There's no sign of the shooter," Tyler said through gnashed teeth. "Anywhere! How did the fucker get away?"

I drew my dagger and pointed it dead center at Ty's sternum. *Ain't love grand?* "Don't you *ever* do that to me again." My voice dripped with poison. "You understand?"

He took a step toward me, his arms outstretched and palms facing upward as if he were pleading for understanding. *Sorry, buddy. That well's all dried up*. Tyler's love was absolute, uncompromising—just as strong as the bond he'd secured when he pledged himself as my genie. And his protection extended to the point of near obsession. Any other girl would have been swooning over his gallant display.

I am *not* any other girl.

I put my free hand out to stay his progress while I kept the dagger's tip held high in front of his face. He walked right into my palm, and I felt the beat of his heart even through the thick fabric of his coat. Strong, steadily slowing from the previous exertion of the chase. "Darian, I—"

"Never again, Ty," I said. "I'm not fucking around."

I could have listened while he apologized and spilled his guts about how he'd only been trying to protect me, how much he loved me. I could have forgiven him on the spot, and we could've gone back to my place, arm in arm, a perfect loving couple.

Instead, I joined the night air and left him right where he stood.

Under the cover of shadow, I came around to the front entrance of the bar. The thrumming pulse of supernatural energy danced across my skin, something familiar and powerful. A woman darted across the street and paused on the sidewalk, glancing anxiously toward the alley I'd just come from. I recognized her from the PNT Summit a few months ago: She was a Sidhe, one of the oldest and most powerful species in the Fae lineage.

Moira.

What the hell was she doing here?

Her gaze settled across the street, on the exact spot where I stood. Eyes narrowed shrewdly, she smiled as if she could see me through the cover of shadow before taking off at a run. She moved so fast, in fact, that I lost sight of her before I could even think of chasing after her.

Sunlight tingles like tiny pinpricks of sensation when it joins with my skin. The gray indifference of dusk and dawn leave me feeling too warm and suffocated, like I'm wearing a scratchy wool sweater in the middle of August. Nothing appeals to me in the way that welcoming darkness does. Like cool satin flowing over my flesh. Despite what I am now, I have always loved the moonlit hours.

Even in my human life, I preferred the night. So I suppose I'd always been a Shaede in my heart of hearts.

Was I still?

I stepped from the cowl of darkness into my solid form. I had no desire to travel unseen, though my near brush with death—or something worse—suggested that traveling under the cover of shadow might have been the wiser choice. Ignoring my better judgment, I walked with a swagger that would have set a gangbanger back on his heels. Throwing myself out there like a fresh piece of meat was a fuck-you to whoever had slung a magic arrow at my head. A *big* fuck-you. I was pissed and didn't care who knew it.

It wasn't quite midnight, and Seattle was barely gearing up. I cut across First Avenue, hit Stewart Street, and headed toward the Market. Along with the Space Needle, Pike Place Market is one of Seattle's most notable icons. Probably why I always felt compelled to go there, no matter the time of day. Humans had always drawn my curiosity, as well as the places they frequented. I was intrigued by the normalcy of their actions, the sense of safety that prompted them to operate with their guards down. False comfort. I knew from experience that ignorance was bliss. I envied them that ignorance, and I wished like hell I could get mine back.

The tails of my duster bounced against my heels as I walked. Heavily scented air caressed my face—a musty smell of brine, fish, and green things—the waterfront making its way to me. My steps against the cobbled sidewalk ticked in precise rhythm to my internal clock. I counted the seconds: *one, two, three, four* . . . until my anger had finally begun to subside. I stared up at the Public Market sign glowing bloodred against the backdrop of darkness. *Blood* . . . A shiver ran up my spine like tiny insects. My blood happened to be special. It had brought Tyler back from the brink of death. I was so unique, in fact, I'd become the prey of an unknown hunter. Tonight's near miss had been proof enough of that.

Tall buildings loomed to my left, their mirrored windows winking in the glowing light of streetlamps, the tops swallowed by dark night. As I paused midstep, the feeling of insects traveling the highways of my skin intensified. Someone, or some*thing*, was watching me. Instinctively I reached with my right hand for my left shoulder blade, where my katana usually hung. I'd left it at home—*lovely*—so I fingered the hilt of my dagger instead. I never used guns. Too impersonal.

"Come out, come out, wherever you are . . . ," I whispered, standing still as a statue as I tried to gauge the location of my hidden admirer. A breeze rustled my hair, bringing with it a tang that burned my nostrils. The scent was unfamiliar, but that didn't mean anything. Friend or foe, I'd learned months ago that creatures scarier than I roamed at the edge of the shadows.

What happened next is still hazy in my memory. Surreal is the best way to describe it, but time meant something different to me. And though I'm sure everything passed in real time, to my perception it passed in the blink of an eye.

A falcon appeared out of the shadowed night, its white belly nearly scraping the top of my head in passing. Something glowed in the grip of its talons, a bright green gem dangling from a silver chain. The keening sound, like a war cry, screeched from the bird's beak, and it dropped its cargo, tinkling at my feet before coming to rest. I looked to the sky, determined to track the bird's passage. Climbing high above the streetlamp's luminescence, it landed atop a nearby building as if waiting to see what I'd do.

The remnant left by the falcon cast a dull green glow at my feet; heat slithered up from the cobbles, warming my ankles through the heavy boots. And as if I needed a distraction—the protesting whine of tires sliding across pavement—a horn blared in warning, followed by the crunch of metal and plastic. *Goddamn it.*

Once the chain reaction started, it could only end in one place—right at my feet. I dipped and scooped the glowing green gem up in my hands and pushed, hard, with both feet, catapulting myself a good ten yards in the air. Shadow joined with flesh, consuming my physical body and concealing me in the safety of my Shaede form.

Both cars ground to a mangled halt where I'd stood, one stunned driver gripping her steering wheel. The other flew from his seat with adrenaline-infused speed, his eyes wide and disbelieving as he searched the space around and beneath his car. "Shit!" he hollered above the mounting commotion. "Did anybody see that? There was a girl standing right here! Right fucking here! What the hell happened to her?"

Feathery wisps, shades of my corporeal form, drifted to the street a good fifty yards from the crash scene. Red and white flashing lights bounced off the surrounding structures as the first fire trucks arrived on the scene. Emergency personnel swarmed their patients, and the man's voice drifted down the street, echoing toward me. ". . . Right in front of my goddamned car. No, I haven't been drinking! Jesus!"

The contents of my hand warmed my preternatural skin. Fist facing the sky, I slowly opened my palm, fingers unfolding like flower petals under a summer sun. A green gem, humming with energy and buried in a nest of pale silver rope, it shone like moonlight bouncing off a green sea. I took the delicate silver between my fingers, letting the gem dangle. *Fathomless.* The stone had an unmistakable depth to it that I could neither understand nor explain. As I looked deep into the softly glowing stone, infinity lay stretched out before me, with no beginning and no end, only endless green.

I'd never been hypnotized, but warmth seemed to blanket me. Calm blossomed from my chest, and the sound of time passing in my soul quieted for the barest moment. My mind went blank, and I felt as though I stood at the end of a long, dark tunnel, staring out at a tiny point of light. It was a universe away, yet just within my grasp.

The sense of peace passed like a breaker rolling in toward shore, and fear welled thick and hot in my throat to replace it. Fingers relaxed, the silver ropelike chain slipped from my grasp, the chiming tinkle of gem and silver against cobbles awakening me from my trance. Strobes of red and white light had been joined by blue, pulsing in my vision like a heartbeat. Green warmth radiated from the ground at my feet. I looked down, retrieved the pendulum in my fist, and stuffed it into my pocket. It didn't want to be ignored, this bauble; its warmth soaked through my pocket and spread to my thigh.

Time to go home. This had been one hell of a night.

Chapter 6

Stepping out of the old freight elevator that served as an entrance to my apartment, I found the studio empty. Tyler had stayed away, and that was saying a lot, considering how he preferred to be stuck to me like Super Glue lately. I was basically over the whole episode, but having a knife held to the chest by a loved one sends a pretty strong message. Though I regretted doing it after my temper cooled, I wasn't quite ready to eat crow. He'd been wrong, plain and simple. And when I've been offended, I'm not a run-away-and-cry-in-my-pillow type of girl. I'm a jab-someone-with-something-sharp kind of girl, and if he wanted to be with me, he'd just have to get used to that.

I discarded my duster, hanging it on a dining room chair, and absentmindedly shucked my boots. I let my feet sink into the deep pile of carpeting that marked my living room and slid down onto the overstuffed chair, propping my feet up on the coffee table. Warmth pulsed at my thigh, and I dug in my pocket, pulling out my strange new bauble by the chain. The gem had grown dark, its previous glow a tiny twinkle of light somewhere in the fathomless center of green. What was this thing? It looked like a pendulum. The gem was a pointed teardrop, and the fastener of the chain was a large silver loop and toggle. Unfastened, the gem dangled from the toggle, allowing the chain to be held by the loop. It hummed with energy, a powerful magic, indeed.

I couldn't just leave it sitting out, and I couldn't trust anyone with the knowledge of its existence quite yet, so

I shuffled to the kitchen, my socks skating across the polished oak floor. A quick jimmy loosened the bricks that made up the false wall, revealing my safe. After a turn to the left, right, and left again, I pulled the heavy door open wide, staring inside at all of the meager keepsakes of my long life, along with a few bundles of emergency cash. I placed my newfound trinket amongst all of my other secrets and on impulse reached deep into the safe, pulling out a stack of postcards rubber-banded together.

The heavy stock was yellowed with age, and the individual cards stuck to one another even after I'd removed the band. I flipped through the images, pictures of landmarks frozen in time, that started coming sometime around 1932. Las Vegas, Atlantic City, the Grand Canyon, San Francisco, New York . . . Lorik had bounced around a lot while running from his father's murderers. I flipped the cards over. My address had been the only thing written on the cards, along with a single message: *Wish you were here!* It pissed Azriel off to no end that Lorik sent the damned things, and he never knew I'd kept them. But it connected me to someone else in the world besides just Azriel. Grounded me when I had no footing. And now, decades later, all Lorik had to show for his life was stacks of old postcards. I rewrapped the cards with the rubber band and shoved them to the back corner of the safe. As I shut the door, the pendant glowed bright green, as if in protest. I turned the lock, secured the loose bricks back into the wall, and tried to forget about not only the past, but the way that glowing stone had calmed the rush of time, if only for a moment.

I had no doubt the mysterious gift had been meant for me. But why? And the identity of my benefactor had me stewing. Could it have been the same person who'd killed the Lyhtan and tried to kill me? Hardly. Why would someone attempt to kill me and then give me a gift? *Hey, great job* not *getting killed. Here's a token of my admiration!* No, whoever had sent the falcon to me had not been my alleged assassin, but the two were more than likely related. And my gift giver obviously had no intention of revealing himself. Otherwise he would have given me the pendulum in person. I leaned against my kitchen counter, massaging the worry line from the middle of my forehead with my fingertips as I racked my brain for some clue.

The studio felt barren—so empty, in fact, the feeling seeped right into the marrow of my bones. I shouldn't have been so testy with Ty. He'd been trying to protect me, foolish though it might have been. And what had I done to thank him? I shoved my knife at his chest. *Good job, Darian. Way to go.* If I felt abandoned, I had no one to blame but myself. I'd been an arrogant ass, and I probably deserved to feel like shit. But it didn't mean I had to like it.

As I settled into my bed, the warmth of my down comforter urging me toward sleep, I tried to ignore the stabbing pain of loneliness that had stuck with me all night. I didn't want to sleep alone; I'd grown used to Tyler's body pressed against mine and needed to feel his reassuring presence. "I wish Tyler were here," I murmured, half asleep, not sure if I'd said the actual words out loud or not.

I rolled to my side and recognized his weight beside me. My lips curved into a sleepy smile as he gathered me up in his arms. "Don't stay away," I whispered. "Even if I'm mad."

"Promise," he said, close to my ear. His breath stirred the hairs near my temple, and I snuggled in deeper to the curve of his body. Now, I could sleep.

My cell vibrated on my bedside table, crawling across the flat surface and making its way closer to my hand. I slid it the rest of the way across the tabletop and dragged the phone up to my ear, not bothering to check the caller ID.

"'Lo?" I said, my face still buried in my pillow.

"We're moving the Oracle today." Anya sounded almost *pleasant.*

I sat up in bed, awake, and looked to my left. Tyler was already gone. At least I could head to Xander's without opposition or worry. Anya didn't wait for me to respond; she probably hadn't expected me to. "She's going to be transported to the PNT's Oregon headquarters in Portland, and His Majesty would like you to accompany the security team escorting her to the rendezvous point."

Easy-squeezy. "I can do that," I said, clearing any trace of sleep from my voice. "But I don't work for free."

Anya snorted through the receiver, and I smiled. "He expects you within the hour."

It didn't bother me that Ty had left while I slept in. He had to make a living just like anyone else, and he'd complained lately that by working for Xander, I'd cost him a few jobs. Though I didn't fully understand the larger scope of all of Ty's business dealings, the area that concerned me was his job as a "death for hire" contractor. If you wanted a sleazy criminal offed, you contacted Tyler. He brokered the deals and contracted the hits, which usually passed down to me. Always understanding, Ty hadn't made it into a big deal that I hadn't been as available lately. I needed a break from killing, even if it meant not taking out the bad guy to make the world a safer place for some other person. Azriel's death had meant more to me than I'd let on, even to Raif. We'd been together; he'd saved me from a life of abuse, and for a while I'd thought I loved him. And in return, I'd taken his life.

I wondered a lot lately if Azriel's spirit lingered somewhere near. Xander had once told me that Shaedes pass forever into shadow when they die, but he didn't really elaborate on what happens afterward. He probably didn't know. Did they go to Shaede heaven, where it was always lovely and dark? Did they stick around, prowling the shadowed corners of the world? Did they remain earthbound to haunt their murderers? A chill raced up my spine, spreading like icy water over my scalp. The last thing I needed right now was an avenging spirit. "Are you here, Az?" I whispered. "Watching me?"

Security detail meant I'd be decked out in black for the day. I needed to look serious, not to mention deadly, and

I wasn't going to pull it off dressed in a lovely white blouse. I pulled out my usual ensemble, nice stretchy pants, a long-sleeved nylon shirt, and, of course, my duster and black boots. I gathered my hair at the nape and braided the long strawberry blond curls before strapping the katana to my back, adding to the severe appearance I'd been looking for. I paused at a pair of black sunglasses and slipped them on, surveying myself in the mirror. "I'll be back," I said in my best Schwarzenegger voice before deciding I looked a bit too cliché—better to leave the glasses behind.

Raif met me at Xander's front door and gave me a brief once-over. "I see you're going for badass today," he said, noting the extra set of throwing knives I wore at my waist in addition to the dagger strapped to my thigh. "I think you overdid it, though. This won't take long."

Sheesh. Somebody woke up on the wrong side of the bed. "Well, I don't care if it takes ten minutes or ten hours. I wanted to look the part."

"You succeeded. Let's get going, then. I don't want her under this roof for another minute."

I wanted to ask Raif why, all of a sudden, Delilah was being hastily ushered from Xander's care. Sure, I knew that eventually the PNT would take her, but I figured she'd be here for weeks until someone came to deal with her. "How is this going down?" I asked instead. "Are we taking her to the airport and loading her up, or are we dragging her all the way to Portland?"

Raif looked at me as though I had an eyeball hanging out of its socket. "Taking her to the airport?" he repeated slowly. "Of course not. She's a high-profile prisoner. We're escorting her to an exchange point, where she'll be housed temporarily. She'll be transported by a PNT team and taken to the Portland facility later."

"Okay, don't get your Calvins in a bunch, Raif. It's not like Oracle Prisoner Transport is something I do on a daily basis. Shit."

Raif's shoulders slumped for the briefest of moments. If I hadn't known any better, I would have sworn he felt bad for copping an attitude with me. But since I did know better, it was only my smart mouth, spurred by ignorance, that frustrated him. In my defense, it's not like I could run down to the corner bookstore and buy a copy of *Supernatural Existence for Dummies* or *What to Expect When You're Expecting Preternatural Company*. I'd been forced into a world I never knew existed, and it hadn't been a gentle introduction by any means. I was learning as best I could, one slow, agonizing step at a time.

Delilah sat on her bed, looking as if she hadn't moved a fraction of an inch since I'd last seen her a couple of days ago. Still cross-legged, still rocking back and forth, still muttering incoherent words to herself. If anything, she appeared more feral. "It's time to go, Delilah," I said, taking her wrists and fastening them in iron cuffs marked with swirling silver symbols. The silver had been woven with magic, according to Raif, and coupled with the iron to ensure Delilah couldn't escape the manacles. Given her willowy, weak form, I doubted she'd be able to fight her way out of a paper bag.

"The Man, the Man, the Man . . . ," Delilah sang as I pulled her from the bed. She weighed no more than a small child. "He's coming, coming, coming. . . ."

"That's right," I said, leading her along, "and you're going, going, going. Move along, out the door, and up the stairs." I looked at Raif and shook my head. This Oracle was off her *nut*.

"Marking time, time's Keeper weeps, along a crumbling path she creeps. Moments long and short she reaps, until the dawning seconds meet!" Delilah laughed as she rhymed, emitting a deep, guttural sound that reminded me of a diabolical cartoon character.

"Sure, sure," I said through my teeth, pushing her up the stairs. God, could she walk any *slower*? "The Man is coming, and his girlfriend too. They're probably crying because they have to follow your slow ass! I get it, Delilah. You're one crazy bitch."

She continued on, babbling and laughing and babbling some more. From the look on Raif's face, he was about to spontaneously combust at any second. It was probably a good thing we were unloading her on the council. Better them than us. Besides, if he'd had to keep her one more day, I doubt I could've prevented Raif from granting Delilah's wish and sending her after her dead sister.

We loaded her into a sleek black Lincoln Navigator, and I couldn't help but feel a little "covert ops" riding around with the SUV's tinted glass windows shutting out the world. Raif sat shotgun while I sat in back with Delilah. A Shaede I'd never met before drove us; his straight back and serious countenance in Raif's presence told me chauffeuring us around town was the high point of his life. Raif was just one of those sorts. No matter whom he met, people wanted to please and impress him. I hated to admit, I did too.

We drove toward the outskirts of the city, away from the Sound and the noise and the people. Crowded streets became an open four-lane freeway, and within twenty minutes we were leaving Seattle behind. "Care to tell me where we're headed?" I asked, willing to test Raif's foul mood.

"Away from the city," Raif said, staring out the window.

"Thanks, Captain Obvious. I could tell that on my own."

Raif didn't take the bait, and I folded my arms, put out that I hadn't been able to engage him. Another fifteen minutes of our prisoner's crazed mumbling filled my aching ears before we turned onto a paved and gated drive. Our driver stopped, pushed a button on an intercom, and waited.

"State your business," a crisp male voice said through the speaker.

"We've come to deliver High King Alexander's prisoner," our driver said. "The Oracle, Delilah."

The gates whined, slowly opening, and we passed through with considerably less fanfare than I expected. Our driver nodded in greeting as we passed the guard station a few yards past the gate, and he waved us on. I marked the passage of another two minutes and forty-four seconds as we drove up the winding drive before coming to a stop in front of a mirrored glass building, bigger than a grocery store, but considerably smaller than a skyscraper.

"PNT Washington headquarters?" I ventured.

Raif nodded his head.

He didn't wear a CIA-issued black suit, but the PNT's security escort looked no less intimidating. My bones hummed in my body, a reaction to the energy projected by the man approaching us, no doubt Fae. I'd become quite astute at recognizing other creatures by the way their energy made me feel, and the Fae, well, standing next to them was like wrapping myself up in a vibrating massage pad. Not an altogether unpleasant sensation.

"Raif." The tall Fae with auburn hair greeted us, his eyes the color of forest moss. His build was lean, though I could tell every inch of him beneath his black military-style garb was corded with muscle. A short saber hung at one side and a set of knives at the other. He reached out his hand, and Raif took it before standing aside.

"Adare, this is Darian. Darian, meet Adare."

I stepped forward, looking him straight in the eye as we shook hands. "So, are you running this show?"

"Cordial, this one," Adare scoffed. "Bet she's fun to hang around."

Raif smiled as he led the way back to the SUV, where Delilah sat, still blathering on about absolutely nothing. "She's been like this since we found her," Raif said. "Frankly, I'm glad to be done with her. Will you be taking her to Portland straightaway?"

Adare looked Delilah over in the way a three-year-old looks with terrified awe at a stalking tiger caged at a zoo. Little bat-shit crazy Delilah had warriors crawling out of their skin. I had to admire her intimidation tactics. Raif inclined his head, and I ducked inside the vehicle. "Come on, Delilah. The train stops here. The PNT is going to babysit you for a while."

I reached for her arm to pull her out when she lurched

forward. Her sour breath hit my face before she laid her cheek to mine, her mouth close to my ear. "You belong to the Man now. Maybe he'll introduce you to Brakae before he kills everyone you love."

My fingers constricted around Delilah's bony arm. Raif was right. We should have killed her and done the council a favor. "I don't respond well to threats," I said. "Especially ones from bony-assed bitches like you. Threaten me again and you won't make it to Portland to stand trial—you got me?"

Delilah giggled in my ear, the sound sending rivers of chills across my flesh. "He will become the master of time and command the Keeper. He will finish what I started. You should have let me bleed you dry. Now it's too late."

I hauled her ass out of the seat so fast, her head lashed back from the force. I'd had it with her smart mouth, and what I really wanted was to shut her up for good. Let her be the PNT's problem. They could try to decipher the crazy shit pouring out of her useless mouth. Threatening my loved ones, whether directly or indirectly, had been the last straw. She could rot in hell for all I cared, dead sister or not.

With a less than gentle shove, I handed Delilah over to Adare. He caught her before she tumbled to the ground and set her right on her feet. "You are hereby taken into custody of the Pacific Northwest Territories Council," Adare instructed. "You are to stand trial for kidnapping, in addition to conspiracy for your malicious acts against the Shaede Nation. You are forbidden to speak or take action against any living thing until the next full moon when the council will hear your case." He touched his thumb to a spot on her forehead just above her nose, the third eye. A glittering gold spark ignited between their skin, and Delilah fell completely silent. Her eyes glazed over; her limbs hung limp. She'd effectively become a rag doll. Since she offered no resistance, Adare was able to lead Delilah toward the mirrored building.

Raif waved in parting and didn't waste any time jumping back in the front seat of the Lincoln. Adare stood stoic at the building's entrance, waiting for the second member of his security team. I watched his partner emerge through the glass doors, his energy hitting me as if a king-sized tuning fork had been driven right into my skull. The vibration nearly sent me to my knees, but I fought the toppling sensation, fixing my gaze on the man whose power barreled toward me like a shock wave.

He was eternally young and vibrant, his dark hair framing his face and making the gray of his eyes all the more startling. A corner of his mouth tugged into a sardonic smile, the kind that invites a challenge. He stared straight at me, ignoring his partner as well as Delilah, who shrank away from his presence, her tiny shoulders hunched and quivering.

I took my seat and quickly shut the door. An involuntary spasm shook my body as I felt the weight of his stare right through the tinted glass window. Power surged from him, as if he knew I could feel it and wanted me to know exactly what kind of heat he was packing. This guy was the Excalibur of otherworldly energy. My vision blurred, and the sound of my blood pulsed in my veins and echoed in my ears. His gaze never left mine, and my chest began to ache, as if he were staring right through my soul. "Who is that?"

"That," Raif said as our driver pulled away from the building, "is Fallon, and if you know what's good for you, you'll stay as far away from him as possible."

"But who is he?" I had to know. No one had ever unnerved me so, not even Azriel. I didn't like it.

"I don't know. But Adare says he's dangerous," Raif said. "That's all you need to know."

Chapter 7

You'd think unloading Delilah on the PNT would've put Raif in a better mood. It didn't.

"Anya!" His voice thundered through Xander's foyer. "Where the hell are you?"

I'd never seen Anya move so fast. To be honest, I don't know how she managed, bound up in her clothes the way she was. As she rounded the corner at a dead run, her breath came hard, as if she'd sprinted ten miles to Raif's beckoning voice. "Sir," she said, her head bowed.

Sir? Oooh, I liked that. Her tone held more reverence in that single word than any groveling title she'd used when addressing Raif's brother. A warm satisfaction grew in the pit of my stomach. It was better than Christmas!

"I want every inch of that cell cleaned," Raif said. "I don't want to smell any lingering trace of the offal that occupied it. Do you understand me?"

"Yes," Anya said, her gaze downcast. "Consider it done."

She took off like a shot, her shrill orders carrying to every corner of the house. Raif would be able to eat his dinner off the floor of that cell by the time she was done with it. I gave a contented sigh. There were days when I just really loved my job. The thought occurred to me, as I basked in smug amusement, I'd forgotten to discuss payment for services rendered. No matter what Xander thought to the contrary, I did not work for free.

"How's this going to work from now on?" I asked as though the previous moment hadn't happened. "Will I be receiving a monthly stipend, or will the royal treasury be cutting me a check per job?"

"You do have a one-track mind, don't you?" Raif ran his fingers through his hair, looking around as if he'd forgotten something. "You'll have to take that up with my brother," he said. "I'm sure he'll pay whatever you're asking. He's around here somewhere. You can find him on your own, right?"

Raif's distraction had me worried. He never lost his cool—never. But the dull sheen of his eyes told me he was a million miles away, his thoughts disconnected from the present. I wasn't sure when I'd lost him, though I was willing to bet it had been the second we'd stepped foot in Delilah's cell.

I didn't have to go far to find my paycheck. Xander was holed up in his office, bent over something no doubt worthy of his precious time. He looked up as I walked in, a broad, seductive smile gracing his face. Gold flecks glowed in his amber eyes, which took their time in absorbing every curve of my body. "Get a good enough look?" I asked, unceremoniously falling into a chair opposite him. I propped my legs up on the desk, crossing them at the ankle as I made myself at home.

"Not nearly good enough," Xander said. "You have far too many clothes on for what I'd like to see."

Charming. "I can safely say my naked body is not a sight you'll be seeing anytime soon. I'm not here to listen to your cheesy come-ons, Xander. I'm here to talk business."

"Cheesy come-ons?" Xander said, leaning forward in his chair. "What if I told you I dream about you nightly? Your skin glorious and bare beneath my hands. What if I said I crave you like a drug and won't rest until I have you in my bed?"

I ignored the pleasant glow that threatened to settle in my stomach from his words. I wasn't completely immune to Xander's charm. Flocks of women would be more than happy to strip naked for him with fewer words than that. But somehow I had a feeling it was the thrill of the chase that really turned Xander on. "I guess you're going to have to look forward to many sleepless days and nights, Xander."

"You're beautiful," he said, ignoring my sarcasm. "Each second without you is torture."

Being the stubborn, arrogant ass he was, nothing I could say would deter Xander from wanting me. I suspected it was simply because I was the one thing he couldn't get with a seductive smile and snap of his fingers. He was laying it on particularly thick today, but I wasn't interested in playing his game. Raif's mood had brushed off on me.

"I'm here to discuss one thing and one thing only. Money."

Xander opened a drawer and withdrew a square ledger book. He flipped it to the appropriate page and grabbed a pen. "What will it take to get this matter of payment settled once and for all? One hundred thousand? Two? I'll cut you a check, and you can never mention the subject again."

My jaw hung slack. The bastard always had to one up me. But it didn't matter. I wanted something from him, and his arrogance would ensure I was going to get it. "Are we talking about a retainer?"

"If it makes you feel better, yes."

I could name my price and Xander would pay it? Well, it would eliminate having to seek him out every time I set foot on his property. Working for the Shaede King brought with it certain advantages I needed, but did I want to work on retainer for him? He'd dangle the money over my head and use any ridiculous excuse to get me to drop everything for him. "I'll consider it," I said. "On one condition."

He waved his hand in a dismissive gesture. Oh yeah, arrogance, thy name is Xander Peck. "I want to answer to Raif and Raif only. I will not wait at your beck and call. If you have work for me—fine. I'll be glad to operate under retainer. But I won't bat a lash unless Raif tells me to do it. And when he doesn't need me, don't expect to see me. I'll reserve the right to work for other employers." *Take that, asshole.*

"Done," Xander said. "How much should I make the check out for?"

How 'bout a billion dollars? "Two fifty ought to cover it." I held my breath, waiting to see how much he really wanted me around.

"I'll make it three," Xander said, his pen scratching against paper, "just in case." With a flourish, he ripped the check from the ledger and slid it across the desk. Shit. He wanted me more than I'd thought. "Now you're paid, and you can quit whining about it."

I took offense at his comment. I had never considered myself a whiner. "Great," I said.

Xander's lips curved in a triumphant smile. Trumped again, I was sure he'd gloat for a long while over this one. If only I could be so outwardly smug. For a moment, I considered tearing the check to shreds and showering him with the confetti. But that would only prove his point and call my bluff. I needed an in, and this was it. So, instead, I brought Xander's check to my nose, inhaling the scent of all those zeroes before stuffing it in my pocket. I swung my legs down off his desk and stood, hoping like I hell I could walk out the door without being ogled in a way that made me feel as though I'd need a scalding-hot shower afterward. "See you around, *Your Highness*," I said.

"Yes." Xander's velvet voice chased me out the door. "You will."

By paying my retainer, Xander hadn't only just given me an assload of money; he'd also gifted me with what I really wanted out of our arrangement—power. No one would question my authority as Xander's agent. And what I'd have to sacrifice through our bargain—my sanity at being his paid employee for starters—was a fair price to pay for what I'd gained. I'd be able to walk right into the PNT facility and question Delilah, at Xander's request, of course, whether or not he'd actually asked me to do it.

Well . . . what he didn't know wouldn't hurt him.

I could get past Adare. I knew from our first meeting that he was an easygoing sort, not prone to suspicion. My only concern with getting in to question Delilah was Adare's partner. Adare wouldn't have told Raif that Fallon was dangerous if he wasn't. And the fact that someone as deadly as Raif had warned me to stay away from him made me even more nervous. With any luck, I wouldn't have to see him at all. I could slip past Adare with a few kind words and a fabricated story. But with the way Fallon's intense stare had unnerved me, I doubted my ability to properly deceive him.

Who was he? Obviously he had a reputation that preceded him. But Raif's explanation simply wasn't good enough for me. Could I Google him? Sure. That'd work. *Fallon on Facebook. View my complete profile here.* I needed to get back into that building to question Delilah. Bringing Raif in on my plan was not an option. He'd shut me down before I could step a foot on PNT property. A few centuries had passed since his daughter's disappearance. Opening up a wound that had long since scarred over would be terrible for him. I'd have to do this alone. I just hoped I had the backbone required to face those piercing gray eyes should I come across them again.

As I made my way down the stairs to the foyer of Xander's ridiculously large house, the sound of Anya barking out frenzied and fear-fueled orders drifted up from the basement-level staircase. I smiled, striding for the door while humming a tune. "Don't scuff your new leather pants on the tile floor!" I called out as I opened the door. The crash of something metal followed by a furious shriek answered me. Yep. Better than Christmas!

Chapter 8

"**D**arian!" Panting breaths followed a wince of pain. "Are you safe?"

I stared down at my cell for a moment before putting it back to my ear. "I'm fine." Fear congealed in a cold knot, settling in the pit of my stomach. "What's wrong? Where are you? Are you hurt?"

"Thank the gods," was Tyler's reply. I could hear the anxiety in his voice, the pain as he swallowed against gasping breaths. "Don't . . . leave your apartment. Stay where—ah—you are."

"Why?" Jesus, was that really my voice? It had escalated into something high-pitched and frantic. "What the *hell* is going on?"

"Someone will be there soon. . . ."

I waited for him to say more, but the line had gone silent. "Tyler?" I whispered. "Ty?"

An angry growling of gears in the background startled me, and the cell phone dropped to the floor. The back panel popped off while the battery sailed underneath my kitchen table. I left the phone in pieces and merged with thin air only to reappear at the gate to my elevator.

"Is there a reason why you failed to mention that someone tried to *kill* you a few nights ago?" Raif's accusing voice drifted up the shaft before the elevator made its way completely up. "My, but you're a special combination of stupid and stubborn, aren't you?"

"Where is Tyler?" I demanded as Raif stepped out of the metal cage and brushed past me.

"Dimitri's gone after him."

"What happened to him?"

"Oh no," Raif said suddenly. "This is not your inter-rogation. I have some questions for you, and you're go-ing to answer every last one of them before you get one *scrap* of information about your Jinn."

Apparently Raif liked being left in the dark just about as much as I did. With Delilah being our main focus, I'd forgotten to mention my near brush with death a couple nights back. Not that it wasn't unusual lately for some-one to try to kill me. Strange what a girl can get used to.

"Tell me first," I said as I tried to control the shaking of my voice. "Is Tyler all right?"

"I suspect he'll be fine. But we'll get to that later. What happened at that bar you like to frequent?"

Raif's dislike of my favorite hangout was obvious. He wouldn't even give it the respect of referring to it by name. I wanted to tell him, *Hey! It's not called The Pit for nothing!* But sarcastic comebacks would only prolong finding out what happened to Tyler. "A Lyhtan sought me out. Said he wanted to warn me about something. But before he could get the words out, someone nailed him in the back of the head with some serious firepower. Tried for me too. But Tyler took after the guy and scared him off."

"Did you get a look at the shooter?"

"No." And I was still pissed off about that.

"The Lyhtan shouldn't have been so easy to kill. What sort of ammunition did the shooter use?" Raif looked thoughtful as he walked past me into the kitchen. He took up a barstool and rested his elbows on my counter, staring off into space.

"Well, this wasn't your run-of-the-mill ammo. It was an arrow. The damned thing was thick; the shaft was made from some kind of metal, I think. And it burned. Hot. White-hot. It disintegrated the Lyhtan as well as the bricks it hit instead of my head. I've never seen anything like it."

Raif swore under his breath. "Sounds like Fae weaponry to me. It's hard to say, though. Many factions keep the contents of their arsenals secret." I raised a brow in question, but Raif just shook his head. "What did the Lyhtan say to you?"

"Nothing that matters. Whoever shot him really didn't want him talking to me. He didn't get anything worthwhile out before he was killed."

Raif's blue eyes penetrated me with a serious stare. "There's nothing else? No other details you've *forgotten* to mention?"

I wanted to jump from the accusation but forced my body into stillness. My eyes threatened to wander toward the false wall in my kitchen, to the safe where the emerald pendulum was tucked away. I didn't know anything about it or the unknown benefactor who'd given it to me. But I did know that something about the mysterious green stone had stilled the pulsing beat of time that never left me. And for now, that was a secret I refused to share with anyone. "Nothing else," I said. "Now tell me what happened to Ty."

"Attacked, an hour ago." Raif's calm delivery made me want to break something. "Ambushed and nearly killed with iron spikes, but, luckily, his attacker was inept. He called me, and I sent Dimitri to fetch him."

Raif talked about Tyler as if he were some stray hit by a car. "How bad is he?" I asked, fearful of the answer.

"He's not going to be running any marathons soon, but he'll live. We're bringing him here. I'm sorry, but I'm afraid my brother's hospitality has worn thin in regard to your lover."

I snorted. That was the understatement of the century. Xander had tolerated Ty in his home when he'd been nearly killed by the Enphigmalé only because I'd been there and I'd wanted it that way. But Xander hadn't eased up in his pursuit of me, no matter how fruitless his efforts. Having Tyler in Xander's home, weakened and defenseless, would *not* be a good idea. "That's fine with me," I said. "I don't want him at Xander's anyway. I can take care of him here just as well as anywhere."

"I thought you'd say that," he laughed.

Raif's cell phone buzzed in his pocket. He brought the phone to his ear with inhuman speed. "Yes," he answered. "I see. . . . Of course . . . Very well . . ."

Fucking hell! I wanted to know what was going on. Raif's nonchalant conversation could have been with the pizza delivery guy, for all I knew. It was a damned good thing he'd snapped his phone shut. I'd been considering knocking it out of his hand. "Tyler has requested that he not be brought here."

Why? The word stalled in my throat. Did he not trust me to take care of him?

"Don't worry yourself into a heart attack, Darian," Raif said as if he'd heard my frantic thoughts. "He's asked to be taken to his penthouse. It seems the security there is better. Not hard to top, really."

Okay, fine. So my apartment didn't have the best security. Anyone who had a mind to come up could just hop on the elevator. In the past, the lack of safety hadn't bothered me. I mean, I'd thought I was unkillable. What did it matter who came up uninvited? But with another near miss in only a couple of days, I could understand Tyler's decision. I strapped my katana to my back and tucked two throwing knives into my belt before jamming the dagger into the sheath at my thigh. If I was going out, I was going out well armed. "Let's go," I said, not waiting to see if Raif followed or not.

Tyler's penthouse apartment left nothing to be desired. Situated atop the Aspira building, it boasted every technological advancement and top-of-the-line security. Controlled-access parking secured the premises from unwelcome visitors, and the perimeter of the building was monitored by closed-circuit cameras. Tyler left word with the guard station and front desk, allowing us easy access to the apartment. I wanted nothing more than to break from my physical form—the elevator ride was taking *forever*—but Raif convinced me otherwise, saying that keeping up appearances was more important than a hasty ascent.

"You have no idea what happened?" I asked for what felt like the hundredth time.

"Like I said"—Raif ran his hands through his hair—"it seems Tyler was a bit occupied with nearly being killed and didn't have time to go into detail about the attack."

I bounced impatiently in the elevator, repeatedly pushing the penthouse button on the elevator panel. If we didn't move any fucking faster, my next move was going to be stabbing the button with one of my knives.

A serene *ding!* registered low and reverberated before the sleek metal doors slid silently open. From there, a foyer led to the entrance of Tyler's apartment, and I walked through the door, coming face-to-face with Dimitri.

Anya's husband held his sword at the ready, easing up only after seeing Raif walk through the door. The comparison between Anya and Dimitri was like night and day. Anya's hard, leather-clad dominatrix persona seemed even more ridiculous when coupled with Dimitri's soft, Zen-like appearance. His fawn brown eyes held a depth and sadness that spoke of hardships overcome. Blond hair the color of dishwater brushed his collar in soft waves, framing an eternally youthful, round face with high cheekbones. He sheathed his sword, bowing his head to Raif before addressing us both in a voice slightly accented with his native Russian. "He's in the bedroom."

If I could have prepared myself for what I'd see once I walked through the door, I might not have acted so rashly. Anya sat on top of Tyler, straddling his waist, bent over him, his wrists pinned beneath both of her hands. With one fluid motion, I left my physical self, appeared at the side of the bed, and yanked Anya's long rope of braided hair, propelling her from Tyler into the far wall.

I turned from the bed, intent on ripping her head right off. Raif caught me by the elbow, pulling me close against him while Anya picked her sorry ass off the floor. "Seriously, what in the hell has gotten into you?" Raif gave me a jerk, and I looked past him at Anya, a red haze of anger preventing me from forming a rational thought. "Darian!" Raif said louder, shaking me soundly. "Look at him! Anya was trying to *help*!"

One more jaw-rattling shake cleared my mind enough to turn toward the bed. Tyler lay sprawled across its surface, blood staining the light gray coverlet as it seeped from the lacerations made by thin iron rods in his wrists. My eyes roamed farther down, and my breath stilled in my lungs as I noticed a larger iron stake protruding from just above Tyler's left pec.

"Motherfucker!" I shouted, converging on the bed in a single leap. "Anya, get your bony ass over here and help me!"

"What do you think I was trying to do?" she asked, "Fuck him? Sorry, not my type."

"Shut up!" I snapped. I did not have time to get into it with her. Tyler was bleeding to death all over his comforter. "How do we get these out without doing any more damage?"

"The stakes are iron," Dimitri said quietly from the doorway. "Jinn, like Fae, are allergic to iron. They must be removed."

"No shit," I said from between clenched teeth. "But I don't want to hurt him any worse—"

"Darian," Tyler said, his voice pained with labored breath, "just pull them out."

"But, Ty."

"Like a Band-Aid," he rasped. "Do it quick."

Anya glared at me but placed one hand on Tyler's palm, the other just below his wrist. She gave a curt nod, and I wrapped my hands around the rod, took a deep steadying breath—and yanked.

Tyler's back arched, and he thrashed against us, his jaw set and teeth clenched tight in obvious agony. Dimitri came around the bed with stacks of sterile gauze and rolls of tape, slapping the absorbent pads against the wound before wrapping his wrist with the tape. Anya shifted, secured Tyler's other hand, and we repeated the process. We allowed Ty a moment to catch his breath, everyone in the room staring at the spike in his chest like a group of kids standing around an arcade game.

I laid my hand against his cheek, my fingers creeping up into his hair and brushing the sweat-dampened, coppery curls from his face. "Are you ready?" I asked.

Tyler tensed beneath me, and Anya shifted, placing her weight squarely on both of his shoulders. "Ready."

Without steeling myself against the pain I was about to inflict, I pulled—hard—on the stake, and I felt the sickening resistance as it fought to hold on inside his body. Tyler lurched once, and I yanked the stake free. Tyler's body went slack, sweat beading on his brow, and he lost consciousness.

I reached for my dagger, ready and willing to do for Tyler what I'd already done for him once before. "What do you think you're doing?" Raif asked, grabbing my hand before I could cut my own wrist.

"Helping Ty! My blood can heal him."

"Gods, girl." Raif shook his head, jerking the dagger from my hand. "You needn't do anything quite so rash. Give him a little time. Now that the iron has been removed, he'll be fine. His magic will heal him."

Dimitri had begun to dress the wound, so instead I unwound the tape from the first wrist we'd worked on. Still ugly, still oozing, but, strangely enough, it did look smaller than it had when we removed the spike. "Why hadn't he healed from the Enphigmalé attack then?" I asked, rewrapping his wrist.

"Your guess is as good as mine," Raif answered. "Why does Lyhtan venom affect us? Who knows these things?"

Who indeed. Fuck it all, I was exhausted. "Thank you, Anya," I said while still looking at Raif. If I had to make eye contact with her while expressing my gratitude, I might've still taken the dagger to my wrist for a completely different reason. "You too, Dimitri. Thank you for going after him."

Anya snorted in response, and Dimitri shrugged as if to say, *Don't worry about it.* "Get out of here, Raif," I said. "I've got it from here."

Raif laid a hand to my shoulder. "I'll set a guard outside the building, just in case."

"No." I didn't want to be beholden to Xander for anything else.

"You forget an attempt was made on your life as well. You're one of mine. And I take care of mine."

Damn Raif for making me feel all mushy when I'd been going for tough bitch. "Fine," I said against the thickness in my throat. "I still think it's a waste of time, though."

"Obviously," Raif said as he headed for the door, "I don't care what you think is a waste of time. Call me if you need anything."

I nodded my head, swallowing the emotion that threatened to leak from my eyes. When I heard the elevator doors slide shut in the foyer, I managed to exhale the breath I'd been holding. I reexamined Tyler's wounds. Already the bleeding had slowed, barely showing through the gauze. Tyler's eyes fluttered, and I sat on the bed, tracing patterns on his fingers as I waited for him to come to.

"Thanks for staying," Tyler said lazily. "I'm going to need help getting out of my clothes, and I sure as hell didn't want Raif doing it."

I bit back a laugh and squeezed his fingers. "I can help you with that," I said. "Gladly."

Chapter 9

I'd shucked my boots and pants and lain on the bed, stripped of its bloody linens, with my arm draped carefully across Tyler's muscled abs. He twirled the silver ring on my thumb as he spoke, as if it bore the memories of a thousand years.

"I'm not used to being the one who needs to be rescued," he whispered against my hair. "I can't say I like it very much."

"Well, you owe me only once." I caressed his silky hair, the strands slipping through my fingers. "You'll have to settle up with Raif for this one."

Tyler laughed, and then his body jerked in pain. The wound on his chest had yet to heal completely. I'd changed the dressings twice, and finally the bleeding had slowed. His wrists were much better, the injuries appearing to be weeks old rather than merely hours. I had no idea he could heal so fast.

"Raif is a good man," he said, surprising me. The previous night he'd been ready to throw down with the guy for spending too much time with me. Now, he was extolling his virtues?

"He is," I agreed. "Like family. I'd do anything for him."

"I think he'd do the same for you," Tyler said, his tone growing dark. "But I'm glad for that. It's nice to know someone else has your back."

"Do you have family, Ty?" I'd always wondered but never asked. Perhaps the conversation would take his mind off the pain.

"Not really." Tyler slid my ring up and down my thumb between my knuckles. "I didn't grow from infancy. Nor do I remember a childhood. Jinn are born from magic. No mother, no father. Just a moment of self-realization and conscious thought"—he shrugged his shoulders—"and I existed."

Shit. That beat my story a millionfold. Granted, I too was a creature created from sheer will. But I'd been a human first—a real person, born and raised. I'd had a mother, a father, a pretty normal existence. It was years later that Fate, or whatever you want to call it, had done a number on me, and I'd been transformed into something more than human. I'd evolved into what I was—not just a force of magic brought to life. "How did you know what you were? How to live?"

"We are never alone." Tyler kissed my temple, and I sensed he'd become lost in his memories. His voice grew thick, and his words were weighed carefully, accented with the remnants of a language no longer spoken. Near-death experiences have a way of rocketing you into the past, to the beginnings of your life as you've come to know it. Ty wasn't here with me anymore; he was back there—in that place. "I was found by another like me as she traveled through the desert one day. Adira. She took me in, taught me what I needed to know. . . . It's been this way since the beginning of time. We can sense the magic in our kind, and we're naturally drawn to it.

"I'm not going to say that my first days were easy ones. Confusion is a given when you seem to manifest out of nowhere. I could speak, but there was no one to talk to. I hungered, yet the desert held no food. I had a want of things I could not describe nor seek solace for, and I wandered the harsh, lifeless land for days before I was found. At the first sight of another soul, I cried out in relief. I understood her words, and she gave me water, which I drank until it made me sick. She took me to her home, a small village inhabited to my surprise by creatures that looked similar to me, but I sensed the mundane in them. Adira had bound herself to the chieftain's

wife, and she watched over their people. I lived with
Adira for a century or more, learning the ways of the
Jinn from her. One day, while walking the desert, just as
I imagine Adira had, I came across a confused and wandering soul, and I gave him water and food. I delivered
the Jinn to Adira, and she cared for him. I decided to
leave not long after that. I'd learned everything I needed
to know, and I was restless to see the world beyond. I
have not seen that place since the day I left."

I realized, as I listened to the soft cadence of Tyler's
voice, that I didn't know anything about his life — his real
life. I knew he was a good man, and loving, and overprotective in a way that made me want to kiss him and rip
his arms out of their sockets at the same time. But I had
no knowledge of his history, upbringing, or existence.

"Xander said your people come from Europe or the
Middle East. Is that true?"

"Africa," he said almost dreamily. "Egypt. Sudan. Desert regions."

"You don't look African," I teased.

Tyler raised a curious brow. "I'm not," he said. "I am
Jinn."

My voice turned serious, "How many others have you
bound yourself to?"

Tyler shifted in bed to look down on me, one corner
of his mouth curving into a crooked smile. "Jealous?" He
smoothed the tangles of curls from my face. When I
didn't answer, he said, "I hope so. I've only bound myself
to someone once before you. And I don't plan to ever do
it again."

My stomach clenched, a warm wave of pleasure burst-
ing outward through my limbs. It was like having someone tell you he didn't plan on sleeping with anyone else
ever again. That he'd found the one person he could
never leave or get enough of. Was it safe for him to
pledge his loyalty to me? One attempt had been made
on my life so far, and now someone had nearly taken his.
"Who attacked you?"

"I didn't get a look at him," Tyler said. "He knew me

and how to stop me, though. Backed me against a wall before I could get at him and jammed those stakes into my wrists so I couldn't fight back. Cowardly bastard. He went for my heart and would have killed me if I hadn't managed to give him a good kick right as he drove the stake in. Fortunately for me, the bastard jumped me outside The Pit. Levi heard the commotion and came out to see what was going on. The guy's face was covered, and he bolted before Levi could get his hands on him. I lucked out."

Understatement of the century. "Did he say anything to you?" The loaded silence between us told me Tyler's attacker *had* said something. Probably something he didn't want me to know. "Tell me."

Tyler sighed in resignation. He knew I'd have no qualms about beating it out of him if he didn't supply the information willingly. "He said, 'I can't have you protecting her,' and then he went for my heart."

"This is because of me," I said. "Again."

"No," Tyler said, holding me tighter. "You are not allowed to take the blame for this. It comes with the job. It's not as though I didn't know something like this could happen. This is how a binding works. I am your protector. Period. And if that means—"

"How can you say that?" I said, sitting upright and putting some much-needed distance between us. "That it's perfectly okay if you die protecting me because it's your *job*? Your reasoning is seriously fucked up. Do you really think I could live with myself if you were killed?"

"I chose this, Darian." Tyler struggled to lean up on his arm. "Me. No one twisted my arm to make me bind myself to you. I knew the risks then, just like I know them now." His tone escalated with every word. "Don't treat me like some kid who can't take care of himself. I've walked this earth for thousands of years, and I am not a weak human for you to worry about!"

"I don't think you're weak," I said.

Tyler gave me a withering look. "Sure as hell sounds like it. Besides, who said this is just about you? Get over yourself. I've got business that doesn't concern you, and you're not the only one who knows what I am."

There was nothing he could say to convince me the attempt on his life had nothing to do with me. There were too many coincidences. Besides, I doubted Ty had many women he was watching out for, and his attacker said, *I can't have you* protecting *her*. My to-do list was growing by leaps and bounds: Sneak into the PNT building to rattle Delilah's chain; find Raif's daughter; flush out this Man from The Ring; and fend off attempts on not only my life but also Tyler's. I truly had a knack for getting the shitty end of the stick.

While I contemplated the way my heretofore good fortune was slowly circling the drain, Tyler's hand had begun to creep from my wrist, trailing up my arm and across my collarbone. Delicious chills chased the path of his fingers, slowly caressing up my neck, beneath my ear. The bed shifted as he sat up. His mouth hovered near my temple, and I shuddered. "I want you," he whispered, causing a molten rush of excitement to ignite every nerve ending in my body. Talk about a one-eighty. Hadn't we just been on the verge of an argument?

"You're hurt," I murmured.

Not that I didn't want to forget about his injuries and lay him out on his back. Tyler ran the tip of his nose up and down my cheek into my hairline and inhaled deeply. "Mmm, you smell good. It's making me crazy."

That made two of us. A warm, heady odor like sweet vanilla and cinnamon wafted around us, Tyler's arousal evident in the mixture of delicious scents. I took his wrist in my hands, unwinding the gauze to find the wound almost completely healed. Repeating the process on his other wrist, I discarded the bloodied gauze and gently kissed the skin that had been marred with a raw laceration just an hour earlier. "Just like magic," I whispered against his skin.

With a fierceness that startled me, Tyler wrapped his arms around me and snatched me close until our lips were almost touching. His breath came heavy as his eyes delved into mine, and his jaw took a stubborn set. One hand slid up my back, and his fingers threaded through the locks of my hair. My eyes never left his, lost in their hazel depths as I reveled in the feeling of his cool breath fanning over my face.

"Don't ever doubt me," he said in a steel-hard tone that set me back a little. His emotions were teetering close to manic—or at the very least, bipolar. I tried to pull away, but he held me, refusing me even an inch of freedom. "I belong to you. Mind, heart, soul." He paused. "And flesh. I'm strong enough."

I know he thought he was. A powerful genie born from magic, he had a right to be even more arrogant than I was. But if I'd learned anything these past months, it was that nothing—not even Tyler—was immortal.

"Darian." Our mouths met, just a glancing of lip to lip. "You belong to me too. You gave me your blood just as I gave you my bond. Don't shut me out, ever."

He was right. The Enphigmalé had given him a mortal wound, and I'd forced my blood down his throat to heal him because I loved him. The thought of him dying was simply too much. I knew I could never live without him. I didn't want to shut him out, but maybe shut him up, to explain my concern had more to do with love than feeling he was an inadequate protector. I'd almost lost him once before. I didn't think I could stand a repeat of that kind of torture.

Tyler didn't give me the opportunity to say another word. His lips found mine with a hunger that set my skin on fire. I reeled at the intensity of Tyler's kiss. This was no shy, lovesick entreating of lips. This was an I'm-a-man-goddamn-it-and-you'd-better-stand-up-and-take-notice kiss. And oh, did I notice! In one fluid motion, he swung me around and beneath him, his lips locked onto mine throughout the entire gravity-defying maneuver. I pressed my hand to the taught muscles of his stomach and managed to break free just long enough to draw a breath.

"Tyler," I said against his mouth. "Your chest. It's still not completely healed."

He gave his opinion on that matter by sliding his hand slowly down my side. "Shhh." His fingers wrapped around the slim strap of my underwear, and, with a quick jerk, he ripped the seams. With amazing dexterity, he pulled the now-ruined fabric out from underneath me without even chafing my skin.

I moaned, nice and loud. I hoped Tyler's walls (and his floor, respectively) were well soundproofed, because at the rate he was going, I'd be screaming my pleasure in just a few moments. Before he could employ any more of his undressing skills, I pulled my shirt over my head in a single sweeping motion. Tyler's gaze smoldered as he took in every inch of my exposed flesh. He wrapped his hands around my hips, and, in a motion too fast and too deft for someone stabbed a few hours ago, he flipped me over to my stomach. He unclasped my bra, laying his lips between my shoulder blades before sliding the straps down over my shoulders. I lifted my body just enough for him to ease his hands beneath me, and he swept the bra away, lingering as he teased my nipples to stiff peaks with his fingers. I was *so* past caring about injuries as his fingers pressed into my skin, sliding around to my shoulders and down my spine. He cupped my ass, kneading the flesh with strong hands before he ventured farther down and underneath, sliding his fingers inside me. Slick, warm, soft, he pulled away and moved a little farther up, finding my pleasure center, sighing next to my ear as he brought me close to orgasm with each teasing stroke.

While his fingers caressed the softest, most delicate part of me, his mouth went to work on my flesh, kissing, licking, tasting, as he worked from one shoulder, across my back to the other, and then downward. I trembled beneath him, my breath coming in short gasps as the sensation brought me to a level of pleasure so intense, I thought I'd see stars—or lose consciousness.

"Take me, Tyler," I said. "Now."

"Not quite yet," he said hoarsely. "Let me taste you first."

Again he grabbed me by the hips and turned me over.

His chest rose and fell with his rapid breath as he shucked his loose-fitting pajama bottoms. I didn't dare blink as I drank in every detail of his muscled body, my eyes trailing from his face, to his bandaged chest and over the ridges of his abs. My gaze wandered lower to the glorious hard length of him. He sucked in a hiss between clenched teeth. Tyler lowered himself to the bed, starting at my knee and working his way up my thigh with his mouth. I arched, writhing with pleasure and wanting him so badly, I thought I'd burst into flames. His mouth fastened over my core, and I cried out, my hips acting on their own, pressing toward the pulsing sensation drawn from Tyler's gently stroking tongue.

I couldn't hold back any longer. I twined my fingers through Tyler's hair, the passion consuming me as the orgasm swept me away from reality. He held me firmly against him as I called his name. "Tyler, please. I need you inside me. Oh God, now!"

A sound passed between his parted lips, more animal than man as he rose above me, positioned himself, and thrust, at first slow and careful, and then with purpose. I gasped, consumed by the building heat of our passion as he showed me with every drive of his hips that I was his and no amount of whining or insisting could convince him to hide in my shadow. "Oh . . . God!" I shouted, arching my back and pushing my hips to meet his. "More. Harder." His mouth grazed the tender flesh of my neck, and he bit, just hard enough to send a zap of electric heat through my body. I dug my nails into his back, sinking my own teeth into his shoulder as his pace quickened. And just as I thought I couldn't take one more moment of blinding pleasure, it exploded upon me again with an intensity that left me quivering in his arms. Tyler called out, uttering an ancient word that meant nothing to me, but I got the gist of it all the same; he collapsed on top of me, panting and placing lazy kisses along my collarbone and shoulder.

We lay immobile for a few moments, each of us coming down from the intense high. Something cool and wet against my skin shocked me back into reality, and I shoved at Tyler's shoulders, lifting him far enough away from me that I could see the seeping bandage covering his chest. "You're bleeding again," I said as I tried to control the panic in my voice.

"It must have torn open a bit." Tyler gave an uninterested shrug. "I'm sure it'll be fine." He rolled away to lie beside me, and I wanted to pull him back on top of me, to feel the comfort of his weight against me. "Besides," he said, his voice becoming husky, "it was worth the damage."

I tried to redress the now-shallow laceration, but Tyler brushed my concern away, saying that he'd heal before I had a chance to retrieve the roll of gauze. I didn't argue. In fact, I could recall a time not long ago when he had insisted on dressing my own wounds, and I'd rolled my eyes at him, knowing I'd heal. I'd brushed his concern aside as well. That moment felt like a lifetime ago. I suppose it had been. I wasn't the same woman I'd been six months ago. Tyler had changed me on the inside as much as I had changed on the outside. If we could just lie here together, safe and sated and needing nothing more than each other for sustenance, I could stay like this forever and never worry again about the troubles banging down my door. I drifted to sleep, wrapped in Tyler's arms with his breath caressing my forehead.

Strange dreams came to me in my sleep, dreams of an emerald pendulum and a woman with raven hair. A great gray beast chased her through an open field, throwing up turf and mangled bushes in its wake. Watching helplessly, I could do nothing for the woman, though she cried out for me, "Darian! Stop him!"

I tried to take a step forward, but something held me. Compelled beyond the physical, I dropped to my knees, the emerald pendulum burning my flesh as I squeezed it. The point of the gem dug into my hand, blood welling from the gash in my skin. "You are the Guardian!" she shouted as she ran. "Please, help me!"

The beast leapt, and the woman fell at its feet. She didn't move as the gargoyle circled her immobile body, its glowing silver eyes trained on my face rather than on its prey. "I've had your blood," the gargoyle said, "and you will obey *me*."

Chapter 10

I woke the next morning with feelings of unease stirring within me. The gargoyle of my dream, the Enphigmalé, caused me more disquiet than the poor woman begging me to help her. I couldn't shake the eerie image of that voice coming from the fanged mouth of the beast, so confident I would obey its commands.

Tyler's wounds had closed completely during the night. At least I had one thing to be thankful for. Dimitri called to check on Tyler, which in my opinion was a nice gesture, considering that he was married to Anya, and I couldn't imagine her compassion cup overflowed for either of us. Maybe I wasn't giving her enough credit. Maybe I was giving her too much.

Though he'd healed superficially, Tyler was still pretty wiped out. Traces of iron had spread through his system, nothing that couldn't be cured with a little R&R, according to him. So I left him to sleep the day away, unofficially borrowing his motorcycle—hey, he wasn't going anywhere—and I doubted he'd even realize it was gone. I left my coat at Tyler's because I didn't need the long tails tangling in the wheels of the sleek Buell street bike, and sped off through town toward the freeway.

I ducked my head, listening to the wind as it whooshed over the motorcycle helmet. I didn't needed it for protection, though I might have gotten a ticket if I hadn't worn one. It kept my hair from whipping around, however, so it served a certain function. I could have traveled as my ethereal self, but even with my preternatural speed, it would have taken a while to make it to the PNT building—and I was in a hurry.

The place looked even more forbidding than the last time I'd visited. But since I didn't scare easily, I pulled right up to the gate and pushed the call button nice and long, just to annoy whoever was on the receiving end of the noise.

"State your name and business," a crisp, thoroughly pissed voice said.

"Darian Charles, here on official business for Alexander Peck to see Delilah, the Oracle." Unless the guard called to check, he'd have no idea I was lying. And I hoped my authoritative tone and use of Xander's given name wouldn't give him reason to doubt my being there.

"One moment," the voice said.

I waited a good three minutes before the gates swung open to allow me entrance. The bike purred as I put it in gear and drove past the guard station and up the steep driveway to the Pacific Northwest Territories nondescript stronghold. I expected Adare to meet me in front of the building as he had the first time I'd been here, but instead of the easygoing Fae, someone I'd hoped not to see waited to escort me inside.

When I'd first laid eyes on him, he'd set me on edge. Now I could say that seeing him for a second time was no less unsettling. I wasn't afraid; on the contrary, I felt strangely drawn to him. As if I couldn't get off the bike fast enough, I parked, pulled the helmet from my head, and hung it on the handlebar. I had to force myself to slow as I approached him, my legs rebelling against the pace and urging my steps to quicken. His gaze, lowered toward the ground, rose slowly to meet my eyes, and a lazy, confident smile graced his face. Holy hell, but he was something to look at.

Fallon wasn't the sort of regal, rugged handsome of Xander, and he was far from the tousled, supermodel gorgeous of Tyler. Rather, he was striking in a way that demanded attention. His features were sharp, precise, and betrayed his lack of humanity. Dark brown hair woven with reddish gold, clipped short in a style that bespoke an active life or military background, framed his face. Eyes, gray like storm clouds, studied me as he folded his arms across a broad chest. His legs were braced apart, military stance, stock-still and straight. His full lips spread into a smirk, and the expression somehow suited him. My body hummed as his energy funneled into me, making me feel too nervous and jittery to stand still. I knocked one boot against the other as if clearing the soles of dirt, and ran my hand through the wind-knotted ends of my hair. I lowered my gaze as I drew closer, unable to meet his eyes, but I could feel him watching me.

I gave myself a mental shake. Jesus, what the hell was wrong with me? You'd think I'd never been in the presence of a looks-and-power combination. Let's face it; the supernatural community had its share of lookers, as well as power players. Many of us were beautiful and chock-full of energy that spoke of strength; it just came with the genetics. Or the magic. Or both. The sound of seconds passing that I'd trained myself to push to the back of my mind pounded in my veins as I walked toward him. Time would not be ignored as it slogged along, each moment like the tolling of a bell, a warning I could not heed. It must have been the power of Fae magic that drew me to him, though I hadn't felt this way in Adare's presence. Maybe I shouldn't have taken Raif's admonition so lightly. Too late now.

Fallon's tongue traced a line along his bottom lip as if he'd just tasted something delicious—or wanted to. "This is an unexpected visit," he said. "What can the PNT do for you?"

I stared at him, wondering why his voice should sound familiar. "The PNT can't do anything for me," I said. "I'm here to question Delilah."

Fallon opened the door. He swept his arm before him as he waited for me to enter. "You can question her all you like," he laughed. "But I doubt you'll get any answers."

The illusion of uninteresting small business carried over from the parking lot to the interior of the PNT's building. A reception desk crowded the front of the open first floor, and seated at that desk was a very perky, very human woman. She greeted me with her best customer-service smile and turned her attention back to her computer screen, fingers flying on the keyboard. A small waiting area, complete with couches, magazines, and one of those pump coffee carafes and cups, looked, for the most part, unused. Beyond the front entrance, a row of elevators lined a far wall, and behind the receptionist's desk were several small offices with closed metal doors. All in all, it was not an overly friendly atmosphere.

I felt Fallon's presence behind me, the power he exuded nearly stealing my breath. He passed the reception desk toward the elevators, and I followed. One set of metal doors slid open, and Fallon stepped inside. I paused, my eyes scanning the small box and its lack of actual space. Anxiety coursed through my blood, and he met my gaze, his gray eyes burning into mine. "Afraid?" he asked.

The look he gave was an open challenge, and I wasn't one to back down. But damned if I wasn't off my game; he unsettled me, and I felt the sudden urge to wish out loud for Adare to be standing here with me instead. I clamped my jaw tight, as if my mouth might betray me and actually make the wish. Shooting a quick glance over my shoulder to the receptionist, I stepped inside and watched as the first floor was closed from my view. "Have you worked for the PNT long?" I asked. Raif hadn't known him, only heard of him, and I assumed Raif to be very connected. If he didn't know Fallon personally, he couldn't have been here long.

Fallon pushed the button marked B for the basement floor. "No," he said, confirming my suspicion, "I've been here only a couple of months. Came over from the Northeast Division. Connecticut."

I didn't think any of this information would be good for anything, but the small talk helped to calm my skittering nerves. "Needed a change of scenery?"

"You could say that," Fallon answered. "Seattle holds something dear to me."

Can you say *awkward*? I stared at my feet as our conversation died a quick and painful death. A million times over, I silently wished I'd stayed in bed with Tyler and wasted the day away. Instead, I was going out of my fucking mind with this stranger standing too close beside me, his unusual energy pulling my nerves so taut, I thought they'd snap.

The elevator stopped and the doors slid open, much to my relief. I wouldn't have lasted another thirty seconds in such close proximity to my escort without clawing my way out of the elevator. I allowed him to walk in front of me, giving him a healthy head start. His gait was calm, easy with the fluid motion of a stalking cat. We made our way down a long hallway illuminated by a single row of fluorescent lights. None of the doors had latches, I noticed, but beside each on the wall was an electronic keypad. Fallon stopped at the end of the hall, turned to his right, and punched a code into the corresponding keypad.

The door slid open and Fallon announced, "The Oracle," as if he were introducing me to the queen.

I stepped past him into the stark white cell. Sadly, this was sizing up to be one bitch of a day. Delilah's accommodations at Xander's house had been like the Ritz-Carlton in comparison to where she was now. I took stock of the room: four concrete walls: check; windows, or rather lack thereof: check; absence of any comfort, even the most remote—oh yeah, the PNT had that covered too. The room was empty. No furniture—not even a dirty mattress for the poor creature to sleep on. No toilet. I didn't even want to *guess* how she was taking care of that issue.

Like a tiny speck of dirt on a fresh-snow-covered field, Delilah sat on the floor. She was no longer rocking, to my relief, but she was huddled close to a corner, her knobby knees drawn up tight to her chest and her arms hugging her body as if keeping it intact. She looked so young, so completely breakable, that I almost felt sorry for her. "Bet you wish you were anywhere but here right now," I said. Delilah completely ignored me.

Fallon stepped into the room, and Delilah's head snapped to attention like a dog hearing a high-frequency whistle. Her unseeing eyes stared straight ahead, but her head cocked in the avian fashion that made her stand out as something other than human. She must have felt his energy as well because, as soon as he cleared the threshold, Delilah began to shake all over, her tiny bare feet scuttling her back against the corner as if she could will the walls to swallow her whole. I stared from Delilah to Fallon, thinking again of Raif's warning that he was dangerous.

"Okay, Delilah," I said, going for my best impression of fed-up mom. "Your weak-and-frightened act is getting a little boring. I've got a lot of questions and not a lot of time. So let's get down to business. If you cooperate, I promise not to hit you—much. If you don't cooperate . . . well, I'll use my fists instead of an open hand. Got it?"

She didn't respond, though her mouth opened and closed, like a fish that had been dragged up onshore. I sighed. I wanted to get the hell out of there—fast—and Delilah was not making this easy for me. "Delilah!" I nudged at her bare foot, and she flinched. "I know you can hear me, you blind pain in the ass! Knock this shit off. Remember the night I hauled your skinny ass over to Xander's? You mentioned Raif's daughter. Where is she?"

Nothing. Unless you wanted to count her fish-mouth routine.

I took a step forward, bending low and wrapping my hand around the collar of her shirt. As I hauled her to her feet, her head cocked rapidly from side to side and a strangled cry escaped her lips. "Answer me!" I shouted, giving her a solid shake.

"She can't," Fallon finally said. "I told you, you weren't going to get anything out of her."

I dropped Delilah to the floor, and she scrambled back to her perch in the corner of the room. Her body shook like a hypothermia victim, her head cocking toward any sound. I folded my arms—more or less to occupy my hands—wishing I had something I could punch just to release my own tension. Fuck it all, this day was going to shit fast. "Why won't she speak?" My voice was hard enough to cut glass.

Fallon stepped forward and passed his open palm in the air above Delilah's forehead. A mark appeared, glowing gold at the point of her third eye. "She's been restrained by magic," he said. "You saw Adare cast the spell the day you brought her here, did you not? She'll be unable to speak or act against anyone until the date of her trial. It's standard PNT procedure."

Oh. Just. *Great*.

I turned on Fallon. "You know, it might have been nice to know that before I hauled her scrawny ass up off the floor and shook her like a wet cat. And if you'd mentioned this when I arrived, I wouldn't be down in this dungeon, wasting my fucking time."

"Whom are you looking for?" Fallon asked, ignoring everything I'd just said.

"None of your goddamned business—that's who I'm looking for."

"Touchy." He leveled his gaze, another challenge.

"You could say that."

"Who's Raif?"

Who's Raif? This guy wasn't from the Northeast; he was from another planet. Raif's reputation preceded him. You had to have been living under a rock not to have at least heard of Raif Peck. Then again, I'd lived almost a hundred years without hearing even a whisper of his name. But I could hardly be blamed for that. The supernatural world had kept a safe distance from me all those years. And I sure as hell hadn't been looking for them.

"Raif is . . ." What was he? The prince? An earl? I had no idea what the king's brother's official title was. "The High King's brother. And all around badass," I added. "I believe Delilah knows the whereabouts of his daughter, who's been missing for quite a while."

"Why didn't Raif come here himself to question the Oracle?"

His tone matched the look in his eyes, an underlying command. And even as I gave up this secret information, I wondered what in God's name would possess me to tell him. I'd had no intention of sharing this secret with anyone. Yet here I was, spilling the beans to someone who made me want to jump out of my skin. It seemed I couldn't wait to provide information to him. I needed to leave before I started rambling on about my fabulous sex life.

"Raif doubts her." I jerked my head toward Delilah. *Shut up, Darian!* "And so I decided to take up the cause myself." *Zip it, for Christ's sake!*

Something flashed in Fallon's eyes, like lightning on a dark gray afternoon. "Perhaps I could help you on your quest?"

Not bloody likely. "I doubt that." *That's right. You don't need to spill your guts to him!*

"What if I told you I could lift the spell before the trial?"

Oh boy. Shit. I bucked my chin up, met his steely gaze. "Do it, then."

"Not now," he said, lowering his voice. "But soon. Be patient, and I'll be in touch."

I didn't want him touching anything. In fact, I didn't ever want to see his face again. "Now or never," I countered.

"If you want this, you'll have to play by my rules."

Lousy SOB. I walked past him, out of Delilah's earshot, and he followed, the door sliding shut with an echoing finality. If I didn't hurry, Delilah would be transported to Portland before I could question her. And after that, who knew what the PNT Council would do with her. They might kill her, for all I knew, and then my only connection to Brakae would be lost. I walked in silence to the elevator, arguing with myself over any course of action. Agreeing to Fallon's proposal felt very much like making a deal with the devil, and I didn't plan on selling my soul anytime soon. But I wanted—no, needed—to do this for Raif. I had to find the child he'd grieved over for hundreds of years. I could never bring his wife back from the dead. Maybe I could give him back his daughter.

"Fine," I said once the elevator doors slid shut. "What do you propose?"

"Just give me a little time. I'll work something out."

"And how will I know when you've finally got your shit together?"

Deposited back on the reception floor, I stepped out of the elevator and waited. Fallon made no move to follow me but held the doors open. "As I said, I'll be in touch." He released his grip and the doors closed, leaving me staring at my own reflection in the silvered surface.

Damn, I hated how supernaturals conducted business.

Chapter 11

I rode home with the helmet secured to the back of the bike. It felt like the damned thing was suffocating me. I'd just have to deal with the ticket if any cop was ballsy enough to pull me over. My hair swirled in a torrent around my face as I weaved in and out of traffic. I couldn't get away from Fallon fast enough.

Since I'd been gone only a couple of hours, I didn't return to Tyler's apartment. Best to let him rest, and besides, I seriously needed to wind down. I parked the bike in front of my building and melted into nothingness. Too anxious for even a quick ride up my own elevator, I became corporeal only once I was safely in my apartment. I paced around the living room for a few quick laps, trying to rid myself of the pent-up energy suspended in my body like a bottled hurricane.

I'd made an unlikely alliance with a perfect stranger. I couldn't even be sure myself if Delilah spoke the truth. Though her words rang with honesty, it could have been another ploy to twist the knife in Raif's back and offer payback for a sister killed centuries ago. And though I'd felt compelled to tell Fallon of my plan to find Brakae, I'd never had any intention of letting anyone from the PNT become involved. My knowledge of the Fae was shallow at best. I couldn't be sure what type of Fae Fallon actually was, or wasn't, as the case might be. Over the months, I'd learned there were Fae belonging to the night and others to the day. Some that held kinship with water and others with the sky. And I'd heard of Fae who made their homes in the earth, for they took comfort from the dirt and growing things.

But of these many types, I couldn't be sure to which family Fallon belonged. Maybe he wasn't Fae at all, but something else. He was powerful, no doubt there. And he had a strange attractive quality that begged to be noticed. I hadn't been able to help myself. The words spilled out of my mouth like water through a broken dam. Whatever he was, Raif certainly had him pegged. Dangerous. I could ask around to learn more about him, but I didn't want to further raise suspicion by asking questions. No, I'd have to wait until he contacted me and then decide if his solution to loosening Delilah's lips was worth finding Brakae. In the meantime, I had to calm the hell down before I wore a path in my rug.

My winding trek brought me to the kitchen, and my pace slowed as I neared the safe hidden in my wall. The bricks came loose with a gentle tug, and I set them on the counter. I gave a quick turn of the dial and pulled the door open. From the back of the safe, bright green pulsed in the darkness. The emerald pendulum hummed with energy, beckoning me with every surge of brilliant light. I'd almost forgotten about my strange gift and its mysterious giver over the past few days. I plucked the bauble from its resting place, the emerald warming my palm. My eyes drawn inexorably to the pendulum, I walked toward the window, the noonday sun nearing its zenith in the sky.

I pinched the silver chain between my thumb and forefinger and let the stone dangle in my line of sight. The sun reflected within its depths, and the sound of time passing within my soul began to slow until the seconds were no longer recognizable as individual beats, but rather, a distant, ominous echo, like thunder rumbling from far away. On its own willpower, the stone swung toward me, enticing me to stare into the fathomless green that devoured everything around me until there was nothing left but me, the silver chain, and the glowing green stone dangling from it. A vibration tickled the air around me, and the landscape of my apartment melted away until I stood atop a knoll, brilliant with spring grass and smelling of fresh rain. The sun had just begun to rise in the east, and moving steadily toward me was a girl in flowing white robes.

Smiling, the adolescent, perhaps thirteen or fourteen, raised a hand in greeting, sauntering through the grass as if she had nothing but time to waste.

"Welcome, Darian!" she called from twenty yards away. "I was wondering when you'd find me."

I looked around at the vast landscape of rolling green hills, a little more than freaked that I was no longer standing in my apartment. Like the pendulum now bunched in my fist, this place stretched on forever, with neither beginning nor end. "How in the hell did I get here?" I asked as soon as the girl made her way to me.

She simply looked around as if her guess was as good as mine. A soft breeze blew her raven hair, and clear blue eyes swept me from head to toe. She looked familiar, this girl, enough like the child and the woman from my recent dreams to lead me to believe they were all related. But how? Related through a dream? That was a lot to swallow, even for me.

"You've been chosen by Fate," the girl said. "And I'm so happy with the choice. You're more than capable to serve your purpose."

Oh joy. Who was I? Anakin fucking Skywalker? "Did you give me this?" I opened my hand to show her the emerald. "By way of a falcon?"

The girl smiled and reached out to close my hand around the stone. "It belongs to you," she said.

"Not that I don't appreciate it . . ." Actually, I didn't appreciate it. Not a bit. "But I've got a lot to deal with right now. And being—ah—transported to wherever this is does not mesh with my already complicated life. So I think you'd better take your jewelry back and go find someone else to play with, okay?"

If the girl noticed my condescending tone, she didn't let on. An enigmatic smile graced her lips, somehow more menacing than pleasant. "Protect the key, Guardian." She looked wistfully to the sky as the morning sun broke through the clouds. "Time is a precious thing."

I felt my body go suddenly slack, the ring at the end of the pendulum's chain still looped around my finger. It dropped from my palm, jerking as the slack ran out. A peace swept over me as if my upside-down world had been set aright. For the first time since arriving on the knoll, I noticed the absence of time's cadence. I could no longer feel or hear its steady beat within me. I closed my eyes, absorbed in the bliss of silence, and when I opened them again, I was standing in my apartment, looking out the picture window as the sun dipped into the west and out of sight.

Five minutes. I couldn't have been gone more than five minutes, but the sun was setting. It had been noon only moments before. How could nine hours have possibly passed in that brief time?

The sound of my elevator grinding to a stop tore me from the shock of the moment. Tyler emerged, panicked and looking for a fight, armed with both a wicked-looking knife and a Glock. He stopped short of storming the kitchen and dropped his weapons at his side, looking just as confused as I felt. "Darian! Thank the gods. Are you all right? What's going on? Where the hell have you *been*?"

I stuffed the pendulum in my pocket. Tyler was already about to implode from worry. I didn't need to give him anything else to freak out about. "I drove out to the PNT building this morning to see if I could get any more information about Raif's daughter out of Delilah." No use lying about that. "I didn't want to wake you, so I borrowed your Buelle. Then I came back here. Must have fallen asleep. I'm sorry. I should have called."

Tyler's jaw dropped, and he looked at me as though I'd lost my mind. "Darian, you've been gone for two days!"

Raif paced around my kitchen, obviously agitated, while Xander sat as serene as ever in the chair in my living room. Tyler sat beside me on the couch, holding on to my hand with an iron grip. He couldn't seem to peel his eyes off me either. I guess he figured if he blinked, I'd disappear again.

"You mean to tell me you have no recollection of the last two days?" Raif's voice had risen to nearly a shout, but it was only frustration that fueled his tone.

"I told you, I remember waking up, taking Tyler's bike to the PNT, seeing Delilah briefly, and then driving home. I'd barely made it through the front door when Ty came storming up." What happened in the five minutes between my arriving home and Tyler's arrival was no one's business but mine for right now, lost days or not.

"Why in the *hell* did you go back there to talk to her?" Okay, Raif was shouting now. And it wasn't because of frustration. He was flat-out pissed. "I told you to stay the hell away from that Oracle!"

"Raif—"

"You were not instructed to visit that facility. You talked your way in under false pretenses. You attempted to interrogate a prisoner under magical restraint! What has gotten into you? Have you lost your mind?" Those last five words roared across my kitchen.

Throughout Raif's tirade, Xander sat stoic, his fingers in a steeple resting against his pursed lips. I could practically see the gears grinding in his mind as he processed every tiny syllable passing between us.

"You violated a direct order, Darian. How should I deal with this?"

Oh no. Raif did *not* just treat me like some low-level greenhorn. "You don't have to deal with this, Raif. I'm a freelance employee. I'm not a royal subject."

Raif raised a brow to Xander, and I suddenly felt as if I'd just dug my own grave. "I'm afraid that's not necessarily true," Xander said in his rich velvet voice. "You agreed to work under retainer; therefore you *are* subject to reprimand. And if you'll remember, Darian, you set out the terms of our agreement. You requested to work directly under Raif, taking instruction specifically and solely from him. If you disregarded his request to leave the Oracle be, then I'm afraid you did, in fact, violate a direct order from your superior."

Fuck me, the asshole was right. I'd screwed myself over with my own stupid rules, making sure Xander couldn't use me to play his adolescent games. I could have kicked myself.

"But since we're on the subject . . ." *God, Xander, leave—it—alone.* "What is this all about? Why did you go back to see the Oracle?"

Shithead. Just had to stick his nose where it didn't belong. I kept my mouth clamped shut. No way in hell was I going to supply him with any information.

"The day we took Delilah into custody," Raif answered for me, "the Oracle tried to trick Darian into releasing her by saying she had information concerning Brakae's whereabouts."

Tyler squeezed my hand. Hard. He'd known what I was after, but his overbearing show of—*ouch!*—affection, let me know he obviously agreed with Raif and felt I should abandon my quest.

"I see," said Xander, having nothing more to offer. "Darian, stop by my home tomorrow. We'll discuss the terms of your reprimand." He stood and stared down at Tyler with a contemptuous sneer. "I assume I can count on you to keep your eye on her tonight? If you need assistance, Jinn, I can send Dimitri over. I'd hate to see her slip through your fingers for another two days or longer."

"She's not yours to worry about, Xander." Tyler's fingers left my hand as he wrapped an arm protectively around me. "I know how to protect what's mine."

Xander's cold smile betrayed the hateful venom in his glare. A muscle ticked in his cheek, and he cast a glance my way before dissolving into shadow and disappearing completely. I stood, shooting a glare of my own in Tyler's direction before crossing the kitchen to Raif, who was about to follow his brother's exit.

"Raif," I said again, unable to form the necessary words to calm his anger. He took a step toward me, and I flinched, thinking he meant to strike me. But instead, he pulled me into a hard embrace, laid his cheek against my head, and like his brother, became one with the shadows.

I stood with my arms hanging at my sides for a stunned moment. The brotherly gesture from Raif had been no less shocking than a right hook to my face. Emotion swelled in my chest, rising to form a tight knot in my throat. Nothing short of an outright plea would have strengthened my resolve more.

I would not rest until I found Brakae.

A sigh from the couch reminded me that I wasn't in my apartment alone. Annoyance replaced tenderness as Tyler's proclamation that I was essentially his property echoed in my mind. I rounded on him, my hands clenched into fists. "Why didn't you just lift your leg and piss on me? It would have had the same effect."

"Where have you been?" Tyler said instead. I'd never heard the tone of his voice so hard; it was low and serious, nearly shaking with controlled emotion.

"I told you"—I looked at the floor, unable to meet his gaze—"I've been here the entire time." It wasn't exactly a lie. Though the emerald had without a doubt transported me somewhere, I'd never *actually* left my apartment.

"Bullshit." He choked on the word. "I've been here more than once over the past two days. You weren't here. I couldn't feel you. It was almost like our bond had been broken or the distance between us was too far for me to sense you." I looked up to find Tyler's head resting in his hands. "Darian . . . I thought . . . I couldn't sense our bond. It was like you didn't exist."

The annoyance melted right out of my body. While I'd felt as though I'd been gone only a matter of minutes, to the rest of them—Ty, Raif, Xander—I'd been gone without a trace for a couple of days. I thought about how I'd feel if I woke up one morning and Tyler had left without a single clue to his whereabouts. In fact, I knew from experience how it felt to be abandoned by someone you loved. I would be crazy with grief and worry if Ty disappeared. Hell, I'd probably slice up anything that walked too close until I found him. But despite that, I just couldn't bring myself to tell him about the emerald. More than once the confession had been at the tip of my tongue. Something had made me swallow it back, however—a compulsion to keep this secret to myself and not divulge the information to anyone. Why couldn't I have had this problem earlier today—well, two days ago—with Fallon?

"Ty, I'm so sorry." I moved to the couch, where I stood before him, burying my fingers in the thick curls of his hair. "I had no idea."

"Raif seemed pretty distraught over your disappearance." Tyler's tone became the same mixture of jealousy and suspicion he'd used days before. "Even more than Xander. I guess the sonofabitch can't handle a couple of days away from you either."

Christ, not this again. "Tyler, how many times do I have to tell you there's nothing between Raif and me besides a deep respect and friendship?"

"Doesn't feel like it to me."

"You're unhinged. Seriously."

Tyler's eyes flashed with emotion. I could see the concern, but just barely. Something else festered below the surface. His emotions were volatile, shifting without notice. I stroked his face, my own fear tickling at the edges of my senses. Call it intuition, or foreboding, but I had a feeling that these sudden flashes of jealous temper were only the beginning. "I don't want him here," he said in a low growl.

My hands shook from a healthy dose of anxiety. I kept my voice calm and even as I tried to soothe him. "That's going to be tough to agree to when we work together, Ty. Take it easy. He's. Just. A. Friend."

Tyler shook his head, as if cleansing his brain of dust. "You're right." God, he sounded exhausted. "You're right. This is stupid. It's the bond; it just needs to settle. I'm still a little on edge. Darian, you seriously have no memory of where you've been?"

"No." The lie escaped my lips so easily, without the bitter taste of remorse I thought I'd feel. "I thought I'd been here the whole time. I don't remember anything about the last two days."

That much, at least, was true. This wasn't my first encounter with a deviance in time. When I'd been kidnapped by the creepy teenagers who'd fed themselves to the Enphigmalé, I'd counted the days with perfect clarity. Though to my perception, I'd been on the island for nine long days, when Raif came to the island, he told me only twelve hours had passed. And now, minutes had slipped through my fingers with the girl on the knoll while days flew by around me.

I stared down at the ring on my thumb, the symbol of Tyler's binding. He lifted his head to stare up at me, his arms winding tight around my waist. Pressing his cheek against my stomach, he breathed in deeply and held his breath. "I couldn't feel you. It nearly drove me mad. I've never been so empty, so scared. How can I protect you if I can't even find you?"

Those words were enough to send me to my knees. I knew exactly how he felt. We held each other for a long moment, the silence wrapping around us like a thick length of rope. I'd almost lost him, not once, but twice. And the emptiness I'd felt was like a razor slicing my heart to shreds. Mere words would not suffice to convey my feelings. He'd be so much better off without me. His life wouldn't be in danger; he wouldn't have to constantly assert himself to Xander. He wouldn't suffer the anguish of wondering if I was dead or alive. And even though I knew all of this, given the opportunity, I doubted if I'd ever be strong enough to let him go. I needed him like I needed air. And the only thing I could offer him in return was an existence steeped in danger and the constant threat of death.

That reminded me. "You're healed from the attack?" The last time I'd seen him, someone had tried to use him as a pincushion.

"Completely."

"And in the past two days," I said, almost unable to bring myself to ask, "have *you* been safe? Tyler, if anything ever happened to you, I don't know what I'd do."

He took my face in his hands, his mouth covering mine. His tongue traced my lip before delving into my mouth with such care, I thought I'd cry. I draped my arms around his shoulders and kissed him deeper, allowing him to coax me into forgetting—just for a while—about the dangers that stalked us both.

Chapter 12

I arrived at Xander's the next day, nearly dragging my ass up the front steps. I knew I was in for it today. First I'd have to tolerate Xander's reprimand—and hope it didn't involve our spending any quality time together. Then I'd have to deal with Raif. And frankly, at this point, I'd have almost chosen to spend the day with his brother over enduring Raif's displeasure.

No one greeted me at the door when I rang the bell. I waited for forty-seven seconds before I let myself in. I didn't usually need an invite to cross the threshold. But since I was in deep shit with Raif as well as Xander, I thought I'd better mind my p's and q's. I paused for a moment in the foyer as I decided on a course of action and opted for the lesser of two evils by seeking out the King of Shaedes. After a fruitless scan of the first floor, I found Xander in the training room in the basement of the house.

He hadn't heard me approach as he delivered a roundhouse kick to the large sandbag suspended from the ceiling. Bare-chested, he was clothed in just a pair of athletic pants. But for our first meeting, I'd only ever seen Xander perfectly coiffed and sitting on his proverbial throne. I couldn't help but admire his form—both his technique and his body—as he followed through with a solid punch, block, kick combination. He moved with the graceful precision of a leopard on the prowl as he twirled and swept his foot at an invisible opponent's leg, came up with a solid elbow to the bag, and spun again, delivering a kick that sent the bag spinning and rocking in a figure-eight pattern.

Disciplined. Skilled. A true warrior. I could respect—or rather, admire—Xander this way, muscles glistening with sweat, stray strands of blond hair falling from the band that secured the hair at the nape of his neck. I leaned against the doorjamb, enjoying the show as well as the stay of execution. I wasn't exactly eager to hear how Xander and his brother had decided to reprimand me.

"Like what you see?" His voice echoed in the gym.

I rolled my eyes. Leave it to Xander's mouth to tarnish his perfectly beautiful body. "I'm here to discuss my formal reprimand." I'd rather eat glass than admit I enjoyed the view.

Xander crossed to a bench and retrieved a towel. Wiping his face and chest, he crossed the gym to the door where I remained leaning in the doorway while trying, at least, to look casual. "Well, since I *am* the king"—he paused to stretch his legs—"your punishment is mine to give, wouldn't you agree?"

"I'm sorry, Xander. I didn't realize I'd come here today to give your ego a good, long stroking. If this is my punishment for using your authority without permission, then consider me properly lashed."

Xander's molten caramel eyes sparkled with a mischievous light. A silent groan stretched long through my mind. Showcasing his preternatural speed, he moved across the gym in almost a blur, reached to the wall of weapons, and grabbed a wicked-looking cat-o'-nine-tails whip with many dangling cords capped with barbed metal tips. "If you're looking for a good lashing"—he swung the whip with menace as he made his way back to me—"I could give you one that would leave you begging for me to stop."

His voice carried a hard edge, but for the life of me I couldn't tell if the threat was violent or sexual in nature. Maybe I shouldn't have been such a chickenshit and avoided Raif. Anything would have been better than this.

"My workout isn't quite over." The whip hummed as Xander twirled it in a circular pattern. "You beat me, we'll consider you properly reprimanded. I beat you"—

his eyes caressed me from head to toe—"and as punishment for your actions, you return my money and continue working for free."

Sounded more than fair to me. I couldn't think of anything I'd like better than wiping the floor with Xander's pretty face. He was going down! There was no way in hell I was parting with that money. "You're on."

I didn't give him time to react before I launched myself from my perch in the doorway. Shedding my corporeal form—I wasn't about to play fair—I appeared behind him, using his own technique against him, my elbow striking between his shoulder blades before I swept his legs out from underneath him. He hit the mat with a *woof!* and I smiled triumphantly. *That's right, Xander, I'm going to fuck your shit up!*

Before I'd finished my premature celebration, something snapped at my ankle, and I looked down just in time to see the barbed ends of the whip biting through my pant leg into my flesh. Xander jerked, and I went down—hard, I might add—before I had the presence of mind to try to escape. The tails of the whip held my corporeal form—the sonofabitch must have been anticipating an unfair fight—and I assumed the whip had been made with Lyhtan hair, soul shadows, or both. I'd seen only one Shaede extract the magic shadows from his soul in Xander's warehouse months ago. I'd watched as Raif exhaled gently over the wide mouth of a bottle, and with his breath, inky black tendrils had pooled in the container. Soul shadows were the one thing that could kill a Lyhtan, no matter what the time of day. That essence of darkness could break bones as if they were nothing but twigs, and I didn't doubt that Raif had enhanced most of the weapons in this arsenal with his magic.

Before I could bring myself upright, Xander straddled me, securing my wrists with one hand above my head. He smiled and bent low over my ear, his breath warm against my skin. "Give up yet?"

"Not a chance," I said from between clenched teeth. I brought my knee up to his groin, but before I could make purchase on his royal jewels, he rolled away and jumped to his feet, putting a good two or three yards between us.

I'd come to the house unarmed, but I had plenty of weapons at my fingertips. Xander charged at a full run, swinging the whip wildly above his head. I spun away and dissolved, becoming solid at the opposite wall adorned with weapons. I could have grabbed the spiked ball and chain. Or even a dagger. But the point of this fight was not collateral damage, so I took the bokken and gave it a few practice swings before returning to the center of the mat to face the king.

Xander smiled and stretched his neck from side to side. "You're not going to win," he said. "And I'll get you for free."

"Xander," I scoffed, "you'll never get me—period." Without thinking, I charged, letting my warrior's instinct and months of Raif's training guide me. I stabbed forward, but the bokken was deflected with a swipe of the whip. I turned so as not to leave my back undefended, and Xander attacked, swinging his arm toward the wooden sword. The silver barbs of the cat-o'-nine-tails dug into the hard wood and he jerked, the bokken flying through the air along with the discarded whip. Okay, so it was going to be a knock-down, drag-out, hand-to-hand match. Perfect.

Xander had a good seventy pounds and a foot or so of height on me. But I was quicker on my feet and had the advantage of not being confined to corporeality. Our fight came down to a strange mishmash of judo, tae kwon do, and straight-up street brawl. I took a hard left to the ribs and doubled over in pain, disappearing before Xander could land a second blow. He'd broken two of my ribs, but, thanks to my preternatural healing, the damage was repaired before I became my solid self again. I managed to connect my fist to his kidney and followed through with a kick to his knee. He went down, but only for a moment before launching himself at me with renewed vigor and a punch-kick-punch combination that had me retreating rather than fighting back.

"I don't know about you," Xander said, his words coming through pants of breath, "but this is turning me on."

Oh hell no! I almost tapped out of the match, just so I wouldn't have to think about Xander being aroused. It was a good strategy, though. He'd resorted to messing with my head when he realized I could hold my own in the fight. A thought struck me, and I slowed my assault. We could go on like this for hours, until one of us tired or until someone intervened, not willing to risk an injury to the king. I imagined Anya would be the first one to throw her body in the path of that bullet. But I didn't have all night to ponder the possibility of taking her down too, so, like Xander, I changed course.

"You're turned on?" I asked, making my voice sound especially breathy. "Why is that, Xander? Do you like it rough?"

He stumbled, and I used the opportunity to deliver a kick to his gut. Lust sparkled in his eyes, and a smile stretched across his handsome face as he recovered from the kick. I tried to hide my own smile. I had him in my crosshairs, and he was going down. Leave it to Xander to always be thinking with his dick.

"You need to be made love to by a proper man." He ducked my left swing, and then my right. "Not that sad excuse for a lover you keep at your apartment."

His slight against Tyler gave me pause, and he used the opportunity to jab me with his elbow. Damn, *another* broken rib. I groaned, struggling for a deep breath while the bone knitted back together. Asshole. "You think you're the man to give it to me, Xander? I doubt you could handle it. I'm not some compliant groupie, ready to fall back with my legs spread just because you snap your fingers."

I blocked Xander's roundhouse kick and parried a misthrown punch. "I like a challenge," he said. "I bet you're very good in bed."

"I am." Xander's attention drifted as his eyes fastened on what cleavage my V-neck shirt revealed. "Wouldn't you like to know *how* good?"

Bang! Kill shot. Xander paused, his mouth hanging a little slack. Glazed-over eyes and the whole nine yards; I'd used his psychological ploy against him to great effect. Playing the seductress, I walked rather than charged, letting my eyes drop coyly past his waist. My gaze raked him from lean sculpted torso to broad muscled shoulders, and when I'd made my way back to his face, his eyes burned with passion. Hips swaying, chest rising and falling with my labored breath, mouth parted just enough to allow my tongue to pass over my lips, I should have earned some kind of award for my performance. Now within touching distance, Xander reached out his hands, and I took them gently. He dipped his head to mine, his warm breath caressing my face in heavy pants. His gaze was locked on my lips. I tilted my chin up, pausing at the intensity of his expression. Xander didn't look so much the arrogant king as his lips moved toward mine. Rather, his expression spoke of longing.

Using my own body for momentum, I fell backward and gripped his hands. I bent my knees, felt my lower back make contact with the mat, and braced my feet against Xander's stomach. In the blink of an eye, I catapulted him over my head, and the sound of the air leaving his lungs in one painful rush put a smile on my face. I joined the light and reappeared just in time to stomp my foot down on his neck. Raif had had me in the same position my very first night of training. I knew from experience it wasn't pleasant to be on the receiving end of this particular maneuver.

"Do you yield?" My voice was no longer that of an infatuated girl, but it carried the hard edge of a fighter. I stomped down on his neck a little harder, just so he'd know I meant business.

Xander cursed under his breath, and his face turned a lovely shade of crimson. The desire burning bright in his eyes faded, though it shocked me to see the flame had not gone out entirely. "To you?" he said, his voice a low growl. "I would yield my throne."

My insides twisted—just a little—at his words. I increased the pressure on his neck for two full seconds before removing my foot. "I win, then. I keep my money, I keep my job, and punishment is considered given." I turned my back on him and headed for the door.

"It nearly killed him," Xander called out. "He loved his child. And Illiana? Worshipped her." I turned around to find Xander sitting upright, an elbow resting on a raised knee, his other hand massaging his throat. "He was right to kill that Oracle for allowing his wife to sacrifice her life. I would have done no less in his situation. Everything he cherished has been ripped from him. When we couldn't find you for *two whole days*," Xander said with a sigh, "that pain replayed itself. I could see it on his face, the worry. He wouldn't admit it, but I saw it nonetheless. Raif cares for you, Darian. Do not cause him pain again."

A knife twisted in my gut would have been no less agonizing. I didn't want to hurt Raif. On the contrary, I longed to help him. I knew in my gut that Delilah wasn't bullshitting me. She'd have used the Enphigmalé to put an end to Raif if she could have. But since her plan hadn't quite worked out to her advantage, she'd tried to use her knowledge of Brakae's whereabouts as a bargaining chip. She had to know her days were numbered. There was no advantage to offering the information if she wasn't ready to back it up. I just wished Raif could see beyond the hurt of his past to find the truth that I felt in every bone of my body. I could reunite him with Brakae if he'd just stop being so stubborn. His orders to quit looking for her only slowed me up. Sneaking around with someone I felt less than comfortable with would hinder my ability to find her quickly. Instead, I'd had to resort to deception. Raif's pain would be short-lived, and he'd forgive me the grief I caused him when I reunited him with his daughter.

Xander stood and began to stretch. The king once again, he paid me as much attention as he would a pet. "I'll find a way to get a rematch out of you," he said absently. "You won't win a second time."

His words were meant to be arrogant, but I knew better. He'd enjoyed himself and would only be looking for another opportunity to play his games. I left the training room as a breath of air, the thrill of my victory buried beneath Raif's sorrow and Xander's arrogance. I couldn't even be proud of myself for kicking Xander's ass because I knew, somehow, he had let me win.

Raif was waiting for me in the foyer. I became corporeal before I entered the room, though what I'd really wanted was a stealthy escape, or a coward's exit depending on your point of view. But avoiding him wouldn't assuage my guilt at having caused him worry, so I straightened my spine and walked up to him, prepared to take whatever he planned to dish out.

"So, you won," he said.

"You heard?"

"Everyone heard," he laughed. "Really, Darian, you didn't expect us all to close our ears and pretend *not* to listen. It sounded like an exciting match."

I shrugged. "I think Xander got what he wanted out of it." *Some rough-and-tumble close contact, sweaty bodies and all.* "Do you want to add to the torture I just had to endure?"

Raif attempted a smile, but it came off as more of a grimace. "I know you think you can take on the world, Darian. But have a care. It would be—unfortunate—if anything happened to you."

Unfortunate, huh? Well, the words didn't carry much emotion, but the expression on his face spoke volumes. Xander had told the truth. I'd managed to open some old wounds. I didn't plan on letting Raif bleed for long, though. "Don't worry, Raif." I swung my arm and gave him a solid pat on the shoulder. "I'll be careful." Without giving him the opportunity to respond, I left.

My cell buzzed in my pocket as I closed the door behind me. I flipped it open to find a text message from an unknown number:

Midnight. @Seven. East Pike Street. Come alone.
    -F

Well, at least he was kind enough to give an initial, though how the bastard got his hands on my number, I had no idea. How would I manage to shake Tyler long enough to meet Fallon? I practically had to apply for a furlough just to come to Xander's this morning. I would be watched even more closely since my five-minute/two-day field trip. But I couldn't waste any precious time. I'd find a way to meet him, even if it meant wishing Tyler and half of the Shaede Nation into a stupefied state. If Fallon was ready to help, I was ready to take the leap. He scared the shit out of me, I couldn't deny that. But I valued Raif's friendship more than that fear. I just hoped I could keep my unease at bay long enough to hear Fallon out.

Chapter 13

"You look like death warmed over."

Tyler shrugged as he stuffed his foot into a tennis shoe. "I'll be fine."

"What's wrong with you anyway?" In all the years I'd known Tyler, I'd never seen him sick—not once. Aside from the injuries from his recent attack, and his reaction to the Enphigmalé bites, he'd never had so much as a head cold. Now, he looked haggard, his usual glowing complexion was ashen, and a sheen of sweat was breaking out on his brow. Anxiety twisted my stomach into a pretzel.

Tyler slumped back in his seat, averting my gaze. "Something's screwing with our bond, I think."

"Something?"

He ran his hands through his hair. "Or someone."

"I don't feel anything. Are you sure?"

Tyler's sad smile clawed at my heart. "You wouldn't feel anything. The bond flows through you into me. You're like a conduit. I just need to find out who, or what, is causing this. And why."

Screw the whos and whys. All I cared about was Ty's safety. "Can this hurt you?"

"Not really. It's just thrown me off, messed with my emotions. I feel a little out of whack. But I need to get to the bottom of this. I've got a contact that might be able to help. The thing is . . ."

I held my breath.

"I can't exactly let you come with me."

And I exhaled.

"Will you be all right on your own tonight?"

Perfect.

"If not, I can wait—"

"No, Ty. I'll be fine. Go take care of business, talk to whoever it is you need to talk to. I want to know what's going on as much as you do. I don't like to see you like this, whether it's just making you feel a little off or not." I couldn't believe my luck. It was as if someone had handed the night to me on a silver platter. Tyler could work on fixing his problem while I went to meet Fallon.

Too perfect.

Seven wasn't your run-of-the-mill club. More of a place to engage in unrepentant debauchery. With areas sectioned off and devoted to each of the deadly sins, you could eat, drink, gamble, and screw yourself straight to hell. Of course, that was just the tip of the iceberg. There wasn't much you couldn't get away with inside the walls of Seven, and I wondered at Fallon's choice of meeting place until I walked through the doors.

An assortment of Seattle's supernatural partied alongside unsuspecting humans. Curious stares followed me through the club while fingers pointed in my direction. My career as an assassin would be shot to hell if my notoriety didn't die down soon. I even noticed a few humans tapping shoulders, asking over the music who I was and what all the fuss was about. I'd become pretty popular since I'd returned from the island. It wasn't every day you came back from a kidnapping a completely different creature than the one you had left as.

The club was made up of a series of rooms more or less. High archways like wooden canopies marked off each area, and at the top of each canopy was a word written in red neon flames. An ambitious partyer could take a tour of hell's temptations all in one night. Under the Wrath canopy, brawlers swung their fists without fear of being removed from the premises. Within the boundaries of the Greed room, gambling tables enticed many a player to build and lose their fortunes. The Sloth canopy protected the partyers coming down from their highs, strewn about the room like garbage littering the sidewalk. Pride showcased rows of large mirrors, and beautiful creatures showcased their bodily assets. Gluttony provided endless food and drink, and from the center of the club, a raised room ringed with glass provided occupants of Envy with a bird's-eye view of all the things they coveted.

I spotted Fallon in the area of the club marked Lust. Over the haunting beats of Marilyn Manson's rendition of "Sweet Dreams" and through the energy of the other inhuman creatures, I could feel him. That inexplicable burst of power stole my breath, and I considered running for the door and never turning back. But I thought of the rushed and fierce hug Raif had given me two nights ago, and I strengthened my resolve. I could grow a pair and deal with my discomfort—for a while.

Red velvet and black silk curtains lined the small room. Instead of booths or tables, I was welcomed by an assortment of beds piled with pillows and dressed in shiny satins. Keeping my gaze straight ahead, I tried not to look at the occupied spaces, but I could tell by the writhing bodies in my peripheral vision that these people weren't too particular about who watched their nocturnal activities.

Fallon seemed to be enjoying himself. Surrounded by Fae—as far as I could tell—with a female at each side and a sweet-faced male behind him, he lounged while many sets of fingertips and mouths caressed his skin. I shivered in the dim light and gripped the handle of my dagger for comfort. Though I could tolerate a lot, public orgies were not on my list of things I cared to witness.

As if he'd only noticed me standing at the foot of his . . . bed, Fallon dismissed his groupies with a wave of his hand. He could have given Xander a run for his money with his regal behavior. His admirers glared my way before bestowing some over-the-top pouty and pleading faces. Fallon answered with a stern expression, and the trio hopped off the bed as if it were on fire.

"Have a seat," he said.

I took a step forward, feeling that strange pull to do whatever he told me. I steeled myself against the compulsion and ground the balls of my feet into my boots as if they could keep me planted to the floor. "I think I'll stand."

Fallon's eyes narrowed, but he quickly erased the menace with a smile. "Don't you like it here?"

"I'd rather hang out in a public toilet," I said. "Whatever you have to say, say it fast so I can go home and sanitize. No telling what I might catch."

He shrugged as if to say, *Suit yourself.* I already didn't like his taste in entertainment; how I'd be able to cooperate with him was beyond me. Delilah's information had better be gold, or I'd kill her just for making me go through all of this. A waitress, clad in nothing but a skimpy push-up bra and a thong, brushed by me. The heels of her stilettos were high enough to kill her if she tripped, but by the way her ass jiggled when she walked, I got the impression she didn't care as long as she looked good while she fell. She placed a drink on a table beside the bed and traced her fingers down Fallon's arm before scooping a twenty from his palm. Flashing an aren't-you-jealous glance my way, she meandered away to other beds and other customers.

Fallon wiped the hand the waitress had touched on the bedsheets as if he'd just dipped it in a bucket of chicken fat. "Humans," he spat. "How do you stand them?"

I didn't justify his prejudice with a response. I'd been human once, after all, and as far as I could tell, some of them far outweighed Fallon on the respectability scale. "What do you have for me?" My patience had stretched very thin. "Either you can help me with Delilah or you can't."

"Oh, I can help you," he said, patting the empty space next to him on the bed. "But nothing in this world is free."

An unpleasant shudder passed from the top of my

head down my spine. My foot slid across the floor, pulling my body closer to him. The other foot followed, and I pressed down on my heels to keep my feet planted right where they were. I found the man utterly repulsive; yet something beckoned me closer. "What's your price?" I asked through gnashed teeth. My foot twitched impatiently. "I'll need to know if it's worth my while."

"Sit," Fallon said.

"Fuck. No."

His eyes hardened; his full mouth became a tight line. "Sit. *Down*."

The force of that last word snapped my resolve and, against my will, I stumbled toward the bed. As if I had no control over my actions, I lowered myself on the edge, my feet still on the floor, and Fallon smiled. "That's better. Really, Darian, you should try to relax. Enjoy yourself."

"This is as relaxed as I'm going to get," I said more to myself than to him. My pulse picked up double time as I wondered what could have made me act against my will. No way in hell was I going to let my body rebel against my mind again.

He sighed in disappointment and downed his drink in a single swallow. "I can lift the entrapment spell Adare has placed on the Oracle. But it's not an easy task to accomplish. I'd be putting myself on the line by doing this for you. So in return, I ask only that you do the same for me."

"Put myself on the line? How?"

"Someone has stolen something from me, and I want it back."

"Doesn't sound like a fair trade to me." Boy, was that an understatement. "Besides, I'm not a thief. I'm an assassin. If you want someone offed, I'm your girl. But burglary is not my forte."

"Well, then, it had better become your forte. Fast. What I'm asking is fair *and* equitable. If I'm caught removing the spell on the Oracle, I won't simply be removed from duty or reassigned. I'll be arrested—or worse. If you're caught stealing"—his eyes wandered longingly to his companions waiting at the next bed— "you'll suffer the same fate. Fair—and equitable."

Fucker. "Can I have a few days to think about it?"

"Sorry," Fallon said, sounding anything but. "I'm afraid my offer expires in"—he checked his watchless wrist—"fifteen seconds. Take it or leave it."

I balled my fists at my sides to control my mounting rage. "Fine. I'll do it."

Fallon snapped his fingers, and his companions returned to the bed with a grace and speed only the inhuman possessed. As if starved without his nearness, the three of them scrambled onto the bed, kissing and petting him with a perverted intensity. He stared right at me and graced me with an indulgent smile before he relaxed back on the pillows and closed his eyes. "You'll understand if I ask you to go first." He peeked through one lid. "Call it insurance."

"No fucking way. Where's *my* insurance? How do I know you won't drop me cold after I steal whatever it is you want?" My hand closed around the dagger's hilt again. I wanted to stab him so bad, I could taste it.

"You can keep my prize until I fulfill my end of the bargain. Is that enough insurance for you?"

Okay, ransom could work to my advantage. If he didn't help me unlock Delilah's mind, I could pitch whatever it was I'd stolen—or give it back. "All right. Now, what exactly is it I'm stealing?" If I played my cards right, I could slip in and out as my incorporeal self, taking Fallon's trinket before anyone even knew I'd been there.

"A piece to a puzzle." His voice was muffled as the Fae to his right stripped him of his shirt. Her eyes bulged at the sight of exposed, muscled flesh. Brilliant red hair spilled over him like a cascade of flames as she rubbed her mouth against one of his nipples. He closed his eyes for an indulgent moment. "One half of an hourglass."

Interesting. "And who will I be taking it from?"

Fallon's eyes snapped open, and a corner of his mouth

lifted in a smirk. "Sidhe. If I thought you could manage it, I'd have you kill them as well. His name is Reaver, and he's the Keeper of the Glass. His sister, Moira, is his . . . security." He spat to the side. "I would shit on their corpses if I could."

My knees nearly buckled. I'd met the brother-and-sister duo at the PNT Summit not six months ago. And I'd hoped never to see them again. But apparently Fate had other things in mind, since I'd seen Moira at The Pit the night those magic arrows had been slung at my head. Had it been a coincidence? Something told me I was about to dig my own grave.

"Not backing out, are you?" Fallon asked.

I swallowed against the fear tugging at the edge of my mind and an urge to scream, *Yes! Yes!* "No," I said, ignoring my nagging better judgment. "Any idea where I can find them?" *Besides slinking around my favorite hangouts?*

"You have a genie, don't you? Ask him."

Blood turned to ice in my veins. If he knew about Tyler, what else did he know? "Leave him out of this. Or you won't need me to steal a damned thing for you because I'll take your head right off your shoulders." Razor blades would not have been as sharp as my warning.

"Tsk, tsk." Fallon unfastened the male Fae's pants. His eyes turned liquid as he looked upon Fallon as if he'd already given him a million-dollar blow job. I pursed my lips, lest my jaw drop right down to my knees. If I didn't get the hell out of here soon, I'd have a front-seat ticket to an orgy whether I wanted one or not.

"You have such a temper. The Jinn is tied to you, no? He can be an asset—or a liability. Which I'm sure you are to him as well. Such is the way of these bindings." He traced his fingertip along the male's cheek. "I'll call you in one week's time. Best have my merchandise by then. If you don't, I doubt I can keep Adare from transporting your Oracle to Portland, and then you'll never know her secrets, will you?"

I hated him—hated him right down to my toenails.

Xander would be pleased to know someone had finally
knocked him from the top spot on my shit list. But I had
to do this for Raif—for his friendship and for the heartache he'd endured. "I'll have it in three days," I said,
throwing down the bravado. "You'd *best* be ready for *me*."

Spinning on a heel, I turned, commanding my body to
ignore the need to flee for safety and walk away with
calm dignity. It wasn't until I'd cleared the doors of Seven
that I allowed my body to respond to the urge to run.
And it wasn't until I was a block from my apartment that
I'd finally stopped shaking with fear.

Chapter 14

"*A*t least it's not getting any worse," Azriel said, examining the slice to my forearm.

That wasn't saying much. I'd never had a wound that didn't heal fast. The fear of what the blade had been laced with scared me more than the damned gash. What could have damaged my inhuman skin to such an extent?

Azriel's expression didn't give me ease. His eyes shone with knowledge, something his mouth had denied.

"Plant extract? Rat poison? What do you think it was?"

"I told you," Azriel replied, his tone more than simply annoyed. "I have no idea."

"You said a magic blade can kill us. What if—"

"No."

"Can you be sure?"

Azriel wrung the soaking cloth from a basin of water and dabbed at my arm one more time before wrapping it with a white gauze bandage. "I'm sure. The bastard was human, after all. No reason to believe he knew what you were. Damn it, Darian, you've got to be quicker than that. You don't have time to contemplate the morality of your actions. Draw your blade and cut. End of story."

He was angry with me for hesitating, but only because he cared for me and didn't like to see me hurt. I should have done as he'd told me and struck with speed. My hesitation would be my downfall someday, and I didn't want to disappoint him again.

"Another postcard came today," I said as Azriel pinned the bandage in place. "From Dallas."

"Hmph," Azriel grunted, carrying the bowl of blood-ied water to the door and throwing the contents out onto the street. "He'll stick out like a sore thumb there. Better for Lorik if he returns to Europe."

"You said yourself it's not safe for him there."

"Nowhere is safe for him. His father's indiscretions have guaranteed that."

"What is he to you?" I doubted Lorik's postcards were meant for me, even though they were addressed to me. We'd never been what you might call close. "You've taken an unusual interest in this human."

"That," Azriel said, kissing the tip of my nose, "is none of your concern, my love." He pulled the sleeve of my dress back into place, refastening the button. "Now, come lie with me for a spell. Let us watch the rain as it runs down the windows. I have need of the feel of your body against mine."

I smiled, my entire being responding to his words. "That sounds lovely."

He's getting worse, I thought as I shook myself from memories and hung up the phone. This time, Tyler had to be escorted off Xander's property after he'd nearly knocked the door down because he'd thought I was somewhere inside the house. The Grim Reaper couldn't have sounded bleaker than Raif as he'd given me the play-by-play of Ty's extraction from the mansion. And apparently, the cut on his upper arm was a scratch compared to what Xander's guards had wanted to give him.

I barreled through the entryway to my apartment, for-going the pleasantries. I still wasn't completely unwound from my meeting with Fallon, and the news of yet another outburst wasn't doing much for my nerves. "Does this have something to do with our bond?" I demanded as I walked in. "Ty, this jealousy routine is getting old — fast. You're acting crazy, for Christ's sake!"

"He wants you to stay close." A sound not unlike a snarl tore from Tyler's throat. "To him."

"I'm not going to get into this with you again."

"You're *mine*," he said, low.

The apartment was dimly lit, the glow from the television illuminating Tyler's features, making them look sharper, less like the man I loved. I curled up next to him on the couch, taking note of his bandaged arm before I rested my head on his shoulder, sighing. "What's wrong, Tyler? This is *not* you. I mean, if you're going to be jealous of someone, Xander's armed you with plenty of ammo. Why Raif?"

"You smell of him," he said as he stroked my hair absently. "I can't stand it. It's driving me crazy." He pulled away and studied my face. "You've been a busy girl tonight. I sense your fear too. And all kinds of other nastiness. Where've you been?"

"Working for Xander." Sort of. A vision of Fallon stroking a bed full of lovers invaded my thoughts, and I ran my fingers through the silky strands of Tyler's hair to keep them from trembling. "Nothing to worry about."

"Strange. Xander didn't seem to have a clue where you were. I couldn't feel you wherever you were tonight. It was like something was blocking our connection again."

"I'm . . ." God, I *so* didn't want to drag him into this. "I'm following a lead on Brakae. Xander doesn't exactly know about it. I'm just using my royal connection as an in."

Tyler tried to seem light and laughed. A weak attempt, the sound barely carried from his chest. "I should've known you'd never be a low-maintenance girl. I don't care. You're worth all the trouble and then some."

And he was getting that "and then some" in spades with me.

"I don't think I can handle being around Raif, though, He shouldn't come here for a while either, Darian. It's for his own good."

I pictured what it must have looked like when Tyler burst through the door and threw Raif against the wall, his forearm pressed tight against my mentor's windpipe while he demanded to know where I was. Distance sounded like a damned good thing—at least, for a while. "Fine. I'll tell him."

"Darian, I know I'm being an asshole. Don't think I can't tell something's wrong here. But until I can figure out why I'm feeling this way, it's going to be better for him to keep his distance. I know you can't do the same, and I'll deal the best I can. This has never happened before. I feel like—I don't know—like *he's* what's interfering with the bond."

"You know that's not true, though." There was no way Raif could accomplish it even if he'd wanted to. I knew the rules. No one could break our bond but me.

"I know, but until I can sort it all out, best to tread carefully."

"What about the friend you went to see? Couldn't he help you?"

Tyler stiffened. His voice dropped to almost a whisper. "I'm afraid we've gone farther than a simple fix will allow." I'd never heard him sound so pessimistic, and my heart raced at his words. "Don't worry, Darian," he said, stroking my cheek. "Nothing is going to touch you."

I wanted to scream. The kind of soul-cleansing sound that rips through your chest, scalding all the way up. But I couldn't muster the anger to bring forth my voice. Tears stung at the corners of my eyes, and I held them back. I forbade myself from filling up with sorrow. All he cared about was me and not one bit about the fact that he seemed to be losing his mind, his health, his grip or that we had no idea who was causing this trouble. That aspect of the bond drove me to the brink. I couldn't stand the way he disregarded his own safety to protect me.

"Tyler, the way you've been feeling lately, this is happening *because* you're protecting me, isn't it?"

He kissed my head, the gesture as good as a yes.

"I can't let you do this. It's killing me to see you this way."

"You don't have a choice, love." His voice was like a soft caress. "My protection isn't like a light switch, something to be flipped on or off. It's uncompromising and something I can't control." Laughter rumbled in his chest again. "Whoever has it out for you—they're powerful. Big mojo. Don't worry about me. I've got big mojo too. And as long as I breathe, *no one* will harm you."

Tyler relaxed beside me, his arms sliding away from me. "I'm tired." He pushed himself up and moved to the bed, pulling me with him. "Just lie with me, for a while. Let me hold you, touch you."

Hell if I know why, but I did as he asked. We should have been out searching every dark corner of Seattle for whoever was wreaking this havoc on our lives. *I* should have been out there, finding whoever had it out for me, no doubt the same person who'd been fucking with Tyler. He'd die to protect my life. Well, I'd kill to save his.

I curled up against him, listening to the sound of his slow and steady heartbeat against my cheek. He seemed weak—even his scent had lost its usual sweet potency, as if it were taking everything he had to protect me from whatever threatened my existence. He might as well have had a fucking target on his back. Murder attempts, magic bonds, theft, secrets, conspiracy all around, and I'd brought it to his door. I had managed to dig myself a damned big hole; if I didn't get my ass in gear, I'd be buried alive and I'd take him with me.

Assuming my incorporeal form, I snuck out of bed with ease once I was sure Tyler was asleep. I sent Raif a text and waited until I saw him appear on the street below my apartment. Raif stood under a streetlamp, the fluorescent light casting the shadow of his corporeal body as a long black gash in the gray sidewalk. I stood next to him, watching my own shadow become one with his. I felt as close to him as our shadows, but my affection for Raif was nothing more than familial. What—or who— could be causing Ty to sense otherwise? I waited beside him and counted the seconds pounding away inside me until he was ready to speak.

"Please tell me this has nothing to do with my daughter."

"Okay, I won't."

"Darian," Raif said with exasperation, "what have you gotten yourself into?"

"Do you know what it's like to be lonely, Raif? Truly alone? I do. I was an only child, ignored by my socialite parents, an abused wife, regarded as worthless. Azriel made me keep myself hidden from the world, and aside from the people I *killed* for, I had nothing. No one. Tyler made me feel like a woman again, made me feel loved. But you . . . Raif, you pulled me out of the dark. Not Azriel, not Xander, and not Delilah and her revenge. You. You're my friend. There's nothing I wouldn't do for you."

Raif closed his eyes, and his head dropped. I was all about the heartfelt words tonight. Must have been Fallon's lack of decency that spurred me to such emotion. But even I had a breaking point, and I wasn't willing to let Raif reciprocate. Or maybe I was afraid he wouldn't. Whatever my reason, I spoke up again before he could open his mouth. "Ty didn't hurt you, did he?"

Raif's brow rose in question, his blue eyes glowing in the dark. "He's strong. Surprisingly strong. I think he broke a few of my ribs, but I'll be fine. Don't worry," he said as I opened my mouth to speak. "I know this isn't his fault. But if this threat to your Jinn's sanity or the attempts on both your lives has anything to do with Brakae, maybe you should abandon this quest. I've come to terms with my loss. Looking for a ghost isn't going to do any of us any good."

"If any part of what's going on has to do with her, then she's not a ghost, is she?"

"Perhaps not." The hope in his voice made him sound so much younger. Vulnerable. "But is it worth the risk?"

"I think you can answer that all on your own," I said.

"Yes," Raif said, "I suppose I can."

We stood side by side, watching the traffic for a while in utter silence. "What do you know?" he asked. I had a feeling it had taken a huge leap of faith for him to make the transition from resignation to hope.

"Very little at this point. I'm going out. I have some things to take care of. Can I count on you if I need help?"

"What about your Jinn?"

"I need to keep him out of this if I can. It'll be safer for him the less he knows." Then again, as I thought of Delilah's warnings and my strange dreams, someone could be fucking with Ty and me for an entirely different reason. I hadn't forgotten about the mysterious Man from The Ring. And if he was truly coming for me, I'd handle that little problem all by myself. "If I need you, I'll call."

Raif answered with a nod, and I joined with the shadows stretching beyond our feet before he might be tempted to follow me.

I walked into The Pit, armed to the teeth and carrying a wad of cash. Levi waved and flashed his boy-next-door smile, pushing up the long sleeves of his rugby shirt. A flock of girls turned from the bar to see what had snagged their eye candy's attention, and a few of them sneered. If I'd been feeling more playful, I would have given them a real show. Instead, I let my natural charm shine. "Back off, ladies," I said, and sidled my way into the middle of their little group. "He's got an appointment. You can come back and drool all you like after I'm done with him."

The downtrodden groupies gathered their drinks and scattered. Guess I'd burst their balloons. Misery loves company. I felt like shit—so should they.

"You're in a mood tonight," Levi said, sliding a Malibu and orange juice toward me. "And thanks for ruining *my* chances at a good mood."

"They'll get over it. And so will you. You can have a one-nighter some other time." I downed half my drink before fishing in my pocket. "Besides, I brought more engaging company. His name's Ben, and he's got a lot of brothers." I slapped the roll of hundred-dollar bills into his hand.

Always smooth, Levi didn't even flinch as he stowed the money. He took my glass and freshened it up before pulling a couple of imported beers from the fridge below the bar. "I haven't found anything out about your ring man."

"That little project is going to have to go on the back burner for now. What I need tonight is information about a couple of Sidhe."

"Playing with the big boys, huh?" Levi motioned to one of the cocktail waitresses. "Can you watch the bar, Monique? I need ten or fifteen minutes."

Monique looked as though she'd walk out into traffic if Levi asked her to. And fortunately, the bar wasn't very busy. I followed as Levi led the way to a quiet corner. He took a seat and I followed suit, sipping the drink he'd made me when what I really wanted was to abandon it and go straight for the bottle.

"Sidhe are the oldest of the Fae lineage. Their magic is the strongest too. Time hasn't been kind to the nonhuman population, Darian. But the Sidhe have held on to their ways and shunned humanity for the most part. They've got power and then some. Are you sure you want to get involved with them?"

No, but it was too late now to rethink my decisions. "Honestly, Levi, I don't plan on making friends. Besides, I'm only interested in two Sidhe. A sister and brother called Moira and Reaver."

Levi let out a low whistle. "Might as well douse yourself in gasoline and light the match, Darian. Why in the hell would you want to tangle with them?"

Oh fucking *fuck*. How did I always manage to pick the baddest of the bad to get involved with? I couldn't tell Levi why I was interested in the siblings. Letting everyone in the city know I was out to steal from them wouldn't exactly help me in the burglary department. But I had to know who and what I was up against. Fallon's request smelled like a trap. Either that or he knew it was a suicide mission and was hoping I'd at least get my hands on the merchandise before they killed me. In which case, he wouldn't need to bother with Delilah or lifting the spell. "Levi, I gave you a shitload of cash. Let me worry about my own ass. Moira and Reaver," I said slowly, "tell me about them."

Levi sighed and looked around as if afraid someone might overhear our conversation. "From what I've heard, Moira is the more dangerous of the two. She's got a lot of magic up her sleeve. A Healer, I believe. And a Herald."

"What's that?"

"A Herald is someone who can talk to the dead or the crossed over. Most of the supernatural don't view death as a finality. They tend to see it as an evolution or a passing into another realm. They don't harbor the spiritual existence as a joining with God or going to heaven. Think Avalon. You don't *die* die. You just leave this realm, and your soul takes up residence somewhere else. But I guess I don't have to tell you that."

I knew Shaedes didn't believe in conventional death. Xander said our physical bodies might die, but we would forever live in shadow. And apparently this Moira could speak to our dearly departed brethren. "What about Reaver?"

Levi leaned close. "Reaver is called the Keeper."

I knew that much already. "Do you know what he keeps?"

Levi gave a nervous chuckle. "I don't have a fucking clue."

Well, I knew something Levi didn't. The thing that Reaver "kept" was the exact thing Fallon wanted me to steal. If Levi was corroborating Fallon's information—that Reaver was, in fact, the Keeper—then at least I knew he hadn't been playing me. It didn't matter that Levi didn't know what the Sidhe kept. Fallon knew. "Do you know where they live? How I can find them?"

"I don't know about Moira, but I've heard Reaver likes to hang out at a place called Atlas. It's a high-end, private club. Caters to nonhuman clientele only. Very exclusive."

"Where is it?"

"Don't quote me on this, but I think it's underground. Industrial District, maybe. They're only open at night;

watch for the flow of luxury traffic—should lead you right to him."

I left The Pit a thousand dollars lighter but rich with information. Levi was good for it, I had no doubt. That preppy bastard knew more about the supernatural world than I did. The waterfront called, and I was itching to check out the Industrial District for any sign of the esoteric supernatural hangout, but the gray-streaked eastern sky told me I'd have to wait another eighteen or so hours before I could begin my quest for the Keeper.

Sandpaper would have been softer than my eyelids as I blinked. God, I was tired.

I hadn't had a decent night's sleep in . . . I couldn't even remember how long. When this was all over and done with, I was going to sleep for a month. I headed toward downtown and my apartment, when the sound of wings flapping drew my attention. As I looked skyward, a golden red form swooped down, nearly clipping my head with its talons. A falcon, the same falcon that had given me the pendulum, dove and spun, twisting in midair and digging at my pocket while it beat against me with its wings.

Insistent shit, I thought as I batted it away. Gaining altitude, the falcon regrouped and began anew, clawing at my pocket and tugging with a swift flapping of wings. I fought the bird off with my left hand while my right ventured to my pocket, which had begun to grow warm. Strange. Since I'd returned from my little field trip, the gem had been dormant, its warmth and otherworldly light seeming to have disappeared. But with the appearance of the falcon, it had awoken. The emerald pendulum pulsed with bright green light as I drew it out into the open air, watching as it swung to and fro before my eyes. With a parting screech, the falcon soared into the sky and out of sight. Guess it had delivered its message.

Two days I'd been gone the last time I had allowed myself to become drawn into the pendulum. And I'd kept the damned thing tucked in my pocket ever since.

But I pulled it out of its hiding place and stared into its depths anyway, unable to tear my gaze from the fathomless green light. The gem swung toward me, pulled by some unknown force of gravity, and I leaned toward the light, mesmerized by the sudden peace and unequivocal quiet it offered. Seconds slowed, the pulsing beat of time came nearly to a halt, and I felt a strange tug at my center, urging me toward something I couldn't identify. I allowed my eyes to drift shut, and when I opened them again, I no longer stood on the gray Seattle streets but at the top of the knoll, looking down into the green valley and at the dark-haired woman who waited for me.

Chapter 15

Another blink of my eyes and I no longer stood on the knoll. Without taking a step, I'd appeared in the valley below, standing face-to-face with a woman I recognized and yet didn't know.

This was the woman who'd run from the charging Enphigmalé in my dream. She had the same thick raven hair, same peaches-and-cream skin, and the exact same sapphire eyes. She looked my age, maybe a little younger, but I realized with certainty there was no mistaking the kinship between her, the child who'd warned me about "the Man," and the adolescent girl who'd brought me here the first time. Sisters? Mother and daughters? Did I really have time to wonder?

She smiled. Again it struck me as familiar—not an openly hostile expression, but not exactly warm either. It didn't suit her. A gentle breeze stirred her hair, and she looked to the sky, her smile fading into something more serious. When her eyes met mine again, there was a depth of sadness there. "I must speak with you," she said.

"Whatever you have to say, make it fast." The sound thumping in my ears now was not the passage of time but my own racing heart. "The last time I wound up here, a few minutes cost me two days. What the hell is going on? Who are you?"

"I'm nothing but a humble servant. A priestess and caretaker. And *you* are the Guardian. You must protect the Key and the natural order. You must give assistance if I call upon you."

Lovely.

"I have to go," I said.

"He will deceive you," she said, taking my hand in hers. "You have to be strong."

"I really, *really* do not have time for this." I pulled my hand from hers. How long had I been standing here? A minute? Ninety seconds? "I have to get back home before someone notices I'm gone. I don't know what the hell you're talking about, and I'm not a damned Guardian. You got that?"

"Please, Darian," she said, too calmly. "You have no choice."

"I'm not sure what you think I'm responsible for guarding, but I don't even own a key to my own apartment. As for giving you assistance . . . this looks like a nice, calm place. I doubt you have anything to worry about." I held out the emerald, trying again to return it, but she took a step back and shook her head.

A couple of minutes gone? A day—or more? I had to leave. Now. "I can't help you," I said. "I'm sorry. I've got my own shit to deal with. Find someone else to guard your keys, and quit bringing me here." I let the pendulum fall from my hand, and it drifted as if it were a feather. "I have to go. I can't stay here." I turned my back to her, and the green landscape melted away as I heard the pendulum land in the grass.

"Look out! Move out of the way!" someone shouted before a horn blared. My eyes flew open just in time to see the bus barreling toward me. I jumped, falling back against someone as I tripped on the sidewalk, the bus whooshing past me to turn the corner. Late afternoon. The sun was just about to sink into the western sky. How long had I been gone this time? I had to get back to Tyler fast, but becoming incorporeal on a street packed with humans wasn't an option. Of course, no one had seemed to notice that I'd just popped out of thin air, so maybe no one would notice if I did it again. Above the din of engines, horns, and people, a high-pitched keen raised my hackles. The falcon swooped down; silver glinted in its talons as it released its cargo just above my head before spinning in midair and flying away.

With preternatural speed, I reached out, catching the pendulum before it hit the ground. I looked at the emerald in my hand and could almost hear a woman's calm voice saying, "You forgot something." Pulling back my fist, I prepared to fling the damned thing into traffic, but before I let it fly, the emerald warmed my palm, absorbing the sound of time and delivering peace to my soul. *Damn it.* Instead, I shoved the pendulum in my pocket and watched as the falcon made its ascent into the sky.

"You're a pain in the ass—you know that?" I shouted. A few people stopped to gape, though I was only one of several people on this street talking or shouting to themselves. I meandered through the pedestrians, fighting to appear unruffled until I could find a hidden place to leave my solid form behind.

On the plus side, I had less time to kill before nightfall, which meant less time until I could track Reaver. But I was terrified I'd lost more than seven or eight hours. What if it had been seven or eight days? I hurried toward my apartment, all the while racking my brain for a decent excuse for where I'd been, when I heard the scurrying sound of insects close behind me.

I rolled my eyes to the heavens. Just what I needed. I fought the urge to turn and stamp their shiny little bodies into the pavement. In the light of day, a Lyhtan could choose to take the corporeal form of an unassuming insect. At night, they were formidable fighters, nearly seven feet tall and with sharp, venomous teeth that could turn their prey's insides into a slurpable goo. I'd once seen one of them partaking of a liquid meal. In a word: Disgusting.

Rather than flee like a coward, I stayed my course, waiting for the right time and the right place to turn and fight. I sensed the approach of sunset, my skin prickling with each passing second. Until the sun slipped completely away, the Lyhtans would be shielded from human eyes by their incorporeal forms. They could attack me right here and now if they wanted to. But I assumed they hadn't attacked me already simply because they were worried that they'd run out of time and would be forced to regain their solid forms before they could kill me. I needed to find cover, and fast. Good thing dangerous, abandoned alleys were plentiful. Gotta love the city.

The evening sun plunged beneath the horizon, and I felt its passage as a rumble that traveled the length of my body. Quickening my pace, I ducked into the darkest, dankest, most abandoned alleyway I could find—and I turned to fight.

Son of a bitch, there were five of the fuckers. I could easily have taken two or three. But five? Fate really had it out for me. I drew my katana, thankful I wouldn't be hindered by my corporeal form. Post-sunset, the Lyhtans would be trapped in their bodies, but it didn't make them any less deadly. Any one of them would be capable of ripping my head from my shoulders if I made one careless move. But if I could take their heads first . . . the better for me.

I assessed the situation as quickly as I could. None of them appeared armed, though their taloned hands could deliver a poisonous slice or two. I wasn't taking any chances as I backed deeper into the alley, drawing them away from the hapless public. "I'm having a serious self-esteem moment," I said. "I mean, five against one? You guys must think I'm pretty damned tough."

One of them laughed, and I shivered at the sound. No matter how many years I lived, I knew I'd never get used to the many facets of sound that made up a single Lyhtan voice. "We're going to enjoy eating you." As a collective body, my five attackers took a step closer, greenish drool leaking from their gaping mouths.

"You'll make a decent meal," another said. "A savory morsel, indeed. The world will owe us a debt of gratitude once we've finished with you. You are Other. Worse than you were when simply another Shaede scum."

Nothing I hadn't heard before. Lyhtans bore a hatred and jealousy toward Shaedes for as long as their species had lived. And since my transformation into something more than both of them . . . let's just say they wouldn't be inviting me to any family functions any time soon. "Okay, you hate me. And might I add, maybe you're just a little jealous that I can do what you can do—but better." I swung my sword in a swirling pattern. "I might be outnumbered, but you're outweaponed, and outskilled. Leave now and I won't harbor any ill feelings."

They laughed, the sound of a thousand mirthful voices. "She's brave," one of them said to his buddies.

"She's not smart, though. Oh no, she is not smart at all."

Their little conversation was grating on my last nerve. Again they advanced, and again I retreated deeper into the alley. Gray twilight melted away into darkening night as they talked—I assumed—in an attempt to scare me.

"I'm not smart?" Hmm. That pissed me off. I considered myself pretty damned smart. Reason enough to kill my attackers, fair fight or not. "Fuck you."

I spun the katana high over my head as I leapt into the air, cutting down with speed and precision. Two of the Lyhtans stumbled back, but the other three charged, converging on me so as to give me no escape. I jabbed with my sword and then cut down. Without pause, I swept the blade back in an upward arc. One of my assailants stumbled backward before falling to its knees, clutching its bleeding torso, while the other died before its body hit the ground. *Two down.* The one I'd missed lunged toward me, teeth bared and poised to bite. Dissolving into dusk, I left my body just in time to miss becoming a Lyhtan predinner smoothie.

Unfortunately, now I had one enemy at my back and two before me. I drew a throwing knife from my belt and turned to the side. With a sweeping throw, I launched the knife and struck one of my three remaining opponents square in the middle of its forehead. *One more down, two to go.* It toppled over like a felled tree, landing on the pavement with a sickening *crack*. I pointed the katana at attackers four and five and waited for them to make a move.

Lyhtans are skilled hunters and adept at hiding. The bastards can literally run up walls, and so I crouched, sword ready, my free hand hovering near my knives. In a blink, one of them moved *fast*. Like a character straight out of a video game, it scaled the wall, running up and sideways, and then flipped as it came to the ground on the other side of me.

Two against one. Piece of cake. I went for another knife, drew it, and let it fly. It grazed the Lyhtan standing at the back of the alley, the damage barely classifying as a scratch. *Great. Way to hit your mark, dipshit.* Raif would've died if he'd been there to see me make such a rookie mistake.

While I was distracted by my utter lack of skill, assassin number five jumped me. We tumbled to the ground in a tangle of long insect limbs before I dissolved from the Lyhtan's grasp and reappeared above it. Gripping the katana in both hands, I aimed the sword for the bastard's heart and stabbed down. It jerked, arching its long, lean back, and died, leaving me man to man—well, woman to thing—with the last remaining Lyhtan. I abandoned the throwing knives—my aim was shit—and went for my dagger instead. Swinging the sword and stabbing with the long dagger, I fought the creature that had nothing more than its talons and sharp teeth to use against me.

The alley was narrow and our quarters close. It damned well might have been blind fucking luck that I'd beaten the other four because, as I grappled with the remaining Lyhtan, it seemed the walls of the alley were closing in on us. It pushed me back, and I slammed against a wall, the katana clanging to the pavement at my feet. The Lyhtan moved in a blur of speed, its long jagged teeth sinking into the flesh of my arm.

Motherfucker! I thought I'd pass out from the pain. Searing venom pulsed through my veins, and had I been a more helpless soul, my insides would have begun to melt within a matter of seconds. It didn't take long for the burning to subside as my otherworldly body took over, expelling the venom from the wound. What had

once been a raw, open tear began to close, the skin knit-
ting back together with amazing speed. Desperate, the
Lyhtan lunged at me again, and I met its advance in a
strange battle dance that put me within gutting distance.
I jabbed hard with the long dagger, careful not to make
a killing blow. Aiming high above the waist, but just below the ribs, I stabbed, feeling the sharp metal penetrate
flesh, meat, and muscle, gouging the Lyhtan's midsection.
I tugged hard, withdrew the blade, and wrapped my free
hand around the bastard's shoulder. I'd have grabbed a
hank of its corn silk hair for leverage, but, damn, it was
tall. With speed and unnatural strength, I threw my attacker to the ground, stomping my boot on its shoulder to
keep it down.

I smiled into the Lyhtan's seething face. *Yeah, that's
right. Nobody fucks with this girl.* "Okay," I said, feeling
my badassedness. "Who sent you after me? And if you
tell me you don't know . . . I'm going to take you apart,
starting with your fingers"—I pointed the dagger between the Lyhtan's thighs—"and ending with whatever
it is you're hiding under that nasty tuft of fur."

The Lyhtan cackled as it strained for breath. "I answer to no one and need no reason to kill you beyond
your mere existence. You are favored by that bastard
king and his warrior brother. What a blow to them it
would be when I delivered your body to their doorstep."

So . . . what? This had nothing to do with me, personally. I was just a pawn in the eternal Lyhtan/Shaede
strife. *Wonderful.* I didn't have time for this petty bullshit.
"What's your name?"

"Mengoth."

Good Lord, couldn't one of them be named Sam or
Brad? *Mengoth?* Give me a break. "Well, then, you're
not worth keeping alive." I bent over him. "Wouldn't you
agree? I mean, if I don't take care of you right now, who's
to say the next Shaede you cross will walk away to tell
the tale."

"If you think I'd be stupid enough to beg a creature
no better than me to spare my life, you aren't worthy to

do the deed," he said. "You seem to be under the misas-sumption that I find you worth my respect." He coughed, and greenish spittle splattered on the toe of my boot. "You may have the privilege of joining with the light, but make no mistake. You are nothing more than a common Shaede. And you deserve nothing better than a slow, painful death."

Mengoth kicked his legs and grabbed my foot with both his taloned hands, giving my ankle a sound twist. I hit the pavement headfirst, white light exploding in my cracked skull. Dazed, I tried to shake the fog from my brain as Mengoth fumbled in the haze of encroaching night for my sword. Metal scraped against asphalt, and the sound of it echoed in the alley, an eerie prelude to my impending death. I lay still, my fingers creeping to my belt as I waited for Mengoth to strike. Through lowered lids, I watched the bastard take up my sword and raise it high above me. He poised to strike, lifted his head to-ward the sky, and took a deep breath. It was now or never. I pulled the last throwing knife from my belt and launched it at Mengoth's head. The silver buried itself to the hilt in the Lyhtan's neck, and it looked down on me, amber eyes wide with surprise. I rolled back and kicked, propelling myself upward, and delivered a roundhouse to his stomach. He slammed against the wall, dropping the katana, which I caught in midfall. With a sweeping upward cut, I ran the blade through his neck, just above the knife hilt, and the Lyhtan's head rolled deep into the alley before his body crumpled to the ground at my feet.

Just my luck to end an evening on a bloody note.

I pulled my cell phone out of my pocket and dialed Raif's number before retrieving my knives from the Lyhtan bodies that were already beginning to dissolve into shimmering light. For all intents and purposes, I had to admire the Lyhtan form; they were perfectly designed for stealth. They could travel invisibly or virtually un-noticed during the day, and they were fully capable of staying hidden at night. Plus, no messy bodies to scare the shit out of the police when they died. Perfect, really.

On the fifth ring, Raif finally answered. "Where have you been all day?"

All day. I could almost sigh in relief. I'd been gone less than twenty-four hours this time. "Out."

"You sound out of breath. What trouble have you found now?"

I wished he'd give it a rest already. Like Tyler, Raif was beginning to sound like a broken record. "Oh, you know, just an evening jog to get the heart pumping. How's Tyler?"

"Not better, but not worse either. Whatever ails him has certainly weakened him. Dimitri has been checking in on him, and your Jinn is growing tired of having a babysitter. It took a bit to calm him down. Sounds like your protector doesn't like to wake up and find his charge missing."

Shit. Night had barely fallen, and I still needed to find Reaver. "Can Dimitri keep an eye on my apartment for a few more hours? I have an errand to run."

"Tyler's not a prisoner, Darian. Or helpless. I don't expect Dimitri to follow your Jinn, should he leave. What sort of errands do you have?"

"Just scoping out a new hot spot." My endeavors to find Raif's daughter, cure Tyler of his magical ailment, and steal a mysterious hourglass would be a hell of a lot easier without everyone's noses up my ass. Raif sighed into the phone, obviously onto me. "I'm going to talk to Levi about a lead," I said, lying through my teeth. "Just looking for some help on the Tyler front."

His pregnant pause made me cringe. Raif sure wasn't helping me to help him. The deception had begun to wear on me. I *needed* help; I couldn't do everything on my own. I didn't want Raif to be a party to my acts of thievery unless it was absolutely necessary. I knew I could count on him. He'd finally allowed himself to consider the possibility that his daughter was still alive. But until I had the leverage I needed, I wanted Raif to know as little as possible about what I was up to. He was much too honorable to participate in a criminal act, and I wanted it to stay that way.

"Dimitri can keep an eye on things," Raif said. "For a while longer. But, Darian, you'll have Anya to contend with if you keep her husband much longer."

Anya. Yeah, that's all I needed. "I'll be home by dawn. Thanks, Raif."

"Darian," he said in a tone too big brother for my taste, "when you're done with your . . . *errands* . . . we need to have a talk."

Sure. Why not? Pile it on! "Fine," I said, and hung up.

Chapter 16

I wandered the Industrial District with one thought: *Find Reaver*. I was through playing fuck-around. Time to locate Raif's daughter and wrap this shit up. Something was seriously wrong with Tyler, and it was getting worse by the day, for all I knew. And the faster I found Brakae, the faster I could focus my attention on the Man from The Ring and the shit storm his mysterious presence had brought into my life.

Shortly after midnight, the flow of traffic increased significantly, and the vehicles became more ostentatious. The supernatural loved their money. And they flaunted their wealth like an oil baron on holiday. BMWs, Ferraris, Mercedes, Bentleys, Aston Martins—the high-end cars drifted by like a parade of self-important aristocracy. Some of Atlas's clientele hadn't come by car, however. I felt the presence of others approaching in the shadows, like a dog pile of energy resting square upon my shoulders to send me steadily to the ground.

Under the cover of darkness, I ventured near the warehouse that housed the private club. It was buzzing with the energy of the inhuman. I couldn't risk being recognized: I got enough attention as it was. This was a good old-fashioned stealth mission. Though invisible to most, I had no idea what I might encounter should I venture inside the supersecret supernatural club. Delilah could see me in my shadow form, and she was as blind as a bat. So, with curiosity raging inside me, I waited outside the warehouse—and watched.

For an hour I stood guard, invisible to the human eye

and crouched atop a stack of shipping crates. All I could think about was the monumental waste of time the whole stakeout was, and how I could be curled up in bed next to Tyler, feeling his bare skin against mine. And then my mark made his appearance.

Alone. I don't know why it surprised me. I guess I assumed Moira would be with him. From the looks of them at the PNT Summit several months ago, I'd doubted one went anywhere without the other. I'd seen Moira alone at The Pit, though, hadn't I? I couldn't shake the feeling that Moira's appearance at the bar was more than coincidence. Had *she* been staking *me* out? Or perhaps aiming an arrow at my head?

Reaver pulled up in a very classy light blue Mercedes AMG. The sports car paid homage to an elegant era long forgotten with its short cab and elongated body. But it also looked like it could kick some serious ass in a street race.

The driver's-side gullwing door opened, and true to its name, it looked like a bird about to take flight. Reaver stepped out into the night. When I'd first met him, he'd issued a silent challenge. Without so much as wiggling a toe, he'd tried to impose his will on me, as if placing invisible hands on my shoulders to push me to my knees. Unlike Fallon, Reaver forced his will with a sort of telekinesis. Fallon's power was like an urging. A natural impulse I didn't know how to fight.

Tall—almost as tall as a Lyhtan—and unusually thin, Reaver walked with the grace only the nonhuman possess. His suit must have cost more than a couple grand, tailored to his body in a way that accentuated his natural endowments and made his very thin form seem more lean than too skinny. He paused before entering the warehouse and looked in my direction. I remained shrouded under the cover of darkness, but as his empty sky blue eyes scanned the area where I stood, I didn't dare draw a breath. His lips rose in a sardonic smirk as his attention was drawn to a black Porsche Cayenne pulling into the parking lot. He waited, the smirk spreading into a warm smile as he waited for the driver to join him.

Interesting. Apparently Reaver wasn't the cold-hearted bastard I'd chalked him up to be. A second Fae approached with a spring in his step, his eyes sparkling with adoration. He took Reaver's outstretched hand and pressed his lips to the Sidhe's fingertips before the two disappeared inside the darkened doorway of the warehouse and Atlas.

Waiting is so much harder when you're aware of every single second. Curiosity burned as I wondered what the secret playhouse of the supernatural looked like. Was it truly underground? Hidden beneath a stack of metal crates? Or did a mysterious doorway open up, allowing the patrons to party the night away in some mystical realm? The mystery enticed me; yet I had no choice but to wait for Reaver to grow bored and leave for the night.

At three in the morning, he'd finally reached his fun quota. It could have been worse. Every minute waiting on Reaver was a minute lost with Tyler. Lucky for me, Reaver didn't seem interested in what might be hiding under the cover of darkness. His companion walked through the door, arm in arm with Reaver, both heading for the Mercedes. Good for me. Great, in fact. If Reaver was occupied with his date, he'd be less on guard, which would make him easier to trail. And since I no longer had Ty's motorcycle, I had to hope he'd travel the city streets slowly enough for me to keep up.

My ears filled with the sound of the wind as it rushed over me, through me. As my shadow self, I followed Reaver in a winding path, in some cases backtracking, circling blocks over again and backtracking some more, before he finally felt safe enough to stop masking his route. The Sidhe was either especially paranoid, or he could feel my presence nearby. I hoped to hell it was the former. I could deal with paranoid. It took all of my energy to keep up; I pushed my preternatural speed to its limits. The city melted away, the houses becoming larger and more scattered as we ventured into Capitol Hill. I recognized the area well. Xander's house wasn't far from here.

Reaver pulled the Mercedes into the garage, and I followed, unsure of what I might find. Three additional cars offered plenty of cover, though I had a sneaking suspicion Reaver would be able to sense my presence if he happened to pay attention. Fortunately, his boyfriend kept him more than occupied. I crouched behind a Maserati while the pair paused near the hood of the car for some heavy petting. Good God, but I was getting some serious soft-core shows these days. Free porn, right here! Reaver paused long enough to make an open sweeping gesture with his hands, and I felt a vibration in the air.

Wards. Most supernaturals didn't have much use for expensive alarm systems. Not when you could cast impenetrable magical protection on your property. This posed a problem. As my incorporeal self, I could easily slide in and out of anywhere with ease. But I'd never tried to infiltrate a magic barrier. The first kink in what was beginning to feel like a much-knotted plan.

Fallon was out of his mind if he thought this was a *fair and equitable* trade. But occupied or not, I didn't feel like traipsing around Reaver's house while he and his boyfriend got busy in the next room—or in the same room. So, I waited for the two of them to enter the house before I slid soundlessly through the garage door, out of sight.

Dawn was fast approaching when I reached my studio. Gray skies smeared with light blues, oranges, and pinks welcomed the sun in the eastern sky. Ty sat in the living room with Dimitri, playing poker. Nothing like a game of Texas hold 'em to cure what ails ya.

"Having fun?" I tried to ignore the fact that Tyler looked worse.

"Sure," Ty said a little too sarcastically for my taste. "I've made a haul. How was *your* night?"

The question was flavored with accusation, and I averted my gaze. I should have been turning the city upside down looking for whoever was making Tyler sick, not playing thief for Fallon. "Oh, you know, boring for the most part." At least that wasn't a lie. Watching Reaver hadn't exactly been action packed. "How are you feeling?"

"Great." Sarcasm aside, he tried to put up a nonchalant front. "Well, Dimitri, I guess we're done here." Ty stretched and folded his hand. "You can try and win it back from me some other time."

"I'll take you up on that offer," Dimitri said, clapping Ty on the shoulder. "Good morning, Darian." He nodded and made his way to the door.

Tyler settled on the couch and held his arms out for me. Smiling, I sank down next to him, sighing at the pure bliss of relaxing in his embrace. God, if we got out of this with my sanity intact, I swore we were going to take a long and much-deserved vacation.

"You've been gone awhile," Ty whispered into my hair. "I missed you. I was about to go out looking for you, but since you decided I needed a *babysitter*, I had no choice but to sit here and take Dimitri's money."

I balled my hands into fists, my fingers slick and clammy with the evidence of my mounting guilt complex. He was *so* onto me. "I missed you too." His lips brushed my temple, and then my ear. "How are you really feeling?" Shivers followed the path of his mouth.

"Tired," he said, "but not too bad. Really. It's just exhausting to put up such a strong shield. I'm getting better at identifying the assaults when they happen, though."

"Ty, are you sure this"—I racked my brain for the right words—"magical attack is aimed at me? I mean, how can you tell?"

"I can tell. I told you, the bond flows through you into me. Since I can feel you, I know where the attack is coming from."

Jesus Christ, the whole "bond" thing confused the hell out of me. "Maybe someone's using me to get to *you*?"

Tyler shifted and sat up a little straighter. "It's possible, I suppose. But I doubt it. Something to look into anyway. All I know is that whatever this is, it triggers all of my protective instincts to the point that it's all I can think about. Anyone who's close to you is suddenly a potential threat. When I find out who's responsible for it—the bastard is as good as dead."

Amen. And I was going to be the one to do the deed. I chewed my bottom lip, knowing what I needed to speed this business with Fallon along, and yet knowing I shouldn't venture down this path. Weakened, Ty could barely keep himself upright; I didn't want to add to that by drawing further on his powers. I opened my mouth, ready to speak the words—no warning, just wish. And then I came to my senses. The wards on Reaver's house would surely protect its contents as well. There was no point expending Ty's precious energy on a wish impossible to grant. I'd have to get Fallon's hourglass the old-fashioned way.

"What are you thinking about?" Tyler asked.

The age-old question. I would have thought it cliché from anyone but Ty. "I'm thinking about time. How it seems to slip through my fingers. I wish I could slow it down."

"Why?" Tyler said, softly. "You have all the time in the world."

"Maybe." Maybe not. Warmth pulsed from my pocket, spreading outward, the emerald's call. What if I was sucked into that strange place again and couldn't get out? What if one of those damned girls kept me there for an hour—or a year or ten years? How much time would pass in the real world; how many decades, centuries? I could lose Tyler. He'd forget all about me while I ran around after a trio of raven-haired beauties, unable to find my way home.

"I think I'd like to live on a deserted island." I slid my hand under Tyler's shirt so I could caress the ridges of his muscled stomach. "Just you and me and coconuts."

"Coconuts," Ty laughed. "You think we could live on that?"

"I could, if I had you." I meant it too. I'd eat coconuts boiled, baked, shredded, and fried every day for the next five thousand years if Tyler was there with me, safe and sound. "Couldn't you?"

"I don't know," he mused. "Just you and coconuts? I think I'd need a steak every once in a while."

"Thanks." I pulled away and gave him a playful swat.

"I could do it." Tyler kissed me and pulled me close. "Coconut stew every day. And you."

As the sun rose, we sat entwined on the couch, devising the many ways we'd eat our imaginary coconuts. If only life could be that simple. But I knew better.

"There's no fucking way." I paced around my bathroom, my voice muted. Tyler and I had spent eighteen blissful hours in my apartment, and I dreaded what I knew had to be done once Reaver left his house for the night. "The place is locked down with wards. I can't get past them."

"What about your Jinn?"

If Fallon mentioned Tyler one more time, I was going to gut him. I strangled my cell phone in both hands, as if it would make me feel better, before bringing it back to my ear. "This isn't a fair trade. I can't use Tyler. He's . . . sick." There I went again, divulging information he *did not* need. "You'll just have to find another way to get your piece of junk. I can't do it."

"Relax." Fallon's power seemed to snake right through the phone. "We won't need your boyfriend. The wards aren't aimed at you. You'll be able to get past them without incident."

Alarms bells blared in my head. "How would you know that?"

"That's none of your business. But I can say in all confidence, you are only one of three people who would be able to pass the wards unharmed."

"I won't do this if you don't tell me how you know that."

Fallon laughed. I closed my eyes, the sound so sinister, it made my limbs quake. "No. You know the terms of our agreement. You bring me the glass; I deliver the Oracle."

I stomped my foot like a three-year-old and kicked at

an abandoned shoe, sending it sailing into the shower. Tyler's footsteps approached, and he knocked on the door. "Everything okay?"

"Fine!" I called. "I just—ah—tripped on the toilet!" *Oh nice, Darian. You couldn't think of anything better than that? Idiot.* "I'll be out in a sec."

His footsteps retreated, and I waited until I could hear him moving around in the living room once again. "I'll have it to you tomorrow night," I seethed into the phone. "And if you even think about double-crossing me, I'll cut you open from stomach to sternum. You got that?"

"Tomorrow night then," Fallon said, and hung up.

I walked into the living room, favoring my right foot. Don't ask me why; it wasn't as if any damage I would've sustained in even a lethal toe-stubbing wouldn't have healed instantly. But I was so wrapped up in keeping Tyler out of my dealings with Fallon that I put my thespian skills to work and went the extra mile.

"Were you talking to someone?" Ty asked as I rifled through the refrigerator. I stiffened and leaned forward, wishing like hell I could disappear in it. "I thought I heard voices."

"Just talking to myself." I grabbed a soda and popped the tab. "I swore a bit when I stubbed my toe. Hurt like hell." I hated lying to him. And worse, I hated that the lies seemed to tumble from my lips with such ease. Was this what happened when you were trying to protect someone? Even the most unimaginable things became acceptable? Hell, I was about to commit larceny to help someone I cared for. What was a lie or two in the name of love?

"I might have a lead on who's messing with our bond," Ty said over his shoulder. "I was thinking about going to check it out tonight, see what I can find out. So I won't be around; is that all right?"

It was more than all right. Again it seemed Fate was clearing a path for me, making the tasks at hand easier to accomplish. No babysitter for Ty. No answering to

Raif. No Dimitri. And no wards for me to worry about. A cakewalk. "Of course I want you to go." Anything that would help Tyler was worth exploring. "If you get any useful information, call me."

"You'll be the first to know," Ty said, heading for the door. "Promise to stay out of trouble while I'm gone?"

I drew a cross over my heart. "I promise." *To try,* I added silently.

"I'll be back in a few hours. Don't go anywhere."

Didn't give me much time for a B&E, but I could make it work. It was almost midnight, and with any luck, Reaver would be gearing up for another night on the town, and if Fallon's information proved correct, I could slip in and out with one half of a broken hourglass, and payment for a charm-free Delilah. "I'll be here when you get back," I said.

"I'm serious," Ty said. "Stay here."

I beamed in his direction, hoping my smile was the reassurance he needed.

I swallowed down the bitter taste of deceit as Ty walked out the door. Damn, I was getting good at this whole deception thing.

Too good.

Chapter 17

"*H*ave you ever wondered why an assassin's life is so lonely?" Azriel asked.

"It's not. Not for us anyway. We have each other."

Azriel traced a pattern between my bare shoulder blades, curling down my spine before stopping at the small of my back. His lips followed suit, bringing delicious chills to the surface of my skin. I buried my face in the pillow, smiling as his tongue teased the area his lips had just been. "True, my love. True."

He seemed worried, which was out of character for his usually cavalier attitude. Lorik's father, Vasily Egorov, had finally met his end. And from what Azriel had told me, it hadn't been a peaceful one. We hadn't received any postcards for a couple of months, so it stood to reason that Lorik was no longer around to ascend to his father's seat of power within the mob. I'd never understood why Az cared. And as for work, we'd land on our feet. We always did. Plus we had enough cash and valuables to keep us afloat and living comfortably for a good, long time.

"You're so very special," Azriel said as his lips found my shoulder. "But if anyone should find out about you, not even an entire Shaede Kingdom could keep you safe. It's for the best that Vasily is gone. Lorik as well. Fear not, my love. I'll protect you until the time is right for your presence to be known."

I let him speak his nonsense. He had a tendency to talk in circles. I rolled onto my back, and his mouth caressed mine, his tongue sliding warm and welcome through my parted lips. Let the world rot, *I thought as his hand cupped my breast.* Vasily and Lorik too. *As long as I had Azriel, I didn't need anyone else.*

My mind swirled with innumerable thoughts and memories, clouding my focus. Azriel had known all along that once my existence became public knowledge, a shit storm was soon to follow—understatement of the century. Rather than slow down, my world spiraled out of control, rotation upon rotation, problem upon problem. And as I made my way to Reaver's empty house, I laid out my troubles like strands of thread, each representing a singular nuisance in the braided bullshit of my life.

The Man from The Ring, the raven-haired Shaedes, and the pendulum became a single strand. And next to that lay Delilah, Raif, Brakae—and unfortunately— Fallon as well. The third strand represented Tyler, his strange behavior, the attempts on his life, and an unknown threat—aimed at driving him out of his mind. Somehow, they all came together, weaving in and out, constructing a solid length of rope. But who or what wove them together was lost on me.

Reaver's house, only a few blocks from Volunteer Park, might well have been considered a mansion by someone who'd never seen Xander's impressive estate. The residences had one thing in common, though: They both favored old-world elegance. Perhaps it connected the owners to their pasts, to eras they couldn't reclaim. The Victorian beauty of Reaver's three-story home struck me as almost too elegant for someone who came off as menacing with the potential for great violence.

After checking the garage to make sure that Reaver had, in fact, gone out for the evening, I hovered near the front door, pacing along the tiled covered porch, sensing the powerful wards designed to protect his property. My body hummed with energy, like an itch just under the skin that I couldn't scratch. The pendulum in my pocket responded as well, heat pulsing from the emerald warming my thigh. I should have dropped the damned thing in the middle of Puget Sound, but for the life of me, I couldn't bring myself to part from it since the falcon had returned it to me.

Wondering if I should trust Fallon's word, I continued to pace. *"You are only one of three people who would be able to pass those wards unharmed. . . ."* How did he know? The sound of my teeth grating against one another resounded in my ears. I stretched my neck from side to side, unclenched my fists, and inhaled a deep, cleansing breath to release the tension that pulled my entire body taut. I would find peace only by unraveling the mysteries strand by strand; finding Brakae was the first step.

I decided believing Fallon was my only option, so I closed my eyes, taking a leap of faith as I passed through Reaver's front door as nothing more than a wisp of darkness. The wards slid over my incorporeal form, like hunting dogs tracking scent. Magic snaked around me, twining and searching, pausing for the briefest moment before retreating and dissipating into nothing.

The air left my lungs in a great rush of breath, and muscle by muscle, I began to relax. Though I felt the presence of the wards, they seemed to ignore me, as if I belonged in the house and posed no threat to the secrets Reaver was trying to protect. Fallon had been right. I could pass through the house without harm. With any luck, he'd tell me why that was, once he had his prize—and I had Delilah.

Five thousand square feet was a rather large amount of space to search for something no bigger than a drinking glass. If Reaver was smart, he would've hidden his bauble in a safe, behind a false wall, as I did. But then again, I deduced Reaver's cocky, deadly attitude, coupled with the wards, might offer him the peace of mind to leave his half of the hourglass on display somewhere that he might look upon it.

I didn't take solid form, but rather swept the house as a wraith, moving from room to room. Reaver kept an especially tidy house. I doubted dust particles dared to rear their ugly heads in his presence. From the foyer, I

wandered through the kitchen, formal and informal dining rooms, the sitting room and the living room. The me-
dia room, complete with home theater and a sixty-inch
flat-panel TV, led to a library and a small office. Two
bathrooms were completely uninteresting, and a coat
closet—again, boring—was empty, save a couple of jack-
ets; it wasn't exactly piled with board games and playing
cards. I got the impression Reaver didn't host many
"family game nights" with the neighbors.

A search of the upstairs proved equally fruitless. He
kept the six-bedroom second floor as immaculate and
uninteresting as he did the downstairs. The master suite,
predictably sporting a king-sized bed and attached sitting room, looked *Architectural Digest* ready. I marked
the passage of thirty-three minutes and cradled my head
in my hands. I was running out of time, and still I had
found no sign of anything more than human, let alone
made of magic. Tyler would be back soon. If I wasn't
there when he got home, I doubted I'd be able to keep
my plans secret any longer.

Drifting through the floor, I found myself once again
on the first floor of the house. I had one more area to
search—the basement. Another flight of stairs led from
a small door beneath the staircase down to the bottom
floor. I expected old and musty and rickety wooden
stairs and crumbling concrete walls. What I saw instead
blasted me with the force of magical energy. The basement was the only floor of the house that hadn't been
kept true to its period design. Marble stairs and marble-
lined walls glowed with silver and gold symbols, the
shapes swirling and moving, illuminating my path deeper
into the basement.

Magic burned hot and heavy here, the sensation of
thousands of tiny feet traveling the highways of my skin
driving me to the point of near distraction. The emerald
in my pocket blazed, no longer pulsing with warmth but
almost searing through my pocket and screaming for me
to notice. At the same time, the sound of time quieted
within me, and I didn't need to gaze into the emerald or

stand in another world to feel it. Iron butterflies swirled in my stomach, much too heavy and foreboding to be light jitters of nerves. I'd need hip boots to get out of this mess because, as I suddenly realized, I was wading in deep shit.

As I descended lower into Reaver's basement, my body became corporeal, the sound of my boots echoing eerily on the marble steps. All around me gold and silver light led the way, runes flashing and symbols swirling. The wards that protected the house felt stronger here, mingling with the already present magic and causing my teeth to chatter. But as before, whatever protected the Sidhe's property paid me no mind.

I took the last step, a feeling of finality stealing my breath as a soft glow of light that seemed to come from nowhere pulsed from the ceiling. Finally, I could see the full scope of the basement, and what a room it was. At first sight, it reminded me of something out of a decadent 1950s reenactment of *Cleopatra*, or some other epic tale. But as I took in the whole of it, I realized it held to an older tradition, dating to pre-Christian *civilization*—Celtic more than likely. Beautiful didn't begin to describe this room. Reverent wouldn't do justice to the emotions swelling in my chest. This sacred place assaulted my senses, my emotions. I'd never felt so safe, or so right. Somehow, a kinship formed between me and this place; I was meant to be here. I had to stop, shrinking to my knees as I caught my breath and stilled my quaking limbs.

Trees lined the walls. Growing out of nothing, they were yet vibrant and living. Rowan, alder, ash, birch, cedar, and other trees I couldn't name shot up into an impossibly tall ceiling—too tall not to be an illusion. Like the sky, it twinkled with stars and then changed, showcasing a dark sky and a full opal moon. White candles burned, the wicks never seeming to diminish and the flames unwavering with the disturbance of my passing. A long, rectangular pool ran the length of the room, splitting it down the middle, and sparkling orbs of different colors swam about in light blue water.

As I walked, the false sky changed again, lightening by slow degrees, streaked with pinks and deep burnt oranges. The basement became bright with the light of morning sun, and I could sense the leaves of the trees shifting and reaching toward sustenance. In the full light, I could finally see to the end of the room, its length and width again too vast to be real. And at the end of Reaver's basement, atop a granite column, sat the hourglass.

It looked like any other, really, except that it was one half of a whole. Grains of golden sand glistened inside it, gathering at the bottom as if they poured from the top half that used to be there. When at last the glass filled, the flecks of gold reversed their path, floating upward and disappearing into nothing. I watched in awe as the cycle repeated itself once more, my hand resting at my thigh, cupping the pendulum in my pocket.

As I stood there staring at the broken—and somehow functional—hourglass, I had an Indiana Jones moment. But I didn't have a bag of sand to trade with the relic, and I wondered at the possibility of setting off an epic set of booby traps, rolling boulder and all. But I thought of Raif: friend, loyal brother, and wronged husband. I thought of his grief, the lengths he'd been willing to go to find his missing child, and the lengths he refused to go to despite his pain and need for answers. And goddamn it, if someone needed a ray of sunshine in his life, you could bet your ass it was Raif.

Screw it.

I plucked the hourglass from its perch.

Closed my eyes tight.

Waited for the boulder to roll on top of me.

And let out a shaky breath when nothing happened. I mean, no darts shooting from the walls? The ceiling wasn't slowly shrinking to crush me? No giant swinging axes ready to slice me in two? The whole thing was rather anticlimactic in my opinion.

That is, until I turned around and came face-to-face with Reaver.

The weight of his stare pressed upon me just as well as

any shrinking ceiling. And the accusing finger he pointed at me was no less piercing than a poison dart striking my chest. He took a step closer, and the sound of his footsteps rang in my ears like sharp metal cutting me down.

Tyler would be home from his meeting any minute. Fuck, fuck, *fuck!* My sword sang as the metal scraped against the scabbard, and I held it at the ready, prepared to fight for my prize.

I can't stop you, Reaver's voice echoed in my mind. *But if you leave with the glass, the damage will be irreparable.*

"That's a neat little trick," I said, backing away from the granite podium, sidestepping Reaver. The glamour he wore for human benefit slid away, and my jaw sagged—just a little—in awe. No wonder all of Fae-kind wore glamours. Any human would be dumbfounded to gaze upon them in their true forms. Though I can only describe him as beautiful, it didn't detract at all from Reaver's masculinity. His once-pale skin appeared deeper now, more bronze with a strange, golden luminescence, as if he held sunlight within him. Eyes, larger than they'd been, slanted in an alluring almond shape, and his ice blue irises ran with veins of the same golden light reflected in his skin. Still tall, still lithe, his limbs seemed even more willowy and graceful, but at the same time, his frame was powerful. Strong. And I knew that if he wanted to, Reaver could have broken me without even batting a lash. With the trees, water, and false sky as a backdrop, he looked like an ancient forest god. And, for all I knew, he was.

You'll be nothing more than a murderer. But then again, perhaps I should expect nothing less than death from an assassin, and now a common thief.

Somebody was high-and-mighty. I took a step to the side, and then another, putting the rectangular pool between us. He mirrored my actions, taking his place at the opposite side of the water and followed me with matching steps.

Time belongs to no one, least of all me. Yet, I beg you to rethink your actions. I am the Keeper, entrusted for a reason.

"You're not going to talk me out of this." Forget the hip boots. I'd been caught in a shit storm of hurricane proportions. Caught in the act and not even denying my role as thief, I was as good as busted. If Reaver decided to turn me in to the PNT Council, I was bent-over-a-barrel-fucked. "I need this thing," I said, weighing the hourglass in my hand. "I wouldn't take it if I didn't think I had no other choice. I'm not a thief—usually. And as for being a murderer . . ." I was.

You have the potential to do good things for those you love. But you will only cause them to suffer.

He continued to walk, mirroring my movement until we'd reached the end of the pool and the foot of the marble staircase. I can't say I particularly cared for his threats, not with Tyler already suffering at the hands of malicious magic. "Are you threatening me?"

I'm providing you with the facts. Reaver's ice blue eyes bore into mine. *You're walking a dangerous path, one that only leads toward destruction. Find your answers elsewhere, Guardian, and leave the glass with me.*

Wasn't gonna happen. His big talk was nothing more than an attempt to get me to return his trinket. This broken thing was my ticket to Raif's daughter. She was the first piece of the puzzle. Through her, I'd be able to link to recent events. And, maybe, solve the mystery of Tyler's illness and strange behavior. Reaver would get his glass back over my dead body. I stumbled as Reaver's words sank in. "Why did you call me a Guardian?" And did he know that my raven-haired antagonist had called me the same thing?

He cocked a brow, and his knowing smile did little to comfort me. False sunlight glittered through the leaves of a birch tree, and I joined its company, fleeing Reaver's presence for the main floor of the house. When I hit the top of the stairs, I slammed back into my corporeal form with all the force of a Mack truck hitting a wall. Katana

at the ready, I looked around for whatever had kept me
from traveling unseen. Near the foyer, my gaze found
Moira.

Reaver's sister blocked my path, her lips moving un-
intelligibly. I don't know how, but she kept me confined
to my solid form. Levi said Sidhe possessed some serious
magic, and apparently Moira was a heavy hitter. Her
eyes narrowed as she took me in from head to toe, and
from behind her back she produced two wicked-looking
short swords, the blades forged into a waving pattern
ridged with gleaming barbs. Superhuman healing or not,
if she managed to cut me with one of those, it was going
to hurt like a sonofabitch.

"Is it true you can talk to the dead?" Well, Levi said she
could, and when would I get another chance to ask her?

Showcasing none of the elegance she'd displayed at
the PNT summit, Moira was dressed for a fight. Her long,
fawn-colored hair had been pulled back, and her outfit
would've had a marine weeping with respect. All the
navy blue ensemble needed was a splash of camo and
she'd be ready for a black-ops mission. A corner of her
mouth lifted in a smirk as she gave me a head-to-toe appraisal. "Would you like to speak with someone? It's not
necessary. Continue on, and you'll be joining the dead
shortly."

Well, crap. This was *not* going to be the cakewalk I
hoped it would be. Fighting one handed would be a
bitch. I couldn't set the glass down, and my balance
would be shit. I'd just have to wing it. "I'm not so easy to
kill," I said.

"Easier than you think." Moira's tone would have
dropped a less stalwart warrior. She crouched in a battle
stance, rocking her weight from foot to foot, and twirled
the crooked swords in her hands. She didn't wait for me
to charge but ran with inhuman speed across the foyer
and into the great room, where I stood like an idiot, awed
by the graceful ferocity of her attack. Too bad I had to
fight against her instead of alongside her.

Moira definitely had the advantage. She swung her arms with practiced precision, leaving me no choice but to parry her attacks. The force and speed of her movements sent me to the floor, and I hugged the hourglass close to my body, using the katana as a shield as she continued to attack. She lunged at me, aiming her blades for my midsection, and I landed a solid kick to her right hip, sending her stumbling back against the wall. While she collected herself, I launched my body from the floor and attacked, slicing my blade across her arm before she could defend herself.

A shriek that should have broken glass erupted from Moira's throat, and the smug look she'd worn earlier transformed into one of mindless rage. Someone was a sore loser. Maybe that was why Reaver didn't keep board games in the house. The break in her attack had given me the advantage, though, and positioned me close to the door. I took off running as if ghoulish fiends were chasing me, but that bitch was faster than any undead creature I'd ever seen in the movies. All I knew was one second she leaned against the wall favoring her injured arm, and the next she had me by the hair, dragging me through the open door and back into the house. I used her movement for momentum, slamming her back against a wall, but froze when I felt the cold barbs of her blade resting just below my jaw.

"No!" Reaver shouted from the top of the stairs. "Moira, you can't!"

Her labored breath caressed my cheek, and her grip on me tightened, the steel biting farther into my skin. I felt the trickle of blood and the fusing of my skin as it healed. Reaver approached us slowly, his arms held out imploringly before him as he calmed his sister with soothing tones.

"Moira, let her go."

What. The. Hell? My eyes widened in disbelief as I took in the worried expression on Reaver's face. How could he possibly be concerned for the person who stole from him? If I'd found someone in my apartment stealing my stuff, the fucker would have been toast. Believe it.

"She's not worthy," Moira said, her voice shaking with rage. "Let me kill her or we'll all suffer for her stupidity."

Not the first time I'd been called stupid in the last few days. I drove my elbow into Moira's stomach, eliciting a grunt of pain. She tightened her grip, grabbing my hair so hard, I felt strands pulling loose from my scalp. "I want her blood!"

"Get in line," I seethed. "Let me go and I won't separate your head from your shoulders."

"A bold statement, indeed," Moira laughed, "considering it's *my* sword about to draw *your* blood."

Reaver might be able to make some ground with his sister. At least, I hoped so, because if he didn't, I was pretty sure Moira was going to chop me into bite-sized pieces. But before he got his chance, the front door blew off its hinges, and shit really hit the fan.

The force of the impact nearly knocked Moira off her feet, and me along with her. Splinters of wood and shards of glass littered Reaver's pristine floors—probably the biggest mess the place had ever seen. Tyler strode through the gaping hole he'd left in the front of Reaver's house, his hazel eyes glazed over with rage and his expression no less murderous.

"Let her go," he said, power emanating from every syllable. "Now."

Moira shrank against the wall, her grip on my hair becoming loose and the dagger no longer touching, but still hovering near my skin. "You shouldn't have come here, Jinn." Moira's tone became sharp as a razor's edge. "This doesn't concern you."

"She's mine," he growled. "Making this one hundred percent *my* concern."

How . . . in . . . the . . . hell did he know where to find me? Then again, I'd always suspected our bond gave him an internal Darian tracking system. God, he was more breathtaking than any avenging angel, standing in the midst of the chaos he'd created, armed with nothing more than his good looks. It might not have been the best timing, but it sent my heart to hammering in my chest, and all I wanted to do was strip him bare and taste every inch of his flesh.

Reaver seemed to share my opinion. His eyes roamed freely enough over Tyler's body, his interest no longer on his sister or me. He took a step forward and then another. But Tyler raised his palm as if to stay Reaver's progress across the floor. Another surge of power wafted from the spot where Tyler stood, and Reaver stopped dead in his tracks, unable to take another step forward.

Your lover has skills. Jesus, even his thoughts projected in my mind carried a sensual appreciation for Tyler. *But if you want him to come out of this in one piece, I'd get him as far away from my sister as possible.*

Agreed. If this was going to boil down to a pissing match between that Sidhe witch and Tyler, I had a feeling I'd be less than happy with the outcome. Reaver gave an almost imperceptible nod of his head, no doubt agreeing with my assumption. Too bad Moira wasn't so agreeable.

She tightened her hold on my hair, forcing my head to tilt back. With deadly purpose, she positioned the blade below my left ear, clearly ready to slice me from ear to ear. My eyes met Tyler's, and through my fear, my guilt, the bitter taste of my deceit, I sensed his anger, his raw power, his determination to keep me safe. God. I *so* did not deserve him. *I love you,* I mouthed, knowing damned well Moira's blade would take my head right off my shoulders in a matter of seconds.

"I'm not going to tell you again," Tyler said to my captor. "Let her go."

The teeth of Moira's wicked blade bit into my flesh, and I closed my eyes, unwilling to see my death reflected in Tyler's face. But before she could send me to my end, Tyler lashed out with a blast of energy so powerful, it sent us both sailing across the room. I waited for the impact, for the jarring of every bone as I hit the floor. I should have known what would happen next: Tyler caught me before I could land.

He held me close, one arm wrapped around my torso, his grip fierce. "Damn it, Darian." His voice broke as he spoke close to my ear. "Why can't you *ever* ask for help?"

Moira pushed herself up from the floor, a gash in her head spilling blood down her temple. She stumbled as she tried to stand, her knees giving out and sending her back to the floor. "She'll destroy everything we know," she said from between clenched teeth.

"Trust in Fate, Sister," Reaver said, still glued to his spot on the floor. His wolfish gaze was locked on mine as Tyler hauled me toward the gaping hole that had once been Reaver's front door. "Have faith."

Moira glared at her brother before turning the full force of her hatred on me—or not. Tyler gripped his head, hissing in pain as he dragged us both onto the front porch. That bitch had aimed her Sidhe magic at Tyler, not me. I felt his anguish as he held me, the confusion swirling in his mind and the pain assaulting his body all at once. I'd never had such a strong connection to him before; our bond seemed to fuse us together in the moment. It had to have been Moira all along. She'd been the cause of Tyler's weird mood swings and illness. She'd been at The Pit. I *knew* she'd killed that Lyhtan and tried to kill me. The pieces fit too perfectly together. "Tyler," I said as he pulled me toward the street. "Ty, wait. I've got to go back. It's her!"

My genie wasn't having it. He held me fast as he murmured a few unintelligible words next to my ear. "No!" I screamed, fighting against him. "Goddamn it, Ty! She's hurting you! She's hurting you!"

"Stop," Tyler said, pulling me farther back. "Leave it, Darian. I've got to get you out of here." His power snaked around me, that same invisible shield that had kept me nice and cozy in the alley behind The Pit. Damn him and his gallantry. He'd die to protect me, and there wasn't a fucking thing I could do to stop him.

As he dragged me away, Moira appeared from out of

the rubble, but before she could come after us, her brother grabbed her by the shoulders and pulled her back. I sent out a thought I knew Reaver would hear. *When I see her again, and I will . . . she's going to die for hurting what belongs to me.*

Chapter 18

I locked the hourglass in my safe and slid to the floor. The cold of the hardwood seeped into my pants, drawing my attention from the warmth of the pendulum. Reaver's words haunted me: *"You have the potential to do good things for those you love. But you will only cause them to suffer."*

Hot tears streaked down my face, and a deep, rich pain bloomed from my sternum, spreading through me. Reaver was right. By staying my course and helping Raif, I had only brought pain to someone I loved. Without a thought to his welfare, I'd put Ty in danger. Assassination attempts, threats from Fallon, and Moira's magical assault. I would *never* be out of harm's way. Never. And because he was my genie, that harm extended to Ty. After I found Brakae, I had the mysterious Man from The Ring to deal with. And after that, the emerald and the raven-haired women. Not to mention, I'd be watching my back for Moira to lop my head off unless I got to her first. She didn't strike me as the kind of girl who let go of a grudge.

Tyler's eyes hadn't left me since we'd arrived at my apartment. I wiped my sleeve across my face to dry the tears that ran in rivulets down my cheeks. "So, do you want to continue going off on your own like a stubborn fool?" His soft voice sliced through me like a blade. "Or are you finally ready to let someone in?"

"She already has."

As Raif stepped out of the elevator into my apartment, a wave of power burst from Tyler, and the temperature seemed to drop by about thirty degrees. I expected him to be pissed, but the deep-freeze routine was unexpected. Pushing myself up off the floor, I got my shit together quick, fast, and in a hurry. From the look of him, Ty was gearing up for a fight. And if our earlier episode at Reaver's was any indication, this was going to get messy.

"I told you to stay the fuck away from her." Tyler's voice brought with it the promise of death. "What part of that didn't you understand?"

"I'm going to take into consideration that you're not yourself, Jinn. Because otherwise, I'd consider your behavior nothing but a lot of jackassed posturing. I'm the least of your concerns. And you know damned well I have no romantic notions about Darian."

"Bullshit." Tyler crossed the space between them in the snap of a finger. "You're on her like a goddamned shadow lately." His voice continued to escalate, the words reverberating with menace, like the echo of thunder. "And if you think you're going to take her from me—"

"Tyler!" I couldn't take it anymore. Moira had worked him over and good. The mindfuck was obvious: He'd never in a million years pull this shit on Raif. I should have killed the bitch when I had the chance, but instead I'd let Ty get me clear of Reaver's house. What really stuck in my craw, though, was that I had no idea why she'd targeted him, not to mention how she could get to him, no matter the distance between them.

Ty stood nose to nose with Raif, trembling with suppressed rage. His nostrils flared with his heavy breath, his chest rising and falling in a quick, steady rhythm. He was magnificent in his anger. Dangerous. Ferocious. Beautiful. Too bad the target of his rage was my best friend.

"Calm yourself," Raif said in a soft, even tone. "Think, Tyler. Consider where you've just been. What you've seen. You'd know there's something wrong with your instincts if you'd settle down long enough to examine how you feel."

"He's right, Ty." Probably not the best idea to take

Raif's side. But my only other option was to let Tyler rip him to shreds. I stepped between them, pushing Raif behind me. "Look at me, Ty. You can see the truth right here. Just. Look. At. Me."

He always had a way of making the world melt away. And as his gaze locked with mine, there was nothing but him, me, and this moment. By small degrees, the spark of rage left his hazel eyes, and his expression softened. The bones in his jaw creaked as he unclenched his teeth, and as I brought my arms to his wide, strong shoulders, they relaxed as well, no longer tensed and ready for a fight.

"I have to leave," he whispered, his body trembling from the immense self-control he exerted. "I'll kill him if I don't."

The last thing I wanted was for Tyler to leave, but I knew he couldn't stay here. "Go." I began to shake from my own suppressed emotion. "Be safe."

He pulled me into his arms and kissed me, a slow, deep, urgent demand that I answered and then some. When he pulled away, I was breathless, on the verge of tears, aching to the point where I wanted to scream in hopes of releasing the pressure. "I love you." He kissed me again, a kiss good-bye, and turned on his heel. "Darian." His voice became strained again. Not a good sign. "I need for you to wish me out of here. I—I can't leave you here with him. My brain is screaming for me to stay. All I sense is danger, as if I leave I'll lose you—forever. Get me the hell out of here before I do something I'll regret."

Where? I wondered. Who could help Tyler? Keep *him* safe? I stepped behind him, wrapped my arms around his waist, and laid my cheek against his back. "I love you," I murmured. "Tyler, I wish you were at The Pit with Levi for the rest of the night."

"I'll see you soon," Tyler said.

I closed my eyes and filled my lungs with his scent. A wave of energy pulsed around me, and I stumbled forward, my once-full arms slack and holding on to nothing but air. My eyes met Raif's, his cold determination echoing mine. "I'm going to kill her, Raif."

"Tread lightly, Darian." I envied Raif's unflappable attitude. "First things first. Tell me everything."

This was going to be a long night.

The next morning, I walked through Ty's door to the delicious aroma of pancakes and bacon. Tyler stood at the stove, a wan smile on his face. My heart lurched in my chest, tearing a little at the sight of him.

"How was your night?" Tyler did nothing to mask his accusatory tone as he flipped a huckleberry pancake onto a stack and handed me a plate.

I shrugged. "How was yours?"

"Not bad." His hazel gaze locked with mine, as if he were trying to see into my soul. "It actually took the edge off, hanging with Levi. Worked better than I expected. Don't think that just because I feel better, you're off the hook, though. As soon as I've got your stomach full and your guard down, you're going to tell me everything that's been going on, starting with why you agreed to turn thief for this Fallon."

He grabbed a plate for himself and joined me at the bar, scooting his stool close enough to mine that our bodies touched. I tried to stop my hand from shaking as I raised my fork to my mouth. Eating was the last thing on my mind. I wanted to throw up. "Was Levi able to help you find a way to resist Moira's influence?" Maybe if I kept him distracted long enough, he wouldn't press me about what had happened the night before.

"Hmm." Tyler shoved a forkful of pancake into his mouth and chewed thoughtfully. "Honestly, Darian, I don't think it's her doing it. I can't explain it, but I feel like someone wants me to believe it's her. I'll know more later. But until I can look into it and talk to my contact, I don't want to jump to any conclusions. I'm checking Fallon out, too. I don't think that's even his real name. I can't find anything about him—not even from the Northeast Division's personnel records. Someone should have picked up on this. And I suppose it goes without saying that you need to stay the hell away from him. I don't care what sort of deal he's trying to make with you. I'm going to handle this situation with Delilah and Raif's daughter from here on out."

Apparently Tyler wasn't messing around anymore either. Last night had been the last straw for both of us. "Ty, I know you're worried, but this situation isn't yours to handle. I can take care of this on my own. I'm not dragging you into it."

Tyler threw his fork down on his plate. I flinched as he turned in his seat to face me and shouted, "Why do you insist on taking on the world by yourself?"

"Because that's all I know, Tyler!" I hadn't meant to shout back, but I couldn't contain my emotions any longer. "Don't you think if I could change that about myself, I would? I've had no one to rely on for almost a goddamned century, and so I've had no choice but to rely on myself!"

His expression softened, and he raked his fingers through the tousled curls of his hair as he took a couple of calming breaths. I know he wanted to understand, but how could he? Even from his first moment of existence, someone had sought him out and taken care of him. I'd been passed off to a governess as a child and then later to a husband, who despised me. Azriel had taken me under his wing, only to train me to shun all personal contact. And after he disappeared . . . ? I'd done just what he'd taught me to do. I'd kept my nose to the ground. The people who paid my salary, and those whose lives I'd been paid to end, were the only contact I had with other living souls. I didn't have the first clue how to relate to anyone on a personal level. God, I was so broken, it made me sick.

"Darian," Ty said, his voice no longer angry but full of compassion, "you have to learn to let go and open up. You're not alone anymore. You have to trust the people who care about you and allow us to *help* you."

From the corner of my eye, I took in every minute detail of Tyler's face as I pretended to pay attention to my breakfast. He looked haggard. Too tired and worn too thin. His coppery hair had lost some of its luster, the curls seeming drab. Under his mysterious hazel eyes, dark circles had begun to form, and the hollows beneath his cheeks appeared deeper. He was still the most amazing man I'd ever seen, despite his exhausted state. And I loved him so much, it hurt. I choked on the emotional overload, and I felt as though I couldn't swallow or take a deep breath. Tears threatened, but I refused to let them come. He wanted me to trust him. He urged me to let him in and allow him to help. But how could I when doing that might put his life in danger? I could work on my many issues for him, but not now. I had to remain hard. I had to stay my course. I'd shed my tears already. I couldn't allow myself the weakness when there was still so much for me to do.

Tyler doubled over the bar, cradling his head in his hands. A moan of agony escaped his lips as he got down from his stool, lowering his head between his knees and taking measured breaths.

"It's her again, isn't it? What's she doing?" Every ounce of frustration and anger I felt over my own shortcomings dissolved into concern. I didn't care what Tyler thought. Moira *had* to be responsible for this. My heart sped to a frantic rhythm as the panic set in.

"Nothing," Ty panted through his pain. "Just a headache."

"Bullshit, Tyler." Visions of my blade piercing Moira's heart grounded my swirling emotions. "How can I help you? Tell me what to do."

I hovered above him, worrying like a mother hen. I was helpless. So fucking helpless! I could wield a sword, cut down my enemies, slit a throat, and deliver a mean right hook. But I could do absolutely nothing to assuage Ty's pain. How could I fight an enemy who didn't have to be present to launch an attack?

Tense, silence-filled moments passed, and Tyler stood. His weak smile was meant to be reassuring, but it did nothing other than fill me with a sense of dread. "I'm fine," he said, caressing my arm as if it had been my pain, not his.

I could tell it took all the effort he could expend to appear fine. He wanted me to think whatever magic assaulted him caused nothing more than mild discomfort. But I knew better. Leaning against the bar, I fixed him with a suspicious gaze. He knew damned well I was wise to his ploy, but he pulled me into his arms and murmured, "Damn it, Darian, your stubbornness aggravates the hell out of me. If I could, I'd go back and punish every single person who ever hurt you. I can't imagine what you must have gone through, all of those years, utterly alone. But you're not alone anymore. You have me. And I love you."

He cradled my face in his hands and slowly combed his fingers through my hair. A sigh escaped his lips, and he bent his nose to my temple, inhaling deeply. "You smell so good," he murmured. "I've always thought so. Like a field of wildflowers after the rain. That first night we met—at The Pit—I couldn't tear my eyes off you. I'd never seen anything so fiercely beautiful in all my life. I wanted to make love to you right there on that bar."

I bit my lip to keep it from trembling. Laughter rumbled in Tyler's chest. "You were such a snarky pain in the ass. Still are. And I could tell from the start you'd be nothing but trouble. But I didn't care, as long as you were mine. Forever."

His words were like razor blades scoring my skin. I couldn't endure the torture of his loving affirmations much longer. If he knew what I planned to do . . . I steeled myself against the emotion that threatened to eat me alive and leaned into him.

"There's nothing I wouldn't do for you." Tyler's lips touched the top of my head and then my brow. "No torture I wouldn't endure." His finger beneath my chin, he raised my face to meet his. "I love you." A light kiss to my cheek preceded the gentle searching of his mouth when it met mine. I let my eyes drift shut as I reveled in the sweet taste of him. His tongue moved with gentle precision, caressing, teasing, entreating. Our lips met again and again in a slow dance, featherlight and full of promise. I wanted to freeze this moment in time, hold on to the sensation of his kisses lingering on my mouth, keep the memory of the taste of him fresh in my mind. I tried to remember every detail of his kisses, etching them into my brain.

My breath caught as Ty's hands maneuvered under my shirt, his fingers kneading and working my flesh as he shimmied my shirt up over my head. He bent down, pressing his lips to my temple, down the side of my face, my jaw, and lower still. His tongue flicked out, unusually hot against my flesh before he nuzzled my neck and continued his descent across one shoulder, and then to the other, branding my skin with every pass of his mouth. With the backs of his fingers, he traced my collarbone and worked his way between my breasts. My head fell back as I pressed myself hard against him, forgetting our previous argument and the pain of my decisions—for a while. A moan worked up from my throat as he unhooked my bra and cupped my breast in his hand, teasing my nipple with his thumb before pinching lightly.

He took the other nipple in his mouth, grazing with his teeth. A thrilling pulse of excitement shot through me, and my jaw dropped, moaning again. "That's right," Tyler murmured, his hand leaving my breast to unfasten my pants. "I want to hear you. I want to make you scream."

His hand slid inside my underwear and found me wet and ready, and he sucked his breath in through his teeth. I shuddered as he brought me close to orgasm, his fingers rubbing in slow circles and flicking with agonizing slow precision over my core. "Darian," he growled, "I don't think I'll make it to the bedroom."

I guided him toward the low countertop next to the breakfast bar and lifted myself up until I perched on the edge. "Make love to me, Tyler, like you wanted to that first night."

I kicked my pants off, and my underwear with them. He stripped his clothes off his body as if they were on fire, and he pressed against me. Cupping the back of my neck in his hand, Tyler kissed me deep, his tongue thrusting into my mouth with a need that I understood all too well. He was hard and ready, the marble-smooth flesh grazing my thigh as he rubbed against me in a rhythm that promised pleasure to follow. I reached down between us, reveling in the feel of his skin, stroking him, and his breath hitched. "Darian," he murmured on an exhale of breath, "I want you . . . right . . . now."

If he said anything after that, I couldn't hear him over my screams.

As Tyler slept beside me, I watched the even rise and fall of his chest. I should have felt guilty for the hours we'd spent pleasuring each other, but I didn't. Those last moments would have to sustain me. When he woke, I tried to imagine that he'd be fine. Healthy. Back to normal.

And I'd be gone.

Looking down, I twisted the silver ring on my thumb, Tyler's gift carved with his symbol of the bear, representing his fierce and loyal protection. I smoothed his hair back with my hand and laid my lips to his forehead. I loved him—more than I thought I could ever love anyone or anything.

My stomach twisted into knots, and my limbs ached with anxiety-infused adrenaline. If Raif didn't have my back, I'd never be able to follow through on my plan. I refused to break our bond. It would be like refusing his love, and that meant more to me than any protection he could offer. But I had to protect him this time, and dragging him along on a quest that had nothing to do with him wasn't fair. I had to finish this and finish it now, or I'd risk losing him forever.

Tyler's brow furrowed in sleep and then relaxed. Was it my imagination that he looked a little better? I crossed the bedroom and found a pad of paper in Tyler's desk. He was probably sick to death of waking to find a note beside him, but I vowed this was the last time he'd have to read one.

*It's time for me to protect you. Please don't be angry
with me. Try to understand. I can't sit by and watch
you put yourself in harm's way. There are too many
mysteries to solve, and all of them could end up with
you dead. I couldn't live with that. Not when I can
do something to stop it. I won't be gone long. Wait
for me.*

"I'm sorry," I said under my breath as I laid the note
on the pillow. "But it's the only way I can keep you safe.
I love you, Tyler." I took a deep breath and quelled the
sob rising in my throat. "I wish for you to stay in the city
until I come home. I wish for you to let me go without
coming to find me." Silent tears streamed down my
cheeks. Tyler stirred, a tremor moving along his beautiful
body before his eyes opened. For a single moment we
stared at each other, the pain of my words etched into
every line of his face. Twilight, as gray and sad as my
ragged emotions, swallowed my physical body whole,
and I fled like a coward under the cover of near dark.

I'd never hated the cold detachment of my own apartment as much as I did when I pulled the broken hourglass from my safe. I held it in my trembling hands,
fighting the urge to smash the thing against the bricks of
my wall. I needed a fucking shower and a stiff drink—
and to sleep for about a year and a half. But I wasn't
going to get any of those things—not for a while.

After I found Brakae, I'd come crawling back to Tyler
if he wanted. My stomach turned at the betrayal. That I'd
left in the night like the thief I now was would probably
piss him off to no end. But I'd spend forever making it
up to him, if he'd let me.

I paced the apartment for five minutes and forty-
seven seconds—God I hated the sound of time!—before
I dialed Fallon's number.

"Do you have it?" he asked in an excited tone.

"I do."

"Bring it to me."

"No." Fallon was as dumb as a sack of rocks if he thought I'd just hand the hourglass over without getting what I wanted in return. "I want the Oracle first. You give me Delilah—speaking and in her right mind—and you'll get this piece-of-shit hourglass. No negotiation."

Silence answered, and I pictured Fallon sitting on one of those god-awful beds at Seven, slowly strangling the nearest human waitress in frustration. I hoped he was—frustrated, that is, not strangling anyone. Though I wouldn't put it past the creepy fucker to be into that shit. "Of course." His smooth reply reeked of barely controlled rage. "I wouldn't dream of not fulfilling my end of our bargain."

"I'm sure you wouldn't dream of it." My voice carried a sarcastic edge I hoped he noticed. Bastard. "Can we do this in an hour?"

"It might raise suspicion," he said. "I'm scheduled to take the midnight shift. Just don't come stomping right up to the gate. I don't need your face plastered all over security camera footage. Come cloaked by darkness, and I'll let you in when I make my rounds. Don't try to scale the walls; they're protected by wards. The front gate is the only way in—or out. I'll meet you at the entrance at one. Agreed?"

As if I had a choice. "One a.m. at the front entrance. I won't be seen."

"And you'll bring the glass . . ."

"Yes." Can you say broken record? "I'll bring the glass."

"I'll see you then."

I ended the call without saying good-bye. Once Fallon played his part, I'd try to find a way to notify someone that he had Reaver's hourglass. A double cross, and dishonorable, but whoever said there was honor amongst thieves?

Chapter 19

My equilibrium was off as I traveled to the PNT headquarters. Up was down, north became south, and the emerald pendulum glowed so hot, I thought it would scorch a hole right through my pants. I don't know why I didn't leave the damned thing at home, but for some reason, I felt I simply couldn't part with it. The pendulum seemed to have a knack for knowing when and when not to make its presence known. And right now, it wanted me to stand up and take notice. After being mostly dormant, the gem had come to life over the past few days, growing hotter and hotter in my pocket, where I'd stowed it away. I had a feeling it was trying to deliver a message, but whatever that message was would just have to wait.

I focused my senses, tried to ignore the flow of time, and sent out invisible feelers for my genie. Even though I knew Ty would be safe while I searched for Brakae, I needed to feel some kind of connection to him, the reassurance of his presence. I'd felt something arc between us when Moira had attacked Tyler with whatever magic she wielded against him. Maybe I could feel our bond again. Tyler claimed he could sense our connection. He'd found me at Reaver's house. He could find me almost anywhere. I'd taken care of that, though. I'd wished him confined to the city, forbidding him to come after me. And the fact that I'd once again brushed his help to the side, not allowing him to be strong enough for both of us, left me feeling empty and lonely—incomplete.

I'd arrived thirty minutes early, too damned antsy for

patience of any kind. I'm sure there were toddlers out there with better waiting skills than mine. My phone vibrated in my pocket, and I checked the caller ID: *Ty. Well, what did you expect? Did you really think he'd just shrug his shoulders and say, "Well, okay then. If you say so."* I stared at the phone, holding my breath until it quit ringing. A few seconds later it started up again, buzzing incessantly, and I pictured Ty's furious expression when the buzzing stopped and my voice mail undoubtedly answered.

Fallon approached the gate at two minutes past one, his swagger evidence of his satisfaction at the turn of events. He walked to the gate, careful to avoid the security cameras, and pressed his face against the metal bars. The wild glint in his hard gray eyes sent a shiver from my head to my toes as he looked to where I stood, as if he could see me in my shadow form. "Do you have what I want?" his cold voice pierced the night.

"Do *you* have what *I* want?" I asked in return. I wanted Fallon to go down so bad, I could taste it. I hated opportunists.

"You know I do," he answered, running his forefinger down the center of the gate. A golden light glowed from his fingertip, and the gate swung open wide enough to permit my shadow form to slide through. "Careful." He looked to the guard station behind him. "If you touch the gate, the wards will react. I'd hate to see you caught when you're so close to getting what you want."

Yeah, right. Like Fallon gave two shits about what I wanted. He'd seen an opportunity to steal something *he* wanted without getting his hands dirty, and the bastard had taken it. Remaining cloaked by night, I slid through the opening in the gate. With another touch of his finger, he sealed up the entrance, effectively sealing *me* in.

Fallon led the way back toward the complex. His black military-style garb seemed fitting for his role as PNT security high roller, but another thing I planned on doing once I had Delilah's information was make sure he no longer carried his position here. My phone vibrated in my pocket and I tried to ignore it, though every pulse came with a mental image of Tyler's furious face. *Brakae.* I kept my eye on the prize: Find Raif's daughter and end the grief that had followed him for centuries and spurred a blood feud that had almost destroyed an entire kingdom — not to mention me.

We entered the building, and Fallon secured the door behind us. He looked at the empty reception desk, his hands balling into fists at his sides. "Can you believe they allow a human to work here?" He ran his hands through his hair. "It makes me sick."

"What the hell do you care about who works here?" This guy had some serious antihuman hang-ups.

"Humans are like insects," he spat as we made our way to the elevator. "Or worse, rodents. They multiply like rabbits — or rats," he laughed. "Humans are filthy rats. A pestilence contaminating the world with their presence."

"Give me a break." I hated him more by the second. "They're not much different from you, or from me, for that matter. Live and let live."

We stepped in the elevator, and Fallon took a step toward me, close enough to my shrouded form that he could have almost touched me. "You're not anything like *them*," he said, inhaling the air where I stood. "You are something else entirely. Special."

His words frightened me. The desire in his tone, laced with violent need, touched every part of me in a way that made me feel violated. There was nothing sexual about it. What I'd felt from his voice ran deeper than physical desire. I suddenly regretted wishing into uselessness the only person in this world who could offer me protection.

"Humans are bred from the mundane," Fallon continued to complain as the elevator took us into the bowels of the building. "Before the humans poisoned the earth with their vile presence, the Fae and creatures like them ruled. We walked in freedom without fear of revealing our true natures. It sickens me how low we've sunk. Hiding, pretending to be nothing more interesting than a leaf dangling from a branch." He leaned in toward me again, tracing the air around me with his hands. "But if you look closely at the leaf, you will see its intricacies. The various patterns and weavings in its construction. You will see the extraordinary. The magic living within each cell. We are passed over as common things when we should rightfully hold dominion over this world."

Wow, evil dictator, anyone? I didn't respond to his tirade. Honestly, I doubted he'd care one way or the other how I felt on the issue of supremacy. Xander believed that Shaedes and Fae, Jinn and Sylphs, even Lyhtans and the rest of the supernatural world, were just as much a part of the natural order as humans, animals, grass, and even insects. He believed that nothing was infallible or immune to the laws of nature. It didn't mean that he didn't recognize the supernatural community's need for discretion, though. Humans weren't superior to the supernatural, but the one thing humans were not good at was stepping out of their comfort zones. And discovering the neighbor could become a gust of wind whenever she might choose, well, that just wouldn't fly with most of them. Best to leave Sylphs, Fae, and the like in legends, where they belonged.

The elevator door slid open, and I stepped out into the darkened corridor leading to Delilah's cell. "You'll soon see, Darian," Fallon said. "And you will be amazed."

For shit's sake, this guy got creepier by the second. If simply turning him in wasn't good enough, I might have been tempted to run him through with my katana if the occasion arose. All I wanted was to get the information locked in Delilah's crazy head and get the hell out of here. I tried not to dwell on the fact that I was trapped inside the walls of the PNT facility until Fallon let me out. I fought for control of my nerves as his presence frayed them to shreds. The emerald pulsed in one pocket, my phone buzzed in the other, each reminding me of unfinished business. But I pushed those things to the back of my mind and followed the path of fear to Delilah's cell.

Fallon entered the security code into the electronic pad, and the door slid open in a flash. Delilah sat exactly where I'd left her days before, huddled in a ball, pathetic and useless. "You see?" Fallon said, nudging her with his booted foot. "I kept her safe and sound for you."

I drifted from my shadow form and raised a quizzical brow. What the fuck was his definition of "safe and sound"? From the looks of her, Delilah was neither. "Let's get this show on the road." I squatted down to Delilah's level. "I've got places to go and people to see."

"The hourglass?" Fallon asked with an icy tone.

"Will be yours once you hold up your end of our bargain."

"How do I even know you have it?" he asked. "I could free the Oracle's mind only to be rewarded with a piece of trash."

I rolled my eyes. Apparently Fallon had been double-crossed before. Maybe then he wouldn't be too surprised when I turned him in to Reaver. I slung a small backpack from my shoulders and dug through the largest pocket, retrieving the hourglass carefully protected in a towel. I took care in unwinding the relic from its wrappings and held it aloft for Fallon's inspection. The sparkling grains of golden sand floated upward into nothing before pouring back into the bottom of the glass. His gray eyes flashed with quicksilver when he saw it, his hands reaching out to take it.

"Whoa, boy," I said, covering the hourglass and stowing it in my bag. "Not until you give me Delilah."

A calculating smile lit up his face. "Can't have one without the other." He knelt beside me at Delilah's feet. "What do you say, my dear?" he whispered near her face. "Are you ready to come out and play?"

Like some kind of freaky Stepford wife, Delilah stood. Her empty milky blue gaze stared straight ahead, though her head cocked from one side to the other. She inhaled the air around her and trembled. Tears pooled in her eyes but didn't spill over her lids. Her bottom lip quivered, jutting out like a frightened child. I stood by and watched, waiting anxiously for Fallon to pay me for services rendered and lift the spells confining Delilah to silence.

Fallon turned to look at me, the same hungry gleam in his eyes. He lifted his hand to Delilah's forehead, the moment mounting to the suspenseful climax Fallon wanted it to be. And just when I thought my goals were within my reach, the shrieking blare of alarms told me I was wrong to have ever trusted Fallon to hold up his part of our bargain. "What the hell is this?" I drew my dagger and leveled it, hovering just over his heart.

Fallon swept the blade away as if shooing a fly. "Don't be an idiot," he said through clenched teeth. "We've got to get out of here. Now. Or we're both as good as dead."

"I'm not leaving without Delilah," I said, wrapping my free hand around her scrawny arm.

"You expect me to get all three of us out of here unscathed?" Fallon's eyes bulged.

"You damned well bet I do." I ushered him toward the door with the point of my dagger. "You're as guilty as I am, buddy. And Delilah comes with me."

Great, Darian. You've gone from trained assassin and royal guard to petty thief and kidnapper. Way to raise your standards. But my mission to find Brakae had become an obsession. No fucking way was I walking away now. I towed Delilah out behind me while I prodded Fallon in front of me. "Don't forget," I said, harsh, angry, the voice of a blossoming criminal, "I have the hourglass. If you want it, you'd better get us out of here."

The alarms continued to howl, following us down the corridor toward the elevators. Delilah wasn't easy cargo to haul. Basically a zombie, she moved only because I pulled her into motion. She didn't speak or make a sound. She just shuffled her feet along, her stringy hair swinging around her empty, emotionless face.

"Can't you get her moving faster?" Fallon asked.

"Not unless you want to employ your fancy brain-restoration techniques right fucking now!" I snapped. "Otherwise, shut up and keep moving."

Fallon shook his head and froze ten feet from the elevators. Three sets of doors slid open simultaneously to admit a fully uniformed security detachment—and at their head stood Moira.

The urge to kill her was a tangible thing, burning in my chest and threatening to override the tiny sense of reason I'd been clinging to. She'd hurt Tyler, messed with his mind and his emotions. And that bitch was going to pay.

"Fall back," he said, no longer needing my dagger to encourage him. "There's a set of stairs at the end of the hallway just past Delilah's cell."

I took a step forward instead of retreating, and Fallon grabbed onto my arm, pulling me back. "Now isn't the time. Unless you want to forfeit your life along with the Oracle's secrets, we've got to get out of here. Now."

I stared at Moira good and hard, hoping that she, like her brother, could hear my thoughts. *This isn't over.* "Let's go." I shoved Delilah at Fallon, and he scooped her up in his arms, retreating the way we'd come. I drew my katana from behind my back—quite a feat considering the backpack—and pointed it toward my biggest threat, the Sidhe with an attitude. I backed away slowly, giving Fallon the lead. Delilah had become my number one priority. If she died, the secret of Raif's daughter would die with her. And after everything I'd done, I doubted any of the fifteen Fae standing before me would lend a concerned ear.

"My brother isn't here to save your pathetic hide." Moira brandished her scary barbed swords with glee. "I don't care who or what you are. You're dead."

"Only if you catch me." No one escaped a dangerous situation by playing meek.

"If Reaver could see who you've decided to consort with," she snorted, "I'm sure he wouldn't champion you. He'd help me rip you limb from limb."

I did *not* want to stick around and chat with this psycho bitch. The bloodlust in her white-blue eyes had me yearning for my own revenge. She had the upper hand, however, and if she caught me, she wouldn't just stab; she'd skin me alive and make sure the feat would take days to accomplish. My phone vibrated in my pocket, and I swore under my breath. As if I didn't have enough to worry about right now. I slowly put distance between Moira and me. She sheathed her swords and drew a bow from behind her back. I paused—curious—and watched as she produced a strange arrow from a quiver hanging at her side. My lips curled into a snarl, and I fought the urge to charge full speed and run her through with my katana. I recognized those arrows well. They could incinerate *anything* they managed to strike—including me.

"Get Delilah out of here—now!" I yelled over my shoulder. I turned to run, feeling as though I traveled in slow motion, melting into nothing as I heard the first arrow fly. Moira cried in battle, a shrill and chilling sound that drowned out the sound of the alarms. She barked an order in a strange language, and I didn't look back as I fled down the corridor, fearful of what I might see if I dared to look. I heard the whooshing of air as the arrow sailed past me, burying itself in the floor. The concrete began to sizzle and melt away, leaving a two-foot hole and no sign of the arrow that had caused the damage.

My bones hummed in my body, my skin crawled with the sensation of powerful magic, and I felt my body leave the safety of obscurity as Moira put the kibosh on my hopes of a stealthy escape. Whatever magic she'd aimed at me earlier at her brother's house held me now, chained to my solid form and making me an easy target to take down.

Fallon rounded a corner just past Delilah's cell and paused before disappearing from sight. "Hurry up, damn it!" he called.

"Darian!" a familiar voice called out from behind me. I glanced over my shoulder to see Adare shoulder to shoulder with Moira. Great. Just great. The whole of Xander's kingdom would know about this clusterfuck by sunrise. "It isn't too late to turn yourself in! Think about what you're doing. Stop!"

I rounded the corner just as one arrow buried itself in

the wall, another barely clipping my boot. Moira's enraged scream put a smile on my face as I took the stairs,
two at a time. With no idea where I was going, I ran up
the stairs, taking two flights before a hand grabbed me
hard around the arm, hauling me through a doorway.

"Be still!" Fallon seethed, giving me a shake. "I'll get
you out of here with your head still attached, but you've
got to be quiet."

"How are you going to do that?" I asked. "This place
is swarming with PNT security, including that Sidhe
bitch. Oh, and did I mention she's got some wicked fucking arrows to sling?"

"Moira," Fallon replied with disgust. "Her power is
nothing. Shut your mouth and don't move."

Fallon set Delilah down, and she stood like a man-
nequin as he went to work. Muttering words I couldn't
decipher, he passed his hands over me from toe to head,
ending by combing his fingers through my hair. He repeated the procedure with Delilah who didn't bat a lash,
and then in the same sweeping gesture, passed his hands
over his own body. "There. We'll walk out right under the
bastards' noses."

"Are you off your nut?" I asked before I really looked
at my companions and my jaw dropped. "Holy hell, how
did you do that?"

Delilah and Fallon were no longer recognizable as
themselves. And as I passed my hand over my face and
through my now-short hair, I realized neither was I. If
Fallon scoffed at Moira's power and managed to do this
to me, he was jacked up with more magic than any preternatural creature I'd ever met—except, maybe, for Ty.

"A glamour," he said. "But it won't last long, so I suggest we get the hell out of here."

I marveled at my hands, no longer small and thin, but
rough and corded. A man's hands. I didn't even want to
think about what other attributes Fallon had given me.
Wouldn't Anya be jealous? I probably had the balls she
wished she had! "Where to from here?" I asked. "I don't
want to look like this for any longer than I have to."

Fallon answered with a chuckle. "The Oracle will be our only problem, as she's a bit on the lethargic side. This corridor leads to the elevators. We should be able to hit the main floor and walk right through the gate."

Yeah, well, the best-laid plans and all of that . . . If it ended up being that easy, I'd shit my pants. Frantic voices echoed throughout the complex and finally, thank God, they shut off the alarms. We walked to the elevator without incident, although I have to admit anyone with half a brain would have noticed we looked a little suspicious with the third member of our party dragging "his" feet as he followed us along.

We rode the elevator to the main floor in tense silence. I was scared shitless to step even a toe out of line. But as the doors glided open and we stepped into the lobby, I let out a deep breath. The search had migrated to other areas of the compound, and we were nearly home free. I pushed Delilah in front of me, urging her out the front entry just behind Fallon. One hundred and fifty yards stood between us and safety. One way in, one way out. Right through the front gate.

"Put your sword away," Fallon said. "That's not a standard-issue weapon."

I tucked the blade in its scabbard, though doing so made me feel twice as vulnerable. "Don't speak to anyone," he continued as we walked down the long driveway to the main gate. "I didn't have time to glamour your voice. You'll betray us if you open your mouth."

Again, no one stopped us or questioned our actions. Fallon played his part well, searching bushes as we walked as if sweeping the property for any sign of—well—*us*. My skin tingled as I sensed the approaching dawn, warm and scratchy, made more stifling by the effects of Fallon's glamour. Already we'd been here longer than I'd hoped. I wanted nothing more than to be rid of both Fallon and Delilah. Now they stood at my side, partners in crime.

The guard at the gate stood at attention, sword drawn and wary. "No one is allowed off the property," he said, moving between us and the gate. "Adare's orders."

"We're not leaving the property," Fallon said. "Just checking the perimeter. Also, Adare's orders."

"What's your name?" the guard asked. "I've never seen you before."

I noticed from the corner of my eye Fallon reaching for his dagger, and I stepped in front of him, not willing to risk any lives for what I'd done. I pulled my arm back and swung, striking the guard square on his chin. His head jerked and lolled to the side before he crumpled to the ground.

"I had the situation under control," Fallon said between clenched teeth.

"No, you didn't. I'm not about to kill innocents doing nothing more than their jobs."

Fallon looked at me as if he thought me foolish. Stepping over the fallen guard, he traced his finger down the center of the gate, using his magic to let us out the way he'd let me in a few hours earlier. Why he didn't just reach into the control booth and open it manually was beyond me, but I didn't care as long as he got us the hell out of there with Delilah in one piece. He retrieved the dazed Oracle and stepped through the gate. "Are you coming?"

I looked over my shoulder and back to the gate. What would Tyler think of what I'd done? What would Xander or Raif think? For that matter, what did I think?

Fuck it. What was done was done. I wasn't coming back without Brakae anyway, and with any luck, I'd have the hourglass with me as well. I looked to Fallon and Delilah in their glamoured forms. I'd walked through these gates a woman on a mission, bent on helping a friend and obsessed with discovering the truth.

I walked out a fugitive.

Chapter 20

"What are you so sullen about?" Fallon asked.

I hadn't said a word since we'd escaped from the PNT facility. Dawn approached, and the eastern gray skies were smeared with red. It seemed appropriate, considering the circumstances. An omen of sorts. Blood before the sunrise. I watched the scenery passing us by through the passenger-side window. We'd left Seattle behind, headed down the I-5.

"Where the hell are we going?" I asked, my nerves winding tighter with every mile we drove.

Fallon shrugged. "As far as this tank of gas will take us. I figure we have enough to get to Spokane. I want to put as much distance between us and Moira as possible."

She definitely wanted both of us dead, so I couldn't really blame him for wanting to get the hell out of Dodge. I wondered why she made him so nervous, though. Fallon wasn't exactly helpless; he'd demonstrated he had power and then some. Yet Fallon was spooked. I only wished I knew why. I decided not to press the matter, though; I had nothing more to say to him and didn't feel like drawing the SOB into conversation. I turned in my seat to check on Delilah, who sat in the back of the unassuming VW sedan, just as much a vegetable as she'd been when we'd hauled her out of her cell. I rode shotgun—lucky me—and the man whose throat I wanted to slit wide open drove. Not well, I might add. Jesus, I'd seen newly licensed teens with better driving skills.

I'd spent the better part of three hours berating myself for letting this situation get so out of hand. If only Adare had met me at the door that day. If only I'd asked Tyler for help. If only I'd quit fighting against Xander and tried to convince him to work with me. Instead of letting people in, I'd done what I'd trained myself to do for years: I'd shut everyone out—everyone, that is, but Raif.

"Are you going to answer me?" Fallon said. "Or are you going to pout the rest of the way?"

I pressed my palm to the pocket holding my cell. GPS was a hell of a safety net. Even though I'd fled Seattle with Fallon, Raif could find me. I never—ever—went out on a job without a backup plan. The night Tyler had come to my rescue at Reaver's had been the last straw. I couldn't bear for him to endanger himself for a task that was none of his concern. Raif, on the other hand, was just as much a part of this as I was. His worried expression was fresh in my mind as I thought back to our last encounter before I'd left with Fallon.

"Raif, hear me out." I turned to face my friend, hugging my arms to myself to ease the emptiness I felt. It worried me that I'd had to wish Tyler out of my apartment and to The Pit, where Levi could keep an eye on him. His control was held together by the barest of threads. "You don't want to reopen old wounds. I get that. But Delilah wouldn't have mentioned Brakae just to piss you off. She knew the PNT would more than likely lock her away for good . . . or worse. She'd planned on using your daughter as a bargaining chip if she happened to get caught."

"It's been centuries, Darian. With no word. Not even a trace of where she might have gone. Why would Delilah keep such a secret for so long?"

I cocked a brow. "Why? Why not? You killed her sister, Raif. I wouldn't have willingly supplied you with that information either. You wanted answers. I believe she's got them. But we won't know for sure unless we can unlock whatever spell Adare put on her so I can get to the bottom of this."

"Why not just go to Adare?"

"Do you think he'd put our issues before PNT justice?"

Raif sighed. "No."

"So let's use Fallon to our advantage. I've already stolen this goddamned hourglass; it's too late to change course now. I'll make the trade, get what we need from Delilah, and when it's all said and done, we'll bring Adare and Reaver into it."

"And what if Fallon double-crosses you?"

The thought hadn't escaped me. He didn't strike me as particularly trustworthy. "When I meet up with him to exchange the hourglass, I'll activate the GPS on my phone. If he tries anything, you can keep track of where we are. If things go south, you call in the cavalry and you'll know how to get to me. It's doable. We can make this work."

Raif gave me a sad smile. "Darian, are you prepared to face PNT justice over this? There could be serious repercussions for what you're doing."

"I know," I replied with a sigh. "And yes, I'm ready to accept the consequences of my actions. Whatever they might be."

"All right, then." Raif's expression changed from concern to resignation. "We'll try."

Though he had no idea how his daughter's disappearance could be connected to the "Man" Delilah had mentioned or the mysterious Shaede women of my dreams, he promised to see this through to the very end—his daughter returned to him or not. Now, I just had to wait him out. He was tracking me—no doubt there—and as soon as Delilah spilled her little secret, I had to trust he'd get me the hell away from Fallon so I could return the hourglass to Reaver. From there, we'd find his daughter together.

"You're not much of a travel companion." Fallon's voice broke into my reverie. As if he had nothing better to do than listen to himself talk, he continued. "I hope the next hundred miles are better than the last."

Since we'd confined ourselves to the ridiculously cramped car, my feelings of unease had mounted. Something about Fallon pulled and repulsed me, simultaneously urging me to flee; yet I wanted to lean in closer. My phone continued to vibrate in my pocket at five-minute intervals, and I was pretty sure my voice mail was full because that alert had quit going off an hour ago. Though I worried he'd run the battery down with his repeated calls, that vibrating phone connected me to Tyler and let me know he still cared about me despite everything I'd done to crush him.

"Darian, speak to me."

"What do you want me to say?" I looked away, preferring blurry scenery and car sickness to Fallon's attempts at conversation. Why had I begun to feel more like a prisoner and less like an accomplice?

Spokane struck me as a city built upon a foundation of churches. From the freeway, they jutted up everywhere and farther out, toward the city proper as well. It was a city of old architecture peppered with new—and a variety of gods watching over it all.

I'd taken jobs for Tyler that led me to other cities, but not often. I liked to stay close to home, to what felt familiar. I didn't like leaving my comfort zone. Despite its size, Spokane felt small at about two-thirds the population of Seattle, and in turn made me feel exposed. I blended into the Seattle scenery. Here, I stuck out like a sore thumb. There wasn't the same press of bodies or quick pace that allowed me to go unnoticed. There was too much room to breathe. Too easygoing. Spokane had more of a Small Town, USA, feel: eye contact, open smiles, and friendly curiosity. Not that Seattle wasn't friendly, but with the big-city pace, people just didn't have time for much more than a passing glance. We wouldn't blend in quite as well here. No one in our trio of preternatural fugitives needed that kind of attention.

Fallon abandoned the downtown area, continuing down the freeway toward the Idaho border. We'd be more exposed as we left the population behind, and I wondered at his choice in direction. "Where are we going?" As though it mattered. Every mile we drove was a mile too far. All I wanted was to return home.

"We'll need to find a hotel. A quiet place where I can lift the magic that imprisons Delilah in her own mind. Isn't that what you want? To unlock her secrets? I can't do it from the driver's seat of this car."

"And then you'll get the hourglass. So don't act like all of this is one magnanimous gesture. Look around you, Fallon," I said, indicating the thinning urban landscape. "You don't think we're going to arouse suspicion?"

"I won't," he said. "Glamour, remember?"

I refused to look at him. And why should his ability to glamour bother me? Fae wore glamour to hide from the human populace all the time. Maybe it wasn't the glamour at all. Since we'd left Seattle, Fallon's mood and personality had done a complete one-eighty. He'd been uptight, done, and demanding before. Now, he seemed relaxed, cheerful even. He hadn't mentioned the hourglass since we'd left the city. Why? He'd been itching to get his hands on it before. The damn thing wasn't out of his reach, though. It was right in the backseat, resting next to Delilah, who might as well have been luggage herself.

As I turned to look at him, the heavy sigh escaped my lips before I thought better of it. The next second, pain and white-hot light exploded in my skull. My head bounced against the window from the impact of the blow, and a swollen knot formed on my temple before healing and shrinking back to nothing. I shook the fog from my brain and tried to calm my suddenly racing pulse and the unpleasant memories that crashed over me like a tidal wave. Too shocked to react, I stared at Fallon in disbelief as he shook out his fist. The coppery tang of blood coated my mouth from the split in my lip, and I passed my tongue over the wound as the skin fused back together.

"You forget, I'm helping you," he said low, the words infused with rage. "You should be grateful, and instead you're acting like a spoiled child. I don't want to hit you, so don't give me reason to do it again."

I was dazed, and my breath came in shallow drafts. My heart beat triple time to the passing of seconds, and

I squeezed my hands together to keep them from shaking. I had been the victim of an abusive human husband nearly a century and a lifetime ago. Erratic mood swings came standard issue with abuse, and Fallon's behavior was no exception. With a single punch and a warning, Fallon had reminded me of the woman I used to be and never wanted to be again.

"Lay your fist on me again, Fallon, and I'll be more than happy to gut you right here on the freeway." I seethed with pent-up anger, fire burning a path through my veins and pooling in the pit of my stomach. My hands clenched into fists, the urge to retaliate overwhelming. But even as I tried to raise my arm to give him tit for tat, something stayed my progress—a strange compulsion to keep my fists in my lap and my mouth shut.

"Now," he said, his tone becoming light once again, "let's find somewhere to settle in."

Fallon took the next exit and followed the ramp toward a cluster of hotels and a strip mall. We pulled into the parking lot of a Best Western, and he cut the engine, leaning so close to me I could feel his breath on my face. "Stay here." It was a warning and a command. "I'm going to get us a room, and I'll be right back." He took the keys out of the ignition, engaging the alarm as he walked toward the hotel lobby. As I watched him walk, his form shimmered for just a moment, like heat rising from asphalt. By his next step, he'd assumed the guise of a well-coiffed businessman, suit and all. I tried to contain my fear and amazement, but it came out anyway in a sort of half-choked sob.

My cell hadn't rung for at least a half hour. I pulled it from my pocket, prepared to call Tyler so I could beg him to come and take me home. When I flipped open the phone, the screen flashed *Low Battery* before going completely black. My chest tightened, constricting the flow of air to my lungs. *It doesn't matter,* I told myself. *Raif knows where I am. He'll come and we'll get the hell out of here.* Fallon might not have been bothered by our situation, but I sure as hell was. "You know what, Delilah," I said. "I'd have been a lot better off if you'd kept your big mouth shut!"

Through the lobby window, I could see Fallon standing at the front desk. He cast the occasional glance back at the car as if afraid I would try to bolt. I don't know why I didn't leave. The same strange compulsion I felt around Fallon kept me welded to my seat, as though an unspoken command prevented me from actually following through. Moments later, he emerged from the hotel, smug and satisfied as ever. He tapped a plastic keycard against his palm, his face thoughtful as he kept his businessman guise.

"We're down there." He pointed to the farthest end of the building. "I told the front desk I was exhausted and needed some peace and quiet." His gray eyes hardened as he took his seat, moving the car down the parking lot closer to our room. "I'll deal with the Oracle; you retrieve my glass."

And, fool that I was, I did exactly as he asked. I wondered at my behavior. It felt like the moment you realize you've had way too much to drink. And even though you know you're acting like a complete drunken idiot and nothing like your normal self, you do nothing to stop it. I slung the backpack over my shoulder, careful not to jostle the hourglass inside. I followed Fallon like an obedient puppy while he led Delilah toward our room. She stared straight ahead, her head cocking to one side and then the other. If she had any inkling of what was happening to her, the only indication she gave was the slight shiver that occasionally shook her lithe body.

Once inside the drab and uninteresting space that was bound to become my personal hell, Fallon flung himself across one of the queen-sized beds, stretching with languid grace. I'd never seen anyone so bipolar. Just three minutes and fifteen seconds ago, his eyes had flashed with rage. And now he looked like a kid on vacation.

"No doubt Adare is hunting us," I said, slumping down on the opposite bed. "We shouldn't have run."

"Don't be ridiculous," Fallon answered. "Where we're going, they won't find us."

Where we're going? Uh-uh. No freakin' way. I'd gone far enough with him. I wasn't going another foot, let alone another mile. My phone was dead, GPS effectively shut down. I wasn't taking another step in any direction until I saw the whites of Raif's eyes.

My assassin's instincts took over as I studied the layout of our room. I needed to be familiar with every corner when shit went down. And it would. The better acquainted I became with my surroundings and my accomplice-turned-captor's mannerisms, the better my chance at escape would become. "I'm not going any farther," I said, though the words carried little fortitude. "Release Delilah's mind. I'll give you the hourglass, and you can be on your way."

Fallon stood, and I felt my head slowly shrink into my shoulders. A wild silver glint chased across his gaze as he approached and seized me roughly around the throat. "You *will* go farther for as long as I say you will," he said, giving me a brain-rattling shake. "Do you understand me?"

I couldn't speak or draw a breath deep enough to produce any kind of sound. His fingers dug into my tender flesh, bruising, nearly burning me with the contact. The emerald flared in my pocket, hot and angry, but I pushed it to the back of my mind. I nodded my head as much as his grip would allow, and he pushed me away, throwing me down on the bed. As I massaged my neck, Fallon paced the room, muttering under his breath. He rounded back to the bed and hauled me up by a handful of hair, pressing the tips of his fingers to the middle of my forehead. I jerked away, but he held me. I bit my lip so I wouldn't cry out at the searing contact. Magic flowed over me, binding my body in a second skin.

"I can't have you leaving," Fallon said, "or disappearing right under my nose." *No. He couldn't have!* But I realized as I tried to merge with the light that Fallon had, in fact, bound me to my corporeal form. "You've done this to yourself." His chiding tone made me want to vomit. "You can be mad all you want, Darian. But this is *your* fault. Behave, and I won't have to further punish you."

I sat on the bed, staring in disbelief as he left my side to tend to Delilah. What the hell was wrong with me? Fallon should have been dead where he stood. If any other man had laid his hands on me, I wouldn't have hesitated to part him from his head. So why, now, did I cower in fear of this Fae who shouldn't have one-tenth of the power he held over me? I thought of the times I'd felt drawn to him, compelled to divulge information he had no business knowing. Could it be that his magic had played a part even then? Secretly stealing my will? The thoughts in my brain began to swirl and mull about like mud meeting a pool of fresh water. I had a feeling someone should be coming to get me, but for the life of me I couldn't remember who.

"Darian, come here."

I walked to Fallon despite the instinctive thought that I should keep my distance. He knelt at Delilah's feet in an almost-meditative position, his palms resting on his knees. "Time to spill your secrets," he said, and pressed the heel of his hand to her forehead.

Delilah came to as if someone had just doused her with a bucket of ice water. As she thrashed her limbs and gasped for air, it took all of Fallon's strength to hold her down. You wouldn't think a twig of a girl like Delilah could fight so hard, but let me tell you, she gave him a run for his money.

"Keep quiet!" Fallon growled. "You'll have all of Washington down on our heads if you raise your voice."

I waited for him to smack her across the face or kick her good and hard. But he didn't. Apparently he saved that affection solely for me. Prick. Delilah calmed, the mere sound of Fallon's voice enough to put the fear of Jesus in her. Not a very hard nut to crack. "Do you know where you are?" I asked.

"Darian." Her voice, unused for a few weeks, rasped in a near whisper. "You're swathed in Fae magic. And separated from your protector. Changed since I saw you last. Have you been to The Ring?"

Come again? "I haven't been anywhere, you crazy pain in the ass. You're up and talking for one reason and one reason only. Where is Raif's daughter? You said you knew how to find her. Where is Brakae?"

Delilah laughed as if she'd just heard the funniest, dirtiest joke ever written. She tilted her head in Fallon's direction, looking very much like the cat that ate the canary and crawling, it seemed, from madness to lucidity. "You don't know, do you?"

Fallon sat back on his heels, taking in every word Delilah said with perverse interest. I ignored the way my body responded to his movements, swaying backward as if attached by a length of string. My mind cleared as if by his will, and I found the pluck to drill right into Delilah. "No more games, no more riddles. Just plain talk here. I've been through hell the past couple of weeks and, goddamn it, I want to take a shower, get some sleep, and go the fuck home. Tell me right now where Raif's daughter is, and I won't beat the shit out of you before I give you back to the PNT."

"In my mind's eye, she's very beautiful. Is she still?" Delilah asked, the epitome of innocence. "Did you know that Oracles are blind and not particularly lovely in exchange for their gifts? I'll never see the sunrise as you do or captivate men's hearts the way you have. The way *she* has. For the right price, I can show anyone his future. Hers. Yours. Even Tyler's. Everyone's but my own. Funny, isn't it?"

I went for the dagger I kept sheathed at my thigh, ready to stab her out of sheer frustration. But when I reached for it, I found it was gone. I looked around the room, confused. Again my mind felt shrouded in fog, and my memory became hazy. Where was the dagger? I reached for my back. The katana was also gone, but I couldn't remember for the life of me where it could be. Had I left it in the car? Put it in the closet? I shook my head to clear my thoughts, and Delilah's face blurred in and out of focus. Damn Fallon and his magic Fae fingers. What had he done to me?

"Where is she, Delilah?" My legs wobbled, threatening to give at any moment, and my arms felt too heavy to lift. "Spit it out already. Where is Brakae? I need to find her."

"Darian." Delilah sat up straight in her chair, her voice laced with bravado. "Darian, Darian, Darian. You broke me out of that prison, abandoned Tyler, and the gods know what else, when what you should have been doing was watching your back."

Well, she'd snapped back into her old snarky self pretty damned fast. What happened to the bat-shit-crazy girl I'd dropped off at the PNT weeks ago? I should have known she wasn't going to be grateful and spill her secrets as if we were the best of friends. Nope. I'd have to beat it out of her. Fine by me. Though I'd probably need a solid night of rest before I could do it properly. Jesus Christ, I was tired. When was the last time I'd slept?

"I warned you," she said. "But you never listen, do you? You're just *so* very tough. What did Tyler say when you left him? Was he understanding of your running off with another man?"

I answered her with silence. I hadn't told Tyler I was leaving, or had I? God, I couldn't form a coherent thought to save my life.

"You didn't tell him!" Delilah squealed like a girl at a pajama party. "Oh wow. He is going to be *pissed*. You've never seen his nasty side, but I can tell you from experience . . . Tyler has an ugly temper when he has cause to show it."

"Shut. Up!" I yelled, clarity singeing a path through my brain. I brought my face nose to nose with hers. "You are not allowed to talk about him. Ever. You used him to get to me. You would have let me die thinking he'd betrayed me."

"Had to get you on board somehow. You were chosen. And the Enphigmalé needed a Guardian's blood to be awakened. A Guardian . . . in love, no less."

Guardian. Again. Fate laughed at my predicament, the separate events of my recent life twining once again into a long, complicated braid. The black-haired Shaede had called me a Guardian. So had Reaver. What the fuck was going on? And why was I *always* the last to find out? "Your plan didn't go too well," I said, backing away from Delilah's stinking face. "I killed your gargoyles. Every last one."

"Are you sure about that?" Delilah asked, her head cocking toward Fallon.

He stood in a flash of movement and brought his fist down hard against Delilah's tiny skull. He knocked her right off her chair, actually. She fell to the floor with a thud, out like a light. My knees finally gave up the fight to support my body, and I crumpled to the floor beside her, staring without emotion at her still and fortunately silent form. Fallon stood above me, stroking my hair as if I'd become some sort of pet, and I fought a wave of nausea so strong, I thought I'd empty my stomach right there on the hotel carpeting.

"Shhh," he soothed as he petted me. "Sleep, Darian."

Magic twined around me, holding me warm and secure. I fell back against him as his arms gathered me close. *Finally,* I thought, *I'm going to get some rest.*

Chapter 21

I awoke to a pulsing warmth at my throat. The sensation didn't disturb me; in fact, it calmed me and turned my bones into Jell-O. A body hovered above me, and warm breath fell on my bare neck as a finger caressed something hard and unyielding that lay against my skin. I felt rested, despite the crazy dream I'd had, as if I'd been sleeping for hours. I snuggled deeper against my pillow, my eyelids still too heavy with sleep for me to open. I recalled the details of my dream as I floated in the hazy realm between sleep and wakefulness. I'd become a thief, a kidnapper, and I'd left Tyler. I groaned as I struggled to fight the lethargy that clung to my mind. Surely my dream was more nightmare than anything. No way in hell would I ever leave Ty.

"Tyler."

The warmth at my throat diminished as fingers lifted the heavy weight from my skin. I felt the rasp of a chain as it slid against my neck, but my brain was still too fuzzy to command my eyes to open. It had to be Tyler sitting next to me. I wanted to open my eyes, to look at him, but holy hell, I was so, so tired.

"I dreamt I'd left you without even saying good-bye. It was horrible." My voice was thick with sleep. My tongue stuck to the roof of my mouth. I tried to lick my lips, but the effort exhausted me.

The warm weight returned to rest against my throat, and what I'd once perceived as a pleasant touch became forceful as a hand wound around my neck, forcing my face upward. "It's time you forgot about the Jinn," Fallon snarled. I came fully awake as if plunged into a freezing lake, and I stared into his angry gray eyes. "Do you understand me?"

My blood turned to ice as my mind regained coherency. This nightmare wasn't something I could merely wake up from. It had become my reality, and my heart pounded against my rib cage like it wanted out as yesterday's details flashed fresh in my mind. I pulled away and sat up, facing the bastard who'd managed to make me his prisoner. He leaned on an elbow and lifted the emerald pendulum, the thing he'd caressed so lovingly, the chain now fastened around my neck.

"I found it in your pocket. There's no need to keep it hidden. Not now. You should wear it. It's your right."

I took a cleansing breath, wanting like hell to wish for Tyler's help. I needed him so badly, and not just for protection. Only Tyler could fill the black hole that Fallon had managed to tear open in my soul. But something prevented me from speaking the words. The wish sat at the tip of my tongue but refused to go any farther. I sat bolt upright and looked down at the deep green gem, glowing softly against my skin. "Do you know what this is?"

Liquid silver flashed in his eyes. *"Iskosia,"* he said. "The Key. And you're the only living thing this side of *O Anel* to possess one."

"What is *O Anel*?"

Fallon laughed, launching himself from the bed with a jaunty bounce. "I'm starving! Aren't you? There's no room service in this dump, and even if there were, I wouldn't eat anything prepared by a human. Stay here. I'll bring you back a delicious breakfast, and you'll see what you've been missing."

Good God, but he was a daffy fucker. He needed a Prozac the size of a golf ball to deal with his personality issues. But if he wanted a contamination-free breakfast, then the better for me that he go in search of one. "I doubt you'll find a meal within a hundred-mile radius *not* prepared by human hands."

Fallon tapped his temple with his forefinger and headed toward the door, the same businessman guise sliding over his skin. He crossed the room to the bedside table, grabbed the phone, and jerked the cord from the wall, tucking it under his arm. "We have a long day ahead of us. I'll be back soon."

I sat on the bed with a silly grin plastered on my face. When I heard the door latch, I ran to the window, peeking through the curtain, and watched as the VW pulled out of the parking lot. I crossed the room with only one thought: *Get the fuck out of here.* I turned the knob and pulled the door, only to find it refused to open. Using the wall for leverage, I propped a foot against it, pulling with every ounce of my preternatural strength. The door would not budge.

"Did you really think he'd leave you here without taking precautions?" Delilah said from where she sat on the other bed. "He's waited for you a long time. He's not going to let you go."

She looked much too comfortable for my taste, lounging against the headboard as if she hadn't a care in the world. "Delilah," I said, coming to stand at the foot of her bed. "Shut the fuck up! I wouldn't be in this mess if you hadn't decided to get all chatty about Raif's daughter. I should have let him kill you when he wanted to."

"Yes, you should have. Never forgive your enemies, Darian. It will *always* come back to bite you in the ass."

"Point taken. Now shut up. I've got to find a way out of here." A locked door wasn't going to stop me. I didn't care if I brought the whole building down around our heads; I was getting out of this room. I grabbed a bulky chair and threw it at the window. It bounced off the glass as if the chair were made of cotton balls and landed at my feet. "Fallon's spelled the entire room, hasn't he?" I whispered. "I'm not getting out of here."

"Is that what he's calling himself?" Delilah mused. "He's fortified the windows, walls, and door with a containment charm. *Fallon* has made the room impossible to escape from. I told you, Darian—he won't let you go. Not now."

Is that what he's calling himself? What the hell was that supposed to mean? Could Ty have been right all along? Fallon had been keeping his true identity a secret. Despair welled in my chest, threatening to choke the air right out of me. I hoped it would. I hoped it suffocated me with its weight and put an end to my miserable existence. I'd taken offense at being called stupid time and again, but lo and behold! I was as dumb as a person could get. I'd orchestrated my own undoing with almost no effort at all. Fuck the world, how could I have been such an idiot?

I sat at the foot of Delilah's bed, rested my elbows on my knees, and cradled my head in my hands. I couldn't let Fallon—or whoever the hell he was—get the upper hand. He'd done something to me, messed with my head without my realizing it. If it happened again, I was as good as dead.

"Delilah," I said, turning toward her, "how long was I unconscious?"

"Fifteen or twenty minutes." She shrugged. "We've been here only an hour."

I massaged my throbbing forehead with my fingertips. Confusion swirled as an anxiety-fused knot formed in my stomach. My limbs were sluggish and heavy, and my head teetered on my shoulders as though I'd slept for days. I had no sense of time. Fifteen minutes? Felt like a fucking week. "You and I are going to have a little talk."

I stalked to the side of the bed, hauled her scrawny ass up, and threw her into a chair. Hell if I know how I kept from beating her to death, because it was all I could do to prevent myself from using her as a punching bag. She deserved it. Oh, she may have looked tiny and defenseless, but she'd eat me whole and spit me out the first chance she got. "Now, I may not have a knife to cut you with, but don't doubt for a second that I know ways to inflict serious pain without a blade. And just because you think I'm one of the good guys doesn't mean I won't enjoy every second of your torture either." Big talk? Damn straight. I needed it. "Now, before Fallon gets back with my human-free breakfast, I want to know what the hell is going on. And if I feel like you're not being forthcoming with me . . ." I grabbed a glass from the counter, smashed it, and took a large shard in my hand. "Well, I'm going to start by using this glass to carve out little bits and pieces of you. You got that?"

Delilah nodded in agreement. But her coy smile caused a chill to shake me from head to toe. God, she was one creepy chick. I wondered how Ty could have ever befriended her . . . *Focus, Darian!* I shook the cobwebs left over from Fallon's influence over my mind and bent low so I could look Delilah in the eyes. Who cared if she couldn't look back? "Where is Brakae?" I asked, my voice steady.

"Brakae is in The Ring," Delilah said as if I should have known. "She's been there since the day she was chosen."

"What do you mean, 'chosen'?"

"Chosen to serve. Just like you were. Though I have to say, Darian, you got the better end of the deal."

I strangled the air in front of Delilah's neck. If I didn't know any better, I would have thought she was stalling. But Delilah just liked to talk in circles. In my opinion, it was her greatest gift. "What is The Ring?" I asked. "And why is Fallon so interested in this broken hourglass? It's connected to Brakae, right? That's the whole point of this little field trip."

"Boy, you don't miss a thing, do you?" She tilted her head to the side, thoughtful. "He was banished from *O Anel* a few hundred years ago. And ever since, he's been looking for a way back."

Fabulous. "Where is *O Anel*? What is it?" She laughed and I pressed the shard of glass to her delicate skin. "I'm not kidding, Delilah. I'll kill you if you don't cooperate."

Sighing, she settled deeper into her chair. "*O Anel* is The Ring, Darian. It's the Faerie Realm."

I fingered the emerald at my neck. "And *Iskosia*. What is that?"

"The Key," Delilah said. "Belonging to only one person. The Guardian. It opens *O Anel*."

"And I'm this Guardian, right?"

"Amazing, isn't it?" Delilah said, picking at her finger-nails. "Do you think they get channel twelve here? I wonder if *Judge Judy* is on."

Jesus Christ. "Stay with me here, Delilah, and you can watch—or listen to—all the trashy TV you want. But not until you answer my questions. So, let's talk about this Guardian bullshit."

"It's not bullshit, Darian. You were chosen. Before your Shaede existence, Fate had your path set out for you. And if you don't like it, well, I guess that's just too damned bad."

A scream built in my stomach and rumbled up my throat, but I swallowed it down, determined not to let her shake me. I, not Delilah, was in charge of this inter-rogation. Running out of time, I needed more informa-tion before Fallon returned. "Okay, so let's say I am this Guardian. What do I protect?"

"Not just what, but whom," Delilah said shrewdly. "You *know*, Darian. I don't have to tell you this one. I sensed it on you. You've been there already. You've seen the Time Keeper with your own eyes."

"That woman. The priestess. She's the Time Keeper?"

Delilah graced me with her Mona Lisa smile.

"Wait," I said, wading through the details in my mind. "That can't be right. There're more than one of them. I saw three different girls. Are they all Time Keepers? Or just one of them?"

Laughter answered me. "Time is a strange thing in *O Anel*."

It couldn't be. Could it? As I slowly pieced the infor-mation together, I couldn't believe I hadn't realized it sooner. Those sapphire eyes, the curling raven hair. And their smiles. All the same, and so familiar. It wasn't the first time I'd seen that expression either. "They're all the same girl," I said more to myself that Delilah. "And"—*holy fucking shit*—"the Time Keeper is Brakae."

"You're finally catching on," Delilah said. "Took you long enough."

"What about Fallon?" I said. "How does he fit into all of this?"

Delilah laughed in astonishment. "Darian, how could you not know by now? We've covered this. *Fallon* is the Man from The Ring."

I slumped back, saved from a fall by my ass bouncing on the foot of the bed. Of course Fallon was the Man from The Ring. Who the hell else would he be?

"I'm sorry, Darian, but I did warn you." Delilah stood and laid a comforting hand on my shoulder, which I promptly brushed away. "You should have killed him like you did the others. But you let him get away. Too concerned about Tyler's injuries, I suppose. Who could blame you? You love him."

"What's going on here?" Fallon walked through the door, slamming it behind him. "Delilah, my dear, you've been running off at the mouth again, haven't you? I thought I could trust you without sealing your mouth shut. I guess I was wrong."

Delilah seemed to melt under Fallon's heated stare, shrinking back down into her chair. "I didn't tell her anything she didn't already know or wouldn't have figured out with a little thought."

I'd run out of time and could already feel the draw of his presence, my will dissolving. I'd be nothing but a dancing puppet as he pulled the strings in a matter of moments. With determined focus, I cataloged everything Delilah told me, praying I wouldn't forget.

"What do you think, Darian?" He beckoned me with a finger and I obeyed, walking toward him as if I had no other choice. "Does Delilah have a big mouth?"

"Oh yeah." I blurted the words as if he'd fed them to me on a teleprompter. "She likes the sound of her own voice."

"My thoughts exactly." Fallon pulled a long knife from a sheath at his waist. Not made of anything metal, the black sheen of the blade ran with veins of emerald. "You've played your part, Oracle. Now it is time to go to your sister."

Delilah clamped her jaw tight and bucked her chin up in the air. The girl had moxie. It was the one thing I admired about her. Her expression softened into that of resignation . . . no, reverence, as if she sat in the presence of greatness. I'd seen that expression before, when the Enphigmalé had sprung to life before Delilah's unseeing eyes. She'd stood in awe of them. Fallon ran his hand over her hair—a loving gesture, really. Just as he'd done to me earlier, he soothed her, shushed her lightly, and kissed the top of her head before running his knife through her heart. He twisted the blade with a jerk and pulled it out, cleaning off the blood on Delilah's own shirt while she died.

And I did nothing to stop it.

Fallon returned the knife to its sheath and put his hand on my shoulder. "Don't mourn her," he said. "She's with her sister. I found us something suitable to eat," he said, letting me go to retrieve the bag he'd left at the door. "Sit and let me feed you."

And, damn it, I did. I rested my arms at my sides as Fallon pushed my chair in. He placed a clear-plastic container of food in front of me: breads, fruits, and cheeses all garnished with flowers.

"I found a Sylph downtown who owns a bakery. You wouldn't think it would be so hard to find our kind in this city, but I have to admit, it took some looking." Fallon set a fork beside me and plucked a grape from a small bunch. "Taste this." He brought the fruit to my mouth, which I opened obligingly. He placed the grape in my mouth, his finger brushing my lip. "Tell me that's not the sweetest grape you've ever eaten."

The fruit burst in my mouth. It was sweeter than anything I'd ever tasted, with a strange floral aftertaste that tingled on my tongue—delicious. "Eat," he said, pushing the fork toward me. "It's all wonderful without a trace of human taint."

I picked up the fork and ate my breakfast as if I didn't have a mind of my own. Eat, drink, sleep . . . What else would Fallon command me to do? I shuddered at the thought. While I stuffed my face with "taint-free" food, Fallon retrieved my backpack from the closet. He sat down beside me, unzipping the bag as if it would explode if he didn't take care. Peering down, he found his prize, and a hungry smile graced his lips. He drew the broken hourglass from my bag and carefully unwrapped the towels I'd used to cushion it.

"The prize," he said, setting the glass on the table between us. "We're so close."

"Close to what?" I asked.

"Freedom," he said.

"What does that hourglass do?" The food must have been charmed. I couldn't stop eating it. Everything tasted so delicious, even the flowers used for garnish. And the more I ate, the more confused I became, having to remind myself that I was sitting at the table of a madman with a corpse for company.

"Broken, the hourglass is useless. It maintains the flow of time in the realm to which it belongs. But we're going to join this half with its mate. And when we do, wondrous things will happen."

Fallon spoke with a passion only fanatics possess. He watched, mesmerized by the golden grains of sand falling upward and passing into nothing before returning to fill the bottom of the glass. I nibbled on a piece of cheese, my eyes wandering to poor Delilah, who had let her grief and need for revenge steer her toward the dark path that led to her death. If she could have seen her own future, I wondered if she would have done things the same way. I reached toward her with my left hand and touched her shoulder, my gaze drawn to my thumb. The skin below my knuckle was smooth, as if something had worn it that way. Had I been wearing jewelry earlier? It seemed a ring was missing from my thumb. And I had a feeling it should not be missing, and that somehow, without it, I was incomplete.

"Fallon," I said, "where are you taking me?" Others would miss me—I thought. I had friends, loved ones, didn't I? I knew just a moment ago. *Remember*. I closed my eyes and forced myself to focus despite the fog shrouding my mind. Delilah had told me about someone. Someone I'd been searching for. My friend's daughter. *Raif's* daughter—Brakae—the Time Keeper. She lived . . . Where did she live? In the Faerie Realm. And I was her Guardian. *Don't forget, Darian. Don't you dare forget again. You've got to find her and kill Fallon before he kills you so you can get home to Tyler. He thinks you've left him.* "Where the hell's my ring?" I stroked my thumb with a forefinger. "And where are you taking me?" I asked again with more force behind the words. I pushed the plate away; I wanted more, craved it, but I couldn't allow myself to eat another bite.

"It's not where I'm taking you," Fallon said, still enrapt by the hourglass. "It's where you're taking me."

"I don't have anywhere to go," I said. Or did I? Yes, I had to find Brakae. For Raif. I couldn't forget again.

"You're taking me home, to *O Anel*. I have business with the Time Keeper."

Chapter 22

"There's one problem with that, Fallon." I held on to lucidity by the skin of my teeth. My mind reeled in his presence. "I have no idea how to get us there."

His expression warned of rage, a storm close to breaking. I slid my hand across the table, picking up one of the shards of glass I'd used to threaten Delilah. No way in hell was he getting his hands on me again. I felt the violence coming, uncoiling from somewhere deep within him, and I watched as his hands clenched into tight fists. "Do it," I warned, my voice low. "I dare you to hit me."

The silver light swirling in his eyes calmed to neutral gray, and he busted out into over-the-top laughter. "I can see why you were chosen to protect her. Such a . . . badass," he said as if searching for the right word, "aren't you?"

"Damn right, I am. I know you've laid some sort of magic on me too. Because if I were in my right mind right now, you'd be dead."

"You're probably right," Fallon said, popping a grape into his mouth. "But you're not in your right mind, are you?"

Thoughts swirled in my head, which suddenly felt too heavy for my shoulders to support. "I *am* going to kill you, Fallon. And I'm going to enjoy doing it."

He laughed again, a half-crazed sort of bark. "We'll see about that."

I tried not to look at Delilah, who for all her treachery had gotten the shitty end of this deal. Well, I hoped revenge was sweet in the afterlife, because she sure as hell hadn't savored any part of it in this world. Fallon seemed oblivious to our dead breakfast guest, paying more attention to his food, all the while caressing the broken hourglass.

My arms were lead weights at my side as I struggled to push against the table, desperate to get away from him. Inch by inch, I moved my chair, the effort seeming insurmountable. And all the while, Fallon paid me no attention, closing his eyes as he enjoyed every bite of his breakfast. Only when I managed to move my chair enough to give myself room to stand did he look at me.

"What are you doing?"

"I'm going to the bathroom," I said. "Do you have a problem with that?"

"Not at all," he said. "As long as you behave."

Though I didn't have the strength of will to do it, I wanted nothing more than to gouge his eyes out with the plastic fork in my hand. Maybe splashing a little cold water on my face would shock me out of the lethargy Fallon's presence imposed. Or better yet, I hoped there was a window that hadn't been reinforced by magic that I could use to get the hell out of here.

I'm not sure how I made it to the bathroom. One second I was standing by the table, and the next I stood in front of the sink, studying my reflection in the large rectangular mirror. I'd come in here looking for something . . . a window. How long had I been standing here, staring at the emerald pendulum dangling from my neck, resting just above the swell of my breasts? *"Iskosia,"* I whispered, wondering how I knew that word. I stroked the gem lightly with my finger.

Water streamed from the sink, though I couldn't remember turning it on. I looked back to the mirror, now clouded with steam. I hadn't moved an inch, had I? I'd wanted a little cold water on my face. Not hot. Fumbling with the knobs, I waited for the water to cool and filled my palms, splashing water over my face and neck. Lukewarm rivulets ran down my shirt and into my bra. Not cold enough. I was still much too groggy. All I wanted was to curl up in bed. . . .

I fought to form a coherent thought, to keep myself in the present. Water dripped from my nose to the tile floor. Suddenly, a rough white hotel towel passed against my cheeks.

"Darian," Fallon said, "I can't have you a mindless shell. Your idle threats of violence wear on my patience. Others may enjoy that smart mouth of yours, but I do not. If you promise to be a good girl and behave, I will allow you some presence of mind. Agreed?"

Fallon. But that wasn't his real name. Delilah had said as much. Clarity returned by small degrees, and I ticked off important facts in my head, securing them like mental sticky notes. The Man from The Ring. He'd killed Delilah and tricked me into stealing something for him. I closed my eyes to better concentrate while he dried my face. Time. I'd stolen time for him. And the emerald . . . I touched the stone at my neck. The emerald was the key to *O Anel*, the Faerie Realm. I was going to kill him.

But not unless I played his game. "I promise to behave," I said. "I don't want to feel this way anymore."

He pressed a palm against my cheek, and already my mind felt clearer. I remembered most of what had happened since we'd left Seattle; only bits and pieces were missing—black holes in my memory. "How long have we been here?" I asked. The last thing I remembered, Delilah—the thought cut off in my mind, but slowly came back to me in pieces. He'd killed Delilah. Yes, I was sure of it. "We checked into this hotel, this morning. . . ."

Fallon tossed the towel into the sink. "We're leaving. Right now. I have business to attend to, and I'm not going to wait any longer for you to come around. We have an accord now, right? You cooperate, I won't turn your mind against you. I want the other half of my hourglass, and you're going to get it for me."

Sure, you keep telling yourself that. The fog continued to lift, allowing me a clearer train of thought. Tyler was no doubt out of his mind with worry. But I couldn't think about Tyler or how I'd make amends with him for all that I'd done. Not until I cleaned house here. Though I had reason to hope I'd be rid of Fallon soon, Raif had activated the GPS in my cell so he could track me. The battery had died when we'd pulled in to the hotel, but Raif couldn't have been more than a couple of hours behind us. Why hadn't he showed? My only option was to stall Fallon and to keep him rooted to our hotel room until Raif found me.

"I told you, I don't know how to get there." I'd made my tone complacent, a trick I'd learned from years of abuse at my human husband's hand. "I'm sorry; I don't want you to be angry with me. But I don't *know* how to help you."

With a sneer, the puppet master ushered me back to the bed. The room reeked of death, so much stronger to my preternatural senses. Delilah's body had been removed, though the chair where she'd died and the carpet below were still stained with her blood. I fought a wave of nausea as I wondered about how, when, and where he'd managed to dispose of her body, and I shuddered. Fallon turned me around to face him and placed his hands on my shoulders, urging me to sit. He went to his knees in front of me, and my pulse picked up double time. Leaning in, he caressed the emerald resting just above the swell of my breasts, and my body went rigid.

His cold laughter filled me with dread. "No need for you to worry, Darian, I've no interest in you beyond the bauble around your neck," he said. "Don't flatter yourself."

By small degrees, my body relaxed, though I didn't outwardly show my complete and utter relief. I didn't want to insult him and give him cause to lay down the "mojo" as Tyler would have called it. Thinking of Tyler again sent a jolt of bitter pain through my body and soul. I missed him so much. "Why were you banished from your home, Fallon?" Delilah had told me he'd been thrown out of *O Anel*. Maybe if I knew why, I could use the information to my advantage.

"It doesn't matter. Not anymore. That was so long ago. What's important is that we're going there, you and I. And you will help me right the world."

I should have known you just can't reason with the criminally insane. And have no doubt, Fallon was as unhinged as one could get. "But you still haven't told me how you think I'm going to get us there."

"*Iskosia.* You have the key. The Oracle said you've been there." He placed his hands on my knees and leaned in close. The wild glint in his eyes flashed silver. "What did it look like?"

The urge to spill my guts overwhelmed me. "Green. Nothing but endless green. Knolls and valleys and rolling hills covered with trees for as far as I could see."

Fallon's eyes drifted shut, and a smile curved his lips. "I miss it. Being surrounded by living, growing things. The world here is crowded, polluted, covered with hard, unyielding surfaces. It's even worse than it was two hundred years ago. Once-blue shining waters now glisten with the sheen of spilled fuel. Refuse litters the forests. Humanity did that. There is no place for green in their self-centered lives. Humans are indeed rats. Their numbers have exploded in the centuries I've been gone."

So apparently Fallon hadn't been hanging out in Connecticut the past couple of centuries, but I didn't have time to ponder this piece of the puzzle. "Where is *O Anel*?" The island of the Enphigmalé had existed in another place, so to speak. Another time. But the concept escaped me. "Is it here? On this planet?"

"You think with the narrow mind of the mundane," Fallon said, caressing my cheek as if in sympathy. "*O Anel* exists behind the veil, Darian. It is here, all around us, though we cannot see it. You smell a hint of it on the wind, just before a rain, or see a glimpse as the sun breaks over the horizon. It is a beautiful and sometimes lonely place, but it doesn't have to be. I am going to change that. I will make it an Eden. And we will never have cause to hide again."

He stood in one fluid, unnatural motion and spun in a half circle, turning his back to me. "Get ready. We're leaving."

*   *   *

I stared out of the hotel room window; a large, dingy rectangle speckled with what looked to be mud obscured my view. Not that there was anything to look at. Freeway, parking lots, the strip mall—not exactly a five-star location. But then again, that was exactly why Fallon had chosen it. No one would bother to ask any questions. I watched the cars speeding by on the freeway. People headed home from work, going to dinner or a movie, living regular lives. My life was far from average, but it had been good. I had a job that paid enough to keep me comfortable and made me feel that I'd been serving a purpose. I'd finally managed to make a friend or two, and I had Tyler. *Had.* I doubted I could claim Tyler as mine anymore after I'd run off on him. And I might never see him again. I had no idea how long Fallon planned to keep me in *O Anel*. And for that matter, I had no clue how I was going to manage to kill him and get home— not when he controlled me so completely.

And what about Brakae? I had to protect her too. How long would all of this take? Centuries? The thought of returning to that green and endless place terrified me; yet I knew I had no other choice but to go and finish what I'd started.

Fallon came up behind me and squeezed my shoulders. How he could have thought we'd actually bonded over my kidnapping was beyond me. But then again, he was off his rocker in a serious way. Who knew what he thought about how I felt about him. "*Iskosia* is what connects the Guardian to the Time Keeper. The hourglass is like yin and yang, each keeping in balance with the other. The Guardian must be able to travel between the realms in order to protect the essence of time and the natural order."

"Reaver?" I asked. "He's a Time Keeper too?"

"Yes," Fallon said with disgust.

"Who is his Guardian? Is there another key as well?"

"You ask too many questions." His features hardened, becoming the threatening guise of controlled rage.

"Azriel used to tell me that." I don't know why I said it. And in the next moment, I regretted it. Fallon back-handed me, closed fist and all, sending me sprawling to the floor. My jaw had to be broken; the pop echoed in my ears like an explosion, the pain searing and instant. Without my quick healing, I'd have been FUBAR. As it was, Fallon's heavy-handed punishments left me bruised from the inside out.

"You must like this sort of treatment to provoke me so often." He spoke too calmly for my peace of mind before grabbing me by the hair and dragging me to my feet. Once, twice, and again for good measure, he slapped me. Blood trickled from a split across my cheekbone, mingling with what had begun to flow from my lip. The bastard didn't need much provocation to rough me up. "What else did he tell you?" He shook me, hard, his face nose to nose with mine. "What secrets did he whisper in your ear before he died?"

"N-nothing," I stammered. God, I did *not* want to be hit again. Banished memories blinded me with their pain. "He never told me anything. Ever. The entire time I knew him, he kept the truth from me."

Fallon's body relaxed, and he let go of my hair. I stumbled back, leaning on the tacky upholstered desk chair for support. Wiping at the trickle of blood from the corner of my mouth, I asked, "Why are you upset?"

He lunged toward me, and I shrank away, trying to make myself as small as possible. In midstep he stopped, closed his eyes, and drew a deep breath. He rolled his shoulders, tipped his head to the ceiling, and exhaled. When he leveled his gaze on me again, liquid silver swirled in his eyes. "Come here."

I only stood a few feet away; yet I felt the pull of his command and the sudden urge to sprint to his side. With hands as gentle as they had been harsh, Fallon released the toggle from the clasp and removed the emerald necklace from my neck, making it once again a simple pendulum. Dangling it in front of me, he commanded, "Take it."

I reached out, drawn to the emerald's call. So far lost to Fallon's control, I hadn't even considered using the pendulum as a means to escape. And if I had, would I have even known how to use the damned thing? My trips into the Faerie Realm had been accidental at best. My fingers brushed the silver chain, and time seemed to suspend itself. . . .

A pounding on the other side of the cheap metal door rattled the hinges that threatened to break from the pressure. "Darian!" A familiar voice called out. "Darian, are you in there?"

Raif.

Jesus Christ, my heart pounded at the sound of his voice, drawing my attention from the pendulum. Fallon seized the emerald from my hand, stuffing it in his pocket before drawing his dagger, which he held tight to my throat. "Not a word."

Raif! I screamed in my head, desperate for him to break down the door. *Get me the fuck out of here!*

My captor pulled me against his chest, one arm squeezing the air from my lungs, the other wrapped tight around my neck. All it would take was a long, loud sigh and I'd be as good as dead. Fallon wasn't the kind of person to waste his time on idle threats. Another round of thunderous pounding followed Raif's shouts, and the door creaked in its frame. Fallon's wards held, though, and Raif might as well have been trying to kick through a solid stone wall.

Despair stabbed at my ragged emotions, sharper than the blade Fallon held to my skin. And even if I'd had the balls to call out to Raif, a nagging thought stole the fight right out of me: *Why bother? You're as good as dead. Don't bring him down with you.*

As if he'd heard me, Raif's struggles with the door stilled and a dead silence settled. Oh God. "Don't leave me," I whispered. What would happen to me if my only hope of escape had actually thrown in the towel?

The air around me became dense, permeated with a sweet aroma that banished the stench of Delilah's death from my nostrils. I stared at the door, my breath stalling in my lungs, and watched as dark threads of glistening shadow snaked their way through the tight cracks between the door and the jamb. The Soul Shadows twined back and forth, in and out, weaving around the doorknob, the hinges, the door itself, before crushing the barrier upon itself like a rag being wrung dry.

Raif stood on the other side of the threshold, sword in hand, a warrior's fierce battle lust shining in his deep blue eyes. He stormed through the entry, Fallon's wards broken by Shaede magic, poised and ready for a fight. Unfortunately for both of us, I stood between him and my captor's death, a shield well used, my body tight against his.

"I thought you and the Jinn would have killed each other by now," Fallon said. "I suppose if you want a job done right, you have to do it yourself."

Raif didn't grace him with an answer. Instead, his discerning gaze raked me from head to toe, no doubt taking stock of my bloodied face, evidence of every bruise, cut, or scrape Fallon had just given me. I wanted to shrink away from his appraisal, my shame at allowing myself to be victimized all the worse from having him bear witness to it. I healed fast, but I couldn't do anything about my disheveled appearance or the blood that remained.

"Darian," Raif said, calm as a still pond, "I'm afraid you're going to have to fight me for the right to kill this piece of shit." Did he know me, or what? "Because I swear to you now, he's going to fall beneath my sword."

God, I hoped so. I could live with knowing it wouldn't be me ripping his soul from his body as long as the bastard was dead. Fallon pulled me back until the bed stayed his progress. Then he hitched the dagger high beneath my chin. "Stay right here." His too-warm breath sickened me as he whispered in my ear. "Don't move a muscle."

Arms limp at my sides, I waited in mute silence, literally unable to move. Raif stood at the ready, looking damned near itchy to launch himself onto Fallon and be done with it. But my kidnapper had something Raif didn't: a determination born of madness matched with fanatical purpose. He didn't waste time posturing for a fight. Nor did he use his voice to issue threats of violence. Oh, no. Fallon was a straight-up killer, and he launched himself at Raif without preamble.

Arms flailed, legs kicked, and fists flew, the muffled sounds of the fight coming to my ears as if through a tunnel. I watched in mute horror, unable to aid my friend, utterly helpless. Tears streamed down my cheeks, and my teeth gnashed to the point of shattering as I fought against Fallon's influence — invisible shackles even the strongest will couldn't break. The quarters were close, their bodies too mashed into the tight space of the room's entrance to gauge who had the upper hand. Raif fought like a man possessed, hacking at Fallon with two hands gripping his sword. But Fallon was fast and deft. He matched Raif's assault swing for swing, defending as though he knew what Raif had planned a second before he executed. Raif raised his sword high, and a shout of pain followed by a grunt drew my attention just in time to see Fallon pull his dagger from Raif's stomach. The deep crimson of his blood was barely visible against the black blade until it dripped from the sharp point, landing on the dingy gray of the hotel carpet.

"Nooooo!" My voice exploded out of me, breaking whatever magical barrier that kept it silent. I swooned from the effort it took to exert the one word, the sound dragging out to a keening cry as Raif's hand fell limp and his head listed to the side.

Fallon stood, his steel gray eyes flashing silver. He cocked his head toward the gaping doorway and then swung his attention back to me, urgency flashing across his cruel face for the briefest of moments. Blood streamed from Raif's stomach; his breath seemed to still in his lungs. Dying? How? Not the quick-healing warrior I'd grown to love like a brother. I refused to believe what my eyes beheld. He couldn't die. *Please. God. No.*

My mind clouded with the force of Fallon's influence.

Against my will, I turned my eyes from Raif's unmoving form and watched instead as that sonofabitch took the emerald from his pocket and held it aloft. I plucked it from his waiting fingers, holding it before me just as he wanted me to. The room blurred in my peripheral vision, the emerald glowing bright as it became the focus of my entire existence. Seconds—time that never left me—slowed to a standstill, and I realized what Fallon wanted me to do. Only when the emerald consumed me so completely could I travel to *O Anel*. And he'd known it all along. No longer patient, through with playing games, he pulled me close—so close our bodies contoured to each other. His hand snaked around my neck, burying itself in the curls of my hair and winding the locks into his fist. With a cruel jerk, he forced me to look past the glowing emerald and into his cold silver eyes.

"You should have left him out of our business, Darian. He'd still be alive. But won't Delilah be pleased," he mused. "She finally got her revenge."

"Fuck you!" I shrieked, desperate to dig my nails into his smirking face. "I am going to kill you, Fallon. Do you hear me? I'm going to kill you!"

His face drew close to mine, and I felt my knees go weak. Again, my mind filled with a foggy haze, and I blinked to clear my vision. What had happened here? The door was gone off its hinges, and someone lay on the floor, blood pooling around his body and soaking into the carpet. Who was he?

Fallon squeezed my cheeks in his hand so hard that tears sprang to my eyes. Somehow, I felt that I deserved his treatment and that I needed to be punished for something I'd done. "Since you're a curious little chit, haven't you wondered how I can manipulate you with such ease?"

My mind cleared, no doubt because he willed it so, and the pain of the moment crashed over me again. Raif lay on the floor, bleeding to death, and I couldn't do a damned thing about it. Eyes narrowed in hatred, I was bound and determined to send Fallon to the hereafter once and for all. One wish was all I needed, and I could laugh while Tyler handed this bastard his ass. The words rose up, hovering on my lips before something gray and evil swirled in my head to swallow them up.

"You've never asked how you came to this end. Why? Don't you want to know when it really happened? When you were chosen by Fate to serve this purpose?" He dropped his gaze to the emerald for the briefest moment before turning his attention back to me. "You weren't the first Guardian to give a blood sacrifice to the Enphigmalé. Your predecessor died during the last ritual." The words sounded as if they'd been wrenched from his chest and ended in a vicious snarl. "And the one before him, and the one before her as well.

"Guardians are chosen for their character, their desire to protect, and strength of will. When a Guardian dies, the next in line is called to serve. Transformation is inevitable. As you moved higher in the ranks of the chosen, Fate prepared you. You became a Shaede because a shadow had been cast on your soul in your human life. And when you found love"—a look of jealousy crossed his face—"you took the light of the sun into your heart, making you even more powerful. The Oracle was my key to freedom. She collected the Guardians and performed the blood rituals. None of the others were strong enough to release us. You were hidden until you grew into the protector you were meant to be. But you didn't hide well enough. Maybe if that Shaede King hadn't paraded you around like some sort of concubine, you'd still be safe. No one can interfere now." The wild tone of fanaticism crept back into his voice. "And you're nowhere near strong enough to stop me."

I couldn't look away, no matter how the emerald screamed for my attention. It glowed so bright, casting a green shadow on Fallon's face as if pleading for me to fight. Helpless, I stared into his eyes, the silver swirls consuming his irises, no longer gray but shining silver orbs. Something reflected in their depths—a great beast—a gargoyle running through the woods in escape. A voice from my dreams haunted me, the familiarity now clear. "I've had your blood," the Enphigmalé said. "And you will obey *me*."

My heart pounded, threatening to break right out of my goddamned rib cage. It was impossible. He *couldn't* be. But how could I deny what Fallon had all but admitted. "What are you?" I whispered, desperate for his words to prove me wrong.

"I am Faolán, the Wolf of Badb, and one of the nine. The first Guardian. Banished. Cursed. Forgotten. And you"—he licked his lips, hungrily—"belong to me."

Chapter 23

I stared at him in stunned silence. Never in my wildest imaginings would I have guessed that the lunatic holding me prisoner by force of will had been the Enphigmalé I'd failed to kill on the island those many months ago. Isn't it great the way life can pull the rug right out from under you every now and then?

Delilah tried to tell me in her strange, circular way. But I hadn't listened. Just like everything in my life, I turned a blind eye and a deaf ear while being beaten over the head with the truth. Even Reaver, though he'd let me steal the hourglass while he watched, had tried to warn me. And Moira, I now realized, had every right to kill me, and probably should have.

"Darian," Faolán whispered in my ear. I almost laughed. His true name suited him much better. Somehow the long "a" sounded more sinister. The gentle tone of his voice sent chills across my skin, and I shuddered. "Take me to *O Anel*."

I couldn't resist the command. Through my blood, he controlled me, and it must have been an ancient, potent form of magic. It prevented me from resisting the compulsion to do exactly what he wanted me to do. *Fight him, damn it!* If I could just break free, get some distance between us, maybe I could form a coherent thought. But he had a death grip on my hair, and when I tried to shake free of him, he held me tighter, crushing me in his embrace. My thoughts clouded, the haze sticky and thick like being bound with cotton candy, and as if I'd planned it all along, I gazed into the emerald with no other thought than going back to that grass-covered knoll.

"I'll take you," I said, my voice sounding thick with sleep, "but you're going to die, Faolán. Believe it."

The emerald called to me, with endless green and beautiful light. The calm spread through me, warm and pleasant like soaking in a hot tub filled to overflowing. Time—the ceaseless cadence that plagued me—slowed again to near silence, and my body went limp in Faolán's arms. Infinity beckoned, and I gave myself over to the euphoric calm. *Don't you die, Raif. I found your daughter, and damn it, I'm bringing her back to you.* I resisted Faolán's influence, holding on to every last coherent thought. My heart sank as the emerald called to me and the haze of confusion pushed farther into my mind. I fought for one last oath, and I was sure as hell going to follow through on it. *Tyler, wait for me,* I thought. *I promise I'm coming back to you.*

I closed my eyes as tight as I could, and in turn, Faolán pulled me even closer. *I'm going to kill you.* I repeated the thought over and over, drilling it into my mind. No matter what, I had to make sure he didn't get his hands on Raif's daughter—not while the responsibility to protect her rested on my shoulders.

A pulse rocked me backward, and Faolán's body relaxed, his grip no longer squeezing the air from me. As if a breeze had cleansed the fog from my mind, coherent thought returned; only then did I open my eyes, though I dreaded to do so. A blanket of green surrounded us as far as I could see. There was no sign of Brakae. At least something had gone right for me in this never-ending string of bullshit. My Enphigmalé companion dropped to his knees and wept, kissing the ground and running his fingers through the grass. I expected him to shuck his clothes and roll around naked for all of his weepy dramatics.

From the moment I'd opened my eyes, I began to count the minutes. Each one that passed helped to guarantee I'd return home to a lonely, changed Seattle—one without Tyler. My accuracy wasn't great—the sound of time had gone silent in this place—but I had to at least try. I looked out across the vast fields of green, turning full circle before letting my attention fall to Faolán, still acting the fool as he smelled the grass.

"I'm home, Darian," he said, wonderment coloring his voice. "It looks just the same as when I left."

"Good for you," I said. Lucky Faolán. He didn't have to hide his emotions. Crazy bastard just let it all out like he were a guest on a Barbara Walters special. But not me. I took every emotion swirling within me and bottled each one up, storing them all in the deepest, darkest recess of my soul. If I allowed myself to feel the despair, the pain, the *loss*—I'd crack. And I was already running at half capacity. Faolán had made sure of that. I needed every ounce of apathy I could muster.

While I waited for Faolán to pull himself together, I took stock of the situation. Preoccupied, I realized he didn't exercise quite as much control over me. His concentration must've been the key to absolute control, and that had definite benefits for me in this place. I stretched my neck from side to side, releasing only a fraction of the tension I felt. No weapon. Not even a goddamned throwing knife. If anything had happened to my katana . . . well, let's just say I'd kill him twice.

Faolán's black dagger—the one he'd killed Delilah with and later used on Raif—hung at his side. The only justice worthy of what he'd done would be to kill him with his own weapon. I could take his knife, but that would require close combat and concentration. With his full focus on me, I doubted I could overpower him. Some Guardian I'd turned out to be—captured, manipulated, without even a stick to hit the enemy with. *Lovely.*

Finally, Faolán's homecoming celebration ended. Silver chased across his eyes as he dusted himself off and came to stand beside me. His influence pulled at my mind, clouding my thoughts just enough to confuse me. But I held on by the barest of threads. *Kill him. Protect Brakae. Get home. No matter what.* From my backpack,

Faolán produced the broken half of the hourglass. The sands no longer passed in a peaceful track up and down, up and down. Now they swirled about the glass in a torrent before traveling up into nothing and back.

"We're so close," he said. "I can feel it. The last time I saw this place, I was beaten, chained. About to face exile and eternal imprisonment. But then she helped *her*," he said to me in disbelief. "My Time Keeper helped Moira and her army to capture me and my brethren. She betrayed me, Darian, and she has to pay. Since she's now yours to protect, you're going to deliver her to me. Come, let's find her, shall we?"

"How do you think we're going to manage that?" I asked. I mean, seriously, did he not notice we stood in an ocean of green grass? There wasn't another soul for miles. "It's not like I can pull her out of my ass."

"You have a foul mouth," Faolán snapped, grabbing me by the arm. His fingers bit into the skin, bruising. If I had to rip him apart with my bare hands, I would. "You have yet to see the true Faerie Ring, Darian. I'll find her without your meager assistance."

"Oh yeah?" I said with a sneer. "What are you going to do—go gargoyle on me and sniff her out?"

Faolán shuddered at my words, his steps faltering. "I was trapped in that form for centuries," he said, none too graciously jerking my arm. "Don't think for a moment that I'm anxious to return to it anytime soon. Besides," he continued, his cruel gaze locked with mine, "I don't need to assume the form of a beast to be deadly."

He pulled me along, and I jerked my arm free of his grasp. But he let me. I knew if he'd really wanted to hold me, he would have. We walked for somewhere close to fifteen minutes, and every step made my stomach sour. Minutes equaled days, and in this place time stretched out in an unfathomable distance. Every step took me farther away from Tyler. Five minutes here was two days in the real world. It had already been almost a week since we'd left the hotel room, and I had just gotten here. Despair constricted my lungs as I thought of Raif, lying

on the floor as he bled out. I couldn't save him. I'd stood
by and watched as Faolán ran his dagger through Raif's
stomach. But I had to hope that he'd lived, despite his
injuries. For the moment, hope was all I had.

I hadn't paid much attention to the scenery as we
traveled. Why? Everywhere I looked was blanketed with
green; it wasn't like I'd miss anything. But as I looked up
and really took stock of our surroundings, I noticed the
landscape had changed dramatically in the short time
we'd been moving. "You could see for miles in all direc-
tions from that knoll," I said. "I didn't see a single tree.
Where did they come from?" A thick forest had sprung
out of nowhere. Lush ferns, bushes of deep green and
light with bright-colored berries, and trees of every species imaginable—and some I doubted existed in my
world—dotted the landscape.

"I told you," Faolán said. I was getting sick of his dis-
dainful tone. "*O Anel* is special. It isn't like the human
realm we've been imprisoned in. Nothing here is as it
seems."

Sunlight streamed through the many branches forming a canopy above us. The eerie yet ethereal light cap-
tivated me, swelling my chest with warm emotion. Beautiful.
Faolán was right; I'd never seen anything so awe inspir-
ing in all of my existence.

Up ahead, the trees began to clear. I squinted through
the muted light, trying to make out the shapes looming
in the distance. They looked oddly familiar, but I doubted
my own eyes. How could it be? Faolán moved with silent
grace beside me, barely rustling a blade of grass as he
walked. My bones hummed with the power he exuded,
growing stronger the closer we came to the hulking
shapes. Something of great importance and even greater
power lay ahead of us, and my stomach clenched in fear
of what I'd see.

"I haven't been here for centuries," Faolán mused,
"but even still, its power calls to me."

The circle of stones stood tall and proud, nothing like
it did in the human world. But there was no mistaking

the pattern: the larger circle and the smaller one inside of it, the rough, natural placement of the stones, and the archways they constructed. And though I'd never seen it in person, and though this circle was complete and not damaged by time and man's interference, there was no doubt of what I was looking at.

"Stonehenge," I murmured.

Faolán laughed. "In the beginning, before the hourglass was split, it was called *Kotja A'ma.* Font of Time."

If I'd thought Faolán's power overwhelming, it was a drop in the bucket to what I felt coming from the ring of stones. I had no doubt *O Anel's* name had sprung from this place. I was staring at the true Faerie Ring, the heart of this realm and probably the twin to the heart of the mundane world. I stood in awe of the structure. A divinity resided here, a connection to something bigger than me—or anything I knew, for that matter. It stole the breath from my lungs to look at it, and I averted my gaze, so overcome by its power.

"Now you see," Faolán whispered, "why I would do anything to return to this place."

I could. In fact, I'd lost track of the minutes as we stood here. Panic set in as I tried to calculate how much time we'd spent behind the veil. Thirty minutes? An hour? Oh God, how I could I have been so careless? Months could have already passed in the human world. I turned in a circle and ran my fingers through my hair, pulling at the roots. I was poised for a full-on anxiety attack.

"Darian, stop your fidgeting and come here." Faolán's voice bounced around inside my brain, bringing with it a foggy confusion. What had I been upset about?

I walked to his side like any obedient pet, and he pulled me close, as though we were simply two friends looking at a blazing sunset or silvery moon. His silence pressed upon me, coupled with the control he exuded with no effort whatsoever. Idly, he traced a pattern on my wrist with his thumb. "There is something special about you. The other Guardians were weak. They died after I'd taken their blood. A powerful Guardian used her blood to imprison me. It took the blood from an equally powerful Guardian to release me. None of the three who came before you could withstand the connection. And their power wasn't enough to release me from stone. None of them loved deeply enough. But you . . . ," he said, trailing off with a sigh. "You are different. Your strength astounds me. This was meant to be, and you have done well. Perhaps I won't kill you after all. If you continue to prove your worth, I will give you a place of honor in the new world."

Through the haze, a small shred of my mind forced its way to the surface. It seemed easier to do here, in this place steeped in magic. Strong? I felt so weak. I let him control me. I didn't have the will to fight him; yet he thought me strong. A force apart from Faolán supported me, holding me up under the pressure of his influence. I felt safe despite the danger. Brakae was close. Somehow I recognized her energy as a pure force of nature, like a breeze that blew the fog from my mind. Maybe with her help, we could undo this clusterfuck after all.

I couldn't let Faolán in on my clarity. So, like a good little zombie slave, I stood passively at his side, accepting his light touch as if I had no other choice. What I really wanted to do was break his arm in two.

"What now?" I asked, ignoring his musings. "I brought you here, like you wanted me to do."

"Yes, you did." He patted the top of my head, and I suppressed the urge to slap his hand away. "But this is only the beginning, Darian. There is much to be done."

"What?"

His lips curved into a sardonic smile. "Why would I tell you?" he said. "No, I think I'd best keep that secret to myself for the time being. First, we have to find the Time Keeper. And after she surrenders her half of the hourglass, all will be set aright."

I could only guess what kind of shit storm would be caused by bringing the two halves together. "What makes you think she'll do that?" I mean, give me a break.

Faolán had to be pretty full of himself to think this would all tie together with a neat little bow.

"I have no doubt she will." His confidence sickened me. "She's going to surrender the glass to you."

"Not likely." But the cold feeling of dread sliding down my spine said otherwise. Reaver hadn't tried to stop me. In fact, I probably could have marched right up to the front door and asked for it. But since I had not a goddamned clue why that was, I had to assume Faolán knew something I didn't. I mean, didn't everyone have one up on me in the knowledge department?

Faolán turned me to face him so quickly and so roughly, it nearly gave me whiplash. He hit me across the face—with a closed fucking fist—a right hook that sent me headfirst to the ground. *Christ*, I was tired of getting smacked around. Blood trickled from my nose, mouth, and cheek, staining the grass that cushioned the unbattered side of my face.

Before I could drag my sorry ass up to a sitting position, Faolán drew the dagger from his belt. The veins of green glowed bright against the black, and he pounced, pinning my legs beneath his and holding me down with his hand constricting my airway. He held the dagger high and looked around us, his eyes glowing deadly silver. "She is beloved by your father!" Faolán shouted to the sky. "Do you hear me, Brakae? Will you sit idly by and watch her die?"

Fucker! Faolán was well versed in the ways of abusive control. Mental, emotional, physical—oh yeah, he had it covered, the triple play of abuse. My entire face throbbed, and my blood continued to flow, which shouldn't have happened. I usually healed fast, almost instantaneously. And I hurt like *hell*. Unconsciousness threatened, the pain sending me into a state of near shock. I hadn't felt this degree of prolonged agony since—well—since the beatings I'd endured from an abusive husband in my human life.

Silence answered us. A dead silence made all the more dramatic for the promise inherent in Faolán's words. He'd kill me and not even bat an eyelash. I'd brought him to Brakae, making me as good as expendable. "Perhaps she thinks I'm bluffing," he said more to himself than to me. "I'm sorry, Darian, but I'm going to have to prove to the Time Keeper just how dire your situation is."

Sure, he warned me, but that didn't mean I was close to prepared when he brought his arm down in one forceful, sweeping motion. He drew the dagger across my skin from my collarbone to my sternum, opening a deep gash in my flesh. Screams pierced the still air. *Shut the fuck up!* I thought, until I realized I was the one screaming. Liquid fire seared from the wound, spreading through my body like poison.

His laughter fueled my rage, and I snarled like a wounded animal, working my broken jaw, despite the hurt it caused me, to toss out a string of curses. Holy shit, I was in some serious pain. My body could start with the healing . . . anytime now. . . . Come *on*, damn it. *Heal.* "Faolán!" I shrieked. "I'm going to enjoy watching you die!"

"Quiet." The command stalled my mind, numbed my pain, and stilled my body. Our surroundings blurred in my vision, leaving only the two of us alone in a sea of gray nothing. Faolán towered above me, looking too far away to be so close. "I'm going to kill her!" he shouted again. "Just like the others! Do you think your father will weep for her? Will he relive the pain of losing his child? Would you be the one to deliver that agony upon him for the second time? I. *Will*. Kill. Her!" His words rent the still air, ragged and strained with his rage. He looked down, his eyebrow cocked, and he whispered the last words for me alone. "Believe it."

Something in the distance stole his focus from the business of sending me to my death. Lucidity returned, and with it an excruciating pain that made me want to retreat back into my mind, anywhere but the present moment. My breath came in shallow pants—all I could manage with Faolán's hand squeezing my throat. Above me the dagger hovered in his fist, dripping my own blood onto my body. He leaned back, his grip slackened, and I resisted the urge to turn my head and look. But when I noticed the half-crazed expression creep onto his face, my heart sank into my stomach. *Stupid girl.* She'd done just what I would've done in her situation.

Brakae had surrendered.

Chapter 24

Faolán eased himself up from the ground, dismissing me like an insect beneath his boot. I could have just closed my eyes and drifted away right there in the fragrant grass for all the attention he paid. He stumbled backward, his eyes glued to the figure standing barely beyond my line of sight. Hate, jealousy, and—could it be?—love twisted his features into something even more otherworldly than he already was.

The longer we'd been in this strange place, the more his Fae glamour slid away, as if he couldn't spare the concentration to keep the guise intact. And I focused on those things: his face, the way his body trembled in Brakae's presence, the slight shifting of his eyes, how they'd become rounder and brighter. Because if I didn't, I'd succumb to my fear and pain, and I'd be damned if Faolán saw me weakened by anything he'd done.

Grass rustled in the distance, and with it came a stirring breeze and the fragrant scent of Shaede, though there was something foreign about it that my senses could not identify. I closed my eyes, the hairs standing on my arms as I felt her presence beside me. She knelt and gathered my head in her hands, cradling it on her lap. *Don't open your eyes,* I thought as she combed her fingers through my hair, sweeping it away from my temple. *Just lie here and sleep.*

"Faolán, my love." Brakae's words jump-started my heart as if I'd been struck by lightning. "What have you done?"

I'd heard her wrong. Of course, she'd said, "Faolán, you *low-life piece of shit*, what have you done?"

But, no, just like all of the lovely surprises in my life, I'd heard her plain as day. "My hand has been forced." The longing in his voice was unmistakable. "You helped them imprison me. And why? For the pestilence known as humanity? I loved you. I love you still; yet you would rather see *me* dead than a race so disgustingly fragile their lives are nothing more than a flash of lightning against a black sky."

Here I was, sliced open and bleeding to death in a realm where time flew by at a blurring pace, with Brakae and Faolán positioned on either side of my battered body having a bittersweet lovers' reunion. Wasn't this just fan-fucking-tastic? Brakae continued to stroke my hair—did the whole of the supernatural community have an affinity for petting?—as Faolán paced back and forth, as agitated as I'd ever seen him.

"This is an old argument," Brakae said. "Too old for us to revisit. Life, *all life*, is precious, and there is not one of us who deserves a higher place above another. I will not reopen healed wounds by entertaining your madness again."

Hello? Anyone remember the bleeding girl here? And why the *hell* was I still not healing? God, I wanted to pass out from the pain. Yet the little *Days of Our Lives* moment unfolding at my head and feet kept me nice and conscious. "I hate to interrupt," I said, struggling to lean up at least on one elbow. "But, Brakae, this should be the part where you stand up and run the fuck away!"

"Shhh." She cupped the side of my face Faolán hadn't managed to break. "Don't worry. I trust you."

You trust me? What the hell kind of thing was that to say at a moment like this? Good Lord, I was beginning to wish Faolán would hurry up and kill me, just to give me a reprieve from all of their cryptic talk and strange behavior.

"Get up," Faolán commanded, and I felt my world go

fuzzy and gray. "I don't have time for idle discussions. Brakae, take us to the glass."

I looked up at Raif's daughter, the deadly smile on her face an exact replica of his. How had I not recognized it the moment I'd met her? A light of calculation gleamed in her sapphire eyes. Maybe she wasn't as harmless as I'd thought. "Yes," she said as she placed her hands under my arms, easing me to a sitting position. "It's time to go."

"Why is my body not healing?" I asked close to her ear. Confusion swirled in my mind from Faolán's influence, countered by the cleansing effects of Brakae's close proximity. A war was being waged within my mind, and I didn't like it one damned bit. "I'm not going to be much use to you beat up and bleeding. Not to mention weaponless."

"A Fae dagger," Brakae murmured. "It has been forged with magic," she said. "You'll heal, but not quickly. If he'd wanted you dead, he would have driven the blade through your heart."

Son of a bitch. For once Azriel hadn't been a complete liar. He'd told me once only a magic blade could kill me. The asshole knew about the blade, and about what I would eventually become. Who would have thought his lies had been woven with the truth? "He's controlling me," I said. "I may not be able to fight him."

"Darian, you're talking too much again." Faolán pulled me away from Brakae, tucking me safely behind him. "Now be quiet and move along."

Brakae remained stoic but pleasant as she led us from the circle of stones down a winding path as if we had nothing better to do than take a leisurely stroll in an enchanted forest. Blood trickled down my chest, soaking my shirt. If I ever got out of this mess, I'd ceremoniously burn this particular outfit. I ignored the lush green forest, the brilliant blue sky peppered with dragonflies and other buzzing creatures too strange to be mere insects. I felt the presence of magic all around me and other creatures watching from their hiding places. But none of this mattered or held me rapt. My mind dwelled on one thing and one thing only: Tyler, and the fact that I would more than likely never see him again.

"You're not really thinking of handing your half of the hourglass over to Faolán, are you?" At least I could use impending death and disaster to get my mind off Tyler. "I mean, you do realize he's not planning to bring peace to the world or anything like that."

"No," Brakae said. "I plan on handing it over to you."

Was everyone out of their fucking minds? I was the last person on the face of the earth who should have that glass. "I don't know how well you've thought this through, Brakae, but I would advise against that."

She looked back and flashed me a very Raif-like smile. "I trust you."

Fantastic.

I worked my jaw back and forth, thankful it had finally begun to heal. The swelling in my eye had gone down, and I traced the cut on my cheek, now scabbed over. It wasn't my usual speedy recovery, though it was better than human. My chest still felt like I'd been gored with a red-hot poker, but the blood no longer flowed. A gentle twist of my shoulders sent a violent spasm of pain clear through to my spine. Bleeding or not, I was still pretty worked over.

"Darian, my father?" Through the strength, I could sense the sadness in her words. "Is he well?"

How was I supposed to answer that? "I don't know," I said as I walked behind Faolán. The last time I saw my mentor, his daughter's ex was driving a knife into his gut. Honestly, I didn't think it would help our situation if I told her Raif might very well be dead. "But he'd better be all right." I lowered my voice for Faolán alone and fixed him with an accusatory glare.

I had to believe Raif had survived Faolán's attack. He was one of the strongest people I knew. There was no way a stab to the stomach would kill him—even if it was with a Fae blade. My mentor was too damned tough for that.

I wondered if she knew about all that had happened since her disappearance. Her mother had died trying to find her, for Christ's sake. How could I possibly break the news that her mother had been dead for centuries? And that her father might have died because I'd dragged him into this mess. "Brakae—" I took a deep breath to calm my nerves and started again. "You've been gone a long time." Shit, this was hard. I didn't often break bad news to people. "Your mother . . ."

"Moira told me," she answered before I could continue. "She brings me news of my loved ones. You can't imagine how frustrating it is to be here, unable to communicate."

Moira. That devious bitch. "She's known you were here—talks to you even—and she *never* told Raif you were alive?" Death was too good for her. When I got my hands on her, I'd make sure her torture was slow and painful.

"It's not like that," Brakae said. "You shouldn't think ill of her. It is not her place to speak for me. She's not a Guardian of this realm, and the natural order must be protected at all cost."

Oh good. More cryptic explanations. Someone was going to give me a straight answer for once, damn it. "Oh yeah, well, what about—"

"Darian, silence." Faolán's voice cut through my mind, effectively stifling my voice and putting an end to any questions I might be tempted to ask.

As we continued to walk, I abandoned trying to speak through Faolán's absolute control. *O Anel* became my sole focus, the Faerie Realm and all its wonders pressing in on me. In the human world, I sensed the energy of the supernatural like an assault on my body. Bones humming, skin crawling, breath stalling . . . I felt it all. But here, the energy of every being, every tree, every blade of grass mingled and became one. And the way it wove around me, permeated my senses, gave me peace instead of pause. Fear did not exist in this place—nor common sense, apparently. But despite my circumstances, the wounds that healed too slowly, and the thoughts of never seeing Tyler again, I was not afraid.

We walked for a good hour before Brakae stopped at the face of a large granite rock. At least fifteen feet tall and draped with moss and clinging vines, a gaping maw of an opening invited us to enter. An ethereal golden light emanated from its dark depths, warm and pulsing with magic. "Brakae," I said, my voice finally coming through, thick and sleepy, "I hope you know what you're doing."

She answered with a soft glowing smile, though the gleam in her eyes screamed of steel-hard strength. This woman was one hundred percent Raif's daughter, and I realized, as she stepped through the curtain of vines and moss, that *I* trusted *her*.

At Faolán's urging, I stepped through the curtain behind Brakae, my breath catching at the sight of her. No longer the poised woman, Raif's daughter stood before me, the child I'd first met in my dreams. Time had no rules here. And wondrous magic ran rampant. I was *so* out of my league.

"Come here, Darian." Her tiny voice urged me forward. "I'll show you what you've come so far to fetch."

Her soft little hand twined around mine, leading me deeper into the cave, which defied the laws of physics with the scope of its size. Like Reaver's basement, this place sprawled out before us, lush grass, a pool of water—and holy shit!—gigantic trees. Brakae padded in front of me, Faolán pressed close at my back. Both were fighting for control of me in one capacity or another. And I walked helpless between them, unable to act to the benefit of either while they played their tug-of-war.

"Stop," Faolán said, winding his arm around my waist. His dagger pressed into the flesh at my neck. "Brakae, my dear, I think it best you stay with me and let Darian retrieve the glass for you."

She shrugged, her tiny shoulders thrown back, posture straight as a little soldier. "If that's what you want, Faolán."

"Yes," he said, beckoning her with a finger. "That is what I want."

She came to me, squeezed my fingers in her hand, and smiled. "As a Guardian, you may retrieve the glass for me. You and no one else."

"Do it." Faolán shoved me forward, his command overtaking any hope of lucid thought.

Brakae's half of the hourglass sat nestled in a tree trunk. The main body of the tree had broken off long ago, and graying spears of splintered wood jutted up around the hourglass, encasing it like sharp, pointed teeth. But for all its menacing appearance, I plucked the glass from its perch with ease, just as I had with Reaver's half. The supernatural world had its mysteries, but it didn't know shit about security. Go figure.

Golden sand swirled in a torrent, probably sensing its other half nearby. As if worried, time ceased its natural rhythm, abandoning order for chaos. I turned to find Brakae no longer the child, but the adolescent just blossoming into womanhood. Faolán stood before her, pain distorting his features as he looked upon her. A deep and scarring resentment flared bright in his silver eyes, and at once I shared that pain. It was the agony only a broken heart could cause.

"Bring it to me." His voice, thick with emotion, choked on the words. My heart raced in my chest as I fought the compulsion to do as he asked. As if unaware of my mind, my body responded, hurrying to his side, despite the burning, throbbing pain radiating from my torso with every step. Brakae stood silent, her face emotionless, save her eyes, which spoke of a sorrow too deep to express.

I could stop this if I played my cards right. Though, to be honest, I had no fucking clue what Faolán planned to accomplish by bringing the two halves of the hourglass together. A few feet would close the gap between us. I stopped, despite the urge to go to his side. "I want to know what you're going to do," I said, digging my heels into the earth. "And then, I'll give this to you."

"I am going to end this perversion." He ground the words through clenched teeth. "I am going to heal the flow of time. There will no longer be two realms between us, but a single place. And our kind will not be forced to hide our true natures from creatures too narrow-minded and filled with fear to accept that which is extraordinary."

"And you will kill all of humanity in the process," Brakae whispered. "Please, Faolán, if you love me, you won't go through with this."

Hang on just a damned minute. "Do you mean to tell me, if Faolán puts the hourglass together, every human in the world is going to die?" Brakae gave me a look as if to say, *Isn't that just what I said?* "What exactly is going to happen if he puts that thing back together?"

"In the realms, time runs parallel to itself, though at different rates of speed. Mending the glass will merge the realms. *O Anel* with the mundane world. The veil between us will be lifted, and that parallel line in the human world will have to accelerate to match the pace of time here. They will age, Darian. Instantaneously. Before our eyes they will turn to dust and be no more."

Well, there was no way *in hell* I was going to let that happen. Sliced open and bleeding, zombie mind control or not, I could not allow Faolán to follow through with this insanity. "Listen to her," I said, taking the diplomatic path first. "I can't let you go through with this."

Faolán laughed, though the humor did not spread to the rest of his face. "You have no choice. I've had your blood, and you are mine by right of the oldest magic. Now, bring me the glass."

Could I drop it? Just smash it into pieces? If the sands of time itself swirled in the hourglass, what would happen if I dropped it? Whom would I kill? The inhabitants of this world? Mine? Both? It was too much to chance. I looked to Brakae. Her body quavered for a moment as the illusion of her young body grew to reveal the grown woman once again. Steel determination mingled with sadness, and I knew by the expression on her face that she would do what had to be done. No matter what she felt for him, she would kill Faolán before she would let him kill billions of people all in the name of his twisted version of love. Thank God she was on my side, because if she possessed even a fraction of her father's prowess in battle, Faolán was shit out of luck.

Toe by toe, my foot began to slip toward Faolán. I fought for all I was worth, leaning away from him as my body rebelled against my mind. *Anytime, Brakae,* I thought, trying to give her a silent signal. *Whatever you're going to do, you'd better do it—now.* No such luck. Either I was a piss-poor nonverbal communicator, or she just didn't think this was the right time to act. Regardless, stalling had gained me nothing more than a renewed attempt by Faolán to control me. His power flooded my body and mind, flowing through my blood with every beat of my heart. And as my mind clouded with only one thought, my feet and legs responded. *Go to him. Give him what he wants. Do. Not. Fight.*

My arms reached out toward him, confusion swirling in my brain, and everything but Faolán blurred out of focus. He smiled, an expression of pure madness, and he plucked the second half of the hourglass from my waiting hands.

I looked at Brakae, her face shrouded as if by mist. An almost indiscernible nod of her head was all I needed. I knew what would happen if I gave Faolán total control. I'd blacked out at the hotel twice. Like a light switch was being flicked off and on again inside my brain, I'd awoken from a state of prolonged unconsciousness, only to find that mere moments had passed. Time would mean nothing once I surrendered to him. I'd have no memories from now until Faolán decided to restore my self-control.

But Brakae wanted me to do this, and I had to trust

that she believed that giving myself over to Faolán was for my own protection. Standing on the precipice of losing myself completely, I looked into that dark abyss and smiled. No fear. No regret. You can't win without losing. And so, with Brakae's faith to support my decision, I stepped off the edge into the darkness.

Chapter 25

"You know what it's like to be separated from your love," Faolán said with all the fervor of the brokenhearted. "Imagine knowing your Jinn lived just beyond your reach, and you were stuck in a place you hated, forced to live there in order to protect the one thing you were forbidden to see."

Blinking to clear my vision, I looked around, completely unaware of my surroundings. As though waking suddenly from the deepest sleep, I realized I'd been brought back from whatever dark place Faolán had cast me into. The last thing I remembered was standing in the mouth of the granite cave. And now I found myself in a darkened forest, lightless save the silvery glow of the moon overhead, while Faolán held his dagger against my flesh and prattled on like a preacher at his pulpit. "You cannot deny you have experienced the pain of separation."

Thanks to you, I do know what that feels like, dickhead. But I thought better of lending my voice to the complaint. Faolán held me close, one arm wrapped tight around my waist. Though his words were for me alone, he gazed past me, toward the woman sitting beneath the swaying branches of a rowan tree. Brakae faced us, the two halves of the broken hourglass resting on the ground beside her, the tears in her eyes reflected in the swirling golden light as the sands of time rebelled against the inevitability of what would soon take place. What the hell had happened since I'd been out of it? Something magical bound her too, her helpless expression proof enough that she could force her way free no better than I. She looked at me and then at Faolán, a silent sob escaping her lips. She had loved him once. And that love had driven him to insanity.

"She is the most beautiful creature I have ever beheld," Faolán said, his voice breaking with emotion. "I never wanted her here. Trapped. Bound to chaos for eternity. How do you think it made me feel to know that the next time I saw her, she might not be the woman I could hold in my arms? What was I supposed to do with a child? Protect her and nothing more. It disgusts me. Time is perverse this close to The Ring—and that perversion is tied to *her*. It doesn't have to be, though. I could never stay as long as I wanted. Every visit was a gamble, and too, too short." Faolán waved the dagger before him in a flourish, as if showing me a point of interest. "Just as you live in the mundane, Moira lives here with Brakae. Of course, Guardians can travel between the realms. She visits the mundane world often, as once I would come to *O Anel* at my pleasure. And why this rule of nature? I ask you. Why could I not live here with Brakae and Moira with her brother? How better to protect the one I loved than to be with her always? But no. That is not the way. We must maintain the balance."

"Faolán," I rasped through a too-dry throat, "it's not too late to stop this."

"I should have stopped this millennia ago," Faolán snarled in my ear. "It is far too late to change course. I will take this hourglass to *Kotja A'ma*, and there I will merge the realms." I stared at him, completely uncomprehending.

"You must understand how it all began, Darian," he continued. "I was a warrior, once. The right hand of the goddess Badb. The Enphigmalé were bred to fight, and we served our purpose, making war against Badb's enemies. The blood of our foes pooled on the battlefield." His shoulders slumped as if the weight of his past forced him down. "It was so long ago, the memories are like remnants of dreams."

I knew how Faolán felt. I had only a century under my belt, and memories from my human childhood were hazy and without detail. I could only imagine what recalling the events from thousands of years ago would be like: lifetimes' worth of memories slipping through the mental cracks.

"The humans kept their distance from the Fae. Soon their curiosity of the extraordinary turned to fear and hatred." Faolán's dreamy countenance faded, and the muscles flexed in his cheek as he clenched his jaw. "War broke out between the humans and the Fae, but they were weak and fragile, and our armies decimated their numbers until few remained. The gods had come to love their human children and could no longer bear to see them killed."

"You sound bitter, Faolán," I muttered. "Upset you couldn't commit genocide when you had the chance?"

"I'd been bred to kill." His voice was a low growl in my ear. "What do you think?"

"You're not inherently cruel." Brakae's soft voice broke into our conversation. "Faolán, Badb would have never made you a protector if you were nothing more than a vicious killer."

His smile was sad as he turned his gaze on her. "The Enphigmalé had sworn an oath to serve Badb, and she pulled us from the battlefield. I was the wolf of war no longer. She made me a Guardian. Chosen to protect . . ."

I pulled away from Faolán's grasp, hoping he was too distracted to hold me. "Be still," he growled, and I had no choice but to obey the command. "You'll hear me out. Badb took the hourglass and broke it in two. The veil was created to protect humanity, and she split the world into separate realms that stood apart from each other, yet existed in a natural accord. Our kind was forced to make a choice: Live openly here, never to visit the mortal realm again, or live there, where we are forced to hide our true selves for the benefit of a lowly, ignorant species. She appointed two Time Keepers to watch over the halves of the hourglasses that maintained the flow of time, and Guardians to protect the doorways to each realm. We were each given a key. My key opened the doorway from the mortal realm into *O Anel*. And so in the mortal realm I would reside.

"For centuries after the realms had been split, there was unrest. Many sought to seize the hourglasses and thereby control time. So many Keepers died. I'd never cared before. The others before Brakae meant nothing to me. But then I fell in love," he almost whispered.

"I loved you too, Faolán. How could I not?" Brakae shifted as if she wanted to stand, but something prevented her. "You were fierce and passionate and loyal. A true protector, though you believed yourself nothing but a heartless warrior." Her voice broke. "You were gentle. Don't you remember how you comforted me when I was afraid?"

Something glistened in Faolán's eyes, pooling like mercury. Tears? He cleared his throat and turned his gaze from Brakae as if her words threatened to convince him to change his course. "Everything changed. I no longer wished to live amongst the mundane and watch from afar. Protecting the doorway to *O Anel* and maintaining the balance of time became an asinine notion. I cared for nothing but her; yet I was forced to abide by tradition and follow the path Badb had laid out for me. I abhorred it. I despise it still. And when I rose up against my goddess, I prompted my brothers-in-arms to do the same. Warriors, bound by oath and blood, they yearned for battle and were more than eager to see an end to Badb's peace. The Enphigmalé were her first children, her most beloved, and she cast us aside for her precious humans. They wanted revenge as much as I did. We wanted to lift the veil between the realms and see an end to her segregation once and for all. I was betrayed by the woman I loved and the goddess I had worshipped for thousands of years. Badb allowed Moira to raise an army, and Brakae, ever the devoted Time Keeper, kept to her vow to protect the natural order, even if that meant destroying our love in the process. She lured us into an ambush.

Well outnumbered, we were easily captured and had no choice but to wait until Badb passed judgment.

"We were sentenced to be frozen in time and made to stand guard for all eternity. And over what?" he shouted. "Nothing! An empty dais and ceaseless time. But before I went to serve my sentence in that solitary green place, I bade an Oracle to help me. Her sister had been killed over the same secret I'd sworn to protect: that of Brakae's existence in the Faerie Realm. She was all too willing to find a way for both of us to be avenged. Love had sent me to my end, she said, and only love would release me from my prison."

As Faolán rambled on, I listened with half an ear while I looked around us in search of escape. I wrenched myself free enough to glance behind me, and I noticed that Faolán had shed his glamour completely. Though it didn't change him much, I found him almost too beautiful for my eyes to comprehend. The strands of his hair glowed faintly in the dark, and his eyes, not a touch of gray left, shone completely silver. Had he been so tall before? And had his skin been so flawless and smooth? He'd fucked with my brain to the point where I had a hard time recalling. But I could see why, in this magical place, Brakae would have been drawn to him. I found it hard myself to tear my gaze away.

"The veil was created to protect *humanity*!" Faolán shouted, breaking me from my trance. "On either side of the veil, *we* suffer! But no more!" He exuded the raw charisma of a dictator. It wouldn't be hard for Faolán to sway others to his cause. "I will set our world aright and rid it of humanity once and for all!"

I expected a Yankee Stadium–sized round of applause and shouts when he concluded his tirade. I'm sure he imagined one. His diatribe did nothing for me except make me want to spit in his face. Clarity returned with every shout of his fervent oration, and I no longer sensed his utter control, though I didn't doubt it could return at a moment's notice. Brakae sat helpless, watching us with the calculation of a hunting cat more than that of a curious kitten. I needed her like this: an adult for starters, mature of mind and body, and able to fight if need be. An unsure teenager or wobbly child would do neither of us any good, and I hoped for once that time would be on my side.

"Faolán," she implored, "this is not you! The man I fell in love with would never have killed innocent people. If you do this, you lose me forever. Is that what you want?"

His demeanor changed from anxious to enraged as he released his hold on me and shoved me to the ground. "I have lost you already!" he railed. "What has passed can never be undone!"

"Exactly!" Brakae said, her tone harsh. "It can never be undone. So why seek revenge? Whom will it punish? No one. This is madness!"

"This is a necessity! And I will do what must be done!"

Faolán had to have fallen far to have once been worthy of Brakae's love. I found nothing in him even remotely lovable or redeemable. But then again, I'd thought I loved Azriel once. The heart wasn't only blind; it was deaf and dumb. Tyler's obsessive nature had infuriated me; yet I loved him fiercely for it. I doubted there was anything he could do to make me fall out of love with him.

Whether Brakae had loved Faolán or not, I had an obligation to protect not only the key to the Faerie Realm, but also time and the natural order. My conscience would not allow me to stand idly by while Faolán killed off every last human on the planet just because he'd suffered a broken heart. Talk about displaced rage. Faolán had been right about one thing: All the events of my life had led me to this one moment. My transformation from human to Shaede; my hidden existence from the world by Azriel's secrets and lies; my eventual discovery by Xander; my love for Tyler; the blood sacrifice to give life to lifeless statues—all of it had led me to this.

Faolán pointed the dagger at Brakae. "Come here, my love."

Standing with fluid grace, Brakae made her way to us.

Her gait was slow, as if she resisted some invisible pull. I recognized that zombie dance, though I wasn't sure how Faolán was able to control her. Faerie magic went way over my head. Another encyclopedia's worth of information I'd have to pay Levi for—if I made it out of here in one piece, and if he was still alive when I got home. Brakae's eyes, glowing soft blue in the wan moonlight, darted back and forth from me to him and back again. The stern set of her jaw told me she was fighting like hell. The way Faolán drew her to him like a magnet told me she was losing.

"Darian," he said, so calm I knew something bad was coming, "you have exceeded my expectations of you. You are the strongest Guardian I have ever known, except maybe for myself. Had we met under different circumstances I would have initiated you into our order, given you a place of honor. But you have worn out your usefulness, and I have no need for useless things. Go well into the afterlife."

He pulled the dagger away from my throat and handed it to Brakae before he shoved me hard into her arms. She caught me against her, looked deep into my eyes, and whispered, "I hope you're as tough as everyone thinks you are, Darian. Remember, I trust you." And before I could ask her what the hell was going on, she plunged the blade into my abdomen, low and to the right, carefully—or not so carefully—missing any major organs, just below my ribs.

"Wake up. You have things to do, and you're wasting time!"

The sound of her voice was a high-pitched buzz increasing in volume as I came nearer to consciousness. A gnat hovering at my ear would have been no less annoying.

"Where is he?" I asked. That sonofabitch was going to pay for what he'd done to me.

The Sprite swirled around my head to the other ear, as if the one she'd been speaking into had malfunctioned or something. "He has stolen time and time's Keeper. It won't be long before everything is destroyed."

Even though I happened to be in the loop on this particular matter, I hated cryptic talk. Just once, I wanted someone to lay it out for me without the fancy subtext. What a serious waste of time.

"Look, Tinkerbell, how about telling me something I don't already know?" I said, batting all four or five inches of her away from my ear canal. "Wait a sec." My torso throbbed with every word, and I laid my head back down on the grass to stave off a wave of nausea. "How do I know you're a Sprite?"

She giggled before circling my head in a dizzying loop. If I hadn't felt like yakking before, that was sure to do it. All around me, I heard the cacophony of tiny wings buzzing. As my vision cleared and the star-filled sky came better into focus, I realized they weren't stars at all, but a scattering of Sprites glowing with a faint bluish light. I felt a lot like Gulliver surrounded by all these Lilliputians.

"Lie still," she ordered in her tiny voice. "You need a Healer, but she hasn't arrived. We'll have to make do without her. You're stabbed."

"No shit," I said, rubbing my temple. Brakae fucking *stabbed* me. What the hell was all that about? Not exactly the best way to ensure your protector is in her best fighting form. "I don't suppose you or any of your little friends up there know how long I've been lying here?"

"Not long for *O Anel*," she said.

Wonderful. Just the answer I was looking for. She might as well have said, *You've been here for-fucking-ever, you idiot!*

I pushed the thought of centuries passing in the mortal realm from my mind and focused on what I needed to do to get out of this goddamned backward place. The calm attitudes I'd encountered so far were starting to get on my last nerve. And that nerve was hanging on by a thread. The wound didn't hurt as bad as the one left by Faolán across my chest, but that wasn't saying much.

Even if I could manage to find a weapon, I doubted I'd be able to wield one. Not to mention that I had no fucking idea where Brakae and Faolán had gone or how to find them.

I looked up to the sky and the floating blue lights descending toward me. Like snowflakes, they landed around me, on top of me, a couple on my forehead for Christ's sake! "Do you mind?" I said, shaking my head. The Sprites laughed, a sound that reminded me of crickets chirping, and jumped to the ground like a scattering of dandelion seeds.

"Didn't you hear what I said? You need a Healer, but we can help to at least mend your wounds." This one seemed to speak for all of them. Maybe they were shy. "If you'll be still, we can get to work."

Her sweet voice couldn't have sounded more annoyed. I had a tendency to get on people's nerves. And on the nerves of Shaedes. And Sidhe. And Lyhtans. And Fae. Now I could add Sprites to my list. If Tyler could see me now, sprawled out on the grass while itty-bitty creatures administered my medical care, he'd bust a gut laughing. I closed my eyes, reliving our last moments together, wrapped in each other's arms. Tears stung my eyes, and my stomach twisted with the anxiety of what I might find when I returned home. What if he hadn't waited for me, or worse, what if he wouldn't forgive me?

A shiver raced across my skin as the Sprites went to work, walking around on my body as if it were a construction site. In my mind, I pictured them with tiny hard hats and rolled-up sets of blueprints. But when I opened my eyes, I saw their serious faces and urgent concern as they poked around the wounds, sewing them up with sparkling strings that looked like cobwebs.

"This has got to be some of the craziest shit I have ever seen." I talked more to myself than to the Sprites. But really, I wished I were talking to Tyler. I needed someone who understood how completely surreal these moments were to me. I mean, even as a Shaede, I never thought I'd see little picturesque creatures with transparent wings sewing me up with supernatural thread. I could almost hear *The Twilight Zone* theme in the distance.

I don't know what they used, how they did it, or what magic aided them. Warmth radiated from the wounds, but not the fiery heat that had pained me before. The sensation comforted me, and I didn't even feel the prick of a needle, that is, if they'd used one. Magic lived and breathed in *O Anel* with a steady pulse I felt all around me. But I also sensed the sadness of this place pressing in on me. "Why is nobody happy here?" I asked. "It seems like a pretty damned nice place to live."

"There is no consistency this close to *O Anel*." This was said by the—what should I call her?—*foreman* Sprite. "The natural order is all about balance. You cannot have order without chaos. The mundane world keeps order, so we are left with its other half."

I had yet to see anything even remotely chaotic in this peaceful place. Obviously this Sprite hadn't seen the real world, where people warred over the silliest things and famine and disease stole the lives of thousands. They'd probably never witnessed a natural disaster or seen the effects of pollution. Faolán had seen it, and it had driven him mad. "You're wrong," I said. "This place can't possibly be chaos. It's way too perfect."

The Sprite laughed. I wanted to call her Cindy or Judy. She had that suburban look about her. She reminded me of a soccer mom: efficient and put together, perfectly coiffed and unflappable, like she ran a tight ship, remembered everyone's schedules, and knew how to keep her brood of children in line. "Chaos isn't always easy to see. You haven't been here long enough to recognize it and form opinions based on more careful observation."

"What's your name?" I had to know. I was moving on to Vanessa or Carri as possible choices.

"Nila." Huh, never would have thought of that one, but somehow the name fit with her large brown eyes, russet skin, and shoulder-length brown hair. "The sun rises and sets just as it should in the mundane world. The seasons come and go according to schedule. The tides ebb and flow. That is the order of your world. And you should feel fortunate to be gifted with its stability."

Stability. That was a joke. But I supposed in a realm where you could see miles of green meadow and suddenly walk into a copse of trees that sprang out of nowhere, the mortal realm might seem to be a fairly stable place. "Where's Faolán?" I steered the conversation back where it needed to be. "I don't have time to waste. I can't let him mend that hourglass."

Nila eyed my wounds, much like the job foreman I imagined her to be. "A few moments more, if you'll just *sit still*." Testing the flesh with her finger as if judging a baking cake, she added, "And even then you won't be completely healed. You need—"

"I know," I said with a sigh. "A Healer." Running at half capacity wasn't ideal, though if it was the best I was going to get, I'd have to take it. But a healed body and all the time in the world weren't going to help me if I couldn't find Brakae and the bastard who'd taken her. "Where's Faolán?" I asked again. "Do you know how to find him?"

"Brakae is no fool," Nila said. "All you have to do is follow the trail she's left for you. Now lie back," she said, stomping her foot down on my forehead, "and let us finish up here. As you said, you don't have time to waste."

Chapter 26

I lay back and waited for Nila and her team to finish sewing me up. Two potentially mortal wounds in one day weren't an all-time record for me, but the rate at which I healed was breaking all sorts of records. It took a considerable amount of concentration to keep from banging my head against the ground in frustration. Too many variables stood in the way of my success, one of those being Brakae's not so gentle handling of me.

She could have been under Faolán's influence when she'd rammed the dagger deep into my flesh. I saw it reflected in her eyes. But she'd spoken to me with a presence of mind that belied his control. Had she simply been playing along so as not to alert Faolán to her stability? If she'd meant to really kill me, I doubt she would've bothered with the prestab warning. No, Brakae had only put on a convincing show for Faolán. She'd been precise in her aim. She'd avoided my lungs and directed the slant of her blade low and to the outside. I'd said I trusted her and meant it. No way would she betray me—not Raif's daughter.

As the Sprites worked on me, my hand wandered to my throat to where the pendulum should have hung. "Where is it?" I asked no one in particular.

"Almost done," Nila said. "Lie still." A pit bull couldn't have been nastier as she pushed at my forehead again with her foot.

Just then, the Sprites looked up to the sky, and I followed their gazes. Dark night had melted away, the sky becoming bright with sunlight. This was the chaos Nila had described. Time couldn't be marked in seconds, minutes, or hours. The sun broke over the horizon without preamble. If dawn had indeed preceded the sunrise, it happened in the blink of an eye—too fast for me to track. Black skies had been replaced with blue as if someone had flipped a switch.

"Are we done?" Not that it mattered. I was out of here. "Time's wasting." Literally.

Nila stepped away as the other Sprites took to the air, floating toward the morning sky, which matured to midday in what seemed like a matter of seconds. Faolán must have been close to following through with his plan; time seemed to move more unevenly than it already did. And I had a feeling, if I didn't get my ass in gear, we were all as good as fucked.

"Go, and be well."

Yeah. Okay. Sure. Time wasn't something I could afford to waste. I took off at a slow jog in no specific direction without a word of parting to the company of Sprites. No "Thanks." No "I owe you one." Nila would just have to take my appreciation as a given. Light glinted through the tree branches, shimmering red and gold and bright green on leaves revealing their fall colors before my eyes. I'd thought spring ruled in this place, but as Nila had so graciously pointed out, the natural order followed a different set of rules.

Where the hell was I headed? It wasn't like Brakae had been so kind as to leave me a trail of bread crumbs to follow. I lacked a decent sense of direction, and as the landscape changed with each passing second, it was hard to find a landmark that might point me in the right direction. My lungs burned from running, the ache spreading into my chest. Slowing to a manageable pace, I stopped in a small clearing as I realized I'd landed myself in the middle of nowhere, alone, without a path to track. "Would've been nice if she'd left me some way to track her," I muttered as I tried to catch my breath. "Like some sort of infrared trail showing me which fucking way to go."

Infrared. Jesus, I was dense. I'd felt her presence once; I could feel it again—just one of the perks unique to my evolution. Although the urgency of my predicament demanded that I keep going at a breakneck pace, I knew the only way I was going to find Brakae was to take things slow. Slow and steady. Fuck.

Plopping down on the grass, I assumed a meditative pose. The sun sank in the horizon, an entire day gone in a matter of minutes. Closing my eyes, I drew several deep breaths—in . . . out . . . in . . . out. . . . A chill wind rustled the brittle leaves now falling from their branches, kissing my cheeks with the promise of winter.

I tilted my head to the north, Brakae's presence coming to me as a slow thrum, pulsing deep into every muscle. It was instantly calming, and I allowed the feeling to spread through my body until I felt as though I could lie down and take a fifty-year nap right in the middle of the forest. God, I wanted to. And I deserved it, damn it. But it would have to wait. First, I had to find my Time Keeper. Then, I had to kill the lousy SOB who'd taken her. Only afterward could I tackle the issue of getting my ass home. Maybe, when all of that was done, I would be allowed to rest.

Slowly, as if I might disrupt the trail with any sudden movements, I opened my eyes and started north. I didn't run this time but kept a steady and manageable pace, allowing myself the concentration I needed to sense the invisible bread crumbs Brakae had left for me to follow. Drawn as I was to her calming energy, my pace quickened as if all I'd needed to do all along was settle the fuck down and lift my nose to the wind.

Twilight melted away as I walked, the sky darkening to a beautiful navy blue, and with the shifting of time, my panic mounted again. How much time had passed at home?

"It's about time you got your head in the game," a voice said from my right.

I whipped around, crouched and ready for a fight. A

fawn-colored ponytail swung to and fro with the woman's gait. Confident. Deadly. Ready.

Moira.

"I'm noticing a trend with you: You seem to always show up right at the tail end of the action." I stalked toward her, trying not to favor my injured torso. Showing weakness could be dangerous since I wasn't quite sure if she still wanted to kill me or not. "And where the hell did you come from anyway?" I'd had a lot to process since I'd wound up in this backward place. Allies had become enemies, and enemies, allies. And just because Moira was apparently one of the good guys didn't mean I wasn't still wary of her.

"You need to seriously work on your interpersonal skills, Darian." Moira's lips twitched, threatening a smile. "You won't win many popularity contests with that attitude of yours."

As if I didn't already know that. I was surprised I didn't walk crooked from the weight of the enormous chip on my shoulder. Miss Congeniality, I wasn't. But since I hadn't exactly been a social butterfly for the past eight or nine decades, Moira would just have to cut me some slack.

"You know, you could have saved everyone a lot of trouble if you'd just come out and told me what the hell was going on. I mean, did it ever occur to you or your brother to say, 'Hold up, Darian. Before you run off with that hourglass, let us clue you in on a few things'? No, you decided to go all Xena Warrior Princess on my ass and scare me off. What the hell is it with you supernaturals anyway?" My temper threatened to get the best of me, but I kept my tone level. Sure, I was angry. But mostly, I was hurt. I didn't want to be a pawn anymore. I had a hard enough time trusting, and it seemed that everyone I'd met wanted to use me for his own agenda. "Why do you all wait until the last fucking second to tell anyone *anything*? You know, I work a hell of a lot better when I've been prepared for a job. Winging it isn't exactly one of my strong suits. If I didn't know any better, I'd think you guys get off on jerking me around."

"Save your anger for someone who deserves it." Moira sheathed her sword and sidestepped me as if I were blocking her view, which only served to rile me more. "We can discuss all of your *many* issues later. But now, you have to focus."

"You haven't seen angry yet." I stepped back into her line of sight so she'd have no choice but to look at me. "Are we on the same side here, or what? I mean, fuck, Moira, way to instill a sense of teamwork. Since I've met you, you've tried to kill me. More than once. Way to welcome me into the bonds of sisterhood."

"I'm not your enemy, Darian. But if you don't stop acting like a fool, I won't hesitate to make you one. Do you understand me?"

"Fuck off." Sure, not a supersnazzy comeback. I wasn't completely convinced I wasn't her enemy. What about threatening to draw my blood with her jagged blades? Arrows zinging at my head? She sure as hell wasn't a friend.

Moira smiled. "You have spirit, I'll give you that. How many times do I have to tell you I'm *not* your enemy? I am a Guardian. And so are you." Her tone indicated this was the one and only time she'd lay it out for me. "We have responsibilities that transcend Fae or human laws. Guard the Keys to the mundane world and *O Anel*, assist the Time Keepers when they need our protection, and maintain the natural order. Perhaps *you* should focus more on your role as well and abandon these petty squabbles over who withheld what from you and why."

"I appreciate your laying it all out so eloquently." I hoped a little sarcasm leaked out in my tone. "Though I'm still not one hundred percent clear on the role I play in all of this." I threw my arms wide in a sweeping gesture. "But since you're so interested in explaining things, would you mind telling me why you let me believe that you were the one hurting Tyler? Because right now, I'm having a hard time being anything but suspicious of you."

"You're referring to the Jinn?"

Why in the hell did everyone insist on referring to Tyler as if he were "the dog" or some shit? It was demeaning.

"Not demeaning," Moira said as if she'd heard my thoughts. "I have nothing but respect for your protector. He is held in high esteem by many. Including me and mine."

I knew deep down—*way* down, past my bitchy attitude—that Moira was an ally. It just made me feel better to vent my frustration. Faolán said that Moira had helped to imprison the Enphigmalé. The enemy of my enemy is my friend and all that. But still . . . "You shot at me."

"I shot—at Faolán."

"No." I'd recognized those magic arrows before the melee at the PNT facility. "In an alley. A few weeks ago. You killed a Lyhtan who tried to warn me about something, and then you shot at me." Not to mention she'd run off like a coward.

"Again"—her voice calmed as if to reassure me—"it was not *I* who shot at you. Besides, I had no reason to kill the Lyhtan. My brother sent him to you."

"Your brother? Reaver sent the Lyhtan?" Why in the hell would he send a Lyhtan to deliver a message to a Shaede? I guess Reaver didn't realize I'd been a target for every Lyhtan within gutting distance since the supernatural community had settled down in Seattle. Or maybe he just wasn't up on his Shaede/Lyhtan history. "He had to have known that was a stupid idea."

"He couldn't reach me and he knew Faolán was close, so he sent the Lyhtan to warn you. By the time I arrived, someone had killed his messenger, and apparently tried to dispatch your Jinn as well. I tried to track the murderer, but I lost the trail. Believe me when I say, those arrows were not meant for you."

"Seriously, though, a *Lyhtan*?"

Moira shrugged. "He's employed by my brother as additional security. He was trustworthy."

If you say so. "So, I suppose that leaves Faolán as the

shooter." That crafty sonofabitch. It fit together perfectly, really. Faolán would have wanted me to stay good and ignorant for as long as possible so he'd have plenty of time to get his hooks into me. And I played right into his hands. *Awesome*.

Moira nodded, sidestepping me again to look past me. "I assume once he killed the Lyhtan, Faolán tried to kill your protector as well. He wouldn't have wanted anything to interfere with his plans to manipulate you into bringing him here. We don't have time to unravel these mysteries now, however. We're running out of time, and we should be tracking Faolán like the dog he is, not standing here, talking about it."

Moira had a point. Every second we stood around hashing this out was time I couldn't afford to lose.

"He's very powerful," Moira said. "And the magic at his disposal . . . ancient."

"More powerful than you?" I asked.

Moira pointedly ignored me, a fact that didn't go unnoticed. Either Faolán had one-upped her in the power department, or she found it insulting that I even asked. It didn't matter to me which it was. Power or not, magic be damned. That bastard was going down.

"Okay," I said. "What now?"

Moira looked to the sky, the once navy blue of night becoming lighter with the rising sun. A day that had passed in an hour. Moira reached around her back and produced a long dagger from her belt. The obsidian blade ran with veins of green and from the looks of it, it was just the weapon I needed. "Take this," Moira said. "You're going to need it. It's time to hunt."

I needed Moira's help if I was going to stop Faolán before he eradicated humanity from the face of the earth. I could sort out the details of this shit storm later—after I was safely home with Tyler and Faolán was dead and gone. I gingerly poked at my side, wincing as my fingers found the stab wound. "Worked over" didn't begin to describe how I felt. I didn't heal as fast as I should have, and I wasn't sure how I'd be able to hold my own in a fight while I was at such a physical disadvantage.

"You'll be fine by the time we find them." *Ugh.* I *knew* she could sense my thoughts.

"You sure about that?"

"I live here, don't forget," Moira said as we negotiated a stream. "It may take longer than you're used to. But you'll be back in fighting form before you know it."

"I usually heal fast. Almost instantaneously."

"*O Anel* isn't like the mortal realm," Moira said. "You became stronger once you were called to serve as a Guardian. Can you imagine how weak you'd be here without that newfound strength?"

My recent evolution had definitely beefed me up in the strength and healing departments. Not to mention that I could become incorporeal no matter the hour. Well, usually, anyway, when someone wasn't laying down the mojo on me. "So, I guess it's sort of like being Superman?"

Moira gave me a curious look.

I rolled my eyes. "You know, he'd have been weaker, fallible on Krypton. But on Earth, he's got all sorts of superpowers."

"I read a Superman comic once. Years ago. Reaver gave it to me. I suppose, yes," Moira laughed. "Something like Superman. In order for you to be strong enough to be a decent protector here, you are afforded the benefit of being superior in the mortal realm."

Comic, huh? I guessed since she lived in *O Anel* most of the time, she wasn't exactly up on pop culture. Or any of the many Superman movies that had been made over the years. "About that," I began, not sure how I wanted to broach the subject. "Faolán said you live here and Reaver lives in the mortal world. Is that right?"

Moira quirked a brow. She'd perfected her snark to facial expressions only.

"Why is that?" I continued, undeterred by her sarcastic expression. "How can you possibly be a decent protector when you're required to live an entire world away from what you're meant to protect?"

"Reaver is the Time Keeper of the mortal realm, and so in the mortal realm he must live. I am the Guardian of the key to the mortal realm. The doorway opens *from O Anel*, and so it is here that I must reside," Moira said. "Balance must be maintained."

"So, since Brakae is the Time Keeper in *O Anel*, she has to stay here all the time? She can't ever leave?"

"It is different for Keepers. When she was chosen," Moira said, "she became one with this realm. She has been bound to the essence of time."

I snorted. "You realize that makes absolutely no sense, right?"

"It is not our place to question Fate—or the gods. We are meant only to serve."

"Serve," I said. "What an appropriate word. Because it seems to me I've just become a slave."

Moira sighed heavily and shook her head. "Think of it this way, Darian. There is a plank resting on a stone. At one end is the mortal realm; at the other, *O Anel*. If Brakae stands with Reaver at the same end of the plank, it will tip to the ground. But if they each stand at one end, the plank will balance straight on the stone. The natural order requires balance in all things."

"I dreamt about her, you know. Brakae. A couple of times."

"Keepers aren't without their own power," Moira responded. "She can't leave *O Anel*, but she has ways to reach out to you if she needs you."

Creepy. But not an entirely ineffective way to communicate with your counterpart when she lived, oh, an entire *universe* away. She'd been trying to warn me about Faolán all along, and even my subconscious had been too stubborn to listen. "I suppose she can send messengers too? Say, for instance, a falcon?" That annoying little bird had delivered the key to me *and* had gotten my attention when Brakae wanted me to use the pendulum. Apparently she had more than a few tricks up her sleeve.

"Certain animals do have the ability to travel between the realms."

"How the hell did you figure all this out?" Because last time I checked, I hadn't been invited to any Guardian orientation seminars. "How did you know the rules? Where to live, what to do? I mean, sorry, but it flat pisses me off that no one prepared me for any of this." Good God, I was starting to sound like a broken record.

"Not that it matters now," Moira said, "but we knew the first time we met you at the PNT Summit. Reaver was quite interested, and had the day gone more smoothly, we would have approached you at the conclusion of the day's proceedings."

By "more smoothly," she meant if Delilah's supposed kidnappers hadn't dropped her off gift-wrapped and beaten to a pulp. The whole of the Summit's participants had fled the facility in the midst of the drama. If I'd only known it was a setup and that I'd end up the kidnapped one, the whole thing would have gone down completely differently. "Reaver was *interested*?" I said. That was an understatement. He'd used magical influence to try to push me to my knees—and right at his feet—but he didn't realize I don't bow to anyone.

"No. I suppose you don't." Moira smiled, once again listening in on my thoughts. "But it wasn't a show of strength on his part like you think."

I stopped her, closed my eyes, and felt Brakae's presence shift to the west and change course. "Then what was it?"

"He was testing your strength."

"Did I pass?"

"That," Moira said as she retrieved the bow slung across her shoulder, "has yet to be seen."

Chapter 27

Moira put a finger to her lips and tuned out everything around her as she closed her eyes and listened. I kept my mouth shut for a change, deciding I was far and above the wingman in this mission. The hairs on my arms and at the nape of my neck prickled, danger plucking at my senses. With silent fluidity, Moira slid an arrow from the quiver at her back and nocked the bow, drawing the string back taut, ready to shoot in the blink of an eye.

What is it? Hey, she'd heard my thoughts before; it was worth a shot.

She opened one shrewd eye and then the other. Letting the bow string slacken, she held up two fingers, pointed to a stand of trees to our left, and motioned for me to flank the grouping at the side opposite her. I drew the long dagger—or maybe it was more of a short sword, depending on your perspective—making sure it would be ready when I needed it, and took off at a trot, careful not to stir even a blade of grass as I moved into position.

I shook off the pull of Brakae's energy and turned my attention instead on the dense cover of trees. Crouching low, I continued to jog, mindful of Moira's position as I went. As stealthy as my shadow-self, I stayed true to my assassin's training, relying on the element of surprise to give me the upper hand. But when I got close enough to look my enemy in the eye, I felt my knees give a little under the weight of their combined energy. The six bodies waiting in the distance paced as if antsy and ready for a brawl. Wide mouths yawned, strong and lithe arms stretched toward the sky, and feet stomped at the earth. I held my body rigid, refusing to allow the tremors that threatened to rip my composure to shreds. One enemy, I could handle. Hell, two or three—piece of cake. Gargoyles, Lyhtans, crazy-ass Sylphs, bring 'em on. But what the hell was I looking at right now? And how had Faolán imprinted them with the signature of his power?

Sea Nymphs. Moira's voice echoed in my mind. *Violent and very dangerous.*

I steeled myself against the fear eating me alive and against the doubts about my purpose and my strength. Teeth clenched to the point of grinding, I moved forward. Gut-check time. Now or never, do or die—all of that inspirational bullshit. Kill my enemies or die trying. But just as I dug my boots into the soft turf, prepared to throw myself into the action, I heard Moira's voice in my mind as clear as if she were speaking right in my ear. *Not yet. Hold your position. If we startle them, they'll be harder to kill.*

Harder than what?

The Nymphs moved with a lazy fluidity that reminded me of water lapping against the shore. Their skin shimmered in the light passing between the tree branches as if their bodies were peppered with droplets of diamonds. Long green hair swayed with every step like seaweed tossed in the surf, and their eyes—gorgeous and swirling with as many shades of blue as made up every body of water in existence. One snapped its powerful jaws, revealing triangular teeth, razor sharp and sharklike. Observation: Stay away from the mouth. Despite their purposeful strides, the Nymphs looked empty, their expressions hollow and detached. Tall, sure. Strong, you betcha. Those teeth, again—stay away from them. . . . But all in all they didn't look like they'd be too hard to take down.

Don't get too excited, Moira's thoughts warned. *Old, powerful magic. Remember? Easier to kill, perhaps. Easier to fight, definitely not. These creatures are under Faolán's influence. Do not underestimate his ability or theirs.*

I'd been as good as Faolán's marionette, strings and all. Who knows what I'd done in those moments when the world went dark and my memory lapsed? With no more exertion than a thought, he'd utterly controlled me. And now, it appeared he had a small troop of zombies at his disposal. I hoped Moira was reading me loud and clear, because we were without a doubt royally fucked.

Not yet.

When things calmed down, this whole telepathy thing was really going to rub me the wrong way.

The silence that followed in my brain sent a zinging blast of adrenaline through my body. God, I needed Tyler right now—needed him like I needed the air filling my lungs. If I'd only opened up to him, I wouldn't be standing here, waiting to go to the slaughter while time sped by at an incalculable rate at home. Why did I always have to shoulder everything on my own?

Darian, this is not the time for such thoughts. Ready yourself for battle instead.

How about you shut up and get the fuck out of my head? I mentally retorted.

If you want to get home to your Jinn, I suggest you put your worry aside and focus.

"Focus" was the million-dollar word of the day. Armed with swords, axes, and spears, the Nymphs were battle-ready and waiting. Good thing I never backed down from a fight. I waited in silence, my mind a blank page, my heart rate slow and steady. Fear tickled at the edge of my senses, but Raif always said fear was what kept you alive in battle. I didn't fight it, but I didn't let it over-take me either.

I gripped the handle of the short sword and tested the balance, surprised that it felt as though it had been made for me. It didn't sit well with me that I was about to fight creatures unaware of their own actions. But war was war, and the rules of morality did not apply. Kill or be killed. Protect the Keeper and the natural order. If I didn't . . . the consequences were too terrible for me to comprehend.

Tension mounted, the air nearly soured by it. The Nymphs continued to pace, their empty eyes staring off into space. I knew it was time to charge into battle when Moira let the first arrow loose, the sound of its passage like a whisper before it struck one of the Nymphs in the neck.

I hurled myself from my hiding place, entering the fray with a battle lust that would have made Raif proud. I dedicated every slice, thrust, and stab to his teachings, a silent vow that I'd keep his daughter safe and reunite them if it killed me. Moira had managed to drop three of the six Nymphs, her aim impeccable and deadly. When she joined the fight with her bow slung across her shoulder, I was grateful to have her by my side. I have to admit, we made quite a pair, our blades ringing out in the quiet clearing, our enemies retreating under our unrelenting attack. It felt so right, fighting with her instead of against her, as if I'd finally found my place in the world.

Moira fought with a sword not unlike the weapon she'd given to me. A black blade with veins of glowing green. Hers was much longer, more of a broad sword than a saber. She handled its weight well. As she swung at the Nymphs coming at us, she maneuvered the weapon with as much precision as she would a dagger. Good thing, too. Those Nymphs were fast fuckers. Flanked on both sides with an attack coming at our center, I had no choice but to concentrate my efforts on one enemy at a time. The Nymphs took us on with a blade in each hand, making it feel as if we stood against six enemies instead of just three. But damn it, I wasn't about to lose. Not when there was so much at stake. I emptied my mind of everything, save the fight. My sole focus became letting as much blood as possible. Swinging with a strength that surprised me, I caught the Nymph on my right with my blade, slicing open a nasty gash in his side.

From my left, the other Nymph came at me, sinking his razor-edged teeth into my forearm. I cried out, spun away from the one I'd cut, and with an upward sweep, drove the dagger through the Nymph's chin and straight up into his head. His eyes cleared for the barest instant, horror and confusion written in the depths of blue. I swallowed down the bile that rose in my throat as he rocked back, careened forward, and crumpled at my feet.

"Look out!" Moira called out just in time to save me from a sword thrust to my face.

I jumped back, narrowly avoiding the injured Nymph's teeth. My sword arm stung, weakened by the tears in my flesh that oozed blood down to my fingertips. The dagger felt heavy in my grasp, but I lunged and swung, managing to nick my attacker's shoulder before he spun away. Moira had her hands full at my side, distracting me as I watched her parry blow after blow, getting in a few good stabs of her own. I had to give her credit—the girl could fight.

A sudden, jarring pain blinded me, a thousand stars against a black sky in my vision. The world slipped away, and I fell, down . . . down . . . through the void until all that was left was welcome oblivion.

"Paris," I said, tossing the postcard across the farm-style table. "You know, he'd be better off hiding somewhere like Wyoming or Montana. Paris is a little conspicuous, wouldn't you agree?"

Azriel nodded absently, his eyes swirling with a darkening storm. He hated the postcards almost as much as they intrigued me. "Lorik is a fool. And he has no intention of lying low. Not now, not ever."

Tapping the postcard on the table, Azriel stared out the window as the rain battered the leaded panes before running in rivulets to the ground. I supposed we'd go out walking soon; he loved to be outside in the rain. "Why does he send them?" I asked, nodding at the postcard. "You know, don't you?"

"There's more to Lorik than meets the eye." I could tell by his tone Azriel would not open the subject for discussion. "That's all you need to know."

"What is he to you?" We'd been receiving the postcards for almost a year. I wanted—no needed—to know why.

"Why don't you trust me enough to share your secrets with me?"

"What do you mean, love?" His words were spoken softly but carried a warning edge. "I share my life *with you. Is that not enough?"*

"Do you not think I can handle the truth? Is that why you keep things from me? Do you not think I'm strong enough? Capable?"

"What I do is for your protection." He'd abandoned the facade of calm, heading down a path I knew better than to follow. "If I keep things from you, it is for your own good. Do not make me regret the decision to save your life, Darian. Leave all things to me and you will be safe. Accept that fact or risk your safety."

"I'm sorry," I whispered. He'd saved my life; he'd cared for me. How could I question him or doubt his honor for even one second? "I—I was just curious, that's all. The postcards, they're like a mystery. A puzzle to be solved."

"Perhaps you need diversion," Azriel said, pulling me onto his lap. His breath tickled where he lowered his lips to my throat. "You need no puzzle to solve or mysteries to unravel." His lips were warm, soft, sending a ripple of pleasure across my skin. "You have me, and I am enough."

My head rolled back on my shoulders as he unbuttoned my dress. Yes. I had him. And he would be with me. Always. I didn't need to know the truth. I didn't need to know anything besides that he loved me. He was enough.

And I trusted him.

Chapter 28

I hadn't trusted him.

I'd done to Tyler what Azriel had done to me all those years ago. I'd taken control of him and the situation, and I hadn't trusted him to be my partner, my equal. I'd used my body to distract him. I'd treated him as if he were weak, beneath me, and he knew it. I'd expected him to blindly trust me without offering anything in return. And I'd left him.

I reached for my thumb, touching the skin that had been worn smooth by Tyler's ring. What had Faolán done with it? I needed it. I needed to feel that part of Tyler on my body.

"Darian," Moira said, not so gently slapping my cheek. "Darian, can you hear me?"

No. Well, I didn't want to anyway. Admitting I could hear her was acknowledging this reality, the fact that I'd dug myself a hole I couldn't get out of, and had more than likely lost the only thing in my life I cared about.

"Darian." She slapped me harder this time, and my head throbbed where I'd been hit. Lovely. Just *lovely*.

"I can hear you fine," I said, venturing to open one eye and then the other. "But if you slap me like that again, you're going to be the one unconscious."

"Get up," she laughed. Apparently she didn't consider me a threat. "We have to keep going."

Slowly, oh, *so* slowly, I brought myself to a sitting position. Damn, I hated how susceptible to injury I was in this place. My head bobbed on my shoulders, and the effort it took to support its weight made me want to lie back down. I reached tentative fingers through hair matted with blood, wincing as I made contact with a large gash.

"It probably feels worse than it looks," Moira said, supporting my shoulders. "Your skin was split clear to the skull. I stopped the bleeding and gave the cut a little jump start in the healing department. It's nothing more than superficial now. You should be fine."

A jump start? Okay, whatever. "What happened?" Besides the fact that I'd been knocked out by a lesser opponent. The shame was almost worse than the injury.

"Pride before the fall?" Moira said. "Not quite. They double-teamed you while I was occupied. You turned your attention to the greater threat, and the other took you down with the pommel of his sword. Better a knock to the head than a blade through your heart."

"Doesn't feel much better."

"Has anyone ever told you that you're very arrogant?"

Sure. In so many words, almost everyone I'd ever met. But in my line of work you had to be a little cocky. "You have a problem with arrogance?"

"In a Guardian?" Moira smiled. "Not at all."

I looked around at the bodies littering the ground beside us—senseless deaths at Faolán's hand. After all, these Nymphs would still be alive and well if it hadn't been for his influence. How many more had to suffer for his insanity? If I had anything to do with it, not another soul.

"What happened when Faolán attempted his last coup?" All I knew was that Brakae had helped to imprison him. There had to be more to the story, and besides, it helped to pass the time as we walked.

"He never should have fallen in love with her," Moira answered. "It was his undoing."

"Yeah. I got that much."

"Faolán's race was bred for war," Moira said. "Fearless warriors, terrifying in their beast forms. Badb kept the Enphigmalé busy for centuries, fighting her battles.

But when the humans became involved, the gods didn't think it was fair to let them fight against supernatural beings. Humans are so very fragile."

From Moira's tone, I got the impression she didn't chum around with many humans. She rolled her eyes at my thoughts, answering my unspoken question.

"The gods decided it was in the best interest of humanity to separate them from the Fae and their kin and rend the fabric of time in two. They gave their extraordinary children a choice: Live in the mundane and hide their true natures or live in *O Anel* openly."

It was my turn to roll my eyes. "Seriously, you expect me to believe that actual gods and goddesses did this?"

"Darian," Moira said with pity, "you're thinking like a human. Your narrow-mindedness is perhaps your most unsavory quality. Badb pulled Faolán from the battlefield and gave him a position of honor: Guardian of *Iskosia*: the key to *O Anel*. He would help to maintain the balance of time and protect *O Anel*'s Time Keeper if need be. I doubt he was thrilled with the appointment, but he tolerated it . . . until Brakae was chosen to serve."

I didn't think the whole mundane world/Faerie Realm thing had been created too recently. Still . . . "Faolán had mentioned that he didn't care about the others, so clearly Brakae wasn't the first Time Keeper."

"Brakae was the fifth. In the beginning, there were many uprisings, and Guardians were busy protecting their charges. Faolán satisfied his need to fight for a thousand years, squashing this usurper or that. By the time Brakae had been called to serve, the hourglass was nothing but a myth."

"I take it peace didn't sit well with our gargoyle?"

"Oh, it agreed with him. He fell in love, after all. But there were too many rules to follow, too many restrictions. Brakae was bound to the essence of time. She had become one with chaos and could never leave *O Anel*."

Moira's story was just too tragic for my usual jaded outlook. "Faolán couldn't stomach the way she aged." He'd said as much already.

Moira nodded. "Amongst other things. And so he gathered his army and set to the task of overthrowing the order the gods had created. Obviously, he did not succeed."

Brakae's energy called to me, and I steered Moira to the left, following her trail. "Badb punished him?"

"Brakae set the trap, and Faolán never suspected her betrayal. I led a small army against him, and we captured the nine Enphigmalé warriors still living. We trapped them between the worlds; I suppose you'd call it purgatory. Through my blood, Badb punished them all for their treason by imprisoning their beast forms in stone. And in that empty place, they were to stay."

"Until I came along," I murmured.

"Yes," Moira said. "Until you."

"Why doesn't Badb step in again?" I asked. "I suspect she could end this pretty quickly, being a goddess and all."

Moira leveled her ice blue eyes on mine. "The old gods don't have much power anymore. No one worships them in these modern times. When there are no prayers to answer, they have no meaning. The old gods sleep."

Damn. Moira just got cheerier by the second. I closed my eyes, her story swimming around in my head. The urge to rest weighed on me, tugging me toward an inviting darkness I had to ignore. *Focus.* I felt Brakae's energy. Close. And something else, too—a power that had nearly brought me to my knees the first time I'd been brought near it.

"They're not far," I said to Moira. Her face came in and out of focus as I willed my eyes to stay open. "And I know where they are."

"The Ring," Moira said as if she'd known all along.

"If you knew where they'd be going all this time, then why in the *hell* didn't you just take us right to them? Jesus, Moira, what a monumental waste of time!"

The sadness in her eyes made me sorry I'd jumped her shit. "There is no constant this close to *Kotja A'ma*, Darian. *Everything* changes. Even the landscape."

Christ. I hadn't thought of that. But then again, how

could I have known? No wonder everyone here was so fucking bummed out all the time. You could leave your house in the morning and the damned thing wouldn't be there when you got back! That is, if you managed to find your way back. It explained why I hadn't seen any permanent structures, or many other living creatures for that matter. I'd go absolutely crazy in this place if I were forced to live here. "I'm sorry." What else could I say?

Moira shrugged. "It is all a matter of the natural order. We are in the heart of chaos, here. That's all. Outside The Ring, there are provinces, villages, just like the mortal realm. Change isn't quite so noticeable. It's not as bad as you think it is. That feeling you have inside you? The magnetic draw that calls to your soul? *You* feel it because you are the Guardian of *O Anel*'s key and are tied to this place."

"Then why can't you feel The Ring?"

"I am tied to time in the mortal realm. I feel the pull there, not here."

Food for thought. But, really, the more time I spent here with Moira, the more I learned. Trial by fire—that was the way for me. Fate sure did have it out for me, but Fate didn't take into account that I was a hell of a lot tougher than most souls. Dish it out—I can take it. "We need to get moving." That was, if I could kick my sorry ass into gear. "They're close, and we're running out of time."

"I feel it as well," Moira said, helping me to stand. "A strange energy charges the air, as if I could reach through time and touch the world beyond the veil."

Fear stomped a path through my chest, down into my stomach, a knot that settled like a boulder. "Well, then, I guess we'd better get our asses going."

Moira checked the wound on the back of my head one more time, deeming me fit to fight. The gash had begun to close, albeit slowly, and I didn't feel as though I were carting a watermelon around on top of my shoulders anymore.

"All right, Guardian," she said. "Where to from here?"

I smiled. Who would have thought I'd actually like

her? I closed my eyes, felt Brakae's unmistakable pull, and thought, *south*, but then realized if the landscape changed in the blink of an eye, direction wouldn't mean much. "This way," I said, jutting my chin to the left.

We continued to walk, though I wanted to run. My head protested, aching every time I pushed our pace. Our surroundings had changed yet again. Autumn had released its hold, the land becoming dormant for winter's sleep. Fluffy bits of white drifted down from a light gray sky, and my breath clouded the air with puffs of moisture.

"He thinks of you often," Moira said, breaking the silence. "Azriel."

I stopped dead in my tracks.

"Does this surprise you?"

Hell, yeah, it did. "Azriel is dead."

"Azriel is crossed over," Moira said. "Nothing is ever truly dead. His soul has merely begun a new existence."

"You're a Herald—is that right?" It was time to put Levi's knowledge to work.

"That's correct."

"So you speak to the dead?"

Moira motioned her hand before us, urging me to walk. "The crossed over."

I closed my eyes for the briefest moment, zeroed in on Brakae's location, and started off. "You speak to the *crossed over*?" Sheesh.

"When they have something to say, yes."

"And Azriel had something to say." My stomach backflipped at the thought. Where was he? Could he see me? Did he know what had happened to me?

"He wants you to know that he holds no ill will toward you. You did what was right and just. He wants you to know"—she paused as if deciding whether she should go farther—"that he cares for you still."

A sucker punch to the gut would have hurt less. "Is that all he said?"

"That is all he wants you to know. For now."

Typical. Leave it to Azriel to jerk me around, even in

death. Control was his greatest weapon, and he'd taught me to use it like a master. "So I guess that means I can expect to hear from him again?" Oh joy of joys. Just what I needed.

"If he feels so inclined, yes."

Let's hope he decides to keep his fat mouth shut. Moira's lips curved into a half smile, and though I knew she'd heard my thoughts, I was glad she decided to keep her own to herself.

The light snow that peppered our heads and shoulders became dense, sticking to the ground and accumulating with each passing minute. I hated the cold, but I loved snow. Silence seemed to accompany its falling, as if the world held its breath for spring's arrival. I loved the silence here. Time didn't hammer like an angry drum, reminding me of its never-ending presence. But despite the peace I felt in this place, it didn't have Tyler. And I'd rather have an entire percussion section take up residence in my brain than live without him.

My bones began to hum in my body, and I knew we were close. The Ring had called to me in an unmistakable way, and beneath that pull I felt Brakae's presence calming me. *You do realize that Faolán can control me?* There was no need to blurt that fact aloud. Moira could hear my thoughts just fine. *If it comes to a fight, I don't know how much help I'll be.*

Faolán's magic is old and strong. Moira's thoughts pushed into my head. *We've already established that. But you, Darian, are a Guardian and have power of your own. Don't forget your purpose: Protect the natural order. Set your focus on the task at hand. Keep your heart and your mind fixed to Brakae and you'll be fine. Faolán is strong, but nothing can overpower a Guardian's protection. Why do you think he now wants you dead?*

Good point.

My boots crunched in the snow as we walked, and I shivered at the cold, though it didn't bother me as much as it usually did. The sooner Faolán fell beneath my sword, the faster I could get the hell out of here and back to Tyler. The Ring called to me, my body welcoming its power the closer we came. I could almost smell Faolán's foul stench beneath the crisp, clean aroma of snow. My fist tightened around the dagger's hilt as I quickened my pace. Time to go to work.

The forest thinned as we approached the ring of stones. My chest ached with the force of its power, but I drank it in, inviting rather than rejecting the sensation. Already I felt stronger, my feet more secure beneath my body. My head no longer throbbed, and as I twisted my torso, the stab wound didn't pull at the stitches. A smile crept to my face as the trees seemed to part in our wake to expose the ancient structure. I was itching for a fight, and Faolán was going to bring one to me.

Cover would be an issue, exposed as we were. My assassin's instincts kicked in, stealth taking precedence over a charge to battle. Moira motioned for me to follow as she kept to the outer ring, crouching low to the ground and using the sparse trees and bushes for cover. Faolán and Brakae were still out of sight, but they were there, somewhere in the innermost ring. I felt them both, each vying for the top spot in my subconscious. I constructed a mental barrier—a brick wall inside my brain, shutting both of them out. If I allowed Brakae inside my head, it would leave me vulnerable to Faolán's influence. She said she trusted me. She'd just have to keep trusting me.

I caught Moira's eye and brought my hand to my temple to indicate what I was attempting to do. She nodded once, and since I couldn't detect her pushing into my thoughts, I had to assume she read me loud and clear.

"I feel you, Darian!" Faolán's voice sliced through the silence. "You can't keep me out, no matter how hard you try!"

Wanna bet, motherfucker? I was going to do everything in my power to ensure he'd messed with my mind for the last time.

As the snow fell around us, collecting on branches and bushes, blanketing the tall stone structures of The Ring, a calm fell on me as well, covering me with a warm composure that this would all end just as it should. I don't know where it came from, whether it was divine intervention or maybe even Fate itself. But one thing I knew for sure: I was going home, and soon.

Moira caught my eye and smirked—a deadly expression if I ever saw one. She took off through the trees, around the ring of stones to the opposite side. With two Guardians against one fanatic, Faolán didn't stand a chance.

"I'll kill her!" the asshole shouted to the sky. "Come any closer and Brakae will die."

Could he actually kill the woman he loved? Sort of pointless if you ask me. His love for Brakae had been the source of all his bitterness. Why would he kill her when everything he was about to do would ensure that they could be together forever?

I wanted to answer him back, let off a string of curses and snarky comebacks just to taunt him. But I kept quiet, fortified my mental barriers, and waited.

"Do you doubt me?" Faolán kept at it, showing his crazy like a poker hand. "I'll do it, Darian! I'll cut her traitorous heart from her breast!"

If I played my own hand right, I'd have him unraveled in a matter of minutes. He'd been slowly losing his mind since we'd arrived in *O Anel*. All it would take to send him over the edge was a few mind games of my own. And I'm a quick study. My silence was pushing all the right buttons, edging him toward the point of no return. I needed Faolán off balance, unfocused, easy to tip.

A strangled cry reached my ears, turning my blood to ice. From the sounds of her screams, Faolán had gone to work on Brakae with the ferocity of the beast he was. And worse yet, his own silence while he took out his frustration on her made me realize that maybe I'd given myself too much credit. It was going to take more than the silent treatment to maneuver Faolán into a position of disadvantage, and I'd risked Brakae's life in the process.

When Brakae's screams finally echoed off into silence, I took a deep, steadying breath. The sensation of her presence was no longer calming but made me so jittery that the dagger shook in my hand. She was alive, but obviously damaged. Damn him. I'd never longed for someone's death as much as I longed for his. My knees shook as I shifted position, and above the crunching of my feet in the snow, Faolán's ragged sobs rose to cover the sound.

"How could you make me do this?" he cried. "*You've* done this, Darian! This is *your* fault!"

I'd never heard anything so . . . pathetic. Faolán was tortured by love and obsession to the point that he'd lost all sense of right and wrong. What he'd done to Brakae had been necessary to that part of him obsessed with merging the realms and eradicating what he felt had kept him from happiness. The racking sobs coming from the ring of stones now were those of blinding grief and heartache.

Shit. No point trying to push his buttons; Faolán's switchboard was already pretty well lit. Only one thing left to do. I took a page from Brakae's book—and surrendered.

Chapter 29

I wanted to run to her, the urge to both protect and avenge a burning acid in my limbs. Was this how Tyler felt when my safety was threatened? Did his instincts urge him to the point that he'd charge out to meet the enemy head-on? Of course they did. Add love to the equation, and that impulse was probably even stronger. I wondered, after all that I'd done, could he love me still?

Faolán's influence poked at my brain, searching for a way past my mental barriers. I took Moira's words to heart. Faolán was strong, but I was a Guardian and just as strong if not stronger than my enemy.

"Slowly." A flash of silver tears glistened in his narrowed gaze before trailing down his cheeks. He held Brakae's whimpering form close, her arms hanging limp at her sides. "Don't do anything foolish, Darian. I *will* kill her."

No problem there. Any sudden movement was bound to bring him to his breaking point. And I had no intention of seeing that up close and personal. "I'm not interested in seeing her killed, Faolán." I slowed my approach to a near shuffle, my movements tedious and precise. "I'm standing here right now because I want to keep her safe."

"She's not dead." The words seemed more self-reassuring than meant for me. "You have no idea how precious to me she is. How much I love her."

Then why the hell did you cut her up, asshole? "I know you do," I said, inching closer. "This isn't exactly the way to show your love."

Faolán pointed his dagger at me, the blade stained with Brakae's blood. "You love deeply. So you should know the pain I feel. Your love freed me from stone. And the symbol of your love will merge the realms, putting an end to this separation once and for all."

That didn't sound good. Though I didn't know what he was talking about, I wasn't going to ask. I couldn't close the gap between us fast enough. Every shuffle of my feet felt like another mile between us. The concentration of power surged around me, the energy emanating from the ring of stones, Brakae's magnetic pull beckoned, and Faolán's influence still searched for a way to control me. My hands began to shake the closer I came to the vortex of energy, my teeth chattering so hard, I had to clamp my jaw tight. It was like walking into the eye of a tornado, the swirling winds of power whipping at my body as I breached its barrier. The short sword weighed down my arm, testing my strength as I fought to keep hold. But it slipped from my fingers, landing in the snow at my feet with a muted thump.

I didn't even try to pick it up. Why would I need a weapon? I wasn't here to fight. . . . I was here to bear witness to something. My thoughts clouded, a familiar peaceful haze blanketing me.

"Come here, Darian," Faolán said.

I closed the distance between us with an eagerness that fired a flight reflex somewhere deep inside me. *Run!* Common sense shouted while my brain answered, *Why?* My gaze drifted from Faolán's silver stare to the woman he held in his arms. Her dark hair cascaded over his arm, and he cradled her as if she were fragile and might shatter if he but shifted in any direction. I knew her. Her name . . .

"Darian." Faolán's warning tone cut through my thoughts. "Pay attention."

Okay. "I'm sorry." Why did I feel the need to apologize?

"We're about to begin, and you have to focus."

Focus. Yes, I was supposed to be focusing on something right now. I had a mission in this place. Something I was meant to protect.

Faolán snapped his fingers, and I lost my train of thought. I shook my head, trying to clear the fog from my brain, but something held my mind in a strong grasp. I couldn't do a damned thing to help myself.

An unspoken command had my arms stretching out, and with gentle care Faolán eased the burden of the woman's weight into my arms. I knelt slowly, spreading her out at his feet as seemed appropriate for some reason. Tears streaked down his cheeks as he looked on her pale face, and I realized this woman must have meant a great deal to him. Her chest rose and fell with shallow breaths, and gory, bloody paths oozed from her arms and neck. Someone had taken a knife to her, and, from the looks of it, had enjoyed what he'd done.

The woman's lids fluttered before opening to reveal beautiful blue eyes. Memorable in both color and the intensity of her stare, I sensed something in this woman that called to me.

"Raif," I whispered, wondering why that name would come to mind.

A hand gripped my own, squeezing hard for how frail she looked. "I trust you," she murmured. "And I'm sorry I stabbed you."

Holy shit, she *had* stabbed me! Brakae. *Fuck*. Brakae was bleeding all over the pristine white of the snow, used like a slab of meat while Faolán doled out his cruel punishment on her flesh. I tore my eyes from her scored skin, brought my gaze to his, and fought like hell to keep my mind closed to his intrusion. "You sonofabitch!" I seethed. "I'm going to kill you for this."

"Not if she kills you first," he said, jutting his chin toward the outer ring of stones.

Resist. Moira's thoughts pushed into my mind as she approached, weapon drawn and ready. *He'll pit you against me. And you know what I'll have to do. I can't allow him to mend the glass*.

She sure as hell wasn't wrong. Already I felt the impulse, the idea being planted in my head: Attack. I didn't have a weapon, but that didn't seem to matter as I left Brakae's side and headed straight for the outer ring of stones. *Darian!* I ignored Moira, my pace quickening at Faolán's urging. *Stop this!* My arms pumped as I ran, my boots kicking up snow behind me. *This is insane! How can you forget your purpose?* My breath clouded as I labored, my lungs ached from the cold. *I* will *kill you!* She would, I had no doubt. Faolán would keep us both occupied with fighting, and Moira would kill me, doing his dirty work for him. *Fight him!*

The toes of my boots dug into the snow and turf, and I launched myself at Moira as I closed the last few yards between us. Time slowed as I cut through the winter air, and by sheer will I forced my mental barriers into place.

I hit Moira with a jarring impact that sent us both skidding through the snow. "Make this believable," I said close to her ear.

Holy hell, what had I gotten myself into? The first crack of Moira's fist to my jaw had me reeling; by the third, I was spitting blood. I had the feeling she was enjoying herself a little too much. I'd wanted it to be believable, though, so I had to grit my teeth and bear it while she attempted to beat me to a pulp. On the plus side, Faolán wanted me to initiate the attack, and it wouldn't have seemed realistic for the scales to be tipped in Moira's favor. So I gave her a decent beating as well, kicking and throwing punches as if I had nothing to lose. And at this point, I didn't.

As Moira and I rolled around on the ground, pounding each other for the sake of entertainment, I noticed Faolán from the corner of my eye. He'd lost interest in our tussle and left Brakae lying in the snow. From my backpack, he produced the broken halves of the hourglass and brought his treasures to the centermost part of the ring of stones, the heart of *O Anel*. I shifted, rolled, and kicked, maneuvering our fight closer to the real action, and Faolán paid us no mind. He set Reaver's half of the glass on a stone pedestal, the golden sands swirling like the snow falling from the sky. Moira had eased up on me, her blows more acted than real by this point. Let's face it—neither of us would have been worth a damn beaten to shit.

The atmosphere seemed to quiver, a ripple in the fabric of time. And as my attention was drawn away from my pseudo-fight to Faolán's actions, a glint of silver caught my eye, and I froze. Sitting at the top knuckle of his forefinger was a ring, old and worn. My ring. The ring Tyler had given to me. God*damn* him. I was going to tear his head right off his fucking shoulders. I dodged Moira's already misguided punch and started off toward Faolán when she grabbed my arm. *Not yet!*

Bullshit. I pulled free from her grasp and lurched forward, but she jumped in front of me. *Wait! We need him to be distracted!* Blind rage guided my fist, and no one influenced my actions now. I swung hard—frustration, anger, and lust for revenge fueling the impact as I made contact with Moira's face. She spun full circle and fell to the ground, snow flying up around her like feathers as she landed.

Faolán's gaze met mine, the silver of his eyes dead and devoid of emotion. His eyebrow cocked, and he plucked the ring from his finger, holding it up for my inspection. He brought it to his lips, blowing gently, and the silver glowed bright as a star. "No!" I shook my head as I left Moira's unconscious body on the ground and took off at a dead run. No fucking way was he going to use *my ring*, the only thing I had of Ty, to destroy the world.

That ring was my lifeline to Tyler, to my own heart. My pulse pounded in my ears as I charged Faolán, anxiety burning through my bloodstream like liquid fire. I didn't have a weapon, but I'd rip his head off with my bare hands if I had to. The ring, carved with Tyler's bear, was the embodiment of his love and undying protection.

His name was a war cry as I advanced, building momentum with every push of my legs. The bastard was going down, once and for all. But when I took the final step and bent down low to throw my body into his, his power hit me like a wrecking ball, and I stopped still in my tracks, my head whipping back from the jarring halt.

Stop.

The command was too strong to resist.

Be still.

Like a fucking statue.

Quiet.

Not a peep.

"Love is such a powerful thing," Faolán mused as he twisted my ring between his thumb and forefinger. "I've seen what your Jinn would do for you and what you, in turn, would do to protect him."

Thoughts swirled in my head, a torrent of vile curses I reserved for only the lowest of bastards. But thanks to Faolán's control, my mouth wouldn't open so I could let the word vomit out.

"In the blood, you will find the most ancient of magic." His voice dropped, becoming soft, almost tender. "But in love you will find power in its truest form. And you, my dear Darian, you have harnessed that power."

Oh. My. God.

Faolán slipped the ring on top of the broken neck of the hourglass. As it made contact, the band of silver glowed white-hot. The snow, swirling into blizzard proportions, stopped in the air, just as still as I was, as if waiting for the command to move again. Even the wind seemed to bow at Faolán's feet, along with the naked tree branches and blades of grass poking up through the snow-covered ground.

All of *O Anel* held its breath, and I was really starting to regret knocking Moira unconscious. Frankly, I could have used her help right about now. My mind was sharp as a razor's edge; obviously Faolán wanted me completely lucid for this particular trick. I imagined the horror of billions of humans disintegrating into dust, a madman's revenge exacted on innocent souls. This was exactly why I only took jobs that involved ridding the world of the dirtiest scum. Faolán wasn't interested in being anything but a blight on the world. It didn't matter whom he killed or whose heart he broke in the process. All he cared about was his burning need for revenge.

My muscles rebelled against my brain's own commands as I fought to move. Snowflakes remained suspended in midair, and the still silence became almost palpable. Two worlds teetered on the brink of collision, and I couldn't help but wonder what was happening on the other side, in the mortal realm.

But in the midst of impending chaos, of death, retribution, and sorrow, I did the one thing that seemed utterly impossible.

I let go.

I swept my mind clean so it became a blank canvas. I focused my gaze on the hovering snowflakes until I lost sight of everything in a blur of hazy white. The fear funneled out of my body, the desperate need to think my way out of this clusterfuck became a nonexistent thing. For the first time since coming to this place, I absorbed and appreciated the calm, the absence of time that never left me in the mortal realm. And in the freedom from everything that weighed me down, a feeling blossomed in my chest—something warm and welcome that fed my soul.

Tyler.

I felt him as if he were standing right next to me, circling me in his strong embrace. I was a world away; yet his love gave me strength. Our connection could never be broken, and from a million or more miles away I *knew* Tyler was the only thing holding me up. Fuck Faolán. Fuck his power, his control, his bullshit Enphigmalé magic. He'd had my blood, but so had Tyler. And Tyler had my heart.

The world came rushing back into focus. Moira still lay unconscious near the outer ring of stones. Brakae rested, unmoving, at Faolán's feet. The snow, wind, grass, and branches waited patiently to do a madman's bidding. A ripple of color like the aurora borealis shone against the darkening sky, the mortal realm pushing at the cusp of the Faerie Ring. My jaw loosened on its hinges, my muscles released their tension, and my heart swelled with the love that had always been there. I should have trusted Ty. I should have let him in. I *should* have allowed him to be the equal partner I knew he could be. Because Faolán was right; there was nothing more powerful than love.

Chapter 30

In one fluid movement, I set my body in motion, throwing every ounce of muscle I had into Faolán's midsection. I'd deal with getting a weapon later. Right now, I had to get him the hell away from the hourglass before he mended the damned thing and sent the natural order to hell.

He wasn't hard to surprise; his arrogance would have never allowed for the possibility that I had the strength to resist his influence. My fist flew, and I clocked him a good one before he found the presence of mind to throw me off. I may have been physically strong—stronger than a mortal man—but Faolán's strength had me beat two to one. I wasn't one to cower from a fight, though, no matter the odds.

I could feel him poking around in my brain, sending invisible feelers to shut me down. *Not gonna happen, asshole. You're done controlling me.* I didn't need to fortify my mental barriers against him any longer; I'd found my power, and that was something Faolán couldn't undo.

"Not so tough anymore, are you, Faolán?" Sticky situations like this required more than the normal amount of cocky bravado. Granted, I wasn't his zombie-puppet anymore, but that didn't mean he couldn't kick my ass the old-fashioned way. I brought my elbow down hard, square on his sternum. "You made a *huge* mistake when you decided to bring Tyler into this. You don't fuck with anyone I care about."

Faolán laughed, fueling my rage. Spitting blood as he chortled, the bastard just couldn't let go of the crazy.

I hit him again and again, expending all the energy I could spare in an attempt to at least knock him unconscious. Fists flying, elbows jabbing, and knees digging in, I worked Faolán *over*, and he took it all with a sick smile plastered on his face, apparently reveling in the pain.

My first misstep was thinking I had the upper hand. My second was failing to consider that he hadn't tried to hit me back—not once. And he'd already proven he didn't mind slapping me around. As the dagger flashed, it seemed to come out of thin air, sinking through the ragged black fabric of my shirt to add yet another hole to the one Brakae had already made. Funny that was what I'd noticed first—that he'd trashed my shirt. As the blade punctured my flesh, it took a moment for the pain to register. But when it did—*holy fucking shit!*—did it burn. Maybe it was because I'd been under his mind-numbing influence before that I hadn't felt the pain to such a degree. Now, as Faolán twisted the dagger's blade in my flesh, I had the distinct impression he wanted me to feel it a hundredfold.

"I should have killed you sooner," he seethed, heaving me off his body. "But not to worry, Darian, I'll remedy that shortly."

The hell you will. Jesus, had it really come down to him and me in the end? Brakae was wounded, maybe even dying. And Moira, well, I'd fucked that up royally. Every other creature in this backward place had gone into hiding, it seemed, and so the fate of both worlds rested on a one-on-one fight to the death. Winner takes all. "I'm not so easy to kill, Faolán," I said through the burning pain. "Don't get your hopes up."

"Spoken like a true Guardian," he drawled before licking blood from his swollen lip.

An invisible force of energy blanketed me, drawing me toward darkness. It wasn't going to work. Faolán had controlled me for the last time, but the fact that he was trying gave me hope. Controlling me meant putting me at a disadvantage. If he needed me incapacitated, he ob-

viously didn't think he could take me without the upper
hand. A grim smile curved my mouth. *I had him*.

"Where's my katana?" I asked, because, well, for one
I was curious. And two, I knew it would throw his focus.
I needed to buy myself a couple of minutes to allow my
flesh to at least *begin* to heal. "I'm taking my ring back
too."

Faolán's brow rose in an elegant arch. "I think I'll
hand-deliver your head to your Jinn. Wrapped in a bright
red bow. Knowing he couldn't protect you will probably
send him straight into madness."

My stomach curled in on itself. "Oh, he'll get a gift all
right." Christ, this could go on forever. "But I think it'll
be your head, not mine."

Posturing is just part of battle. Elk paw at the earth
and thrash their massive racks of antlers; birds display
and puff their feathers; canines circle one another, hackles raised and lips curled. We upright animals, we talk
shit. Faolán's threats were meant to make me cower and
reconsider an attack. "I'm going to kill you, Faolán."

"You've said as much. A few times. And yet I still
live."

I eased back a step, crouched in a defensive position.
The big talk would last only so long; one of us would have
to make a move soon. Snow stuck to my hair as I moved,
as if walking through cobwebs, and I wanted nothing
more than to see the white flakes drift to the ground as
they should. Faolán's eyes narrowed as he tracked my
movement like a cat about to pounce. He palmed his dagger, rotating it in his hand as if the movement soothed
him.

I tensed.

Faolán sidestepped, one foot over the other, circling
me and turning his back on Brakae. A flutter of movement from her body caught my attention, but I refused
to break eye contact. I stared at the center of his face,
right at his nose. I wanted it to seem that I was looking
right through him, as if he mattered as much to me as the
snowflakes hovering around my head.

He smiled.

Chills chased a wave of adrenaline as I waited for him to make his move. Better to be on the defensive, ready for a head-on assault. He was armed and I wasn't. Charging him wasn't in my best interest. Brakae stirred again, her movements more lively this time. I watched her in my peripheral vision, unwilling to rat her out with a sideways glance. Faolán continued to circle, making me nervous. With just a few more steps, Brakae would come into his line of sight, and he'd know she was regaining consciousness. Damn it. I had no choice. I had to protect her. . . .

Weaponless, defenseless, I did what I'd planned *not* to do. Faolán saw it in my eyes, and his own flashed silver as he dug his feet into the snow-covered earth and braced himself for the attack. There wasn't enough space between us for me to pick up any kind of momentum, but I led with my feet, letting the thick soles of my boots take the first slice of Faolán's blade.

The sonofabitch was fast, bringing the dagger up and stabbing down before I had a chance to stand. The blade nicked my thigh, and I rolled away before he could put his weight behind the action and stab through to the muscle. My legs scissored, and I caught him in the groin. He fell to his knees, his face a snarling mask of rage.

"When I'm through with you, I'm going to describe your death to your lover in detail." Really? I'd thought we were through bullshitting. "I don't think just your head will do. I'm going to cut you into tiny pieces and present each little bit to him on a silver platter."

I didn't dignify him with a response. It was what he wanted after all. And what I wanted was to keep him nice and occupied—away from the hourglass and away from Brakae. With a quick roll, I was off my back and leapt to my feet. First thing I was going to do was break his jaw so he'd shut the fuck up.

Faolán parried the blow, striking with the dagger. The blade swept down my forearm, my heavy sleeve tearing open, no longer there to add extra protection. Shit. I was going to be plated up like sushi if this kept up. I jumped back, the dagger missing my jugular by inches. I blew out a heavy breath of relief that clouded the air, mingling with the suspended flakes of snow.

Faolán had been bred for battle, a true beast of war and a goddess's strong arm. He was a warrior right to the marrow of his bones. He fought like one too. Ruthless, with a savage instinct. Raif hadn't been able to keep the advantage in a fight with him, and I was suffering. Blood oozed from my many wounds, and my head swam as my vision darkened at the periphery. I fought to hold on to consciousness. My arms and legs felt like lead weights dangling from my body and, damn it, I was *tired*.

Blow after blow, kicks and stabs, slicing into my skin over and again, Faolán made it apparent he had no intention of losing. I stumbled, then wiped the blood from my forehead to keep it from running into my eyes. He was playing with me now, like a cat with an injured mouse. *Tyler,* I thought, kicking out with my leg and hitting nothing but air, *I wish you were here. I need you.*

I caught Faolán's foot as it rocketed toward my head, but I didn't have much strength left, and as I tried to twist it and break his knee, he pushed against me and threw me off balance. As I landed on my back, the breath left my lungs in a jarring whoosh, and I couldn't draw new air to replace what I'd lost. Chest aching and eyes bulging, I was desperate for a deep breath. Faolán capitalized on my distress and brought his heel down on the center of my stomach. "Bastard!" I wheezed.

I hated this place—hated it with every fiber of my being. I was weakened, nearly impotent in this fucking Faerie Realm. I wanted to go home. I wanted to throw my hands up and just—

"Surrender." Faolán finished my thought, kneeling so he could stare into my bashed and bloodied face. "You can't stop what's going to happen. So don't try. I'll kill you quick. I owe you that much for the part you've played. Just lie there and be still, and I'll put an end to your suffering."

My mind must've been addled, because I thought about closing my eyes, nice and compliant, as I waited for Faolán to deliver the sweet, blissful oblivion he promised. But, as always, Fate had other plans for me. I wasn't thinking when I let my eyes wander to the spot where Brakae had been lying unconscious—the spot that was now unoccupied.

Faolán spun on the balls of his feet, rising to his full height. Brakae stood before him, the long dagger I'd discarded held aloft in her shaking hand. Bruises marred her beautiful face, blood dried and crusted on her robes. So much for true love.

I rolled onto my hands and knees and dragged in ragged gulps of breath. My lungs burned, and I wanted to throw up. But I didn't have time. *Get your shit together.* I sniffed, pulling dripping blood back up into my nose and choked as the coppery taste blazed a trail down my throat. *Come on, Darian, get with the fucking program.*

"What are you going to do, my love?" Faolán's voice was tender, concerned, as if the SOB hadn't beaten and sliced her up earlier. "Would you kill me?"

"Y-yes." Brakae's voice quavered, her eyes brimming over with tears that spilled down her cheeks. "If you don't stop, I will have no choice but to kill you."

I pushed myself back up to my knees and took a moment to stabilize before standing. Brakae had Faolán's undivided attention, her sapphire blue eyes glistening with a steady stream of tears. Her jaw trembled as she fought to keep it raised in a defiant set. But she was struggling; I could see the almost-imperceptible breakdown of her resolve. She'd loved him. Hell, she might've loved him still. I knew better than anyone what that felt like. I'd taken Azriel's life, and despite everything he'd done to me, I'd held him close to my heart.

Faolán inched closer to Brakae. Her eyes darted from side to side, frantic like a trapped animal, and she flinched as he brought his hand up toward her face. "Don't touch me." She raised the dagger as a warning.

"If you feel nothing for me"—Faolán edged closer to

Brakae and I tensed—"then do what you must." He made a show of bearing his chest to her and lifted the tip of her blade with his fingertip, positioning it over his heart. "Your new Guardian couldn't protect you. It was *her* fault you were hurt. I never wanted harm to come to you. If you don't believe me, take my life."

The heavy dagger vibrated under Brakae's trembling hand. She couldn't kill him. Not the man she'd loved. She was Raif's daughter, a warrior's blood coursed through her veins, but she was no killer. If she had been, she wouldn't have needed a Guardian to help protect the natural order.

Slowly, her fingers uncurled from around the dagger. Faolán had his back to me, but I didn't have to see his face to know the triumph written there. He'd kill her, I had no doubt. He'd come too far, and his insanity had taken him to a place he couldn't return from.

I no longer wobbled on my feet. My lungs rose and fell as I drew deep, steady breaths. I watched as the dagger slipped from Brakae's hand, falling soundlessly in this place frozen in time. Faolán reached out, his hands curled into claws, and a snarl tore from his throat. I pushed at the ground, the heavy tread of my boots slipping and then catching hold of the snow.

"I'm sorry," Faolán said as he reached for Brakae. "I will always love you."

I jumped, arms outstretched, and shoved her out of the way before Faolán could seize her. It wasn't a graceful maneuver by any standards as Brakae went flying, but it got the job done. I rolled in a swift, fluid motion and scooped the dagger into my grasp.

With a quick, upward stab, I aimed for the spot Faolán had laid bare for Brakae. The dagger sliced through skin, muscle, and bone as though his body were nothing more than a sheet of silk fabric. Veins of green glowed against the obsidian blade as Faolán pitched forward, knocking me backward. As he fell, the long dagger drove farther still, burying itself to the hilt.

I shimmied my legs up between us and used the leverage to roll him off me. Blood, red and bright, stained the pristine snow and covered my hands with a slick warmth that nauseated me. I'd never had such an attack of conscience before—unless you considered Azriel's death. The tragedy of it all hit too close to home for me to feel anything but regret. Only love could drive a person so completely into the arms of madness.

"You are a Guardian worthy of the Order," Faolán rasped. "My Enphigmalé brothers would be proud to have you amongst their ranks."

I knelt beside him, speechless.

"Thank you." His breath labored in his lungs, an ugly, gurgling sound. "For protecting her."

A scrambling noise drew my attention, and I looked up to see Brakae crawling through the snow, silent sobs catching in her throat. The dagger still protruded from Faolán's chest, and I pulled with everything I had left, determined to provide Brakae with a slightly less gruesome image to remember her beloved by.

Taking the dagger with me, I turned my back as Brakae gently lowered herself on to his torso and wept in earnest. Had she been able to look into his eyes one last time before he faded away? I refused to intrude upon her private moment by turning back to see. Brushing away hovering snowflakes, I limped to the stone podium at the center of the ring of stones. A *pit-pat* sound accompanied every step, blood dripping from my scored and stabbed flesh to stain the snow-covered ground with shiny red tears.

I approached the hourglass with caution. It wasn't every day I attempted to set time aright. My ring glowed white on the neck of the broken half as if waiting to be put to work. Love really was an amazing thing. It could mend hearts, break them, and bend the very fabric of time and space. It bowed to no one, and could bring you to your knees for the right person. My eyelids drooped; I was keeping my eyes open by sheer force of will. Damn, I wanted to sleep for a century or more. But my job wasn't finished—yet.

Chapter 31

I stared unblinkingly at the hourglass for what seemed like forever. I looked around past the ring of stones at the naked tree branches and snowflakes dotting the air. *Time to set the natural order back in balance.* I shivered, finally feeling the chill. Or was it fear that shook me? How much time had passed at home? Were my loved ones safe?

All I had to do was reach out and pluck my ring from the neck of the glass, but my brain was having a hard time getting my arm, hand, and fingers to obey the command. How could I face Tyler again? My actions had been a betrayal of our love. Shame boiled in my stomach, twisting it with regret.

"Just reach out and take it, Darian." Moira's voice was soft, soothing.

She stood behind me, and I didn't turn to face her. "When did you come to?"

"Too late to be of any use."

"Sorry about that." I really was. "I shouldn't have knocked you out."

"No. And I won't forget it either." She sounded playful, but the moment was too somber for comic relief. "You did well."

I choked on a sob, swallowing it down. "Yeah, well, I don't think I'll be counting it as a victory."

"No," Moira whispered. "This is indeed a tragedy."

Understatement of the century. "Just reach out and grab it, huh?"

"The ring belongs to you."

"It's not going to explode or spontaneously burst into flames?"

Moira laughed without humor. "Not likely. Just take it, Darian. Trust."

Trust. Like I had any idea what that was. But I reached out anyway, my fingers trembling. God, I was afraid. I wrapped my fingers around the ring—*my ring*—and the warmth pulsing from the silver put me at ease. If the ring hadn't burned my hand to ash, then maybe that meant Tyler could forgive me. I pulled it from its perch, and as I did, the snow left its stasis and began to float in a slow waltz to the ground. A warm breeze kissed my cheeks, and the branches of the trees quivered, tiny buds of green dotting their once-bare arms.

"Holy shit," I whispered.

"Darian . . ."

Brakae's voice, tiny but somehow strong, drew my attention from the natural wonder before me. Slipping my ring back on my thumb, I left Moira to collect Reaver's half of the hourglass and went to check on Raif's daughter. *Raif's. Daughter.* My God, I'd really found her. Well, more to the point, she had found me.

She left Faolán's body in the now-melting snow and walked toward me with slow, measured steps. Like a hollow representation of her former self, she limped along, gripping her side to stem the flow of blood from one of her many wounds.

"Are you all right?" What a stupid question.

"No," she said, and I respected her for her candor. "But I will be."

Time heals all wounds, right? "I—Brakae—" Fuck, what the hell was I going to say? *Sorry I killed the guy you used to love.*

"We are nothing more than the servants of destiny," she said, holding her hand out to me. I took it, and, well, it didn't even feel a little awkward. "Leave this behind like a stone on the road."

Raif had said that to me once. I felt the sting of tears at my eyes and bit back the emotion. I missed him.

Brakae looked as tired as I felt, as emotionally raw and worked over. We'd both passed through the eye of the storm and come out on the other side. And I *knew* neither of us would ever be the same for it. Her gaze lowered to my neck, and her lips curved in a sad, wan smile. From her robes she produced a glowing green emerald suspended from a length of silver chain. "The Key," I said, taking it from her waiting hand.

"It's not an easy job," Brakae said, "being the Guardian of Time."

"Or the Keeper of it," I added. Her gaze dropped to the ground, and sorrow consumed her expression. She had it much worse than I. She'd suffered and sacrificed. She needed a ray of sun in the dark of her life. "Can I bring your father here?" Hope swelled within me at the thought. I refused to believe Raif had died in that hotel room. Damn it, he had to be alive, and I was going to reunite him with his daughter. "So he can see you?"

I saw a trace of sunlight in her expression, maybe the beginning of a long road toward healing. "I would like that," she said. "Very much."

Suddenly, I felt a little sun as well.

Moira joined us, carrying Brakae's half of the hourglass in one hand and Reaver's half tucked in the crook of her arm. Weren't we just the embodiment of girl power? "Brakae," she said, "your wounds need tending."

Her knees wobbled beneath her, and I reached out to support her. Where were those trauma nurse Sprites when you needed them?

"I can help her," Moira said.

"You're a Healer." Levi had mentioned that. I was going to have to keep that guy on retainer. "Right?"

Moira nodded and made her way to Brakae. She touched her fingertips to her skin, and a soft blue light flowed from the wound, moving outward like rings on glassy water. She began to hum while she worked, a rhythmic, melodious tune that snaked around me and filled me with emotion. It struck me as strange, the way lives and events intertwined to form the knotted chain of destiny. It made me think that, maybe, life wasn't just a random pattern of bullshit tied to bad luck or good fortune. "Moira . . ."

"Do you really want to torture yourself with the truth, Darian?"

Damn mind readers. "Can I talk to him?"

"No. It doesn't work that way."

"He knew. Azriel had to have known all along what would happen to me. It isn't coincidence. I just want to know the why and how of it."

Moira sighed. "He made you what you are."

What was that, exactly? Damaged? Distrustful? A control freak who refused to open up to anyone?

"He made you *strong*," Moira said. "Perhaps Azriel strayed from his path, but without him, you would have died today."

"Raif made me strong." No way was Az going to get the credit.

"Raif made you a fighter," Moira corrected. "Azriel made you capable."

I opened my mouth to argue. I didn't want to acknowledge that Azriel had done anything but permanent damage by taking me under his wing. But Moira's gaze locked with mine, a warning—or a suggestion. *Do not speak of it.* Her voice echoed in my mind. *Leave the past in the past, Darian.*

After a moment, Moira stood. "Brakae, Reaver's glass must be returned. Things are still too volatile here for my peace of mind."

"I agree," Brakae said, and I suddenly felt like an outsider in a private conversation. "Go with my blessings."

Moira handed over Brakae's half of the glass and bowed her head before looking to me. "See you on the other side."

She held out her hand, and I clasped it. "Count on it."

"Brakae," Moira said, turning to leave, "I shall see you soon."

She nodded and raised her hand to gesture her off. "Good-bye, Moira."

A ripple of energy stirred the air, sending the snow-flakes swirling, and then Moira was gone. "Will it always be like this?" I asked, feeling centuries old. "Constant threats and me here fighting while time flies by at home?"

"No." Was it my imagination that she actually sounded disappointed? "You won't be often called upon. So few know of the hourglass, of me, of *O Anel*. It is nothing but legend now, and besides Moira, you have the only other key. That is what you're meant to protect."

She was lonely. Bitter. I knew that tone well. I'd been alone for almost a century, hiding away at Azriel's command. I could only imagine how bad it was for her, here in this place where her deep connection to time aged her at a whim and in any direction. "I'll come visit when I can. And I'll bring Raif too."

She pulled me into her arms and squeezed me—hard. My ribs wanted to crack under her fierce display of affection, but I totally didn't mind. I put my arms around her as well, to let her know she wouldn't feel so separated from the world she'd once known now that I had something to say about it.

"Now, you go home," Brakae said. Was it my imagination that her voice sounded younger, more childlike?

"Just click my heels together?"

Brakae pulled away, gave me a strange, innocent look. "No, just use the Key. Why would you click your heels together?"

Wouldn't she get a dose of culture shock if she came home with me. "Right, use the Key. Honestly, I'm not sure how."

"Just concentrate. The Key will do the rest."

My heart pounded a staccato against my ribs, and my stomach twisted like a pretzel. Christ, was returning to the mortal world so hard to face? I wanted to go home. I *needed* to see Tyler, but I was so afraid to face him, I didn't know if I could bring myself to leave.

"Go with my blessings, Guardian." Brakae's voice calmed me, slowing my racing heart. "And I will see you soon."

My gaze swept past Raif's long-lost daughter one more time to the place where Faolán's body lay. Hourglass in hand, she turned away from me, toward her dead lover, and left me where I stood.

"I'll be back sooner than you think." She didn't acknowledge me, but I knew she'd heard. I left her to grieve and dangled the emerald pendulum before me. Just concentrate. Okay. I pushed my fear and anxiety aside and stared into the glowing green depths of the gem as I had so many times before, allowing infinite green to consume me. *I want to go home,* I thought, Tyler's face looming in my mind. *Time to go.*

A chill breeze blew my hair back from my face, stealing my breath. And a dark, cold, cloudless sky welcomed me, stars blinking in the inky blackness of a new moon.

Ruins.

In the mortal world this place was nothing but weathered granite with stones leaning and pieces missing, but the feeling of power was no less strong for its decrepit age. My body hummed with power, my bones singing under my skin. The energy here was unmistakable, but somehow I didn't feel the magnetic pull of the stones the way I had in *O Anel.* Time once again ticked within my soul, seconds passing like a dual heartbeat, and I welcomed it. I was finally home, where I belonged. My knees buckled from sheer exhaustion, and I sank down on one of the toppled slabs of cold stone, rested my head in the crook of my arm, and allowed my eyes to close for the first time in what felt like forever. God, I was so . . . fucking . . . tired. . . .

Chapter 32

"**O**i! What do you think you're doin' out there?"

My head scraped against stone as I cracked my eyes open. Shards of sunlight pierced my vision like a thousand daggers digging their way into my brain. Turning my head toward the sound of shouting, I shielded my face with my hand. Two security guards ran across the expanse of short-clipped green grass, nightsticks drawn and at the ready. Not what I needed, considering I didn't have a passport or ID, not to mention that I wasn't exactly human. The faint glow of my eyes would raise more than just suspicion if they got a good look at me. I couldn't lie here like a dazed disaster victim any longer.

"Charlie!" the security guard shouted to his partner. "Call it in! What the bloody hell does she think she's doin'?"

The last thing I wanted to do was move. But being arrested wasn't going to help me out *at all*. I rolled to the side, off the slab of granite I'd fallen asleep on, and became one with the light. Ghosting past the charging guards, I barely avoided the one in the lead as he skidded to a stop. Eyes bulging in disbelief, he pointed to the stone where I'd been lying a few moments before, mouth agape. His partner nearly crashed into him as they exchanged amazed expressions. I doubted seeing a woman's phantom form disappear before their eyes was the strangest thing they'd ever witnessed here. This was Stonehenge, after all. The magical energy was palpable.

Careful to remain hidden in bright sunlight, I wound

my way along the footpath, avoiding the crowds of tourists. It took longer than I expected; I didn't have my usual energetic pluck. I managed to break away from the masses and put the ancient ring of stones behind me as I left the viewing area and passed through the main entrance into the parking lot. I had one thing on my mind: Find a phone. Meandering through the rows of parked cars, I finally came across an empty tour bus, the door left wide open by the driver. A cell phone rested on the dash. Thank God. I had no idea how much an international phone call would cost the poor guy, but I only needed a few minutes of his airtime. I wasn't thrilled about stealing anything ever again. But hell, I'd already stolen time itself—pretty hard to top that act of thievery. Besides, the owner could dispute the charges later. I ducked behind one of the seats with the phone and stared at the blank screen.

I left my coat behind.

I didn't think about dialing, or the fact that I'd scared the shit out of two security guards and stolen some poor guy's cell. No. My only thought was that I'd left my fucking duster in that hotel room in Spokane.

I stretched my neck from side to side, lowered my legs from their drawn-up position against the back of the bus seat, and pushed myself upright. Stiff didn't begin to describe how I felt. More like frozen in joint-locked agony. I felt through the tears in my shirt finding nothing but smooth, unmarred skin. Just like a comic book superhero, I'd healed during the night. I breathed a sigh of relief. It made me feel just a little less fallible to be my not so easily wounded self again. If only all of my troubles could be solved so easily.

Hands shaking, I flipped open the phone and dialed. A burst of nervous energy set my feet to bouncing as the call connected. I waited as the phone rang, and rang, and rang to the point that I almost gave up hope he'd answer. *Just pick up. Answer, damn it. Please.*

"Hello?"

Tears sprang to my eyes at the sound of his voice. I'd

had no way of knowing for sure if he'd survived the attack at the hotel; it was only at this moment that I realized I'd been making myself believe he was okay. Knowing it for sure made my limbs weak with relief.

"Raif." I choked on his name, a half sob.

"Thank the gods," he said on an exhale. "Darian, are you all right? Where are you?"

"Wiltshire."

I waited through the pregnant pause on the other end. No doubt Raif's mind was going a mile a minute. "England?"

"Yes. Well, more to the point, Stonehenge. How fast can you get here?"

There was another space of silence. I almost wished I could see his expression.

"Xander has some connections, and I can call in a few favors as well. I'll be there as soon as I can. No more than twelve hours."

"Raif." God, I couldn't believe I was about to say this. "Come alone."

His response was slow. "If that's what you want . . ."

"It is. And one more thing—"

"Darian," he said, cutting me off, "is everything okay? What the hell is going on? I would have expected—"

"I know what you expected." It was my turn to cut him off. Of course he'd expect me to want Tyler to come instead of him. "But you don't need to worry about that right now. Can you do something else for me? Stop by my place and grab a change of clothes. I have a spare coat in my closet. Bring that too."

"Anything else?"

Yeah, my katana. But even I didn't know where it was. "Just get here."

"I'm on my way."

I snapped the phone closed and put it back on the dash. For a second, I thought about curling up in one of the bus seats and going back to sleep. But it would be just my luck that the bus would take off to God knows where and I'd sleep through the whole excursion. I'd had enough adventure to last a lifetime in the past several hours. I didn't need another one.

Stepping down out of the bus, I found a quiet spot away from the parking lot and sat down in the grass, my shoulders sagging in exhaustion. Drawing my legs up to my chest, I rested my arms on my knees and my forehead on my arms, effectively shutting out the rest of the world. Five words—five little words were all it would take to have Tyler by my side. But that was not the way I wanted it to go down. I didn't want him to think I had so little respect for him that I'd leave without a trace and then just wish him out of thin air. I wanted him, though. I needed him. I ached to feel his arms around me, his breath on my face, to hear his voice whisper in my ear. Tears scalded my cheeks as they trailed silently to my chin. I missed him so much, it was a physical pain, a fist squeezing my heart. All I could think of was seeing his face again, but instead I'd done the right thing and called Raif to come get me. This journey had been about him, after all. I owed it to him to reunite him with his daughter.

As the day progressed, the tourists filtered in and out of the area. I did the smart thing and remained in my incorporeal form. It had been so long since I'd been able to join with the night, day, or anytime in between that I'd almost forgotten I could do it at all. It felt good to be invisible, uninteresting. If I could have, I would have lived the rest of my life this way, the wraith of Stonehenge scaring curious onlookers away.

It wasn't long before I slumped over to curl up on the grass. I was still beyond tired, having been awake the entire time I'd been in *O Anel*, and who knew how long that actually was. The sun rose higher in the sky, its warmth lulling me back to sleep. There was something to be said for constancy. The sun rose, it set, it rose again—all in a glorious twenty-four-hour period. I appreciated that. My thoughts wandered as I drifted, and as I succumbed to sleep yet again, it was with thoughts of seeing Tyler comforting me.

*   *   *

"Darian!"

I stirred against the cold and felt around for a blanket.

"Darian! Where the hell are you?"

Right here. Sleeping. Leave me alone.

"Darian, it's Raif. Show yourself."

Damn. I wasn't in my bed, was I? And my memories couldn't be attributed to a restless sleep riddled with nightmares. *Wonderful.*

"Darian!"

Raif's voice penetrated the sleepy haze pulling me back toward endless oblivion. I rolled, my body becoming corporeal as I came to my knees and then to my feet. The sun had set long ago, and night had descended over the sacred ring of stones. I listed to the right, then stumbled toward the dark outline of Raif's body, shaking off the dregs of sleep. "I'm here," I said, my voice weak and hoarse. "Raif, I'm here!"

He spun around, and I couldn't help the cry of relief that burst from my lips. He raced across the dark landscape of the parking lot, closing the distance between us in six quick strides. I would have barreled right into him if he hadn't reached out and wrapped his hands around my shoulders. Holding me at arms' length, he looked me over from head to toe, then spun me around, inspecting me for damage.

"Darian, where have you been?" The fear, mixed with relief, in his voice caused my heart to slam against my rib cage. "Are you hurt?"

"How long have I been gone?" I was afraid to hear it; my ears cringed away from an answer, but I had to know. "How long, Raif?"

"A little over three months," he said.

No. I shook my head and clenched my fists. *Fuck!* I'd feared it had been years. I'd hoped like hell it had only been days. But over three months? It was still too goddamned long. "How is he?"

Raif let go of my shoulders, then ran his fingers through his tawny hair, which had been, until lately, neat and pulled back. In fact, he'd trimmed it short since I'd seen him last. It looked good on him. He opened his mouth, paused, and looked away as if trying to decide how much to say.

"Tell me the truth," I said.

"He's mad with worry," Raif said with obvious concern. "I haven't seen him for a while. He had to be forcibly removed from Xander's house when he accused me and then my brother of playing a part in your disappearance."

My heart stopped its erratic beating and took a nosedive straight into my stomach. I'd done a number on Tyler. I'd been so stupid! Like a note on his pillow would have been enough reassurance to convince him I was coming back to him. My stomach turned with nausea, or was that regret making me feel as though I could throw my guts up? "I had no idea," I said, helpless. "Raif, when I left, I had no idea I'd be gone so long."

"Darian"—Raif stepped toe-to-toe with me so he could stare right into my eyes—"where *have* you been?"

"O Anel."

"The Ring?" Raif translated the words, confused. "What is that? Where's the Oracle? Fallon? What's happened to you these many months?"

God, where to begin. He knew part of it, but the way everything intertwined made *my* head spin. And I knew it all forward and backward. "Fallon," I said, still weary from lack of sleep. "Or rather, Faolán . . ." I thought of Brakae, her grief. "Raif, I was afraid he'd killed you."

"You should know better than that," he said. "It will take a better man than him to send me to the shadows for eternity. But you disappeared. You were there and then—gone."

"About that—"

"You're wanted, Darian." He blurted it out as if he'd had to force the words out. "Adare has ordered that if you are found, you're to be turned over to the PNT for questioning. Despite my testimony of what I saw, that you were in fact a prisoner and not an accomplice. He wants answers."

Shit. I'd forgotten about that. Just one more thing to

pile on my plate. "Adare will get his answers," I said. "Later."

"And what about me?"

"Raif," I said, "you're going to get *your* answers right now."

I reached inside my pocket and pulled out the emerald pendulum. It glowed bright green in my hand, pulsing with warmth and power. It knew what I was going to do, and apparently it didn't object too much.

"What is that?"

"The Key," I said, for the first time not hating the weight of the damned thing as I looped it around my neck. The sound of time's passage left me, and I breathed a sigh of relief. "Are you ready, Raif?"

"For what?" he asked, bemused.

"To see your daughter."

His jaw dropped. I smiled. I couldn't help it; I'd never seen him thrown like that before, and I was happy it had been me to do it to him. I stepped in, laid my cheek on my friend's shoulder, and he instinctively wrapped his arms around me. It didn't matter that we weren't blood related. Raif was as much my brother as if we'd been born of the same parents.

I held the emerald before me, concentrated on where I needed to be, and lost myself in its depths. Next up: one family reunion.

The darkened landscape melted away, and we appeared right where I'd left Brakae in the center of the ring of stones. Raif let go of me, turning a circle as he took in his surroundings. "I know. What a mindfuck, right?"

"Amazing," Raif said. "But, Darian, what does this have to do with—"

"Father?" Her voice was younger than when I'd left, that of an adolescent girl, not that of the grown woman.

His eyes widened in disbelief, glistening with tears. I swallowed the baseball-sized lump that had grown in my throat and squeezed his hand before taking a step back. This was his reunion, not mine. And they both deserved this moment of happiness.

Chapter 33

One advantage to keeping royal company was the perk of a private jet. Xander happened to own a Gulfstream, and for once I didn't feel like wringing his neck for flaunting his extravagant possessions. It was damned comfortable too. I'd added another three and a half weeks to my MIA status by returning to *O Anel* with Raif, and we still had a thirteen-hour flight before we'd be back in Seattle. But if I had to endure the agony of more time away from Tyler, at least I endured it in style.

Knowing he could see Brakae whenever he wanted put Raif at ease. He hadn't felt as if they were parting forever when he'd left *O Anel*—just for a while.

"You're worried, aren't you?" Raif said, interrupting my thoughts. He regarded me with his fierce blue eyes, and it reminded me of the first time we met at Xander's warehouse. Nothing got past him.

"I left him."

"Yes."

"He might not forgive me."

"He's not worthy of you if he doesn't."

Always pragmatic, Raif didn't know how to mince words.

"I'm afraid to face him."

"Nonsense." Raif sat up straight in his chair and leaned forward. "You're not afraid of anything."

I didn't answer him because I didn't want him to know the truth. I was scared shitless to face Tyler.

Raif leaned back in his chair, and his expression softened. "Sleep, Darian. By gods, you've earned it. I'll wake you when we get home."

He didn't have to tell me twice. I was asleep before my chair fully reclined.

"I missed you, Darian."

Oh God, I loved the way he said my name—like a prayer or something sacred. The sound of his voice touched every minute part of me, right down to my hair follicles, like sparks of electricity. For the first time in a long, lonely while I felt *alive*. We were two parts of a whole. Unlike the broken hourglass, my world had been out of balance *without* my other half. And now he was here—right here next to me—and if I'd wished him here in my sleep, then thank God I was a sleep-talker.

But really, I didn't care how he'd gotten here. Raif was nowhere to be seen; maybe he was in the cockpit with the pilot. Whatever, it didn't matter. I had *everything* I needed now. "Tyler . . ." There was so much to say. Where should I start? The dim lighting of the private jet's cabin barely illuminated his face, but I knew every detail. I'd etched a vision of him in my memory. He brought his finger to my lips, effectively silencing anything I'd planned to say. Did words really matter when you loved someone this much?

He replaced his finger with his mouth, his lips so soft, they were nothing more than a light brush against my own. Tyler pulled me out of my seat while he closed the privacy partition around us and settled into the seat I'd been sleeping in. He pulled me down without a word, and I straddled him. I traced my hands up the muscles of his arms, reacquainting myself with the topography of his body. His shoulders were firm in my grip—solid—before I continued my exploration, moving downward over his chest, my fingers tracing the hard, muscled expanse of his stomach.

He thrust his hips, and the hard length of him pressed against me through our clothes, causing a jolt of pleasure that sent my head lolling back on my shoulders. Slowly, and so gently, his fingers laced through my hair like the stirring of a breeze, and he urged my head back while he tasted the flesh just above my collarbone. Tyler's tongue teased and enticed as it traveled up my neck to just below my ear. His teeth grazed my flesh, and I gasped, wrapping my arms around him to draw him closer. The plane could have gone into a nosedive spiral, engulfed in flames, and I wouldn't have noticed. All I knew was I wanted more of Tyler. Right. *Now*.

I threw off my coat and worked at getting Ty's T-shirt up and over his head while he did the same to me. The possibility of getting caught made it all the more exciting as he pulled the straps of my bra down over my shoulders, shoving the silky fabric away from my breasts. It had been so long since I'd felt his skin against mine, and I reveled in the taste of his cool mouth. Hours in *O Anel* had been months, but it felt more like years. Every minute away from him had been a century.

He took one breast into his mouth, sucking and biting gently. I arched my back, pushing closer, and he caught the other breast in his hand. God, yes! I missed this—*him*—so much. He pulled away, and I brought my lips to his, a greedy kiss, a wanton claiming of his mouth. I parted my lips, and Tyler followed suit, our tongues searching, tasting, lingering. *I've died,* I thought as his hands traced down my sides to pull at the waistband of my pants. *I'm dead and this is heaven.*

I rose up on my knees so Tyler could unfasten the button on my pants. A quick tug and they were down around my thighs, not exposing near enough of me for what I wanted to do. I stretched out one leg, and then the other, and kicked my pants and underwear to the floor. I looked down to the bulge in Ty's jeans, pulling my bottom lip between my teeth before meeting his heated hazel gaze. It was all the encouragement he needed before his pants and underwear joined mine. I smiled as I took in the impressive sight of his naked body. He'd put a Greek god to shame with his perfection.

Tyler pulled my head down, kissing me fiercely. No

time for sweet whispered words and foreplay. I needed him inside me. Now.

I positioned myself above him and guided him in. My breath caught as he invaded every inch of me, and it was a sweet torture that made me only want more. He kissed me again, leaving a blazing trail from my lips to my chin, neck, and collarbone, ending again at my breasts. His hands settled at my hips, and I began to move, slow at first, rocking back and forth at a measured pace. Tyler groaned, the sound vibrating across my flesh, and I sped up, unable to control the frenzy he'd created in me. His breath came heavy—or was it my own rasping in my ears?—as my pleasure mounted to unbearable degrees. *More*. I needed more of him. I could never get enough. I vowed silently as he brought his lips to mine that I would never leave him again.

He thrust his hips, driving deep into me as I rocked and pressed down hard on top of him. A wave of pleasure so great, it stole my breath, crested and threatened to crash over me. . . .

"Darian!"

My eyes shot open as though I'd been doused with a bucket of ice water. I sat bolt upright, nearly throwing myself from the chair. Eyes wide and frantic, I looked around the cabin, disbelieving I'd dreamt the whole thing. My body—still warm and pulsing from his touch—felt too real for it all to have been just a dream.

"Are you all right?" Raif asked. "I had to shout to wake you up. I tried several times."

Heat rushed to my cheeks. Jesus Christ, what sounds had escaped my lips in my sleep? I might as well have been caught in the act. I sure as hell felt embarrassed enough. Tears of disappointment and heartache prickled behind my eyes, and I bit my cheek—hard enough to draw blood—to prevent my ragged emotions from taking me over. I swallowed down the coppery taste coating my mouth and took a deep breath to cleanse the remains of the dream from my mind. I could still smell his warm, spicy scent. . . .

"Darian?" Raif snapped his fingers in front of my face to get my attention. "Maybe we should have Xander's physician check you out now that we're home. We're taxiing off the runway right now."

"I'm not going to Xander's with you." I didn't have another minute to spare for anyone. "I'm going to Tyler's as *soon* as I'm off this plane."

"About that." Raif's tone was sour, tentative. "The last time I saw him, he didn't look so good. Haggard. Exhausted. I don't think the man had shaved in months." He cleared his throat. "And he smelled as though he hadn't showered in as long as well."

Ugh. It was just like Raif to let his royal lineage, or rather inner snob, show. Definitely channeling his high-and-mighty brother. I didn't give a shit what Tyler looked like. He could have a beard like Sasquatch's and smell like an outhouse for all I cared, as long as I could see him and feel his arms around me. "Then it's my fault he's in the shape he's in. I've got to see him. Now. I'll tend to myself later."

"Take care, Darian." The brotherly tone had returned to Raif's voice. "He's not himself."

The plane came to a stop, and the pilot stepped out to open the hatch. I wasn't about to waste time walking down the stairs. "I'll talk to you later, Raif. Thank you for coming for me." I didn't wait for a response or reciprocation on his part, though I knew Raif was dying to show his gratitude again. Instead, I became one with the shadows and headed straight for downtown and Tyler's apartment.

Chapter 34

I'd missed the hell out of Seattle, but the cityscape passed in a blur as I raced with preternatural speed to Tyler's penthouse apartment. I'd gawk at the scenery later. Right now, I had to make sure he was okay.

I didn't bother with decorum as I glided like a wraith to the top floor of the building. Waiting on a slow-as-fuck elevator would not have been conducive to my mounting impatience. When I got to Tyler's front door, I became my corporeal self. The door was open a crack, and a sliver of light shone out into the hall. Strange. Tyler was usually so concerned with security, it didn't feel right that his door was open.

Tentatively, I pushed it open and stepped inside. The place did smell a little like Xander's training room after a workout—musty, sweaty—and my stomach twisted into a tight pretzel that felt like a fifty-pound weight. Tyler liked to have his place lit up like a Christmas tree, but tonight the only light came from his bedroom. I walked, silent as a shadow, my gaze drawn inexplicably to the island counter in the kitchen. The granite slab of the counter was cracked down the center, and the island slumped in on itself as if a giant had tried out his karate chop on its surface.

In fact, the whole apartment looked pretty damned trashed. Forget college dorm room; someone had partied like a rock star in Tyler's penthouse—or thrown a king-sized shit fit. My mouth went dry, my hands shook at my sides, and I felt like dry-heaving. What was I going to find on the other side of Tyler's bedroom door? Did I really want to see the havoc I'd wreaked?

I pushed open the door, and it didn't even squeak to betray my presence. Bathed in light, Tyler stood at the foot of his bed, an open suitcase in front of him and a stack of clothes ready to be packed beside it.

"I felt you the second you came back," Tyler said without turning to face to me. "It was like someone had switched a light on in my soul. And then you left again for three weeks, and snap! The light came on again."

His voice was hollow, emotionless. Too calm. My heartbeat kicked into high gear, pounding against my rib cage, and I felt as if I needed to swallow ten times more than usual. "Tyler—"

"Do you know how that feels, Darian, to have that light flipped on and then extinguished over and over?"

"I didn't know." God, what a lame-ass response. "When I left, I had no idea what I was getting myself into."

"No, I suppose you didn't." His voice became hard. "If you had, you probably would've included it in your *note*."

"If I told you what I was going to do, you would have tried to stop me. Or worse, come with me. I was trying to protect you."

Tyler turned to face me, and the fist squeezing my heart constricted at the sight of him. He looked freshly showered and shaved. In fact, his hair was still a little damp, and he smelled of shampoo and body wash on top of his natural scent. His hair was a bit longer, curling at the base of his neck and over his ears. He raised his brows in question and those too disappeared into longer, curling, bronze-streaked locks. But what did me in was the look in those beautiful hazel eyes of his. His gaze was empty, dull, completely hollow, and I realized at that moment that what I'd done—leaving without a trace—had nearly killed him.

"Where did you go?" His tone was that of a demand.

"The Faerie Ring."

"O Anel?"

I opened my mouth to speak, too astonished at his knowledge to put a coherent string of words together.

"What, Darian?" He became agitated, almost defensive. "You didn't think I was smart enough to know what that was? I'm older than your friend Raif and twice as clever as that asshole who managed to gain your trust and lure you away. Fallon," he scoffed. "The least he could have done was picked a better alias. It didn't take long for me to figure out who—and what—he really was. Maybe if you'd checked one of the twenty or so voice mails I'd left you, you would have realized that I was already one step ahead of you. You knew I'd been talking to people. Investigating. You didn't even give me enough time to confirm what I'd learned before you took off on me." My eyes widened, and he gave me a bitter smile. "I guess you didn't think I was strong enough to help you, so why should I be any smarter?"

"That's not true." *Goddamn it*, I needed more saliva in my mouth. It was too dry to even form words.

"That *is* true." He sat down on the bed, crossing his legs at the ankle and his arms in front of him. The laidback attitude he'd adopted put me on high alert. "You didn't think I could hold my own with what you had going down. You lied to me, deceived me, withheld information I could have used to *help you*. And then, to top it all off, you left in the middle of the night with a cryptic note for explanation and fled the city with *another man*. A man you obviously trusted and held in higher regard than me."

"Tyler, that's not what happened at all. *I* was deceived. It was a trap."

He pushed himself off the bed and walked toward me. I had to fight the urge not to cringe away from him, his expression was so dark. I'd seen fury boiling under the surface like that before, but never from Tyler. That terrified me.

"I thought I could prove myself to you," he said, almost murmuring. "I thought if I gave you space and let you think I wasn't just another user trying to control you,

you'd learn to trust me. I bound myself to you out of *love*, and I prayed the gods would let you love me too." He traced his fingers along my jawline, and I felt the tears welling in my eyes spill over onto my cheeks. I couldn't bring myself to speak; the tenderness was killing me. "I should have known better," he whispered. "I should have known you'd never let your guard down. Not for me, not for anyone."

"Tyler," I said as I fought to talk through the dryness in my throat, "I'm so, *so* sorry."

A slight, sad smile curved his lips. "I know you are. But sorry isn't good enough."

"What do you want me to do?" At this point, I'd have done whatever he asked me to. "Just tell me what I have to do to fix things between us."

"You were gone, Darian. I told you how it was for me, but you didn't listen. It was like part of my soul had gone dark. After you left here, I could still feel you. You wouldn't answer your phone, the PNT was looking for you, and I knew you were running. But at least I knew you were alive. Your wish made me damned near powerless. I couldn't come for you even when I sensed you were in trouble. But then—" He paused, and his voice seemed to catch somewhere between his chest and his mouth. "You just disappeared. The light went off. *Nothing*. It was as if you'd never existed."

My throat closed up; I felt as though I were suffocating. There wasn't enough air in the world to fill my lungs. "I did what I thought was best for you. I would have died if anything had happened to you and you were already in danger—"

"You don't get it, Darian." He locked his gaze with mine, and I bit back a sob. "I knew you weren't dead. After all, we're bound. My life force is tied to yours. But at least with death there's some sort of finality! There's nothing worse than *not* knowing. And I had no idea where you'd gone, what had happened to you. Once . . ." He brushed a tear from my cheek with his thumb. "Once I could've sworn I felt you reaching out for me. Right here." He pounded a fist against his chest over his heart. "And it felt so real. But there wasn't a goddamned thing I could do about it! I couldn't go to you. I couldn't *help* you. No, I knew you weren't dead, but I mourned you just the same."

I couldn't hold back the flood any longer. His calm voice, the way his gaze bored right through me, the pain in every syllable he spoke; it was just too much. My entire body seemed to compress against the emotion I was trying not to let bust out of me like a broken dam. "I love you."

"But you don't trust me. You don't consider me your equal. You don't think I'm strong enough to protect you."

"No!" Was that my voice that had erupted into a high, keening cry? "Tyler, no."

"I wish it weren't true." He dragged his hand through his still-damp hair, and my knees threatened to give out beneath me. "I wish to hell that weren't true. But this will happen again. And again. You draw danger like a magnet, Darian. No matter how much I want to be your protector, you'll continue to push me away."

I shook my head. The words wouldn't come. I couldn't get my mouth to work properly.

"I think you need some time—"

"No!" The word exploded from my lips. "Damn it, Tyler, don't do this! Get mad, yell at me, throw something! Set the fucking bed on fire and take a baseball bat to every lamp in the house. But *do not* say what you're about to say."

"I'm sorry, love." He laid his lips to my forehead and stayed that way for a few moments before pulling away. "I think you need to decide what you really want. I won't tag along after you anymore. I won't sit at home and wait while you risk your life."

"But the bond . . ." It was my ace in the hole. He couldn't leave me. He'd bound himself to me.

"Is intact," he said. "I told you, only you have the power to break it. I will protect you with my dying breath. If you need me, you know what to do." He turned away, left me leaning against the doorjamb for support, and returned to his suitcase. He didn't take the time to fold his clothes, instead shoving them in the case before stuffing the lid down and zipping it closed.

I was frantic to keep him where he was. He couldn't leave me. He couldn't. "Ty, please don't go. Please, Ty. Don't—God, please—don't leave me."

"I won't be gone long," he said, throwing my own words back in my face. I wished like hell I'd never written that damned note, that I could turn back time and undo it all. "I tried too hard." He grabbed the suitcase and crossed the room toward me. "I tried to force you before you were ready. Maybe without me here, you'll find the closure you need to let me in. I hope that when I come back, you'll be ready to trust me, to believe in me."

"You don't have to leave for that to happen, Tyler." My world was crumbling around me, and there was nothing I could do about it. "Stay. Please."

"I love you," he said as he leaned in to kiss me one last time. "Good-bye, Darian."

His lips on mine caused a ripple of energy to flow over my body, and the room swam in a dizzy blur. I closed my eyes to steady my careening world, and when I opened them again, he was gone.

I don't know how I got back to my apartment. I was worse than a fucking zombie, more brainless than the walking dead without even hunger to motivate my shuffling steps. I got out of the elevator and stared at my surroundings as if I'd never seen the place before. Someone had come in and turned up the heat. At least, I thought someone had. The vents were blowing warm air, stirring my hair and drying my wide, unblinking eyes.

I'd been back in Seattle for only a few hours. But somehow it felt like years. As if I'd been watching from a distance, the scene with Tyler played over and over in my mind, and I searched for the right word, the perfect phrase I *hadn't* said, that might have convinced him to stay. God, I'd fucked up. Pushed him too far. Expected too much and at the same time, not enough. I loved him the way I'd been taught to love—through control and manipulation. I'd failed him—miserably. I didn't know how to share my life with someone. Tyler deserved someone so much better than I. And though I knew he should have gone out and found that better someone, I prayed to whatever gods that listened that he wouldn't.

"I love you."

He'd said those words to me.

"Good-bye, Darian."

Right before he left me.

What was I going to do without him? He'd been a constant presence in my life for so long. I took for granted the knowledge that he'd always be there for me, no matter what. I took three shuffling steps toward my kitchen when a long black scabbard caught my eye. Sitting atop my dining room table were a note, a stack of mail, and—my katana.

My chest loosened a little when I looked at the sword I thought I'd lost back in Spokane when Faolán had taken control of me. I loved that goddamned piece of metal, and seeing it there on my dining room table brought a fresh wave of tears to my eyes. I picked up the note, staring at the words that seemed nothing more than incoherent scribbles until my eyes finally made sense of them all and recognized Raif's swirling script.

> *You left this in Spokane. It was my pleasure to retrieve it for you. Checked your mail while you were gone as well. This is not the dark hour you think it is, Darian. Have Faith.*
> *—R*

I caressed the scabbard, thinking of the shining blade encased within it as I crumpled Raif's note and threw it somewhere toward my kitchen. He'd known Tyler was leaving. Shit, he'd more than likely talked to him before flying to England to meet me. I felt so lost. Directionless.

Immobile. I didn't know if I could even function without Tyler. I didn't want to be alone. My hand brushed over the stack of mail Raif had left, the shiny surface of a postcard waking me from my stupor. I picked it up, the modern-day depiction of San Francisco covered with bright red curling letters of the city's name. I tried to take a deep breath, my pulse racing out of control as I turned the card over to find a cheerful message from an anonymous sender, though the handwriting was unmistakable: *Wish You Were Here.*

Jesus Christ. *Lorik.* He should have been long dead, but there was no way in hell that postcard was from anyone other than the Armenian gangster's son Azriel had helped to hide decades ago. A renewed sense of fear peppered my skin like flecks of ice, and I shivered. "Azriel," I whispered, "what the hell have you gotten me into this time?"

Turning the postcard over in my hand, I looked for some clue as to what this was all about. I couldn't explain the dark foreboding that cast its shadow on me as I stood staring at the simple laminated cardstock, but I knew trouble was headed my way.

"I will protect you with my dying breath. If you need me, you know what to do." Tyler's affirmation reverberated in my mind, heart, and soul. I hoped that sentiment held true, no matter where in the world he'd gone, because I had no doubt I was going to need Tyler's protection in the very near future.

"Come back to me, Ty." I said, loud enough for the sound of my voice to bounce off the brick walls of my studio. "Soon."

Read on for a look at the next novel in the
Shaede Assassin series,

Crave the Darkness

Available from Signet Eclipse in March 2013.

Shadow.
   That's how I started out; all I was again. A casting of mottled dark. The real me, the me that knew happiness and light left with him.

"Darian, pay attention." Raif nudged me with his elbow, and I brought my eyes up to meet the faces staring back at me.

"Can you repeat the question?"

The seven members of the Pacific Northwest Territories judicial council exchanged frustrated glances. A murmur spread from one end of the long table to the other and the speaker—a Fae with dark eyes and shining blue-black hair—shuffled through her notes before addressing me.

"Let me see if I can get this straight. You refuse to answer to the charges brought against you. Which are—" she shuffled her papers once again—"the kidnapping of a high-priority PNT prisoner, as well as . . ."

I love you.

Tyler had said those words to me.

". . . aiding and abetting a treasonous . . ."

Good-bye, Darian.

Right before he'd walked out the door.

Raif elbowed me again, and I snapped to attention.

". . . in addition to evading PNT authorities and violating section 15-372.1 of chain of command standard operating procedure. Does that just about cover it?"

My gaze drifted to the Fae woman, her face coming back into focus. They might as well throw me in jail right here and now. I wouldn't deny my guilt, and I sure as hell wouldn't explain myself. Silence hung heavy in the room, and Raif cleared his throat. Apparently, it was my turn to speak.

"You forgot breaking and entering, conspiracy, and all-around willful disobedience. *That* about covers it."

Raif pinched the bridge of his nose between his thumb and forefinger, closing his eyes as he released a heavy sigh. When he finally had his temper under control enough to look at me, he slowly shook his head and mouthed the word: *Seriously?*

Yeah, well, it wasn't like I was going to throw myself on the floor and beg for the council's mercy. Besides, I'd lost everything in this world I gave a damn about. At this point, I had nothing left to lose. The seven PNT council members brought their heads together, throwing furtive glances my way while they discussed my fate. This was my third hearing in as many months, and I hadn't given them any more information today than I had at my first arraignment. What had happened after I'd kidnapped Delilah, the Oracle who'd plotted against Raif and the entire Shaede Nation, and left the PNT's Washington Headquarters with her partner in crime, Faolán—known to the PNT as simply Fallon—was no one's business but my own.

"You do realize that by keeping this secret, you may very well face imprisonment or worse." Raif's worried tone didn't change my mind. And though I knew he was grateful for my secrecy, he didn't want to see me punished, either.

"Doesn't matter." I couldn't even muster an ounce of concern in my own voice. I leaned in to Raif so only he heard me. "They can threaten me all they want. It's taken centuries for legends of *O Anel* and the hourglass to fade from memory. I'm not going to endanger Brakae or the natural order by reminding anyone of things best left forgotten."

I didn't give two shits about the PNT's discipline. According to Moira, as a Guardian of the doorway to the faery realm, also known as *O Anel*, I was above the laws of man and Fae alike. Besides, nothing they could dish out would punish me more than I'd already punished myself. I'd hurt the only person in this world I gave a shit about, and destroyed us both in the process.

Tyler.

God, it hurt just to think his name. I broke his heart by leaving without a word of where I was going or when I'd be back. I betrayed our love by wishing for him to stay put in Seattle, unable to leave the city, while I traipsed around on my adventure to find Raif's daughter. And in the end, my reward was exactly what I deserved: time away from him and the space I needed to decide what I really wanted.

I already knew what I wanted.

I wanted Tyler.

But he wasn't here with me, was he? Apparently, he didn't think an appropriate length of time had passed for me to get my shit together. I'd tried wishing for him. In fact, I'd wished for him three or four times a day that first month, but he never showed. Jinn magic is full of rules, regulations, and limitations. One of those being that I could only wish for things I really, truly needed. And somehow, the powers that be had determined my want of Tyler wasn't good enough.

"Will the accused stand?" So polite, as if she was asking if I'd stay for dinner or something. You'd never have guessed the council was about to bring down the hammer.

I scooted my chair back and shoved my bound hands against the table for leverage. The iron cuffs swirled with silver light, charmed to negate my ability to wreak any havoc, if the whim struck. Whenever an accused stood before the council, they were bound with the cuffs. In my case, they prevented me from leaving my corporeal form and weakened me to the point that I couldn't break the bonds. Lucky for the council, I'd given up a long time ago. I had no intentions of wreaking havoc of any kind. Not now, or in the future. The fight had pretty much drained right out of me.

"Since you refuse to speak on your own behalf, and considering we have sworn statements from many eyewitnesses, this council has no choice but to—"

"If it pleases the council . . ." The double doors of the chamber swung wide, and the Shaede High King himself swept into the room as if he owned the place. "I beg a moment of your time." Alexander Peck—or to me, just Xander—never turned down an opportunity to show off his dramatic flair, and right now, he claimed center stage.

"With all due respect, Your Highness," the dark-haired Fae said, "the time to testify in front of this council has passed."

Decked out in what had to have been a ten-thousand-dollar suit, Xander looked as regal as he did imposing. Though his stance was relaxed, his molten caramel eyes sparked with a cold light that dared anyone to turn his request down. I could only imagine what he was up to. Maybe he couldn't stand that I was the center of attention. Or worse, maybe he just wanted to prove that he could throw his weight around.

"Do I have to remind you about Edinburgh, Amelia?" Oh yeah, Xander definitely just wanted to throw his weight around.

The Fae looked at the questioning faces of her colleagues before she cleared her throat, fidgeting with the cuff of her sleeve. She scooped a glowing pearlescent ball in her hand and knocked the faery equivalent of a gavel down on the table twice. "We'll adjourn for fifteen minutes. Alexander, if you'll follow us to our quarters, we'll hear what you have to say."

Xander flashed me an arrogant smile. He waited patiently as the seven council members stood and followed in their wake as they walked, single-file, from the room. "Sit tight," he said as he strolled past Raif and me. "I'll be back shortly."

We sat back down at the same time, and I asked Raif, "What the hell is he up to?"

"Your guess is as good as mine. We're talking about Xander, after all."

Raif leaned back in his seat, staring at the ceiling as if his brother's plans were written there. I, on the other hand, had no interest in wondering what His Royal High and Mightiness had up his sleeve. Instead, my mind drifted to where it always did lately: the clusterfuck that was my life.

You'd think I would have lost track of the days since that night. The emerald pendulum, *Iskosia*, the key to the Faery realm that I wore around my neck, silenced the sound of time as it ticked within my Guardian's soul, but I had invisible tally marks etched on my heart. Eighty-seven days, six hours, fifteen minutes, and twenty-two seconds. Twenty-three ... twenty-four ... twenty-five ...

It's not like I'd been brooding the *entire* three months. Well, almost three months. I had a system going, alternating between outings for my hearings with the PNT's judicial council, setting up camp on my bed, answering the door for grocery delivery, and occasionally crashing on the couch while I let the TV lull me to sleep with mind-numbing entertainment. I wasn't proud of the fact that I knew every single cast member of *The Jersey Shore* down to their cocktails of choice, but it was better than the alternative. The alternative being: allowing my tortured thoughts to drive me to a state of near-insanity.

I leaned forward in my chair and massaged my sternum. The imaginary fist that had been squeezing my heart for the past seven months clenched tight, leaving a hollow ache I couldn't get rid of, no matter how long I rubbed. I'm not a fool. I realized that the blame for our separation rested solely on me. I ran—and spent four months away—from the one person in this world I should have sprinted *toward*. I shunned his protection, disregarded his strength, and stomped all over the love he offered ... all in the name of arrogance.

Ty showed me how much he appreciated my treatment of him by returning the favor in classic "eye for an eye" fashion. I'd come back to Seattle after a months-long excursion spent in *O Anel*, the faery realm, protecting Raif's daughter, Brakae, aka the Time Keeper, from her ex-boyfriend, a nasty Enphigmalé asshole named Faolán. It was my job, after all, to protect the doorway and the key to *O Anel*. I'd failed miserably, taking Faolán to the very placed he'd been banished from so he could mend two halves of the hourglass that controlled the flow of time in both the mundane world and the faery realm. If he'd succeeded in his plans, Faolán would have killed every human being on the planet, aging them instantly as time sped up in the mortal world to keep pace with time on the other side of the veil in the faery realm.

According to Raif, during my absence Tyler had become temperamental, angry, and resentful, not to mention dirty and disheveled. I arrived at his apartment expecting to find a broken man. What I found broke *me*. Calm, clean, showered and shaved, and packing a suitcase for an extended vacation, Tyler gave me one last kiss and left. And he'd stayed gone. Three months and counting . . .

I took a deep breath, tried to slow the frantic beating of my heart that signaled the onset of another panic attack. Dredging up memories of my many mistakes caused my palms to sweat and my breath to stall in my lungs. The floor seemed to tip beneath me and the room swam in and out of focus in a dizzying blur. Oh man, this was going to be a bad one . . .

"Darian, stand up." Raif's voice was nothing more than a whisper, but it echoed in my mind as if shouted down the length of a tunnel.

The door to the council's private chambers opened, and I just about fell on my ass as I shot to my feet. Raif reached out to steady me, his face etched with concern. I would have given him a reassuring pat to the shoulder if my hands weren't bound in the damn cuffs. A few deep, steady breaths managed to calm me down enough that I was no longer seeing stars at the periphery of my vision, and my head finally felt like its normal size, not floating above my shoulders like a balloon.

Xander sauntered out of the council's chambers much

the same way he'd entered. Only this time, the smugness of his expression spoke of victory, not just the prospect of success. *Great*. If he had any pull with regards to the council's decision about my sentence, I'd never live it down. Just one more thing for his royal pain in the ass to hold over my head.

The Fae with the deep brown eyes—Amelia, Xander had called her—cast a cautious glance in the king's direction before turning her focus to me. "The accused is officially absolved of any wrongdoing against the PNT and any charges brought against her are stricken from the official record." She brought the opalescent orb down against the table with a resounding *crack*. With the sound wave, a pulse of energy swept through the room and caressed my face like a kiss of warm breeze. The cuffs around my wrists loosened on their own and dropped to the floor. Amelia's eyes narrowed shrewdly as she addressed me. "You are free to go."

Xander turned to leave, his chest puffed out with pride. "You can thank me later," he said, and strode from the room.

As the council members rose once again to leave, I said to Raif, "He really gets off on throwing his weight around, doesn't he?"

Raif's laughter was the only answer I needed.

ABOUT THE AUTHOR

Amanda Bonilla lives in rural Idaho with her husband and two kids. She's a part-time pet wrangler and a full-time sun worshipper, and she goes out into the cold only when coerced. When she's not writing, she's either reading or talking about her favorite books.

CONNECT ONLINE

www.amandabonilla.com
facebook.com/amandabonillaauthor
twitter.com/amandabonilla

ALSO AVAILABLE FROM

Amanda Bonilla

Shaedes of Gray
A Shaede Assassin Novel

In the shadows of the night, Darian has lived alone for almost a century. Made and abandoned by her former lover, Darian is the last of her kind—an immortal Shaede who can slip into darkness as easily as breathing. With no one else to rely on, she has taught herself how to survive, using her unique skills to become a deadly assassin.

When Darian's next mark turns out to be Xander Peck, King of the Shaede Nation, her whole worldview is thrown into question. Darian wonders if she's taken on more than her conscience will allow. But a good assassin never leaves a job unfinished...

**Available wherever books are sold or at
penguin.com**

facebook.com/ProjectParanormalBooks